SAVAGE REBELLION
BOOK II

SAVAGE BOUNTY

ALSO AVAILABLE

Savage Legion

SAVAGE REBELLION
BOOK II

SAVAGE BOUNTY

MATT WALLACE

1230 AVENUE OF THE AMERICAS, NEW YORK, NEW YORK 10020

This book is a work of fiction. Any references to historical events, real people, or real places are used fictitiously. Other names, characters, places, and events are products of the author's imagination, and any resemblance to actual events or places or persons, living or dead, is entirely coincidental. ✦ For information address Saga Press Subsidiary Rights Department, 1230 Avenue of the Americas, New York, NY 10020 ✦ First Saga Press trade paperback edition July 2021 ✦ SAGA PRESS and colophon are trademarks of Simon & Schuster, Inc. ✦ For information about special discounts for bulk purchases, please contact Simon & Schuster Special Sales at 1-866-506-1949 or business@simonandschuster.com ✦ The Simon & Schuster Speakers Bureau can bring authors to your live event. For more information or to book an event contact the Simon & Schuster Speakers Bureau at 1-866-248-3049 or visit our website at www.simonspeakers.com. ✦ Interior design by A. Kathryn Barrett ✦ Manufactured in the United States of America ✦ 10 9 8 7 6 5 4 3 2 1 ✦ Library of Congress Cataloging-in-Publication Data is available. ✦ ISBN 978-1-5344-3923-8 ✦ ISBN 978-1-5344-3925-2 (eBook)

For everyone who survived 2020,

and everyone who didn't.

CRACHE
Sixth City
Ninth City
Tenth City
Fifth City
Crachian
Border
Sicclunan
Front
Eighth City
Seventh City

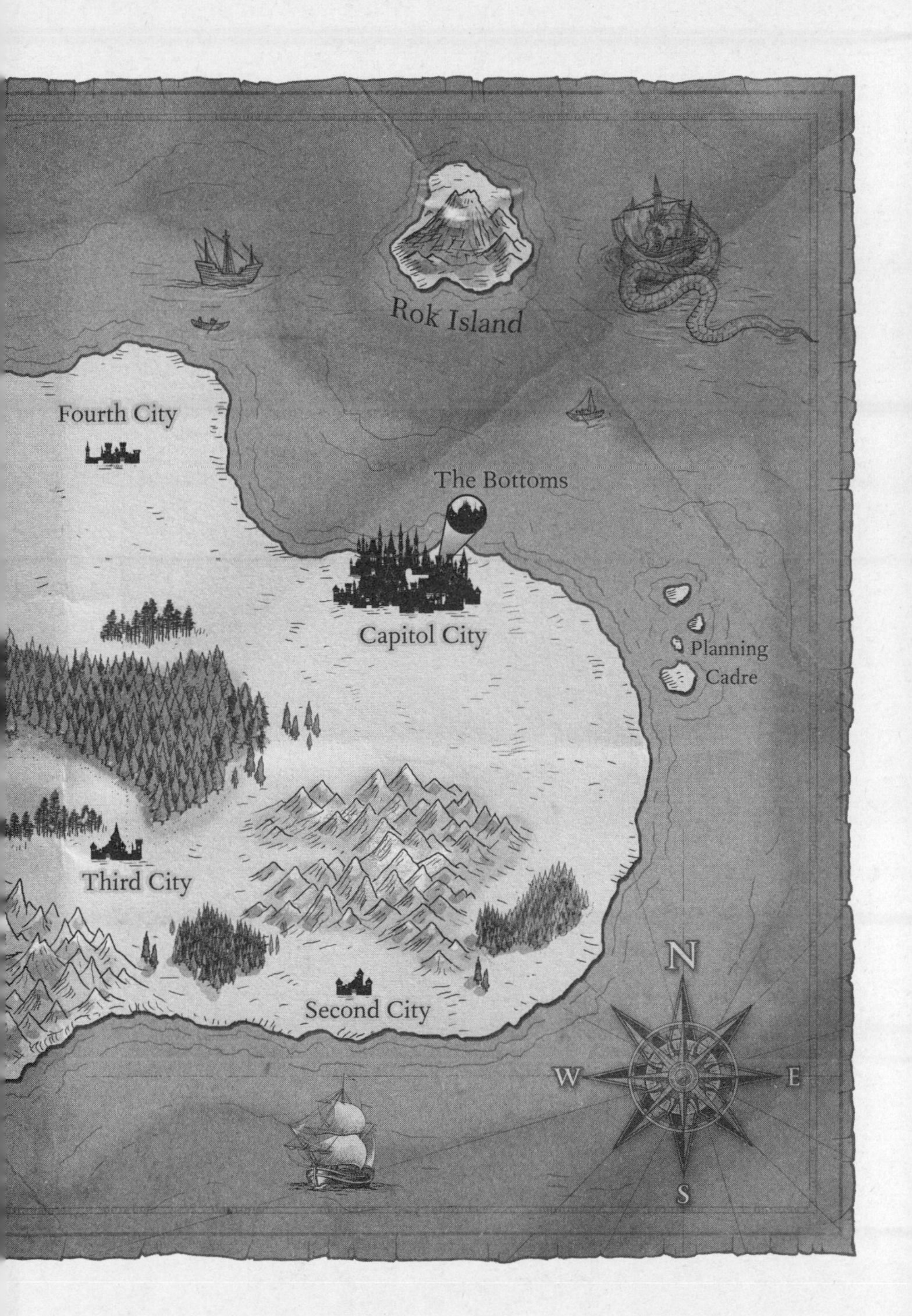

Rok Island
Fourth City
The Bottoms
Capitol City
Planning
Cadre
Third City
Second City
N
W
E
S

PREVIOUSLY, IN *SAVAGE LEGION* . . .

CRACHE APPEARS TO BE AN EVOLVED SOCIETY. IT HAS NO monarchy. No nobility. No aristocracy. No rulers. Just a nameless, timeless utopia. Or upon first glance, that's what it seems.

One of its greatest weapons has always been the Savage Legion, an army of conscripts culled from the dungeons of Crache's cities and hurled on the forefront of battle at the empire's enemies. But the Legion has another clandestine purpose, which is to dispose of dissidents, the homeless, and any others deemed undesirable by the state. It is an instrument of conquest and oppression, the true guiding principles of this "evolved" society.

Evie entered the Savage Legion with a simple mission: infiltrate its ranks and locate her first love, Brio, an advocate from the Capitol who disappeared after asking too many questions about the Legion. In the course of this mission, she has found herself the unlikely leader of a rapidly fomenting rebellion against Crache. With her makeshift army of ex-Savages and common enemies of the Crachian army, the Skrain, she is now poised to lay siege to the Tenth City, and with that, open an inroad to the heart of the nation.

Lexi, Brio's wife and the one who first sought Evie's help, has successfully battled Crache's bureaucracy to take over as leader of Gen Stalbraid in her husband's absence. She has also become the unwilling "guest" of a secret order known as the Ignobles, descendants of the blood nobility that once ruled. The Ignobles want that power back, and Lexi must play a role in their plan in order to keep her life.

Dyeawan lost the use of her legs in an accident years ago, but was able to survive on the streets by virtue of her brilliant mind. Having grown up in the disenfranchised outskirts of the Capitol known as the Bottoms, she was eventually arrested and rejected by the Savage Legion because of her disability. Dyeawan was then brought into the service of the Planning Cadre, a secret keep where equally brilliant minds run Crachian society in all its wonders and horrors. Upon learning an unforgivable secret, she has murdered her mentor, head of the Planning Cadre, leaving behind no evidence and claiming his place.

Taru was once the trusted retainer of Gen Stalbraid, protecting Lexi at every turn. But upon recovering the evidence collected by Brio, meant to expose the truth behind the Savage Legion, Taru has been arrested and conscripted into the Legion themself.

These four each have a role to play in the now-uncertain future of Crache, though what those roles are and their consequences have yet to be determined.

SAVAGE BOUNTY

PART ONE

FLIP OF THE COIN

BURIED IN A JAGGED CROWN

THE SMALL ATOLL RISES A MILE OFFSHORE, LITTLE MORE than a halo of sharp rocks anointing the slate gray waters. From a distance one would scarcely take notice, and upon closer inspection their perception wouldn't be much altered. Yet this nothing of a stone formation has been, since the Planning Cadre took up residence on the island, the closest thing to a sacred site observed by the brilliant and unknown conspiracy of men and women who secretly control the destiny of Crache.

Mister Quan dutifully crews the tiny rowboat, ever the pleasant stoic as he guides the oars smoothly through the lapping tide. Dyeawan sits at the bow, her back to the atoll. She isn't entirely ready to take in the scene that awaits them there.

She studies Quan's face, its broad and congenial features. Dyeawan has always possessed the ability to read people. She never knows their thoughts, but she sees their nature and intentions revealed in the smallest tics in the flesh of their face, or the way they move their body, or the quiver in their voice, no matter how slight.

Mister Quan does not speak, and Dyeawan has yet to witness a single crack in his veneer, not even when he discovered her spying on Edger and Oisin's private conversation and displayed sympathy by not exposing her. He is perhaps the only person she has ever met who appears to act purely and selflessly in aid of those around him.

It has been weeks since Dyeawan ascended to the center of the planners (for there is no "head" of their winding circular table), supplanting Edger, Crache's modern architect and unnamed ruler. What everyone save Dyeawan knows is that Edger's death was an accident. The wind dragon ever affixed to his neck, which enabled him to speak, prematurely entered its frenzied mating cycle and tore out Edger's throat.

What no one but Dyeawan knows, at least not for certain, is that Dyeawan triggered Ku the wind dragon's violent mating cycle in order to kill Edger. It wasn't something Dyeawan planned, not exactly, but it was something for which she'd prepared. She knew what kind of person Edger truly was, even if Dyeawan hadn't wanted to believe it when she first came to the Cadre. She also couldn't have known the depth of his cold, passionless view of people, or the ultimately genocidal impact of it.

Killing Edger was necessary.

Maintaining the Cadre's perception of his death as an accident is also necessary.

Dyeawan sees no dishonesty in Quan, and certainly no malice, but neither can she be certain what he knows or suspects. Quan served Edger with unwavering dedication for more years than Dyeawan has drawn breath. He obviously cared for the old man, yet Quan seems to care for everyone he encounters.

She wonders if inwardly he suspects, as Oisin clearly does, that

Dyeawan played a part in Edger's demise. She further speculates whether or not those suspicions, should Quan harbor them, place her in jeopardy.

Dyeawan hopes the stoic attendant will continue to keep those thoughts unspoken. She has come to like him very much, and has even begun to depend on him.

Their rowboat approaches the rocky shore of the atoll as dusk dims the light of the world. Other skiffs are anchored there, harmlessly knocking against one another as the current sweeps them back and forth. Mister Quan ceases his slow, steady rowing and draws the oars into the boat. Dyeawan watches as he delicately rolls back the wide sleeves of his robe, and then takes up a bell-shaped anchor tethered to a chain. Quan leans over the side of the rowboat and gently lets it slip below the surface of the water, carefully feeding the chain to the end of its length.

Dyeawan finds there is something calming about watching Quan's silent, precise, and unobtrusive movements. She wishes she could feel the inner peace he seems to represent.

The other members of the Planning Cadre are already lining the tops of the stony barrier. They stand shoulder to shoulder with their fellows, each of them denoted by their disparately colored tunics, each color representing their divisions with the Cadre.

The divisions—builders, architects, and so on—are grouped in their own rows, separate from one another. The planners are different. All of them wear their gray tunics, but the planners are represented by two separate rows opposing each other across the atoll. One of the groups is composed of elder planners while the other is significantly and consistently younger in age.

One of the reasons Edger elevated Dyeawan to planner was to tip the balance between the younger, forward-thinking members of the planners and the older guard, whom he labeled as too set in their ways and accomplishments. Before her ascension, the planners numbered twelve. With Edger gone, the unspoken ruling body of Crache would have been evenly divided once more.

Dyeawan has already remedied that by inviting Riko to join her amongst the planners. It was Dyeawan's first act as their leader, and not strictly a calculated maneuver. She genuinely trusts and respects Riko, who is one of the Cadre's most gifted minds and able inventors.

The fact her presence allowed the younger members of the planners to maintain that newly won superiority is simply an added boon.

Riko spots the rowboat docking tenuously beside the atoll and quickly separates her slight figure from the rest of the younger planners. She darts across the tops of the rocks with the speed and nimbleness of a cat to meet Dyeawan and Mister Quan.

"I should have built a ramp for you," Riko says breathlessly. "I'm such a taro head sometimes."

"Don't say that about yourself," Dyeawan replies, mildly chastising her friend.

"They've been having funerals here for a thousand years or something. You'd think someone would've thought to construct a dock at least, yeah?"

"People whose legs obey their commands rarely think of those of us whose legs do not."

Mister Quan rises carefully. He bows to Dyeawan, awaiting her permission to aid her out of the boat. It has become a common gesture between them, and one that always creates a warm, syrupy sensation deep inside her chest.

Dyeawan nods with a gentle smile. She's spent so much of her relatively short life being treated as part of the landscape, both as a girl, and even more so as an urchin seen by most as wholly immobile and incapable. Too many have viewed her as an obstacle they are allowed to move or adjust at their whim. Of all the indignities and hardships of scraping her existence literally from the floor of the Bottoms, that feeling was often one of the absolute worst.

Being given that courtesy by Quan and exercising control over her body is healing in a way Dyeawan could not have anticipated or identified before coming to the Cadre.

Mister Quan carefully and respectfully gathers her up in his arms and lifts Dyeawan from the boat. He steps onto the rocky shore, and despite his long, billowy robes and Dyeawan's weight, easily negotiates the way up the uneven terrain to the summit where the rest of the Cadre is gathered.

Riko follows closely, though Dyeawan can see she's already deeply lost in thought as she examines the spot from which they just departed.

"Maybe a rope and pulley system that moves a pallet up from the shore to the top of the rocks—"

"Perhaps now is not the time, Riko," Dyeawan suggests, not unkindly.

"No, yeah, you're right. Sorry. You know how I am."

Dyeawan stifles an amused grin. "I do."

They reach the summit of the atoll's rim, the spot where the younger members of the planners are gathered.

There is a sturdy chair awaiting Dyeawan, its thick wooden legs standing on a flat, level rock. Quan eases her onto the cushioned seat and steps away quickly to allow Dyeawan to adjust herself as needed. She grips the arms of the chair and settles her hips and spine comfortably against its back. Her own arms have lost some of the strength they developed in their years of pulling her body along alleys on a pig-greased sheet of tin, but they remain as hard as sprung steel and adept at compensating for her lack of control over her other limbs.

Dyeawan stares down into the middle of the atoll. The interior rocks and the waters between them are awash in light, a dozen shimmering colors folding into one another like the reflection of some invisible aurora. The true source of the light is a scattered fleet of paper lanterns floating atop the water. The flame of the candle cradled within each lantern is specially treated to produce different colors and shades, from bloody red to emerald green to sun-fire yellow.

The lanterns swim around a pyre bobbing gently in the center of the calm water. The pyre is draped in white silk to conceal the eternally still form beneath.

Edger's body is merely an outline, barely a silhouette, suggesting a shape rather than defining one.

At first it helps Dyeawan that she cannot see him, and then it's all somehow worse *because* she can't.

She distracts her mind from the matter at hand by scanning the assemblage surrounding the small funereal lake. Dyeawan spots Matei amongst the builders. He's standing behind a large wrought iron wheel encumbered with heavy links of chain. The pudgy young man has his head bowed respectfully, his hands clasped in front of his body. Dyeawan can't see his face. She wishes she could read his expression, and perhaps take comfort in his smile.

The two of them haven't spoken since she put on the gray tunic of a planner. He and Riko were Dyeawan's first true friends at the Cadre, and Riko insists to her that Matei wanted more than Dyeawan's friendship. All of that seems to have changed. Riko says he's jealous of Dyeawan's unexpected rise through the ranks. Dyeawan knows Riko is right, but she still wants to believe Matei is capable of dismissing such petty impulses.

Dyeawan's gaze leaves him, continuing to sweep over the summit of the rocky halo. After a few moments her eyes single out another figure among the rest before Dyeawan is even consciously aware of the person's identity.

One of the other planners is standing apart from both factions. She is, in fact, the only member of the Cadre occupying her own space there on the atoll. Dyeawan remembers her, like most everything she sees, but she realizes she never truly *noticed* the woman before.

She stands a head taller than Dyeawan or Riko, and appears to be several years older than either of them. She is thickly and powerfully built, with long hair the color of dying embers. The features of her face are large and strong. She has painted her cheeks with violet rouge, and her eyelids with a powder that sparkles in the last light of the setting sun.

Dyeawan studies that face, looking past superficial observations. The woman's expression is solemn, as suits the occasion, but there is more beneath that. Her eyes and her posture project something like defiance. It's reserved, dignified, but it is definitely there.

"Who is that?" Dyeawan quietly asks Riko. "The planner standing alone?"

"Her? Oh, that's Nia. She was kind of like Edger's pet planner. Before—"

Riko stops short of finishing the observation.

"Before what?" Dyeawan presses.

"Nothing."

Dyeawan studies her briefly. "You were going to say, 'Before you came along.' "

Riko frowns, looking down at her with regret. "Yeah, but I didn't mean it like that."

"I know what you meant," Dyeawan replies without judgment or reproach.

Riko seems to realize how intensely Dyeawan is studying Nia, and her friend looks with new eyes at the woman across the atoll.

"Why *is* she standing by herself?" Riko wonders aloud.

"She's making a statement," Dyeawan says.

It is clear Riko doesn't follow her line of thinking. "What do you mean?"

"By joining neither us nor what Edger called the 'old guard,' she's protesting the division that exists among the planners."

"Maybe she just made it out here late, yeah?"

Dyeawan shakes her head. "It's symbolic. It's also smart. A bolder gesture than using words, but less . . . antagonistic. You can argue with words. You can't argue with a silent gesture. She's placing herself above our petty squabbling. Setting an example."

Dyeawan looks up at her friend to find Riko wearing a strange, delighted smile.

"Why are you grinning? This isn't a festive occasion."

"I was just thinking about when you first came to the Cadre. You never would've noticed something like that."

"I would've noticed, I just wouldn't have understood what it meant."

"That's life, yeah? Trying to understand what it all means."

Dyeawan says nothing to that. She's studying the other planners now. The rest of them have also taken notice of Nia's gesture. The younger planners on either side of Dyeawan and Riko are staring across the atoll with what appears to be open admiration. It's clear they look up to Nia, which makes sense. If she was a protégé of Edger, whom both sides revered, Nia would be the natural object of envy and aspiration.

Even the old guard seems compelled by Nia's stance. Many of them look confused, some even appear slightly embarrassed or ashamed by the mirror Nia is aiming at them all, but none of them are wearing expressions of anger or resentment. And that surprises Dyeawan the most.

She is left contemplating why, if Nia is such a galvanizing figure, did Edger pass over his "pet" and name Dyeawan as his successor.

Mister Quan now respectfully presents Dyeawan with the narrow end of a large paper cone that will amplify her voice so that she may be heard throughout the atoll.

Dyeawan blinks up at him, unprepared for the cue to speak about Edger to the entire Cadre. As their new leader, it is appropriate, of course. She supposes she should have expected this, but perhaps she didn't want to think about her role in his funeral.

Dyeawan reaches up and takes the cone. Uncertainty clouds her mind. There is so much the rest of the people gathered around the atoll can't know about Edger's life. There is so much they can never know about his death. How can she speak about the man without giving any of that away?

In the end, Dyeawan decides to simply tell the truth.

She speaks into the mouth of the cone: "Edger raised me up from nothing. He was the first person to truly see what not even I perceived; that I am worth more than scraping out a meager existence along the broken cobbles in the shadow of the Capitol. He also showed me how to become more. I imagine many of you have a similar story, and similar thoughts about him.

"I am *not* Edger. He taught me much. He prepared me as well as he could in the time he had. But I am not him. I will use his lessons to guide the Planning Cadre as best I can, in the direction I believe is best for the people we serve. Whether that is enough . . . we will all see in time."

Dyeawan pauses, aware she's revealing too much of her interior thoughts about what is left in Edger's wake. These words are meant to commemorate and eulogize the dead.

"Edger believed in function, not legacy. He didn't want his name known, or his story told. He knew the power of such stories; stories that become legends, and legends that become myth. I will not mythologize him or his life or his impact now. He served his function, and he served it perhaps better than even he could have hoped. Now that function has come to an end. And so has he. I like to think . . . he would find it fitting."

Dyeawan returns the cone to Mister Quan. No one speaks, but the mood of the crowd seems to her to be one of satisfaction, at least with her eulogy.

She stares across the atoll at Nia in particular. The lone planner meets her gaze. More than anything else, and instead of the suspicion or even resentment Dyeawan might have expected, she reads curiosity in the woman's expression.

Mister Quan hikes the hem of his robes and carefully treads down to the edge of the interior rocks. He kneels above the water and removes a small pouch from his belt. He loosens the strings of the pouch and empties its contents, a pale and grainy powder, into the nearest floating lantern.

The reaction is energetic. The lantern's color darkens and the light it casts swells until the small vessel bursts. The paper is incinerated and colorful flame spits forth in every direction. The lanterns closest to it catch fire and quickly combust.

That single lantern coming aflame creates a domino effect spreading across the water inside the atoll. Tendrils of rainbow fire reach out from each affected lantern and touch all those within a few feet. The chain reaction continues until the lanterns swaying at the edges of the funeral pyre are touched.

As they explode, so too is the pyre lit ablaze. The silken white sheet covering Edger's body is quickly consumed.

Stationed at his wheel, Matei begins turning it by its dimpled iron spokes. There are heavy chains running through the rock and beneath the waves linking to the bottom of the pyre. As those chains retract, the fiery heap is slowly drawn underwater.

Dyeawan feels her hands begin to tremble. Watching Edger's body being lowered beneath the surface of the water sparks her recall, and images of the horrors she saw before her last conversation with Edger at the God Rung fill her head.

Since that day, her thoughts have stayed with the bodies that formerly occupied the bottom of the bay; bodies belonging to the disabled people of Crache liquidated on Edger's orders. Dyeawan sees them every night. She's barely been able to sleep since Edger showed her what lay beneath the God Rung, hoping she would understand the necessity of his actions and be willing to carry them forward in his stead.

Edger believed there was no meaningful or useful place in Crachian society for those people. He believed they were a drain on Crachian resources the state could ill afford. The few of them he took into the Cadre to perform menial tasks, like Dyeawan, were his paltry way of assuaging what conscience he had left. Dyeawan knows that now.

On her orders, Oisin and the Protectorate Ministry have moved in secret all of the remains to the deepest part of the island forest. The remains were separated and each soul was put to rest in the ground, in their own grave. The graves cannot be marked, and the names of the dead were not recorded, but Dyeawan instructed Oisin to bury each person with a Planning Cadre medallion.

It doesn't mean much, she supposes, but Dyeawan feels that at the very least the Cadre should claim those bodies in some way.

The *click* of that large iron wheel on the other side of the atoll breaks Dyeawan from her dark reveries.

As the pyre is finally sucked under, the blaze is extinguished, until all that's left of Edger is a phantom made of black smoke, dancing eerily atop the water.

THE KNIFE BEFORE

POLISHED STEEL DRAWS LIGHT THE WAY THE EARTH PULLS A falling body down to meet its embrace. Even in a darkened room, the scantest scrap of light will cause the flat of a blade to shine like the sun. Dull steel is an assassin's best friend, and the truly masterful killers coat their blades in the blackest metal powder if the knife is their preferred method of dispatching a victim.

However, if one's goal is to stab a sleeping body in the dark with a polished steel dagger, the safest technique is to keep its blade sheathed until the last possible moment before the strike.

These are lessons Crachian assassins have apparently never learned, and that gap in their murder education is the only reason Evie is still alive at this moment.

Oddly, that is at the forefront of her mind as she grapples with the shit-smelling man currently attempting to drive the tip of his very shiny blade through the ripe center of her throat.

Evie isn't thinking about dying in the commandeered bed of a Skrain captain, or her army attempting to lay siege to the Tenth City in the morning without her there to lead them. She doesn't see the faces of those she'll leave behind.

Instead, she's silently marveling at how the littlest details often have far-rippling results on the world around them.

She has long trained herself to be a light sleeper. It's a necessary skill for a bodyguard. It doesn't take much to wake Evie, even during the latest hour of the evening. It served her well when her assassin made his entrance. He managed to keep the door from creaking as he opened it, and he had the wits to allow just enough space for him to slip through. The light from the hallway sconce that reflected off the polished blade in his hand just happened to flicker over her closed eyelid.

She didn't wake with a start. Her eyes fluttered open and she was immediately aware of the malevolent presence attempting to creep silently across the floor. Evie had stayed still. Her sword was sheathed and resting on the floor just under her side of the small bed. She had to decide if it was worth going for, if she could retrieve it *and* free it from its scabbard in time for the blade to be of any use to her.

The alternatives, at least the ones she could come up with in a rush, seemed far bleaker.

Evie made her move, whipping the blanket from her body and rolling over to reach under the bed. Her assassin's reaction had been more finely tuned than his knife-handling skills, however. He took one long step forward and leaped over the foot of the bed with surprising speed and grace for a very large man. She only had time to roll onto her back and raise her knees to her chest before the bulk of the man's weight landed atop her. She also managed to brace her neck and face with her forearms, blocking his wrists as he brought the dagger down with both hands.

She can't see very much of his face in the dark, and what features she can discern aren't terribly attractive, but Evie can make out the runes raised just beneath his flesh. She can't know whether he's an actual Savage, or whether the Skrain or Protectorate Ministry have painted one of their agents to resemble a man who has had a blood coin forced down his gullet.

She's already called out for Bam several times to no avail, which means her hound dog–faced self-appointed protector is either absent from his post, or he's already dead. Evie knows she can't afford to dwell on that now. She also knows there's no point in cursing the fact Sirach, who has shared her bed virtually every night since they overran the border and seized the Skrain barracks, is currently out on a final stealthy reconnaissance mission.

She remains calm even as they struggle, reminding herself to breathe steadily in through her nose and then out through her mouth. Panic is not an option. Panic saps one's strength as quickly as it drains the will and overcomes the wits.

Still, the man is incredibly strong and Evie can already feel her arms weakening. She digs what nails she has into his wrists, and her assassin grimaces and growls in pain. She contorts her body beneath him so that she can raise a leg and drape it over the top of the arms pressing the knife down on her. She angles the hard bone within her shin beneath the attacker's chin and digs it against his neck, then straightens her body as much as she can with all her remaining strength. The pressure forces her would-be killer back in order for him to continue freely drawing breath, mitigating his strength advantage and easing the advance of the blade for just a bit, at least.

Evie begins rocking from side to side, trying to unbalance him, but his mass upon her is too much to allow her to build any real momentum. She gives up on the tactic and frees one hand to reach for his face, hoping to dig her thumb or even forefinger into one of his eyes. His arms are now fully extended and his reach far exceeds her own, putting his face beyond her grasp. She briefly considers relaxing her body to allow him to press toward her again, but decides she'll probably be overwhelmed before she can inflict any significant damage.

She desperately casts her gaze about. There's nothing within arm's reach of her except pillows stuffed with chicken feathers.

It's in this moment that Evie realizes she's going to die.

He is simply too big and too strong. She has delayed the inevitable as long as possible, and it has taken all of her skill and experience and will to accomplish that feat.

Evie thinks about Stirba, the woman who completed Ashana's training after she left Gen Stalbraid—when Evie thinks about herself before joining the Savage Legion, she's begun to consider Ashana as another person entirely. Stirba taught Ashana how to be effective in combat as a woman dealing with men who are far larger and possess superior strength. She instructed her how to bleed them out with a knife in seconds, as well as how to evade, to attack and retreat, hit and run, and utilize her surroundings, bashing them against the hardest surface or with the heaviest object available.

Once, Ashana asked the older warrior what happens when one can't evade, retreat, or run, and when one doesn't have an edged or blunt instrument handy. And what happens when one is pinned down by someone twice their size.

You lose, Stirba had told her without sympathy.

These words echo in Evie's head as her arms are on the verge of collapse. She closes her eyes, unwilling to watch her blood spray her assassin's ugly face before the darkness takes her. Evie doesn't want that image to be the last thing she sees.

She doesn't even feel the tip of the blade pierce her throat. There is the sound of what must be a metal dagger hilt colliding with flesh, and she feels the warmth and the wet against her neck and face as blood is released. There is no pain. Her assassin's arms relax and she can only assume he's plunged the blade of the dagger enough to his satisfaction. Evie waits for death to claim her mind and the thoughts and memories to stop.

After several moments longer and still drawing breath, Evie begins entertaining the idea she hasn't actually been stabbed.

She opens her eyes to find her assassin newly backlit. It's enough for her to recognize that his head is hanging limply to one side on a neck that appears to have had the air let out of it. His head is also horribly misshapen and obviously the source of the blood she's now wearing.

The man slopes to his right and Evie sees Bam standing over them and her bed, holding his mallet. A large portion of the assassin's skull is splattered on the flat of the mallet's hammerhead.

Bam grabs the neck he's snapped and in one easy motion pulls the man's corpse off Evie and over the foot of the bed.

Having so much weight lifted so suddenly is jarring for Evie, but she's also relieved. She reaches up with hands that feel like they've had the life sucked from them and wipes the blood away from her face. A moment later, she sits up and slides her legs under her, kneeling on the bed. The door to the quarters is open and the light from the hall is now filling the room.

Bam shakes the gore from his favored weapon and upends it, leaning the mallet against the foot of the bed.

"Sorry, Evie," Bam says, still holding the would-be-killer's body by the scruff of his neck, as if the man were a mad dog he just put down.

Evie's breath is shallow and uneven, and she doesn't yet have the words to answer. She can only shake her head to reassure Bam she's not angry with him and that this isn't his fault.

Bam pats his bulging stomach, which Evie knows is as solid as coiled steel.

"Think that bear meat I ate had turned," he explains. "I hadta go . . . y'know . . ."

"Oh. That's . . . that's fine, Bam. Thank you for coming back. You saved my life."

Evie notices Bam is staring at the floor between them, trying very hard not to look at her.

"What's wrong?" she asks. "I told you, it's all right. I'm not angry. You saved me."

Bam doesn't answer; he only shifts his weight from one booted foot to the other uncomfortably, still not looking up at her.

Then Evie remembers she's completely naked.

"Oh."

Bam reaches out and snatches up the blanket she cast aside with his free hand. He offers it to her, eyes still affixed to the floor.

Evie takes it and wraps it around herself. "Maybe from now on, when it comes to bear for supper, you should skip eating the liver," she suggests.

Bam immediately frowns, lowering his head even more so the stringy tendrils of his hair hide his face.

"I like the liver," he mutters.

Despite having just come within an inch of having her throat opened, Evie begins to laugh.

She's still doing so when the rest of the Elder Company come pouring through the open door, armed to their teeth, which Evie has also seen them use as weapons in several battles.

Mother Manai, the squat, weathered woman twenty years Evie's senior, and who has proved to be invaluable to the budding general as both an advisor and a soldier, leads the charge. Lariat, the boisterous barrel-torsoed pugilist, and Diggs, the most inscrutable member of the group, flank her.

"You all right, little sparrow?" Lariat asks.

Mother Manai prods the mustached man in his ample gut with the barest tips of the forked blade that substitutes for her left hand.

"Dammit, woman!" he yowls.

"She's your general," Mother Manai says in a reprimanding voice.

"It's all right, Mother," Evie tells her. "And I'm fine."

Mother Manai cocks her head as she stares at Bam, still gripping the dead flesh of the assassin's neck.

"You planning to take him home with you?" she asks.

Bam just stares back at her and shrugs.

"Bam, you can drop him," Evie assures the hulking Savage.

He does as bidden, and the other Elder Company members gather around the corpse.

"Those runes painted on?" Lariat asks.

Mother Manai licks her thumb and rubs the tip against the dead man's cheek without hesitation.

"No," she concludes. "He's got a blood coin in 'im."

Lariat kicks the corpse in the ribs, breaking several of them.

"Traitorous dung pile."

Diggs is less moved. "I'm sure they're telling the rest of the Savage Legion the same thing about us."

He's the third assassin Evie's forces have rooted out since they established their base camp, but he's the first one to make it this far.

"They're gettin' desperate," Lariat says.

"How'd he get in the barracks?" Mother Manai demands of the rest of them.

"It's getting harder to sort through newcomers," Diggs explains, unruffled by her tone. "Word's spreading. We've got runaway Savages, defecting Gen servants, refugees, and all manner of put-upon folk wanting to join the fight."

Evie nods. "Good. We'll need them."

"And what of the others like this one?" Mother says, persisting. "They only have to get lucky once, you know."

Evie is unconcerned. "I daresay they've missed their last chance before the morning."

"What about after tomorrow?"

"It may not matter after tomorrow, Mother," Evie says.

Those words land heavily upon them all.

"Let our general rest now," Diggs urges the rest of the Elder Company.

Evie looks up at him. She is still uncertain about this man. He says and does all the right things, but Diggs always seems to be removed from the others. Mother Manai, Lariat, and Bam are all possessed of great passion and emotion, existing fully in every moment. Diggs, on the other hand, never seems to let any particular moment touch the whole of who he is.

They file out of the room, Bam leaning down to snatch the dead assassin by his collar and drag the body away.

Mother Manai lingers.

"What is it, Mother?" Evie asks gently.

"I don't like hearing you talk that way."

"Which way is that?"

"Like we're going to lose tomorrow, or at the very least like you won't be there to see it even if we do."

"You're right. I shouldn't discourage the others."

Mother Manai waves her forked appendage and shakes her head in annoyance.

"I don't care about that. They'll fight with everything they've got even if you tell them you're marching them to certain death. I don't want those thoughts rattling around in *your* head, that's all."

"Vanquishing thoughts is much more difficult than vanquishing an assassin."

Mother frowns with every line in her face. "Are you retiring from the business of revolution to be a poet?"

Evie smiles, swelling with affection and respect for the older woman.

"Perhaps the truth just sounds better," she replies.

Mother Manai sighs, and it sounds more like a predator rumbling in the darkness. She reaches up with her remaining hand and places it gently against Evie's cheek.

Her touch is rough and calloused, and brings Evie great and immediate comfort.

"I love you, girl, as one of my own. We may very well die tomorrow trying to storm that city, but that's no reason to expect it. You hear?"

"Yes, Mother."

"Sleep now. Bam will stay at that door if I have to nail 'im to it."

Evie nods obediently, suppressing the laughter tickling her throat.

Mother Manai finally leaves her, unknowingly taking with her that brief moment of comfort and consolation.

Alone again in her borrowed quarters, Evie hugs the blanket tighter around her body and stares down at the floor beyond the foot of the bed.

Her would-be assassin has left a puddle of blood in his wake.

Evie does not see a small puddle, however. She sees a river of blood, the one that will drown the battlefield in the morning, and she knows that, win or lose, they will all swim in it.

SCREWING, WITH YOUR HEAD

"HE'S HERE, LEXI," THE TWO-FACED KILLER WHISPERS IN HER ear with mocking jubilation. "Brio is here. That's what you wanted, isn't it? That's what all of this was about?"

They haven't bound her to the chair, but Lexi finds it just as difficult to move. Whatever was in the tea Daian forced her to sip (the threat of that force contained solely in the coldness of his eyes when he handed her the cup), it has made her limbs feel as heavy as felled tree trunks.

Lexi's eyelids have no trouble remaining open, however. In fact, she can't seem to close them even when she wants to.

"Say hello to your one true love, my lady," Daian urges her.

For once, he isn't lying. It's Brio, the man she has loved practically since they were both born, or at least as long as she can recall. Raised together, the children of the kith-kins that came together to form Gen Stalbraid, long-serving pleaders for the Bottoms.

Brio manages to make his simple pleader's tunic resplendent. He looks healthy and happy and pleased to see her. His smile is warm and open, and exactly the way Lexi remembers it. He enters the receiving room of her guest quarters/prison cells on Burr's hidden estate. There is only an ornate, antique table between them.

She wants to speak to him, to ask him how he's come back to her, come to be here in this place. Lexi can't seem to command her voice.

"Oh, he's brought a friend," Daian observes. "You aren't the only one who has made new acquaintances in your time apart. Isn't that the girl you hired to find him?"

A smaller, more slender figure steps in front of Brio. A woman.

It's Ashana, who renamed herself Evie in order to infiltrate the Savage Legion, to find and rescue Brio at Lexi's behest. She was a member of Gen Stalbraid once, an orphan they took in off the street to train as a retainer, like Taru. But unlike Taru, the girl was put out by Brio's father when it became clear Ashana was in love with his son.

The last time Lexi saw her, she was wearing the costume of that Evie character, the stinking rags of a poor woman from the Bottoms who had taken to the bottle. Her hair had been greasy and disheveled, her face streaked with muck.

The Evie who has stepped into her line of sight is beautiful, draped in a shimmering silk shift that seems to barely touch her smooth skin. Her dark hair is crisp and clean and framing her face in perfect ringlets.

She stands so near to Brio that her back is touching his chest, and noticing that knots Lexi's stomach. She squirms as much as she's able to against the chair.

"They seem to have become quite close, no?" Daian asks her, suggestively.

As he says those words, Brio slides his hands over Evie's shoulders. Lexi watches her childhood rival for Brio's heart shiver visibly under his touch.

Confusion bubbles in Lexi's brain. She feels her heart begin to race faster.

"Yes," Daian whispers seductively. "Very, very close, from the looks of it."

Brio's fingers curl beneath the straps of Evie's shift. In one quick, almost violent movement, he jerks them over her shoulders and down her arms, exposing her breasts. As he encircles her with his arms and cups her breasts in his hands, Evie reaches up and digs her fingers into Brio's perfectly sculpted hair, gripping his head and forcing his face into the crook of her neck, where he sucks and bites hungrily.

Lexi's chest painfully constricts. She tries to close her eyes and shake her head in denial, but her muscles are still frozen.

"Doesn't seem like a man who needs rescuing to me," Daian remarks. "If he was ever lost, he seems found now. It just wasn't *you* he wanted to find him."

Lexi feels acid rise in her throat. It burns her lips as she finally manages to force out some sound.

"N—no . . ."

"I'd never ask you to trust me," Daian assures her. "Trust your own eyes. Are these the people you've been fighting so hard to honor with your actions? With your service to Crache?"

Lexi has no choice but to watch as Brio tears away the illusory material of the shift still clinging to Evie's body. As he pulls off his own tunic, Evie grinds her naked hips back against him.

She sputters and shakes, but she still can't will her limbs to respond.

"I know this is hard. Not as hard as Brio, clearly, but I am sorry for how difficult this is. But you need to see this. You need to know who your friends are, and who they are not."

The false sympathy in Daian's voice is an added edge to the dagger in her heart.

Lexi wants to claw out her own eyes as Brio enters Evie. In the next moment, they are fucking like animals three feet in front of Lexi, both moaning and screaming as if they're moments from exploding into a thousand pieces.

"They're not worth saving, Lexi," her captor insists. "Nothing about the world in which you were raised is worth saving. It's all made of lies and betrayal and pain. It's time to embrace a new world, and new friends, ones who would never hurt you like this."

He's right about the pain of it all. The agony of what she's witnessing is unbearable.

This was a deep fear she'd had, one that Lexi never voiced even in her own mind. Now it is happening right in front of her, and nothing about the world makes sense. Nothing can matter if this is truly happening. Nothing she has done means anything.

You don't really believe this, do you? another voice asks her, one that doesn't belong to Daian.

For the first time, Lexi is able to slightly shift her gaze from the sickening scene in front of her.

Her mother is somehow there in the room with them, alive and vibrant and not beset by a trace of the deteriorating sickness that took her from Lexi so long ago. She's standing off to the side, looking at Lexi with features twisted in anger for her daughter. Her mother's eyes, however, are soft and filled with sympathy.

She can't be here, Lexi thinks. *It doesn't make sense. She's dead. None of this makes sense.*

There is a reason for that, her mother says, as if she can hear Lexi's thoughts. *This isn't real, daughter. It may look and sound and smell and feel real, but it isn't. It can't be, because these people care about you, and they would not betray you. Brio would not betray you. Would he?*

But he has. He is. She's watching it happen.

Concentrate! her mother demands. *Look at them and focus! You are stronger than this! Be the stem, not the petal.*

We are not flowers. We do not wilt.

Those words have guided Lexi through most of her life, through all the hardships of the past year. They were her mother's words, when she was alive. Her mother was always the one she went to, always the voice of reason and truth and resolve and encouragement.

Lexi forces herself to watch Brio still thrusting lustily into Evie, and Evie gratefully writhing against him. Lexi strains with her mind, her gaze narrowing as if she is trying to look through them.

The two lovers humping each other like rabbits don't disappear, but they change before Lexi's eyes. The man no longer looks like Brio. He's younger and far fitter, his muscles chiseled and sculpted. Neither is the girl Evie. She is some pale, blond waif.

A cold relief spreads through Lexi's body. That same icy wave seems to shake free her voice, as well.

"I don't know who these people are," she says through gritted teeth. "But they are *not* my people. That is not my husband. I can see them now. I see the truth."

She hears Daian sigh.

"That will do, you two," he says, speaking to the couple splayed upon the table.

The pair immediately stops. They are both still breathing hard and labored from their coupling, but all of the passion vanishes from their faces, from the language of their bodies. Their enraptured moans cease as quickly as if they'd been echoes brought by the wind.

It's clear the lust was also an act.

The image of Lexi's mother *has* disappeared, however, gone with the rest of the illusions in the room.

Lexi laughs, bitterly, feeling tacky sweat covering most of her skin.

"That is very clever," she commends Daian. "Mixing the real with the imagined. It makes it quite difficult to tell them apart."

"That was the idea, anyway," Daian says, not even attempting to mask his irritation.

They are trying to change her. That much is clear. They are trying to break her down and turn her against all that she loves. It must be so Burr and the Ignobles can use Lexi to achieve whatever their ultimate goal is. They want her to willingly give herself and her allegiance to them.

As the two performers climb down from the table and begin to gather up their strewn clothing, Daian paces in front of the chair, gazing down at her with a wry grin.

"Burr puts so much stock in this meddling of the mind. I told her, giving me an hour of solitude with you and a few of my favorite forged implements would be quicker and far more effective."

She stares up at him defiantly. "You can hurt me. You are undeniably good at that. But you cannot change me. That power is beyond you, beyond any tool you possess. And if you cannot change me, you cannot win."

Lexi thinks she detects the briefest crack in his maniacal veneer. However, Daian is now smiling wider than before. He leans down, resting his palms against his knees, his face inches from hers.

"Those are truly beautiful words, and they express a lovely, worthwhile sentiment. But you and I both know they aren't true. I've already changed you. Quite a bit, I imagine."

"Only in the way an infection changes you. Infections heal."

Daian nods, casually. "Or they kill you. Wouldn't you say death counts as change? What's more transformative than that, really?"

Lexi's eyes turn deathly cold. "I'm too tired to bite your nose off," she says. "You should be grateful for that."

Daian laughs. He leans away from her, standing to his full height.

"I like you more and more every day, you know. I'm very glad you're here. This place can be quite boring."

He turns and begins following his performing sex minions from the guest rooms.

"The immobilizing effects of Burr's potion will wear off in a bit," he calls to her without looking back. "This was fun. We'll do it again soon."

After they're gone and the doors have been closed, Lexi can

only wait for the privilege of free movement to return. She tries to shake Daian's words from her head.

You're going to have to kill him first, you know.

It's her mother's voice again.

Lexi casts her glance to every corner of the room, but the image of the woman has not returned.

"What do you mean?"

Whatever their plans for you, however you acquiesce to them, whatever else happens, that man is going to kill you one day. You can see it in his eyes. He dreams about it. The thought gives him pleasure.

Lexi closes her eyes, feeling the truth of that. The realization churns her guts.

"What if I can't?" she asks the ghost in her head. "I'm not . . . I have never harmed anyone that way . . . let alone . . ."

You have to decide whether you value your life more than not taking the life of another. And you have to know there is nothing you can't do to survive. If you have not learned that by now, no one can teach it to you.

Tears are welling up in Lexi's eyes.

"I wish you really were here," she whispers.

RUNED

A GRAYING, PEG-LEGGED SKRAIN FILLS TARU'S CUP WITH muddy water. They look up into the soldier's withered, joyless face. His eyes don't even see Taru. He moves to the next wretch waiting for refreshment, toiling along like a weary spirit shuffling endlessly through limbo.

The grizzled, hobbling veteran is one of only a handful of Skrain detailed to "guard" the Savages, though mostly the Skrain seem to ignore them in favor of huddling together, drinking and gambling and commiserating sullenly among themselves. Those of the soldiers who have not aged beyond the battlefield have taken injuries that would prevent them from effectively fighting by Skrain standards, mostly missing arms and legs.

Apparently, the Savage Legion is also where Crache sends its forgotten soldiers.

The former retainer newly conscripted into the Savage Legion is seated on a stump in one of the many clearings dominating the great forest immediately east of the Capitol. When they were young and first came into the service of Gen Stalbraid, Brio's father would bring Taru along with him and his boy to fish the ponds and hunt green pheasants. The forest was vast then, full and lush, the trees tall and ancient. Now the saplings outnumber their more mature fellows, and huge sections of the forest have been clear-cut to the ground.

Even as they sit there with the other newly coined legionnaires, Taru can hear the crews of three different Gens with lumber concessions working in other parts of the forest. The sounds of chopping axes and sawing blades echo through the clearing in all directions.

Taru stares at their reflection shrouded in the murky waters of the cup. Bluish-green runes have already formed in both of Taru's cheeks. It took a half-dozen unenthusiastic Skrain to hold them down while the minter forced a freshly pressed coin down the retainer's gullet. A portrait of every one of their faces, including the dead-eyed minter, has been added to the walls of the revenge museum inside Taru's head.

They take a sip of the water that is more brown than clear, gag, and immediately spit it out onto the ground. Taru angrily tosses away the cup and scratches at the stubbly sides of their scalp. Their blond hair is rioting wild down the back of their neck, and Taru would murder for a razor or even a proper knife without an edge full of chips and rust.

Erazo scurries past Taru, toting the short, bulbous bludgeon that is somehow wholly appropriate for the stubby man and his blunt and wooden personality. The legionnaires' chief wrangler ascends another one of the permanent stumps pockmarking the clearing to address his company.

"You've watered your filthy holes!" he shouts at them in his raspy voice. "Now get on your feet! We're moving!"

"Where're we going?" a scrawny, white-bearded dungeon rat of a man asks the wrangler.

Erazo nods to one of the brutes on his staff, who smartly slaps the man across the ear, eliciting a high-pitched squeal.

Taru takes a deep breath, hanging their head in order to compose themself. They never could abide bullies, but these are special circumstances.

The irony is that, in a way, the brutal little man treats Taru more fairly as a slave than they were treated by most in the Capitol as a free person and retainer of a Gen. There doesn't appear to be any prejudice against the Undeclared here.

In the Savage Legion, they are all equally inhuman.

"We're marching to the northern coast," Erazo informs them. "Where you'll be loaded onto boats for the journey east to the front line. There is glory, gold, and freedom waiting for you in the fight against these rebel scum!"

Taru cannot help themself. They laugh openly and bitterly at that statement.

The retainer doesn't have to raise their head to know Erazo is staring nine-tailed lashes at them from his perch, but they bring their eyes up to meet his anyway.

"Did I say something funny, Savage?" he asks them.

Taru shakes their head. "Not at all. I was just wondering, how many have actually claimed this glory, gold, and freedom? How many marked like us?"

Erazo hops down from the stool and wades through the withered crop of emaciated new recruits seeming to sprout weakly from the ground.

"Haven't you learned yet?" he barks at the retainer. "I don't answer to you or anyone!"

Though Taru knows they shouldn't, they stand to stare down at the wrangler.

"We all answer to someone," the retainer says, coolly.

Erazo, with surprising speed and agility, swings his bludgeon into the back of Taru's left knee, folding their leg and dropping the former retainer down to all fours.

Taru groans more from the frustration and anger than the pain, though there is a copious amount of that, too. They push themself up from the ground by their hands only to have Erazo kick one of their wrists out from under them.

"That knee'll be hell on the march," he tells Taru. "But it'll heal. That's me pulling my strike. You talk pretty, so I bet I seem a brainless hoss to you. But I know my job. You're a big bitch. Or bastard. However you like. You've had training, it's clear enough. You are better stock than I usually get. So I'll see you to your first battle healthy enough. But don't press me. Around here, even good stock is easily replaced by enough of the bad, and I get plenty of that."

Taru has already made the decision to punch the little man in his balls, hopefully with enough force to permanently recede both tiny orbs into Erazo's body. The retainer leans back and balances themself on one knee, cradling the other as it begins to throb in earnest.

Even on their knees, the top of Taru's head rises to the height of the chief wrangler's chest.

Erazo clearly sees the menace in the retainer's eyes, but rather than being alarmed or frightened, he is deeply amused. He crouches down to meet Taru's violent gaze despite the fact he does not have to travel very far.

"I explained the rules to you," he says. "Do you want to die here or in battle?"

"I don't want to die at all," Taru replies coldly.

Erazo laughs in the retainer's face. His breath is surprisingly fresh, scented with the slightest hint of spearmint.

"There you go, then," he concludes, rising and walking away from them.

Taru allows him to go unscathed, fists white-knuckled at their sides.

In truth, the retainer is not afraid to die, but in that moment they decide they do want to outlive Erazo.

SLAB

"YOU ARE ALL PROBABLY WONDERING ABOUT THE TABLE," Dyeawan begins her first address to the rest of the planners.

They are gathered around a long, thick rectangle of darkly grained wood. The table has been freshly carved from a single great, ancient tree felled in the island's forest at Dyeawan's command. The oaken surface sits in place of the planners' previous meeting table, which was chiseled from stone and wound in concentric circles like a maze, matching the emblem they all wear on the breasts of their tunics.

Not surprisingly, Nia is the one who answers Dyeawan. "Among other things we are all probably wondering, I expect."

Dyeawan nods. "I took the liberty of . . . updating our accommodations."

No one else speaks right away. She can feel the frustration and boiling anger of the old guard without even looking to see it written clearly on their faces.

Finally, a planner with a shaved head that is mottled from age, and who Dyeawan remembers as Trowel, bursts forth, "That table was crafted by the masons who helped *found* the Planning Cadre on this island!"

"It shows," she calmly responds. "That table was a monument to form over function, and that is the opposite of our purpose."

"Is there no function in honoring the past and what it has given the present?" Trowel demands.

"We honor the past by using its lessons to shape the future."

"I agree—"

"As well as its mistakes."

Dyeawan lets the implications of that statement settle over them all like the ash from a blazing wildfire.

"*Mistakes*—" Trowel begins to protest.

"She's right," Nia proclaims.

That statement takes the older planners aback, while the younger members of their group seem excited by her show of support.

"That table was a contradiction," Nia adds. "And I was tired of craning my neck every time someone spoke. It is also the absolute last item on our current agenda requiring the attention of this assemblage. Let us move on."

That seems to soundly defeat any further objection from Trowel, or the others.

Riko flashes a secret grin at Dyeawan, who does not share her friend's apparent appreciation of Nia's actions.

Dyeawan is more interested in the display of authority by Edger's former protégé. Nia obviously has the respect of both factions within the planners.

Dyeawan wonders then why Edger never told her about Nia. Perhaps he simply didn't have the chance.

She refocuses on the task at hand, gathering her voice and her thoughts to address her fellow planners in earnest.

"I could barely read when I first came to the Planning Cadre," she begins. "I had never even held a book before. I'd only seen them through shop windows. Now I've read hundreds. I've learned many, many new words from all of that reading. One of them is 'politics.' It seems a necessary idea, the process of governing a people, until you delve into what the word really means. Politics has less to do with governance and more with seeking to gain and hold power. Those are two different pursuits, and the latter demands all sorts of . . . unsavory tactics, like scheming and lying and betraying people to whom you're supposed to be loyal.

"I have concluded I do *not* like politics," Dyeawan assures them. "I do not like the illusions and falsehoods and machinations that come with politics. I wish to speak plainly, honestly, and directly. I didn't replace the table as a symbolic gesture, much less a warning to those of you who hold the past dear. I did it because it was an inefficient monstrosity that was an obstacle to our progress rather than an implement of that progress."

She pauses to give them all time to absorb those words. Dyeawan makes sure to look around the table and hold each of their gazes unflinchingly for at least a brief moment.

"Half of you do not want me to lead. The other half does not know me, and I suspect you are just happy to see a change in leadership, and hopefully, direction. Does anyone wish to correct my view of things?"

No one does, or at least no one chooses to make their voice heard on the matter.

Dyeawan nods, breathing a small sigh of relief. "Good. It's important to know where we're beginning, I think. I'm not sure I want to lead you either, to be honest. I only know Edger entrusted me with this task, and that there are things I would see done to help the people of Crache, because, ultimately, that is our purpose, to improve the lives of Crache's people. If we can agree on that premise, then we can argue and debate the how or why of doing it as much as we need to."

Dyeawan watches their faces, studying as many of their immediate reactions to her words as she can take in before each of them has time to raise their guard. She isn't as concerned about the younger planners as she is the old guard, but to her surprise many of them seem begrudgingly satisfied with the address Dyeawan has just delivered. Several of the older planners even look placated. They all quickly remember they don't or aren't supposed to trust her, however, and a suspicious pall laced with contempt settles over their features.

That's all right, Dyeawan decides. The important thing is her words did placate them on impact.

Most of them were placated, anyway. Trowel, she notes, held that contempt in his expression the entire time.

She suspects he'll be her biggest problem among the old guard.

Finally, Dyeawan turns her gaze to Nia, who smiles subtly back at her.

This surprises Dyeawan once again. It is difficult for her to read. She can't decide if Nia is in agreement, or simply sees what Dyeawan is attempting to do and appreciates it as a strategy.

Being uncertain of Nia is truly beginning to frustrate her.

Dyeawan steels herself to press on with her next gambit, but she is interrupted as Quan glides inside the light of the torches surrounding the perimeter of the meeting table.

Dyeawan looks past the other planners to her stalwart attendant. "Yes, Mister Quan?"

The towering stoic bows deeply and motions toward the shadows of the room with a sweep of his draped sleeve.

Heavy boots trudge through that darkness. A moment later Oisin emerges, leading a small squadron of Protectorate Ministry agents, all of them clad head to toe in their night-black uniforms. The only pieces of them to catch the torchlight are their emotionless eyes and the golden eagle pendants stamped on their chests.

Four of the agents marching in Oisin's wake are carrying a heavy burden. These men bear the corner of a thick stone slab being ferried between them. The rough-cut edges of the slab are jagged and uneven, as if it were hastily carved or bashed from the middle of a larger piece of granite.

Spying that cargo, Riko whispers to Dyeawan, "You think it's a welcome present for you?"

Dyeawan deftly covers her own mouth to stifle the laughter threatening to break through her lips.

She shakes her head at her friend, both in the negative and as a reprimand.

Oisin appears to be in even less of a joking mood than usual. He snaps his gloved fingers, and the other Protectorate Ministry agents unceremoniously lift the slab and drop it down atop the meeting table.

Thankfully, the strong oak holds.

Dyeawan frowns at their callousness, but her thoughts toward them are interrupted as she glances at the top of the stone slab.

Its smooth surface is stained red. The crude image of a sparrow in flight has been painted on it.

"This is how it begins!" Oisin thunders ominously, and with genuine fervor.

"Begins what?" Riko asks with wide, innocent eyes. "Are you taking art lessons?"

Oisin's gaze falls on her. There is fire in the circles of his eyes.

"This is a section of wall from the Spectrum," he explains. "It was vandalized some time in the night. The mark is that of the so-named 'Sparrow General' who is leading the Savages in revolt."

"Did you consider washing the wall before you dismantled it?" Trowel asks.

"The stain runs too deeply to be cleansed from the stone," Oisin says through a mouthful of grinding teeth. "A fitting metaphor for the situation developing in the west."

Trowel dismissively waves a hand. "A temporary nuisance, nothing more. The Skrain march to eradicate it even as we speak."

"And in the meantime," Oisin fires back, "we will be lucky to intercede before these rogue Savages and their forces lay siege to the Tenth City!"

Trowel is unmoved. "The city has been sealed. The citizens have been told they are being protected from an oncoming calamity of the weather. The general public will never even know what masses outside the walls."

Oisin points at the sparrow. "And yet word of it has already reached the heart of the Capitol!"

“And you have very neatly excised that word,” Trowel mockingly compliments him. “Thank you as always for your service.”

Oisin draws in a deep, frustrated breath. Rather than bandy words with the old man further, he looks to Dyeawan. “Removing a piece of rock is hardly dealing with the issue. We must stop the seed of this from spreading.”

“Seeds can be uprooted and destroyed,” Dyeawan says. “Ideas are different.”

“Semantics!” Oisin sweeps his arm over the slab. “We must find whoever created this insidious abomination and liquidate them! Immediately!”

“Every time you try to kill a secret, you create two more,” Dyeawan chastises him, adding pointedly, “I would think *you* in particular would have learned that by now.”

It’s clear by his reaction that Oisin takes her meaning, and no one else at the table does. Only Edger was privy to how Oisin and the Protectorate Ministry ordered and then botched the assassination of Lexi Xia.

“Then what does the head of the Planning Cadre suggest?” Oisin asks tightly.

Dyeawan meets his hard stare with one equally as firm. “I do not have any suggestions, but I will *tell* you what you are going to do.”

The color drains from Oisin’s face, an impressive feat for one as pale as he is normally.

He does not, however, protest.

Dyeawan looks down at the crimson graffiti marring the age-old stone. She lets the rest of the room and everyone in it fade from her awareness as she concentrates solely on the problem presented before her.

"We aren't battling people, at least not in the Capitol," she muses. "We are battling ideas. Steel and poison aren't the weapons to use against ideas."

Oisin begins impatiently shifting from one booted foot to the other.

The rest of the planners are watching Dyeawan, some with that same impatience written on their faces, but most with an air of genuine curiosity.

Dyeawan recalls Edger's lessons in the archives, as she sat among relics of ages the Planning Cadre swept from the memory of Crache.

"We need to seed our own ideas," she concludes.

"How?" Oisin demands.

Dyeawan considers that, too. She drops her head, hiding a grin from the rest of them as a solution occurs to her.

"I know just the man for the job."

She ignores Oisin's continued impatience and frantically questioning eyes.

"Get me Yilik, the drafter," she bids Riko. "I've been meaning to catch up with him."

BLOOD GARDEN

ONE SUFFERS MANY INDIGNITIES IN CAPTIVITY, SUCH AS being drugged and psychologically tormented and indoctrinated by a murderous maniac. Even held against that, however, Lexi has decided being drooled upon by a giant meat-eating plant as it attempts to devour you whole ranks highly in the indignity realm.

It's not really spit, she realizes. In fact, it's more like juice, and it even smells rather sweet and appetizing.

At first, she'd been puzzled by Burr, her captor, proclaiming Lexi had the run of the estate while she was their "guest." They even ceased locking the door to her quarters. Lexi resisted venturing out, first from fear and then simply due to stubbornness. She quickly grew bored with the rooms in which they'd installed her, however.

She discovered the cavernous halls of a castle outside her rooms. It felt like being underground, surrounded by huge and ancient stone block walls. There was nothing like it in the Capitol. The same was true for the decorations, consisting mostly of massive ceramic vases set on pedestals. They were all like the gown Burr wore when receiving Lexi after she awoke in this place; unbelievably ornate and intricate in design. The artisans of the Capitol were among the best in Crache, but embellishment and ornamentation are not valued in their trades. The crafts of Crache were functional and elegant in their plain simplicity.

She also viewed woodblock paintings and tapestries the like of which one would never find on a Capitol wall. They all depicted either scenes of history or literature, neither of which Lexi found familiar. There were battles featuring soldiers clad in unrecognizable armor, although the backgrounds of several scenes resembled the features of Crachian cities. She could only guess how many hundreds of years ago the works of art spread throughout the castle were created.

Lexi found the gardens to be expansive, lush, and immensely beautiful, but neither did they appear to be surrounded by high walls, barred gates, or any type of barrier that would impede her simply fleeing the estate and taking her chances on foot across the outlying terrain. In the distance, she could see the peaks of mountains rising high, and Lexi wondered how difficult a crossing they would make on foot.

The main body of the grounds consisted of lantern plant gardens. The large bulbs hung from tall green stems bent at their tops by the weight of each colorful pod. There were bulbs of purple and crimson and bright yellow. Their folds protected the sweet fruit within and resembled a paper lantern.

Lexi wandered the skinny, sandy paths between the flowering patches. The paths themselves had been carefully and meticulously raked. Lexi almost felt guilty disrupting the perfect lines drawn in the sand.

We are not flowers. We do not wilt.

After several moments of marveling, she'd encountered a gardener tending to the lanterns. He was a short, ancient-looking man, clad in a simple smock that was slightly frayed and obviously well worn, but clean and kept with pride. She noticed several spots that had been stitched with a shaky hand. The man's head was covered in a straw hat whose brim cast a shadow over most of his thin, frail body.

"Your lanterns are beautiful," Lexi ventured.

He neither answered nor acknowledged her presence. She might've been a ghost.

"When I was a girl, my mother told me the word for 'gardener' was 'teacher' in one of the old tongues, spoken before the Renewal. She told me a garden teaches one much about life, and that learning to tend properly to a garden could make you the master of your life."

If he had any thoughts on the implications of that statement, he chose not to share them with her.

"I imagine tending to a garden as grand as this one, you've learned a lot."

Once again, he seemed to feel less than compelled to share any of that perceived wisdom with her.

Lexi took a deep, cleansing breath to snuff out her frustration.

"I am sorry to have bothered you while you're working," she offered, genuinely. "I will leave you now."

She walked past him.

"I know only my garden."

His voice was like a blade scraping its whetstone. It was a voice that is rarely used.

Lexi turned back, unsure she'd heard him clearly. "What did you say?"

"I know only my garden," he repeated, mechanically, without emotion. "That is how I am still alive."

He never looked at her or stopped tending to the delicate hanging bulbs. He might have been speaking only to himself.

A deep sympathy swelled inside Lexi.

She wondered how long the man had tended to these lanterns; perhaps the length of his whole life? Had he ever left this estate? Burr lived her secret life here as the Ignobles did long ago, when Nobles still reigned over these lands. Did Burr keep people as her ancestors did, as slaves in all but name, subject to every whim of the privileged? Did she steal infants from the Bottoms, or did the Ignobles go so far as to preserve the bloodlines of their servants, as they had preserved and continued their own bloodlines through the ages?

If so, then the gardener's parents, and their parents, and their parents had all suffered his fate. For generation upon generation, they'd lived as if the Renewal had never happened.

Lexi's mind swam in the horror of it all.

"Well," she began, speaking softly, "you have taught me something today. Thank you."

She thought she detected the slightest of nods from the ancient gardener.

Repelled, Lexi had turned and strode up the path with a renewed urgency and determination. She would not be trapped in this place as everything, including time itself, seemed to have been trapped.

Past the lanterns she soon found a large gap in the lush wreathed walls of the garden. Beyond, she spied open fields leading to the mountains. Lexi had already determined they must be located south of the Capitol based on the position of those mountains, though she couldn't possibly know how far.

There was no gate protecting the gap, but there was an iron frame supporting a long beam running across the top. Several plant pods hung low from that beam, their vines winding around the whole of the iron frame after what appeared to be years of growth.

They were the largest lanterns Lexi had ever seen, if lanterns they were. The pods were almost as long as she was tall from the look of them, and wide enough to birth a calf.

She had approached them slowly, studying them with genuine fascination, until Lexi was standing directly beneath the gargantuan bulbs.

At first Lexi thought the giant pod was simply swaying in the wind until she realized the air was still. She further realized the pod shifting over the top of her head was without question moving on its own.

Then those papery folds peeled back and Lexi was suddenly staring into what was undeniably a mouth. There was no fruit inside, unlike the lanterns in the rest of the garden—only a wet recess filled with dripping glands and a dark hollow resembling the entrance to a throat.

The sound from within began as a chorus of rattles. Then the pod trembled violently and Lexi was blasted with air and a terrible, ear-splitting shriek was unleashed from within that hideous mouth.

Her blood turned cold, and stinging bumps were raised over what felt like every inch of her skin.

Lexi turned to flee back into the garden, but in her panic, she tripped over her own feet and fell forward onto the sandy path.

Above her, the pod dipped toward the ground, its vines uncoiling around the beam to allow and support its descent. Lexi felt an unpleasant wetness around her ankles and calves, and she glanced back just in time to watch the bulb effortlessly suck her up into its mouth. She screamed, but the plant possessed nothing resembling ears. That, or her terror didn't bother it. Once it held her securely, the pod raised itself back into the air and she found herself staring down at the outline of her body in the sand.

In its maw, she has remained. Thankfully the monstrous plant has no thorny teeth, but the pressure of its folds around her is almost unbearable.

"Magnificent, is it not?"

Lexi cranes her neck as much as she's able in order to locate the source of the voice, though she immediately recognizes it.

Burr is serenely watching Lexi being eaten alive from a few feet away, Daian at her side.

His arms are folded across his chest, the hilt of his Crachian dagger filling one hand. The renegade Aegin looks positively delighted by the current proceedings.

Burr is again draped in her ornate and frill-covered garb from a largely forgotten age, a far cry from the simple and drab tunics worn by members of the Gen Franchise Council and the rest of Crachian government.

"What . . . *is* this thing?!"

"The height of Crachian engineering, my lady. They were originally bred to protect the entrances to homes of Gen members. It was thought to be a much more elegant and aesthetically pleasing solution to security than armed guards or trained beasts. The Planning Cadre's brightest minds crossed lanterns with several species of meat-eating plants. They spent the better part of a century attempting to perfect them."

"Perfection is not the word I would employ!" Lexi manages through gritted teeth.

Burr turns to her loyal killer.

"Daian, if you would . . ."

Daian bows his head dutifully, and walks away from them.

As Lexi watches, Burr steps beneath another one of the giant pods.

As it did when Lexi approached the one currently sucking on her like a candied nut, the bulb above Burr sways and lowers itself to meet her.

This twisted plant does not open its maw or shriek, however—it simply hovers passively around the Ignoble's head.

"You see there?" Burr asks her brightly.

Lexi would find it all quite fascinating were she not currently trapped in the slimy maw of a similar mutated plant.

"The Planning Cadre abandoned the pursuit. The pods were deemed too volatile, and also they did not want to create the perception that Gen homes needed such security measures. It would send the wrong message to the people. Crache is a nation free of such concerns, after all. Most of the pods were destroyed, but I managed to reroute a few to my estate and have them planted in the garden. Walls of stone and wrought iron gates are so unsightly, don't you agree? Hardly in keeping with the aesthetic."

Lexi watches the pod as it appears to nuzzle Burr like an obedient pet. The implied intelligence is a disturbing sight to behold.

"It's my blood," Burr explains. "The pod is drawn to it. That is how it knows me and recognizes my authority, and that I belong here. It's also how it recognizes that you do not."

"How is that possible?"

"It is not unlike training a dog to know your scent. The pod is given your blood as a sapling. Any living thing that does *not* carry your blood is seen as a threat, and . . . well, you are currently reviewing the consequences. That was the truly difficult part, as I understand it. Cultivating the pods to recognize the blood without attempting to absorb it. The trick is to feed it a bit every few weeks or so. Arduous, yes, but how can I reject perhaps the only creatures in all of Crache who recognize the quality and purity of the *right* blood?"

A stinging sensation begins to spread through several parts of Lexi's body.

"It burns!" she cries.

"Yes," Burr confirms, calmly. "It is beginning to preemptively digest you. Breaking down your body enough to slide easily past its gullet."

Fortunately, Daian returns, holding the end of a long, lit torch in one hand while the other swings a bucket filled with what appears to be water.

Lexi instinctively turns her head away and shuts tight her eyes as he approaches her with it.

"You wound me, Lexi," he says, his tone full of mocking hurt. "I live only to protect you."

"Forcing mind-altering chemicals down my throat and trying to turn me against everyone I love is a funny way to express that," Lexi spits back.

"Growth is a difficult process, often in need of outside aid."

Daian holds aloft the fiery head of the torch and very gently presses the edges of the flame to the papery skin of the pod.

Lexi's burning skin crawls as the rattling shriek of the pod causes every fleshy bit of its interior to vibrate around her. The pressure eases and Lexi is slopped forth from inside the pod's maw. She lands awkwardly on the ground in front of them.

Daian dumps the bucket of water over her. The burning sensation roasting her flesh subsides almost immediately.

It takes several moments for Lexi to catch her breath and regain her faculties. She looks up at Burr, towering above her like a school matron, beatific smile pasted to her face, hands folded delicately in front of her body.

She cocks her head and regards Lexi. "It is not unlike being born again, no?"

"I wouldn't know. I don't recall being born."

Daian shoves the head of the torch into the bucket, where the damp remnants of the water extinguish the flame. He sets both aside and bends down to haul Lexi to her feet by her arm.

Lexi begins to voice a protest, but it comes out as garbled noise rather than actual words.

Standing shakily, she attempts in vain to brush away the remaining pod slime with her hands, tugging at her nearly destroyed wrap to straighten it.

"You'll want to bathe thoroughly and replace those clothes," Burr advises her.

Lexi gazes at her with open hostility. "How have you managed to keep this sprawling garden of horrors concealed from the state for so long?"

"We Ignobles, as your history so disdainfully calls us, have learned not only to navigate Crachian bureaucracy, but to wield it as one of our most effective and lethal weapons."

"I don't understand."

"The Capitol is well aware of this estate's existence. However, on parchment at least, all of this land is a rice farm. Gen Hsu is tasked with overseeing rice production in this part of Crache. The member who oversees this place is well compensated to never make the journey."

"What about the rice you're meant to be sending to the Capitol coffers?"

"It also exists. Again, on parchment. As do the stores it is meant to replenish, and the invisible Skrain battalion it is meant to feed."

"How is it possible no one in the Spectrum notices these things are not real?"

"Because no one in the Spectrum looks. If it exists on parchment, and every middling bureaucrat involved receives their copy stamped with an official seal, then it *is* real."

Lexi cannot accept it.

Burr seems to enjoy her bewilderment. "How do you imagine

the Savage Legion remains concealed from both public knowledge and the knowledge of most in the Spectrum?"

It's true. Brio only managed to suss it out because he sorted through the endless reams of parchment to which Burr is referring and took the time to investigate the reality behind their words.

"Bureaucracy is truly magic made flesh. Your ancestors meant it to replace the rule of nobility and royalty over the people. Which it did, for a long time. But nobility is not as easily fooled as the people are."

"I'm certain you're only fooled by yourselves."

Burr's smile never wavers. "Truly sharp wit for a woman who was just regurgitated by foliage."

Though she seethes, Lexi has no answer to that.

"Daian, please escort our guest back to her quarters."

Lexi levels a finger at Daian. "Do *not* touch me!"

Daian responds with a smile and a grand gesture of his arms, motioning for her to start back down the garden path toward the castle.

They leave Burr to marvel over her pet pods. Lexi is silent as they walk together.

"You're unusually quiet," Daian observes.

Lexi barely hears him. She is still turning Burr's words over in her head.

"You might at least threaten or insult me."

"I find your torment very boring, Daian."

He grins. "That's more like it."

Lexi says nothing in response.

"You're beginning to see it, aren't you?" he asks her.

"See what?"

"How truly dangerous that bitch is."

Lexi stops walking. She stares up at Daian.

"I thought she was insane," she says, measuring her words carefully. "I *still* think she's insane. But I didn't understand how deeply the Ignobles have rooted themselves in the Spectrum, in all of Crache."

"Obsession is the most powerful force in nature, next to water. Burr and her friends have been plotting and scheming for far longer than either of us have been alive."

"I still don't understand why you're helping her. You're not an Ignoble yourself. You will always be her servant."

"We all serve."

"But why her?"

"She's going to give me what I want."

"What is that? You don't strike me as a man who craves power or riches. What is it that you truly want, Daian?"

He shrugs. "Chaos, I suppose. Very little else seems to satisfy me. I get bored so easily."

Lexi studies him, and she quickly realizes he's serious.

"You do know you're mad, don't you?"

Daian laughs disturbingly. "My *dear*, it is my favorite thing about being me."

GENERAL DECISIONS

EVIE SPENDS THE MORNING OF THE SIEGE VOMITING REPEATedly into a chamber pot.

Mother Manai lovingly and dutifully holds Evie's hair back as the young general empties her stomach of the last remnants of the breakfast they shared together not an hour before.

"There you go, dear," the older woman says as Evie begins dry heaving. "I think that should do it."

Evie sits upright on the floor of her commandeered quarters and Mother Manai dabs at the corners of her mouth with a damp cloth.

"How's my color?" Evie asks.

"Once you have your helm on, no one'll notice. Trust me."

Evie laughs weakly. "The mighty Sparrow General."

Mother waves the cloth, dismissive. "I still begin the morning of a battle by taking a nervous shit. Which end it comes out of is not a judgment on our character."

Evie laughs again, stronger and heartier this time.

She stares up at her battle-hardened elder with genuine affection and admiration in her eyes.

"I really don't know what I would do without you, Mother."

"You'll find out one day."

There is no malice in her words. They are spoken gently, and Mother Manai never stops smiling.

Evie nods, understanding that, as in all things, her friend is trying to prepare her for the inevitable.

"I hope you've taught me enough, then."

Mother Manai grins wryly. "Not nearly as much as you've taught me, General."

She helps Evie to her feet. Surprisingly, Evie no longer feels sick. Slightly hollowed out, perhaps, but she feels lighter, less burdened, her stomach tighter and relieved of its recent chaos.

"Are you ready?" Mother asks her.

Evie takes a deep, cleansing breath. "Was I ever?"

Mother Manai assists Evie in strapping on her armor, beginning with her breastplate. The leather has been dyed as black as pitch. The shape of a sparrow has been painted over the chest in bloody red. The wings drip down the abdomen in ominous, waxy trails.

"This leather was trained for a bosom a might bigger than yours," Mother says as she clasps the straps over Evie's shoulders, "which is a good thing. It's not enough to get in the way, but you'll have an extra half-inch or so if the chest is pierced by an enemy blade or takes an arrow."

"Then why aren't they all trained like this?" Evie asks.

The question gives Mother Manai pause. "Good question. Maybe they are. I've never been one for armor. Slows me down, and I'm slow enough as it is."

"No, you're not."

"I hide it well."

"You're fast enough to still be alive, anyway."

"That is true."

Thin steel pauldrons, the metal coated with blackened metallic powder, protect her shoulders and upper arms, but are light enough not to inhibit her movement.

Evie fits a pair of matched leather gauntlets around her forearms. Flaps shield the backs of her hands while giving her fingers total freedom.

As she cinches the gauntlets' straps, Mother Manai sets about tying a belt around Evie's waist. The belt supports two scabbards, one for a short, curved sword and another for a dagger, and a large ring meant to cradle the haft of a single-handed ax, a tool Evie came to favor in her brief career as a Savage.

The steel that calls those scabbards home is laid out on the edge of the bed beside them. Evie holds the sword aloft and quickly examines the freshly honed edges. The Sicclunan smiths have fashioned the round hand guard of the sword into the shape of two sparrows chasing each other.

Evie sighs. "This has really gone too far."

"It needs to go further if any of us wants to continue aging at length."

"That's not what I meant," Evie says as she sheathes the sword.

"I know that's not what you meant, dear."

Evie takes up her dagger. Its blade is flared, winding like the trail left by a snake. The design ensures that once the blade penetrates an enemy, the wound won't easily close. Evie fits it into the other scabbard on her belt and gives it a testing tug to check that it is secure.

Finally, she picks up her short ax, its hooked beard meant to snatch the tops of enemy shields or trap their blades, and slides its haft through the ring on her belt.

"Don't forget your little friend here," Mother Manai says, presenting Evie with a simple push dagger.

Evie smiles. It's the same weapon she took from Sirach the night they met, after she stopped Sirach from poisoning the Savage Legion and the two of them came within inches of murdering each other. It's also the push dagger she used to kill Laython, the brutal head wrangler of the Savages.

Evie takes the weapon and tucks it carefully inside her right boot.

"It saved my life a few times already," she says.

"*You* saved your life."

The final item of her battle dress is laid out on the bed. Mother Manai begins gathering it up to affix to Evie.

"I'm not wearing the cape," Evie insists.

"You're wearing the cape!"

"I will *not*. That is a ridiculous thing to fight in. Why not just put me in a gown?"

"You're meant to inspire those who've risked everything to fight alongside us. This is exactly what Crache doesn't want."

"What's that?"

"A symbol. A hero. A legend, even."

"I am none of those things."

"No one is. It's just a story, dear. But you're meant to *inspire* that story. We were Savages, nameless, unknown. You need to be known by all. The people will take it from there. They'll spread the tale of your great deeds across the ten cities."

"You mean lies."

"Stories, I said!"

"Lies!"

"Wear the damn cape," Mother Manai orders her, fixing Evie with a hard stare.

"Fine! I'll wear it while we ride to the line, but I'm taking it off before we storm the city!"

"As you like, General." Mother is placating her as she latches the edges of the cape to her breastplate straps. "Do you want me to row your hair?" the battle matron asks.

Evie shakes her head. "Just tie it back. My nerves won't hold for sitting right now."

Mother Manai purses her lips. "Fine, but I'm going to bind it tight. Hopefully your brain won't need too much blood flow for the siege."

"I'm just the general. My brain is purely decorative."

Mother Manai produces a length of catgut from inside her belt. She holds it between her teeth as she gathers up Evie's hair, which has grown out considerably since she was conscripted into the Savage Legion. Mother pulls it tightly, until Evie feels it tugging at her eyelids, and begins tying it off at the roots.

A fist that could only belong to Bam pounds on the chamber door from the other side.

"Come, Bam!" Evie calls to him.

The door swings open, but Bam doesn't come striding through. Instead a filthy little man in ragged clothes, his wrists bound behind his back, is flung into her chamber. A gag has also been shoved into his mouth. He crumples into a pile of tatters at her feet.

A hooded figure enters in the captive's wake. Despite the fact that her head is completely covered, Evie immediately recognizes her enemy-turned-ally-turned-lover.

Several other hooded, black-clad figures enter behind her, joined by Bam and his comically large mallet.

Sirach removes her hood, revealing that perpetually satisfied smile she so often wears.

Evie breathes a small sigh of relief. "I was wondering if you were going to return in time for the siege."

"We were delayed, but I assure you it was worth the wait."

Evie grins. "You always are."

Though she did not admit it to Mother Manai, Evie had begun to worry. Sirach and a company of her night fighters had been sent out the night before the siege to gather any last-minute intelligence or information that might be useful to them before they stormed the city.

Sirach bows her head. "The General flatters me, but that's not exactly what I meant."

"Of course," Evie says. "I imagine *this* person has something to do with that."

"Unless you arrested him for refusing to bathe," Mother Manai offers.

"Don't let the grime deceive you," Sirach warns.

She bends down and grips the man roughly, one hand snagging his hair while the other takes hold of his right shoulder. Sirach dips him forward and forces his chin into his chest.

There is a tattoo inked on the exposed flesh of the back of his neck.

It is an ant, the symbol of Crache.

"A Skrain scout?" Evie asks.

"There were three of them," Sirach confirms. "The other two were clumsy and fell on my sword."

The remaining scout begins growling a protest around his gag.

"Can the Skrain be that close already?" Mother Manai asks, alarmed.

"I don't know," Sirach says. "But he clearly does."

"He hasn't told you?" Mother presses.

"Not yet."

"Perhaps watching you kill his friends made him belligerent?" Evie says.

"They were clumsy! I explained that!"

Evie frowns heavily at her, and then crouches low to meet the level of the bound scout's eyes, her leather armor creaking softly. She reaches out and yanks the gag from his mouth. "What is your name?"

The man spits on the floor.

Sirach thrusts her palm against his right ear. It clearly hurts. A lot.

Evie sighs. "You understand everyone in this room besides me will very happily torture you until you tell them what they want to know?"

The man nods.

"Do you imagine you'll be able to resist?"

He has no answer to that.

"I didn't think so. Then why bother? Pride? Duty? Fellowship?"

"Something like that," the scout manages, hoarsely.

"My friend, regardless of what happens in the immediate future, no one will ever know what you did here. No one will compose a song about how you bravely resisted interrogation for several long minutes before the excruciating pain broke you. Neither will they curse your name for betraying your Skrain brothers and sisters and Crache. Your name will not be committed to history. You have free reign to act without the judgment of time."

The scout stares at her, the resolve in his eyes faltering, but he again maintains his silence.

"If you answer my questions, we will bathe you, feed you, clothe you, and shelter you comfortably. Securely, but comfortably. If you do not answer my questions, Sirach is going to horribly maim you until you do, after which I will probably kill you simply to end your misery. I will feel very guilty about all of it, and if I survive the first day of this siege, I will still be so plagued by your death that I'll find no rest, even in sleep. However, I would submit none of that changes or improves your position, or how you'll feel about the outcome."

The scout looks up at the rest of them surrounding his prostrated form. After that he stares at the floor for quite a while. Blood from the night before still stains the stone there.

"They will arrive by nightfall tomorrow," he mutters.

Evie nods. She feels somewhat relieved.

"How many?"

"Six companies of Skrain, mobilized from the Ninth and Eighth Cities. They have a large complement of Savages. I don't know how many, exactly."

"What else?" Sirach demands.

The scout inhales deeply before answering. "Word around the camp is a much larger force is readying in the east. But they want to stop you from gaining any more ground, or reaching city gates."

Evie doesn't try to hide her surprise. "They're willing to sacrifice a thousand soldiers just to slow us down?"

"Of course they are," Sirach says. "Once we attack a city, this all becomes real, and ten times harder to hide from your people. If it ends here at the border, they can keep pretending none of this has happened."

Evie knows the truth of her words.

"Bam, see that he is cleaned up and fed," she instructs her trusted guard, "then lock him in the barracks cells. Don't let anyone hurt him."

The hulking stoic nods obediently, his hand swallowing one of the scout's biceps and dragging him to his feet.

"You can't win," the scout assures Evie, desperation in his voice. "None of this will matter in the end."

"It matters a great deal to us," she replies before Bam hauls him away.

Evie looks to Sirach. "How likely is it the siege will end and we will have fortified our position by tomorrow night?"

"How likely is it I'll swallow the moon and piss moonbeams?" Mother Manai asks in return.

Sirach points at the older woman. "What she said. Sieges can last weeks, months, or even years."

Evie looks to them both. "What are our options?"

"Fortify our position here and wait," Sirach offers, sounding less than enthusiastic about that course of action. "We can't begin the siege and leave ourselves exposed to an attack. If we deal with the incoming Skrain first, we have the same problem. They've sealed the Tenth City because they know we're coming. If we ride past them to fight, they could muster enough soldiers and Aegins within the city to hit us from behind."

"We could split our forces," Mother Manai suggests. "Begin the siege while a smaller force meets the Skrain."

"We don't have the numbers for that," Sirach insists.

"That hasn't stopped us yet," Mother fires back at her. "If we wait here, then we have to deal with the Skrain they've sent after us *and* whatever reinforcements the Tenth City has to offer. Not to mention this larger force they're gathering to completely wipe us out."

"There is one more choice," Evie interjects.

The two women fall silent.

"We retreat. Abandon the border and return to the wastelands."

"If we retreat, it is as good as disbanding," Sirach warns her. "Half the force we've gathered would flee. They're joining you to take Crache back, not follow you into the wastes."

"And even if they didn't," Mother Manai adds, "we won't have the food or water to keep all of these folks upright. We've already run through the stores in this keep. We need to take the city to feed this new army of yours."

"Beyond the wastes, then?" Evie asks Sirach.

Sirach shakes her head, her eyes darkening. "There is little left beyond the wastes but the sea, and what is left is barely keeping the Sicclunans alive. We've been surviving on scraps for years. Our time was already running out. That hasn't stopped your former masters from wanting to kill us all over that last patch of fertile land, of course."

Evie turns from them and paces across the room, digging her fists into her leather-clad hips. Her chest beneath the breastplate feels hot, and she can't seem to draw enough air into her lungs. Her mind feels as though it is boiling in acid. She tries to keep her struggling breath quiet, hoping desperately they don't see the panic attempting to seize her.

There is a cracked and dusty mirror standing in the corner. In the midst of fighting off the shakes threatening to overtake her every muscle, Evie catches sight of herself decked out for battle, her sparrow-emblazoned armor and weaponry, her ridiculous cape. All of it has been fashioned for her by the Sicclunans.

Once Evie believed, as all Crachians do, that Siccluna was a great rival nation threatening the Crache way of life. Now she knows the truth, that they are a collection of nomads whose entire existence is based around channeling their every meager resource toward defending themselves against Crache's genocidal conquest. Every ounce of steel is precious to them, as is each strip of leather.

Yet they believe in her enough to task their smiths with creating resplendent arms and armor to match the name that those who choose to follow Evie have bestowed on her.

She turns to face her closest allies once more.

"We take the city," she proclaims. "All or nothing."

Evie knows they all feel the weight of those words, but to her surprise they seem to readily accept them.

"I suppose there never really was a choice or options," Mother Manai laments, though she musters a smile for Evie.

"If nothing else," Sirach says, "it'll be nice to fuck up one of their cities for a change."

Evie nods, and the silence that follows is as good as a dismissal. There is nothing left to discuss.

Mother Manai and the Sicclunans turn to leave her.

"Sirach?"

The others filter out of the room, while Sirach remains behind, waiting.

"Did you have to kill those other scouts?" Evie asks when they're alone.

"No," she replies simply. "I chose to. Just as they chose to serve the armies that annihilated my people, stole their kingdom, and purged their history from living memory."

"I served the Skrain as a Savage. I don't want to become them."

The way Sirach looks at her in that moment is not unlike a mother beholding their child's naivety. "I learned long ago that you have to be willing to become a monster to defeat monsters."

"Fine," Evie replies. "But do you have to enjoy it?"

"Can we possibly have this conversation after the war?"

"I hope so."

Sirach forces her pursing lips to form that knowing smile. "I enjoy these verbal sparring sessions of ours, you know. Not as much as our non-verbal sparring sessions, of course."

Evie wishes it weren't so difficult for her to remain angry with the woman. Sirach's actions still disturb her, but Evie also knows there is an inherent contradiction in her, a Crachian, lecturing Sirach on the morality of warfare.

Evie collapses onto the foot of the bed, leaning forward, forearms braced against her knees.

"Do you have any idea what's beyond the sea?" she asks Sirach. "To the west?"

"We've sent ships. We sent them to search for a new home for us all, away from the Crachian machine, though I'm sure it would find us eventually once it's done eating this land and realizes it will never be enough."

Evie waits.

"None of them ever returned," Sirach confirms. "Either the ships we sent found nothing, or what they found they decided to keep for themselves."

"Or something found them," Evie posits.

"Yes. Or something found them."

Evie looks up at her. Sirach is perhaps the fiercest warrior she's ever met. Evie may very well be the better fighter, but she can never hope to match the ferocity imbued by a lifetime of resisting extinction with every breath. She also cannot fathom carrying the weight of that struggle every single moment of every single day.

"Maybe we can find out for ourselves one day," Evie suggests.

"Maybe," Sirach says, though it is clear she can't bring herself to commit to the possibility. "In the meantime, shall we go wage a war?"

Evie nods, slapping her hands against her knees and standing up from the bed. She regards Sirach with a bitter smile. "Coincidentally," she says, "I don't have any other plans today."

BLOODLESS

LEXI ONCE ASKED TARU ABOUT COMBAT. WHILE IT'S TRUE that Lexi has witnessed very little fighting in her life, she can't imagine a fighter more proficient than her Gen's retainer. She has seen Taru best Savages and Aegins, several of whom were trying to take their life, and from Lexi's admittedly limited perspective, Taru dispatched every foe decisively and expertly.

Her retainer stated that effective combat operates on two basic principles: knowing the terrain and knowing your opponent. Taru went on to explain that studying one's opponent revealed weaknesses, while studying the terrain revealed your advantage. Once you've delved thoroughly into those two issues, the task becomes combining that information to form a plan of attack or defense.

When it comes to dealing with a superior enemy or larger force, Taru further explained, two elements often make the difference between victory and defeat. The first element is distraction. The second is surprise. According to Taru, the experienced fighter can use misdirection as deftly as a magician, whether it's in the feint of a single blade, or the arrangement of troops on a battlefield. That misdirection allows one to create tide-turning surprises for their foe. Smaller forces have used these tactics to overcome the odds for centuries, Taru insisted.

Distraction and surprise, Lexi finds herself repeating inwardly as she awakens in the fine, plush bed Burr has given her.

The memory of her retainer's lecture on combat theory is at the forefront of her mind for a single reason: Lexi has decided to take action. She will no longer wait for her captors to decide how best to fit her among the cogs in their conspiratorial wheel. She will no longer have them decide her fate.

Lexi begins the morning by visiting the gardens, as she often has, taking care to stay away from the monstrously manipulated pods that guard the gaps in the surrounding hedge wall. The lanterns are as lush and vibrant as any fruit-bearing plant in Crache. They have thus far provided her sole source of comfort and serenity in this place. She walks among them, dabbing the morning mist from her forehead with a silken handkerchief provided by her captors, among a slew of other lavish grooming items.

The old man moves silently among the lanterns, his withered face cast in the shadow of his straw hat's wilted brim. He gently mists the green stems and colorful folds of the lanterns with a water-filled bellows. His cart filled with pungent pig manure is parked beside the row.

"Good morning, Chivis," she bids the gardener, having learned his name several days ago.

"My lady," he replies, never wavering in his work or meeting her gaze.

It still grates Lexi, the way in which those dwelling in this secret estate use the antiquated greeting when addressing her. She feels no ill will toward Chivis, however. He is, in his way, as much a hostage of this place as she is.

"They look particularly lovely today," she comments, stroking her knuckles against the papery fold of a golden yellow lantern.

Chivis doesn't answer. She imagines he only speaks when he has something of value to say. She also considers that he rarely views what he has to say as valuable.

Lexi turns her attention inward for a moment, thinking of what she has in store for the rest of the day. Her resolve quivers, and she isn't certain she'll be able to follow through with her plans.

In the shadow of that doubt, she thinks of Brio. Of Evie. Of Taru. They are all out there fighting to get home while she sleeps in warm, soft beds and eats food grown, harvested, and prepared for her by the Ignoble's secreted indentured servants.

Lexi owes it to those others, and most of all to herself, to join the fight.

She reaches out once more and very carefully, as not to harm it, rolls back one of the lantern's folds to expose the fruit concealed within the bulb. A dozen plump berries the colors of bruises are bunched together, lush and ripe on their vine.

Lexi glances in Chivis's direction, but the old man shows no sign of protest, or even notice.

She extends a fingertip and gently tests the skin of the largest berry, finding it waxy and slightly moist.

"Poison, my lady," he warns her.

Chivis sounds neither concerned nor particularly alarmed by her actions. He is merely conveying to her a fact.

Storm clouds swell in Lexi's eyes as she stares at the lantern fruit.

"I know," she says darkly.

She carefully picks the ripened fruit from the pod, tucking a handful of berries inside her wrap.

For perhaps the first time since she encountered him, Chivis stops tending to his garden and looks directly at Lexi.

He says nothing. His expression remains dispassionate, but in his eyes she registers awareness. The old man cannot possibly know her plans, but Chivis clearly recognizes her intentions.

In the end, he returns silently and passively to his unending task of tending the garden.

It is as if the brief moment never passed between them.

Lexi smoothes her hands over the front of her wrap, ensuring the berries she has spirited there won't bulge too noticeably. Before she turns to exit the rows of lanterns, she leans close to the old man's mottled ear.

"You deserve to know more of the world than your garden," she whispers. "There is so much beauty beyond these hedges. I'm sorry you've never been allowed to see it. I truly am."

Chivis's rough hands halt in their work. Standing so close to him, Lexi sees his lower lip tremble at her words, and the corner of his eye become glassy with the beginnings of tears.

She touches his bony shoulder briefly before leaving him to his garden.

Pausing beside the manure cart, Lexi quickly and deftly uses her handkerchief to gather up a large clump of the foul-smelling pig droppings. She balls her fist around it tightly as she moves on.

Lexi returns to her rooms. She strides past the fire still burning in the hearth, lit in the coldest part of the morning. She enters the bedchamber and carefully unpacks the items she's sequestered from the garden, laying them out in a row on the foot of the plush feather-stuffed mattress. Examining each, she realizes the one item that is missing.

Lexi gathers up the hem of her wrap and begins tearing a long strip of material from the garment.

Daian fetches her every day around noon for a truly delicious and luxurious luncheon. Lexi cannot accuse her captors of being poor hosts.

She meticulously prepares the rooms that have served as her prison cell. The most important piece of the puzzle she constructs involves one of the many large, antique vases spread throughout the castle. Lexi pulls one down from its pedestal in her bedchamber. It takes her several minutes to administer to it before the vase is ready and suitable to her purpose.

There is a dressing closet standing in one corner of the front room, just down from the archway leading into the bedchamber. Lexi wedges it away from the corner just enough to allow her slender body to squeeze through. Before she does, she lifts the vase over the top of the closet and lowers the ceramic monstrosity behind the ancient piece of furniture, settling it gently on the floor.

Her final act is to open the doors of the dressing closet, exposing its barren innards.

Lexi slips into the empty space behind it and waits. She tries to think of anything except what will happen when Daian comes to get her. She tries to remember those unremarkable moments shared with Brio and Taru, moments of simple laughter shared between them, or the mere comfort of their presence. She finds she longs for those things the most right now.

Eventually, inevitably, she hears hundreds-year-old wood creak and equally aged iron squeal as the doors to her chamber are pushed open. She hears footfalls, gentle and steady at first, then hesitant as Daian fails to immediately spot her within the confines of the quarters.

"Lexi," he calls to her, tentatively.

She holds her breath, terrified an errant gasp or brief catch in her throat will give away her position.

"Lexi!" Daian beckons, more forcefully. "I know you're here. You may not be aware of it, but your door is kept under very attentive watch."

He waits, silent, for several long moments for an answer that doesn't come.

"I thought we'd moved beyond these games, especially after your trip down the plant's gullet."

For a single panicked moment, Lexi reconsiders what she is about to do. She knows if she comes out now, there will be no consequences. If she follows through with her plans, she may very well never leave this room alive again. Daian takes orders, but he is insane. Lexi knows that without any doubt. She also knows his is a cruel madness. He has reveled in killing the men he murdered right in front of her, just as he'd revel in killing her if she gave him the slightest reason.

She can't see it, but Lexi can almost feel him smiling salaciously around his next words.

"All right then, Te-Gen," he says with an almost melodious lilt, "if you want to play, we'll play."

The next thing she hears is several retreating footsteps, and then the sound of a metal bolt snapping home.

Daian has just locked the chamber doors, from the inside.

The next sound she registers is the unmistakable whisper of a dagger's blade clearing the leather of its scabbard. It is followed by a dense thud, and she imagines him stabbing the blade into the surface of the round table that greets entrants to the front room with an assortment of flowers atop it.

"Let's agree to keep this civil, yes?" he asks the rooms.

His footfalls mark him as walking to the hearth, and then back across the room. He takes his time, and each moment elevates the rushing of Lexi's blood.

She waits for him to investigate the corner of the front room in which she's secreted, but she never hears those footfalls approach.

Instead, from hiding she watches him pass into the bedchamber.

Lexi slips out from her concealment, desperately and quietly passing that vase once more over the top of the dressing closet as she does. It is not particularly heavy, but it is bulky and awkward, and her fear she'll drop it and expose herself almost makes that worry come true several times.

In the end, she manages to free herself from behind the closet and bring the vase down into her grip without making a sound.

Lexi edges along the piece of wall around which he just disappeared.

As carefully as she dares, she peers into the bedchamber.

Daian has paused, his back to her, staring intently at the curtains gathered on the left side of the window. The curtains on the other side are wafting and shimmering in the breeze. Their fellows on the left, however, are still, as if they are being anchored in place. Those curtains are bulging unnaturally.

"This is a very bizarre, unbecoming game you've chosen," he comments. "If you don't mind me saying."

Daian steps forward and rips away the curtains. The pillows Lexi bunched there passively meet his expectant gaze. Daian cocks his head, taking in the scene. "Huh."

Lexi breaks cover with the vase clenched between her fists. She openly rushes him, raising her makeshift weapon and readying herself to smash it over his skull.

Daian turns and calmly raises his arms, easily blocking the blow. He catches the bulbous ceramic urn by its rim and base and instantly halts her strike.

Lexi feels an unyielding weight slam against the pit of her stomach. She's knocked backwards off her feet and all the air in her lungs rushes out as Daian kicks her to the floor.

He wrests the vase from her grip as she falls. Daian holds it in front of him, a strange grin on his face.

Lexi practically slithers from the bedchamber, using her elbows to move her along the floor.

Daian pursues, in no particular hurry, exiting the bedchamber behind her. He idly turns the vase in his hands.

"So then," he says in the exhale of a deep breath, "your master plan to overcome me was to bash me in the head with this?"

"Not exactly."

Daian stares down at her curiously.

Lexi watches that curious gaze shift to the vase as he becomes aware that the ceramic is heating unnaturally in his grip. He turns it to peer inside the curved top of the vase, finding it has been plugged with wadded-up bedding from the chamber behind him. He can't see the burnt fuse Lexi fashioned from the material of her wrap, the smoldering pig manure to which it was tethered, or the fire devouring what's left of the air inside the vase.

Daian looks back at Lexi, opening his mouth to question her just as the vase explodes in his hands, peppering his face, chest, and neck with ceramic shards even as the concussive force sweeps him off his feet. His body is hurled against the wall, where the back of his head meets the unforgiving stone.

Lexi crosses her arms in front of her face as the ceramic flies, but she's able to safely peer between her forearms and watch Daian collapse to the floor, rolling lazily onto his back, disoriented.

She stands, holding her throbbing stomach and aching and wincing slightly with every step. Lexi walks over to the round table impaled by Daian's dagger. It takes her several moments and both hands to dislodge it.

Daian is scarcely moving, albeit breathing heavily, as she kneels above him, pressing the tip of his own blade to his throat. There are small cuts crying red tears all over his face and neck. His hands are even worse, each seeming to wear a crimson glove. His wide, vacant eyes stare up at the ceiling, blinking only occasionally.

"Can you hear me, Daian?" she asks breathlessly.

His voice is raspy and distant. "My ears are ringing and the world sounds like I'm underwater, but yes."

"Can you feel the blade at your neck?"

"Everyone seems to want to cut my throat lately."

"You would have to admit, you bring it on yourself."

He laughs hoarsely, convulsing from the chest as the laughter gives way to a fit of coughing.

Lexi waits patiently for the bout to pass.

"I want you to tell me how far we are from the Capitol," she orders him. "How close and in what direction is the nearest town?"

His eyes roll toward her, though his head remains unmoved.

"And if I don't?"

Lexi presses the tip of his dagger into the soft flesh of his throat. "A man who abhors boredom should fear death. Death is very boring."

"And final."

"Then I would answer my questions."

Daian attempts to lift his head, and quickly gives up on it as the slightest motion causes him to wince terribly.

"You've never killed anyone, Te-Gen," he states quite definitively.

Lexi says nothing.

"Fatally piercing someone isn't as easy as it seems," he assures her. "Particularly up close like this. You'll misjudge the amount of pressure required. Odds are you'll knick me just deeply enough to start the blood spurting. Once that happens, you'll panic. You'll withdraw the blade, and I'll be flailing on this floor like a docked fish, spraying blood every which way. At that point, you'll either have to start stabbing me, again and again, until I succumb, or run away. If I were a betting man—"

Lexi removes the tip of the blade from his throat and quickly and steadily draws it across his cheek, deep, slicing open his flesh.

Daian hisses painfully, shutting tight his eyes.

Lexi returns the dagger to his neck.

"I'm sorry to say I'm becoming accustomed to murder," she informs him. "I've witnessed so many as of late. My hands don't even seem to shake anymore."

"I lament your lost innocence," he says through tight, pain-strained lips.

"Answer my questions, Daian. I will not repeat them because I am certain you recall."

"So you can dash away on foot? Why not take me hostage, as your guide? Are you afraid you couldn't keep me subdued?"

"You are *not* leaving this room," she says resolutely.

"Neither are you," he calmly breathes.

Daian moves with a speed she wouldn't have thought possible, considering the state of him. He slaps the dagger from her grip with a single swipe of his arm, and then backhands her across the face with frightening power.

Lexi's cheek burns and her eye waters and swells shut. She doesn't feel her body flying across the floor, or even the impact of hitting it.

The next moment of which she is aware finds her lying several feet away from Daian, a deep throbbing in her left side from the awkward landing atop the stone floor.

Daian rolls over and uses the archway leading into the bedchamber to pull his body up.

Lexi watches, dazed, as he claws his way along the stone like a mountain lion scaling a rock face.

He stumbles with his first few steps, clearly still affected, but quickly finds his footing. Daian scoops up his dagger from where it landed in front of the bed. He hefts it in his hand a few times experimentally, and then closes his fist tightly around the handle.

Daian's eyes find her across the room.

Looking back at him, Lexi sees nothing of any version of the man she's known in that gaze.

All that remains is a monster, something burning from the inside that will only be quenched by blood.

She turns and crawls weakly across the room on her hands and knees. It's useless, of course. The only things in front of her are the dying embers in the hearth.

"Where would you go, Te-Gen?" he asks between hot pants of breath. "Would you crawl into the fire to escape me? Am I distasteful to you even when compared to burning? You seemed so fond of me once."

Hearing those words, and remembering the tender moments she shared with his alter ego, Lexi stops, dropping her head and closing her left eye; her right has shut all on its own from the blow it sustained.

She turns from resting on all fours and seats herself on the floor, opening her eye and staring up at him with unmasked contempt.

Daian smiles down on her.

"Lady Burr is going to be so *very* upset with me," he says, the implication clear.

Daian takes a final, menacing step toward her, and then falters.

Lexi waits, a steely calm spreading through her body, warming even the agonized parts.

He begins blinking rapidly, his eyes seeming to lose focus on her. Daian's ragged breath begins catching in his throat, until he seems as though he's suffocating.

"What is—"

His legs visibly shake before giving out on him. Daian drops to his knees. Lexi can hear bone cracking against the stone floor. The dagger drops from his limp hand.

"I told you," Lexi says. "You are *not* leaving this room."

"What . . . did you do?" he asks foggily.

"I coated the inside of the vase with juice from the lantern plant berries. You have been dead for several minutes. Your body is only now discovering it."

Again, Daian laughs. This time, however, a ribbon of blood spurts in its wake, dribbling over his lips and chin to drip onto his chest.

"You have never been boring, Lexi," he says, grinning grotesquely through the blood. "I'll give you that."

There is no humor in Lexi, dark or otherwise. She stares at him, fire in her single open eye.

"I don't know what manner of thing you truly are, or what made you that way. I may not escape this place, but I will not allow you to be unleashed back on the world, either. Goodbye, Daian."

He tries to speak more words, but only pushes up a sickly gargle from his throat.

Finally, he pitches forward onto the stone tiles, curling into an awkward ball and convulsing a few violent times before succumbing utterly.

Lexi waits until she is certain he's dead. Forcing herself forward, she tries to crawl over to his body, thinking to retrieve his dagger and take it with her. Her insides feel like they're on fire, as does the right side of her face. She begins to wonder if several of her ribs aren't broken. Lexi manages only a few inches before the pain of moving overwhelms her, and she sinks onto her right side where the agony is the least.

She quickly loses any sense of time. At some point a wetness touches her wounded cheek, searing the tender flesh, and she realizes she's crying.

Somewhere behind her, wood is smashed to what sounds like splinters as the doors to her rooms are battered open. There are half a dozen sets of footfalls this time.

They surround her, and for a brief while there is silence as those who have arrived take in the scene.

"Oh dear," Burr says high above her, "this is a dismal sight, isn't it?"

Lexi would laugh if laughter were a thing that still existed within her.

"Are you alive, my lady?" Burr asks her.

Lexi decides in that moment she would much rather pass out than speak with the odious woman, and so she does, gratefully.

DIVISION

"YOU MUST THINK OF CRACHE AS A CAREFULLY MAINTAINED garden," Trowel urges Dyeawan.

It is, by her count, his fifth explanation to her during this single meeting of the planners.

"Must I?" she retorts.

He ignores the barb. "Anything you extract from or introduce into the soil of one patch affects every other patch. We have designed this garden quite carefully, and every ounce of that soil is perfectly calibrated."

"I definitely see where the fertilizer comes from, anyway," Riko mutters to Dyeawan beneath a strategically placed hand.

Dyeawan is too weary to laugh, and she does not want to provoke more of Trowel's bluster, besides.

Trowel is responding to a proposed measure introduced by Dyeawan to shutter the Selection arm of the Spectrum. Growing up in the Bottoms, Dyeawan heard tales of backrooms where surgeons tended to babes born with the sensitive parts of both a man and a woman, but she had no idea the state sponsored an official service for such a procedure.

In truth, Dyeawan never had much contact, nor gave much thought, to the Undeclared, those citizens of Crache who refused Selection, refused to choose to be distinguished as either man or woman. The very notion that there is a classification for such people that separates them from the rest of the populace in that way is appalling to Dyeawan.

She discussed it with Riko, who wholeheartedly agreed the practice of and emphasis on Selection should end. She also agreed it is an outdated and barbaric process, and a poisonous attitude to cultivate among people.

Yet when Dyeawan asked her if an Undeclared has ever served the Planning Cadre, even her friend seemed surprised by the very idea.

That is how insidious such notions are, Dyeawan has come to realize.

She has to admit to herself that she possesses an ulterior motive for moving forward with the proposal. Selection seemed a good test case for her to introduce change to the other planners.

Apparently she underestimated the old guard's attachment to resisting change of any kind.

It is the third meeting over which she has presided, and thus far it appears to be producing the same fruitless results as the two before it, consisting primarily of Dyeawan introducing a notion and Trowel bloviating endlessly about why that notion is ridiculous and impossible to implement.

It is, however, the first meeting Oisin has chosen to attend since Dyeawan faced off with the Protectorate Ministry agent during her ascension to head of the planners. He haunts the back of the meeting room, arms folded beneath his dark half-cape as he surveys the planners' progress, or lack of it, silently and with what Dyeawan reads as a small measure of smugness.

Trowel continues his elaborate and nauseating analogy involving the various elements of effective garden tending, but she has finally stopped listening.

Nia, for her part, has yet to offer the table anything. She merely listens and observes passively, never making direct contact with Dyeawan's eyes.

"The prejudice against the Undeclared is counterproductive to advancing the minds of the people," Dyeawan argues when Trowel finally takes a breath.

"We do not want to advance their minds—we want to mold them."

Mold.

There are several other words among the many thousands she has learned since studying at the Planning Cadre that Dyeawan imagines better fit Trowel's intentions.

"The Undeclared as a group were fashioned to *breed* prejudice," Trowel informs her. "Long before your time, experiments were conducted by this body concerning both the effect and uses of prejudice. Minority groups, and their exclusion, are necessary to galvanize a populace as well as placate them. They are also keys to redirecting the majority's ire from the bureaucracy as necessary."

"I understand," Dyeawan says. "I once blamed a goat for breaking a window I hit with a rock."

Beside her, Riko giggles before she can check herself.

The behavior of the two appears to frustrate Trowel enough to silence him for at least a moment.

"Prejudice creates discord," Dyeawan says. "Discord creates civil disruption and violence."

"There is no violence in the streets of the Capitol, or in any Crachian city," Trowel says, haughtily dismissing the very notion.

"I've seen it. In the Bottoms."

He waves a wrinkled hand. "Not meaning to diminish your . . . origins, as it were, the Bottoms and districts like it were created to house the baser concerns of our nature. Much like opening a window to clear out a smoke-filled room. It is where the people of the city can go to indulge in depravity and barbarism. It also gives our bureaucracy a place to store population overflow. Resources are not infinite. Our people live well because we regulate those resources."

"People who matter, you mean," Dyeawan says.

"People who *produce*," he fires back.

"I am not arguing why the Bottoms are necessary," Dyeawan reminds him, knowing that that debate will have to wait for a day much later in her tenure. "I am speaking of the Undeclared."

"All of these mechanisms, my dear young one, were put in place for reasons beyond your understanding."

"There is nothing you know that is beyond my understanding," Dyeawan states plainly. "Or is ignorance as integral to your methods as prejudice?"

"I know a great deal that you do not."

"Then why did Edger name me to succeed him and not you?"

That stifles Trowel, obviously cutting him deeply.

"Your ideas are intriguing," Nia admits, probably to dilute the tension in the room. "There is, however, a process for ideas, a process you are unfamiliar with, Dyeawan, having skipped service in the Cadre's other departments. Ideas must travel through the proper channels before they reach this body, to be tested and refined."

"I never liked that part of the process as a builder, myself," Riko says.

"But as a planner, surely you understand it, Riko."

Dyeawan finds the way she keeps invoking the names of those to whom she speaks very grating.

She also finds it intensely annoying that Riko seems slightly charmed by it.

"Perhaps we should conclude for the day," Dyeawan suggests, tightly.

Trowel is out of his chair by the time she has finished speaking. "I hope you found this session illuminating," he says to her in passing, already walking away.

The old guard follows him readily, while the younger planners remain a moment longer, looking to both Dyeawan and Nia for guidance.

Dyeawan notices the division in their attentions, and it also concerns her.

"We'll try again tomorrow," she assures the others gently.

They part from the table with that, shuffling, disheartened, out of the room.

Nia finally favors Dyeawan with her gaze before she departs as well, but the older woman's expression tells Dyeawan very little.

"I don't think I like being a planner," Riko says honestly after the rest of them are gone.

"I'm not certain I do either," Dyeawan replies.

"Dinner, yeah? Take our minds away from this mess?"

Dyeawan dredges up a smile for her.

"I'll meet you there," she says.

Riko springs from her chair and practically bounds out of the room with that limitless energy of hers. It actually warms Dyeawan to watch her go.

Oisin lingers. When the table is empty save for Dyeawan, he finally saunters over to her.

"Your new regime seems to be going swimmingly," he says.

Dyeawan is in no mood to feign civility as she is forced to do with the others. "I can do without your commentary."

"I'm sure you can. I am here for our private briefing, on matters Edger always felt were best discussed away from the rest of the planners."

"I understand."

"We have implemented the street art campaign you devised," he relates to her. "Which, admittedly, is an inspired way to combat the rumors and graffiti circulating throughout the Capitol concerning this Sparrow General and her rebels. Our agents in other cities are doing the same."

That is only a preamble, Dyeawan knows, and not a particularly sensitive matter that couldn't be discussed in front of the others. She waits for him to express his true concerns.

"Secondly, if we will no longer be . . . liquidating certain less functional elements of the populace—"

"We will not," Dyeawan reaffirms, stiffly, the mere allusion to Edger's former atrocities setting her on edge.

"I understand. However, it will create population control issues. Not immediately, but after a time."

"Then we will have the cities reallocate resources. That is what they do."

"Not gladly, and not when it is to benefit those who do not serve the greater good."

"As they see it."

"As we have trained them to see it."

"What about the other task I appointed to you?" Dyeawan asks, changing the subject deliberately.

Oisin appears confused, but she sees that for the ruse it is. The Protectorate Ministry agent knows very well to what she is referring.

"Ah, yes—the question of your parentage. I have assigned the appropriate and necessary personnel. They will glean whatever information is available, but I would not hold out hope."

"I do not have to hope. They will do as I've ordered them to do."

Oisin frowns. "Such records are not kept in the Bottoms. The orphanages there are little more than larders for storing children."

"I remember."

"I'm sure. And our census only tabulates population numbers in such districts. We do not keep tabs on individuals."

"We're not important enough, I know," she says impatiently.

"You are *not* one of them, not anymore, and you would do well to cease thinking of yourself as such. It might help you better assimilate in your new role."

Dyeawan stares up at him coldly.

"I know what I am."

"That is good to know. Is there anything else for the time being?"

She sighs. "What of the uprising in the east?"

"It may be quashed even as we speak," Oisin says, sounding genuinely unconcerned.

"I do not want the hollow confidence spread around this table," Dyeawan tells him. "I want the truth."

"The rabble will never see the inside of the Tenth City. That is the truth. The pressing issue is containing stories about the rabble, and your notion in that vein should work well."

Dyeawan nods, satisfied enough.

Oisin smiles emptily. "Good. I believe you and I are beginning to find our own rhythm."

She chooses to remain silent until Oisin takes the hint and retreats.

"Good day, planner," he bids her as he walks away.

Dyeawan is left alone at the long slab of the meeting table. She looks to each empty seat, finding something foreboding in the absence of the others.

"I'm not certain I do either," she says to no one, repeating the words she spoke to Riko.

SIEGE THE DAY

THE REBELLION IS MASSED HALF A MILE OUTSIDE THE TENTH City gates, writhing as a single entity made of steel and leather and flesh.

Evie rides alongside Sirach, who has traded her shadowy camouflage for light leather armor that won't inhibit her catlike movements. The two long, thin, half-moon-curved blades she favors are sheathed in a crisscross over her back like the outline of a scarab's wings. Sirach also covers her face and skull in plated leather that is more mask and hood than helm.

Evie can't help admiring her enemy-turned-lover's odd sense of combat fashion, or more precisely how Sirach makes it work for her when the fighting is thick and bloody.

Their mounts carry them to the rear of the formation. The walls of the city loom large overhead in the distance.

"I've never been to the Tenth City," Evie muses. "It's strange to see a Crachian city with high walls around it, protected by gates."

"You forget, it isn't a Crachian city," Sirach replies. "It's a stolen kingdom. The last one Crache conquered. Its previous occupants knew very well what was coming. They built these walls to protect them from your people."

"So it fell once," Evie concludes.

Sirach smiles bitterly. "It pleases me you homed in so keenly on the point of my story."

"I understood your story," Evie says. "If I didn't agree with the sentiment, I wouldn't be leading an open revolt against the largest and most brutal nation in the known world."

Sirach nods, still grinning. "Fair enough."

"What was its name?" Evie asks her after the agitation has faded. "The kingdom that existed here before it became the Tenth City of Crache. Do you remember?"

"Of course I remember," Sirach says, more somberly this time. "It was my people's kingdom."

Evie turns her head to regard the woman with surprise. In all their time together, Sirach has never divulged that information.

Sirach does not look at her, nor does she actually reveal the name of her ancestors' lost kingdom.

They approach the vanguard of the attack. Their advanced forces are composed of soldiers and warriors from all three main rebel factions, each supplying an equal measure of their people.

The issue of the vanguard very nearly caused a riot in the rebel camp several nights before. When drawing up their plans for the siege, Mother Manai suggested the B'ors act as vanguard in the attack, her reasoning being the B'ors are the rebellion's fiercest close-quarters fighters.

While Evie certainly agrees, she knew as soon as Mother said it that the B'ors would not take the suggestion as a compliment.

She was right.

The B'ors refused to be used as fodder for the very people who have frequently enslaved and very nearly extinguished their story from the world. The ex-Savages argued the Skrain for far too long had used them as fodder. The Sicclunans countered that both the ex-Savages and the B'ors, willingly or not, had helped the Skrain exterminate their nomadic assemblage for decades beyond count.

They all had legitimate points, and they all knew it. Voices grew louder and angrier until the assemblage was seconds from drawing weapons when Evie put forth that each faction would supply an equal number of soldiers to the vanguard, and that they would act as one force.

It was a reminder to Evie that her generalship consisted primarily of keeping her own army from abandoning their shared cause and slaughtering one another.

Spud-bar, the Savage Legion's former armorist, is kneeling beside a repurposed wagon wheel, attending to its spoke. It is one of four wheels attached to a long rectangular platform fitted with handholds along each side. The platform is supporting a massive battering ram fashioned from a felled oak tree. The business end of the tree has been capped with steel forged to a spiraling tip for piercing the thick wooden gates of the city.

Evie gently guides her mount toward Spud-bar until she is peering down at the armorist from her saddle.

"Can I have the first ride on your new sled?" she asks them.

Spud-bar glances over their shoulder without humor, snorts with the derision of a hog sniffing rancid truffles, and returns to ministering to the spoke.

"I've done the best I can with what I have and the time I had to do it," Spud-bar explains. "The Sicclunans didn't bring any siege weapons."

"We don't have any siege weapons," Sirach informs them, sidling up beside Evie on her own mount. "We rarely siege, and never whole cities. Our military focus has traditionally been on surviving outright extinction, you see."

"That a fact, now?" Spud-bar replies noncommittally, and without looking back.

"I notice your former Legionnaires haven't supplied the war effort much more than rusty steel and their own largely grooming-neglected bodies."

The frown Evie levels at Sirach is as disapproving as a hurled dagger.

Spud-bar halts in their work. Evie watches the armorist's head drop for several silent moments. Finally, they stand from the undercarriage of the mobile battering ram and turn to face Sirach's mount.

"We didn't bring any siege weapons because we *are* siege weapons," the armorist ruefully reminds Sirach. "The Skrain maintained the artillery. We were just fleshy pieces."

Sirach cocks her head with a vicious twist to her lips. "I hear 'we' and 'us,' but did you not stay behind with your wagon full of kitchen knives?"

Evie decides to step in before this discussion devolves into a real argument between the two.

"So what is the final tally?" she asks the armorist.

Spud-bar's eyes linger menacingly on Sirach a moment longer, but in the end the armorist sighs, resigned, and turns their attention to Evie.

"Two battering rams, three dozen or so ladders, one complete siege tower that's mostly sticks bound with jerked cat intestines, and another siege tower that's half-finished, but makes for an excellent spot for a bit of bird watching."

"Your sense of humor is improving, at least," Evie compliments them with a wry grin.

Spud-bar snorts once more. "I'd rather our chances were improved."

"All we have is chance, my larger comrade-in-arms," Sirach says.

Spud-bar ignores her this time. "Fortunately for us, there isn't a living Skrain who remembers defending a city under siege. Crachian cities aren't readied for one, neither. They're as unprepared to defend the city as we are to take it. They won't have any catapults, and I doubt they'll field that many archers, or at least ones worth a damn. Odds are fair they'll hide behind the walls and just wait for rescue."

"Considering we'll have to defend the city as soon as we seize it," Sirach says, "it's probably a good thing we aren't setting it ablaze with fiery catapults or knocking over the walls."

"Sure, we'll call it strategy," Spud-bar replies, their voice dripping with irony. "That sounds much better."

Sirach laughs at that, heartily, though she is the only one of them who does.

"It's simple, then," Evie calmly affirms. "We batter down the gates, fight our way inside, put down the Skrain and the Aegins, reseal the doors, and prepare ourselves for the rest of the Skrain to attack."

"This tactical mastery is clearly why you are the general, General."

"We go with what we've got," Evie says, ignoring Sirach's customary gentle mocking.

"That's all any of us can do," Spud-bar says.

Their words sound begrudging, and certainly unhappy, but Evie appreciates the armorist's assent all the same.

"You need to see to your tribespeople before the war starts," Spud-bar says to Evie. "They've broken formation to have some kind of row or something."

Curious, Evie rears her mount and leaves them behind as she trots along the front line.

Several dozen yards away, she discovers that the B'ors warriors among the army's vanguard are gathered around their Storyteller, Yacatek; a revered leader among her people.

One of her primary responsibilities as a B'ors Storyteller is to record the history of their tribe, the most common and traditional way being on the blade of a dagger carved from stone. When the space on that blade has been exhausted, the Storyteller buries the dagger. It doesn't matter where; the B'ors trust such implements will be unearthed in their own time, by whomever is meant to find them.

Yacatek cradles the leather-wrapped handle of such a dagger in one hand. She delicately chips away at the flat of the stone blade with a tiny arrowhead-shaped piece of rock pinched between her thumb and forefinger. The markings it leaves are impossibly small and intricate.

When she is finished, the Storyteller kisses the blade of the dagger before giving it to the nearest tribesman. Evie watches as each warrior presses their lips reverently to the flat of the inscribed blade before handing it with equal reverence to their next closest comrade.

By the time the story dagger has been returned to Yacatek, it has been kissed by a hundred lips.

The warriors slowly disperse to rejoin the loose formation of the vanguard. Yacatek remains behind, kneeling in the grass.

She returns the miniature chisel to a pouch on her belt, drawing in its stead a wooden scoop that looks like an unfinished cup. Yacatek uses it to dig in the ground at her feet, creating a shallow pit just deep enough to welcome her storied blade.

Evie urges her mount forward, watching the Storyteller bury the dagger.

"What is written on that one?" she inquires.

"Their names."

"All that fits on one blade?"

Yacatek smiles wryly. "I write small."

"Shouldn't you wait to bury it until after the battle is over? It seems to me that's a story without an ending."

"It is not the story of a battle. It is the story of people."

"Just as well. I imagine you'd need a fairly big dagger to record what's about to happen here," Evie remarks.

Yacatek slowly shakes her head.

"No?" Evie asks, genuinely surprised and confused by the woman's response.

"Battles receive little storytelling. My people believe in passing on who we are and how we live, not how we die."

"Isn't the fight for life part of all that?"

"So is breathing air. So is emptying your bowels in the morning. Do you sing songs about that?"

Evie blinks down at her in silence, unsure how to respond.

"Revering battle only births more battles," Yacatek assures the younger woman.

"Yet your people have joined this fight."

Yacatek nods. "We have joined this fight. And we will see it through."

"And we are grateful. The B'ors *are* fierce warriors."

Yacatek looks up at Evie with an expression of disappointment.

"Is that all we are to you, Sparrow General?"

Evie opens her mouth to answer, but halts her words. She takes the time to truly think about the Storyteller's question.

"I suppose I don't really know who you are, do I?"

Yacatek contemplates Evie silently for a moment longer, and then dips her head, seeming almost satisfied.

"I hope you live," the Storyteller says. "You still have much to learn, but you have the head to learn it, I think."

Evie grins. "You once told me you're not here to be my teacher."

"I am not," Yacatek remarks, and says no more. Having filled in the hole cradling the B'ors' story dagger, she flattens the repackaged earth with the bottom of her scoop and begins to rise.

"Do you fight alongside your warriors?" Evie asks.

"My name is on the knife," Yacatek says as if that is answer enough.

The Storyteller parts from her. Evie watches the B'ors leader go, marveling at the air of serenity that seems to encompass Yacatek even amidst such chaos. She is at once strengthened by the woman's presence and disturbed by the notion she is responsible for leading Yacatek and her people into this battle.

Evie then proceeds to gallop up and down the line, performing one final inspection of their formation. The faces of former Savages, refugee Crachians, freed warriors of the B'ors, and Sicclunan soldiers all blur together into a single visage. Not being able to distinguish their faces makes it easier for Evie, at first, but with that comes feelings of guilt. Regardless of the success of their siege, she is about to order many of them to their death. She should have to see each of their faces, and never forget a single one.

Evie draws her sword from its sheath, holding it aloft as she rears her mount to confront the city gates and the walls that extend around them. She feels the blood pounding between her ears like the drums of war carried by the Skrain. She already feels out of breath, though the exertion of battle has yet to begin.

In the distance, from high atop the city walls, Evie hears scattered shouts. It briefly occurs to her they don't sound like military officers bellowing commands, but she doesn't have time to puzzle over it. She is ready to give the order to begin the siege.

Evie's mouth opens wide, her throat rumbling with the cry to charge that will send the vanguard screaming across the field.

At that exact moment, Mother Manai steps forward from the

front line. She raises the honed steel that has replaced her right hand, pointing its prongs at the city gates.

"Evie!" she calls to her general, more in astonishment than alarm.

Evie allows the battle cry to die on her tongue, lowering her sword.

She watches with a dropped chin as the Tenth City gates open wide, seemingly of their own accord.

Two figures emerge from inside the city, both of them appearing to be prodded reluctantly forward.

Evie recognizes the tunic of an Aegin and the armor of a Skrain soldier. The Aegin bears first-class stripes. The Skrain is wearing a captain's insignia on his armor emblazoned with the symbol of the Crachian ant. Neither of them is armed—their scabbards are empty and they carry nothing in their hands.

The Skrain captain abruptly collapses to his knees as if pushed from behind, and that's when Evie sees several figures walking behind the pair. One of them is tall, bald, and thickly muscled. He wears the apron and the dark, sooty smudges of a blacksmith. His trade is also clearly revealed by the hammer he wields in his hand. He's joined by an old, round woman with shocks of white hair and a withered face, clothed in tatters and brandishing a meat cleaver stained with dried blood and bits of crusted entrails.

Evie can see many more behind the two, throngs, all of them appearing to be people like those who live in the Bottoms of the Capitol. Still more are armed with makeshift weapons.

Sirach breaks formation on her mount and urges it quickly across the field, bringing the horse to heel beside Evie.

"What's happening?" Sirach demands breathlessly.

"They've taken the city," Evie marvels. "They've taken the city without us."

It is as though Sirach doesn't understand the language Evie is speaking.

"Who?" she asks, genuinely confounded.

"The people," Evie answers.

BLOOD LIES

THE SCENT OF THE TEA IS PUNGENT, EARTHY, AND INVITING. Lexi watches Burr prepare it with slow, deliberate movements and what seems to Lexi to be strange and unnecessary gestures. It is almost performative, the way Burr uses a silken cloth to carefully clean the tiny ceramic cups and bowls and thin wooden instruments, ladle and spoon and stirrer. When she's finished, Burr lays the cloth upon the table between them and deliberately folds it in halves until it forms a perfect, compact triangle.

Lexi soon realizes what she is witnessing is a ceremony.

Burr collects a spoonful of the tea in its dark green powdery form, scooping it into the cup in front of her. She ladles boiling water from a larger bowl into the cup. Hot steam rises from the top like angry spirits.

"I thought I would favor you with a taste of the world as it was when my noble ancestors ruled."

"I've had tea before," Lexi assures her.

"Of course you have. The *way* of tea, however, the *ceremony*, has been lost to Crache for many generations."

The older woman gently stirs the tea half a dozen times.

Afterward, she carefully cleans the slim reed before setting it aside.

Finally, Burr takes up the cup in both hands and offers it to Lexi, who draws a deep breath before reluctantly accepting.

She sips cautiously. The tea is deliciously hot on her tongue. It soothes her throat as she swallows. It comforts her entire body as it warms her stomach.

Lexi briefly ponders the ramifications of smashing the now empty ceramic cup into the side of Burr's skull.

"How are you healing?" Burr asks her.

"Fine," Lexi replies tightly. "Your surgeon is very talented. Gen Stalbraid hasn't been able to keep a surgeon on staff for quite some time. I've been relegated to seeing the Gen Circus healer for years."

"And how are they?"

"Drunk, usually."

Burr gives her unpleasant, disingenuous laugh. "It seems a shame, a crime even, that a Gen contributing so selflessly to the welfare of the Crachian people is allocated so few resources by Crache in return."

"Wasn't it you who said my Gen is obsolete?"

Burr issues a dismissive breath. "A mere performance for those fools on the Franchise Council. I have the utmost respect for Gen Stalbraid's compassion and advocacy for the people in the Bottoms."

"I suppose nobility sees more value in the lives of the poor and forgotten."

"Nobility is a caretakership of the common people, my lady. There are good caretakers and bad caretakers."

Lexi says no more on the subject, knowing the futility of these arguments between them. Burr is a fanatic. There is no way to rationally debate such a person.

Burr finishes preparing her own tea, and sips idly in the silence that follows. Finally, she says: "And how are you coping with the emotional strain of your deathly struggle with our dear, departed Daian?"

Lexi feels her every muscle tightening. "He was a madman."

"He was that," Burr says. "His madness had its uses, but perhaps you killing him was a blessing in disguise. He could no longer serve my interests as an Aegin, after being targeted by the Protectorate Ministry and killing the other Aegins they dispatched to eliminate him."

"A terrible loss," Lexi replies with a distinct absence of sympathy.

"Not an altogether irreplaceable one, however."

Lexi narrows her eyes at the woman, not following.

"Sir Kamen!" Burr calls out.

Lexi looks past her to the chamber doors.

An affable-looking man in the middle of his life enters her quarters. He wears an Aegin's uniform with second-class markings and carries a leather folder under one arm. His smile is warm and friendly, so much so that he seems wholly out of place in such sinister company.

"This is Kamen Lim," Burr says. "The Capitol knows him as an Aegin in good standing. His comrades-in-arms know him as an honest, reliable man of unflappable character."

"I'm happy for you," Lexi says pleasantly.

"In truth, Sir Kamen is an anointed knight."

It takes all of Lexi's self-control not to laugh openly at Burr's antique and fantastical language. The woman might as well say Kamen Lim is a dragon.

"He serves my house by posing as an Aegin," Burr continues.

"So he is like Daian," Lexi concludes, darkly.

"I'm not nearly as volatile, I promise you," Kamen says, bowing his head respectfully, his smile unwavering and unchanged.

"He is, however, every bit as resourceful," Burr says with menacing impetus.

She looks up at Kamen Lim, giving the slightest of nods with her chin. Lim obediently removes the folder from beneath his arm and places it on the table in front of Lexi.

She peers down, disinterestedly at first, but one feature sparks recognition within her.

There, burned into the leather, is the symbol of Gen Stalbraid. Beneath that, much smaller, are two characters representing a familiar name. Lexi reaches out and traces the markings with a fingertip.

"This belongs to my husband," she says. "It was his father's when he served Gen Stalbraid as pleader to the Bottoms. This is the old man's monogram."

Burr sips her tea with a noncommittal expression. "Curious."

Lexi's gaze moves from the charred leather to bore into the other woman. "I dispatched my retainer to collect this."

"More curious."

Lexi takes up the folder and uncoils the cord that binds its flap. She reaches within and unsheathes a ream of inked parchment. She immediately recognizes the official seal of the Spectrum. Even a cursory examination of the parchment's contents is enough for her to know these are the documents referencing the Savage Legion and its true purpose that were collected by Brio.

"Where is Taru?" Lexi asks her stiffly.

"He . . . she . . . which is it? I have never understood how these Undeclared choose to categorize themselves."

Burr glances up at Kamen Lim, who shrugs good-naturedly.

"Neither," Lexi offers in an exasperated breath.

Burr stares back at her. "Pardon me?"

"Neither he nor she."

"How very radical. What say you to that, Sir Kamen?"

Lim rubs his jaw pointedly. "I would categorize the lady's retainer as a good fighter."

Burr nods. "Well enough."

"I assume you have a reason for informing me, in your maddening way, that you hold Taru's life in your hands," says Lexi.

"Motivation," Burr says simply. "It is time for an alternate approach to our partnership. You've proved resistant to my original plan of action."

"You mean to assault my mind and break me down until I bend willingly to whatever you want from me?"

"As I said, you have proved resistant. It is time for another approach. If you will not see the wisdom in Ignoble rule, you will simply have to fear the consequences of not helping us."

"What do you want me to do?"

"Why, precisely what you have taken it upon yourself to do in your husband's absence: be the caretaker of those residing in the Bottoms. Not their pleader, mind you, but their true matron."

"What does that mean to you? What do you want me to do in the Bottoms?"

"Feed the people, for a start. More than a few meals, I mean. We will provide for you amply from our larders to that purpose."

"Why should you care that the people are well fed?"

For the first time, Burr appears impatient with her. "I care that *you* feed them," she says. "I care that the ardor they displayed for you in the gallery of the Spectrum blossoms into outright fervor."

Lexi falls silent, turning contemplative. The full weight of what is being proposed here is beginning to settle upon her. "How will I account for all that food?" she asks carefully. "It will be far beyond the allocation for Gen Stalbraid. The Franchise Council will ask questions, or at least the members who are not you."

Burr waves her free hand while taking a sip of her tea. "We have other Gens loyal to our cause. They will supplement whatever you need. Failing that, we have endless ways to redirect state resources. You needn't worry."

"Very well, but how do I simply . . . return after such a prolonged absence? And what of the Protectorate Ministry agents who Daian murdered in my home? How do I explain all of that?"

"The bodies were removed from your home and the scene was thoroughly cleansed of any sign they were ever there. No one can connect you to the disappearance of those agents, at least not directly or with any proof. They might as well have just walked off a cliff. You've done nothing wrong. Taking time to one's self in seclusion violates no Crachian law."

"The Protectorate Ministry will never believe any of that. They already tried to kill me once."

"Which is all the more reason to return to the people in the Bottoms who have taken you so passionately in their embrace. The Protectorate Ministry cannot simply erase someone so visible. Your safety will be assured by the task to which I am assigning you."

"What is the real reason you'd have me do this? What do you gain?"

"As you feed and clothe and elevate the people of the Bottoms, I want you to tell them a story."

"A story?"

"Yes. You will tell them a story about an age of nobility, when benevolent lords and ladies of ancient and royal blood took care of their people, who knew neither hunger nor strife under their rule."

"So you want me to lie."

"I want you to light a fuse, my lady. That fuse will burn slowly, but it *will* burn, and when it finally reaches every heart and every mind in the Bottoms, you will have served your purpose."

"And then?"

"And then you will be rewarded," Burr assures her.

Another acid-laced reproach is poised on the tip of her tongue, but Lexi stifles it. She recalls her moment of realization in Burr's gardens, after Lexi came within inches of being swallowed by a giant plant. It was the first time she understood the depth of influence and power Burr and her Ignobles had amassed beneath the surface of Crachian bureaucracy, unbeknownst to the nation they pretended to serve.

Now Lexi truly grasps the focus of all that hidden machinery. Burr is waging a secret war against the Protectorate Ministry and all the powers behind Crache. She and the former nobles want to topple, or at the very least take control of the state; not for any altruistic purpose, and certainly not to help people like those subsisting in the Bottoms. Burr wants a return to nobility, and she wants to ascend to what she feels is her rightful place in that hierarchy.

Only a few months ago, Lexi would've thought the woman insane. Now she sees the genuine threat Burr represents. The Ignoble is wily and lethally cunning, and possesses the will to enact her fantasies of restoring the bygone era of lords and ladies and knights.

Burr knows to accomplish such a monumental shift in power and culture that she will need the people of Crache to embrace the idea of nobles and nobility once more. She obviously sees Lexi as part of winning that support.

Lexi wants nothing more than to spit in the woman's face. The Ignobles seizing control of the state would just be swapping the head of one beast for another. In either case, the people will continue to be eaten.

However, they not only hold Lexi's life in their hands—they have Taru.

Lexi knows they both need more time, at the very least.

"Very well," she says. "If all you are asking me to do is feed the people, then I accept."

"Whatever else would I expect of you, my lady?" Burr replies with the sweetest of smiles.

CHOP

IT IS THE SECOND TIME IN THE PAST HOUR SOMEONE HAS vomited on Taru's boots.

The hold of the Skrain galleon is among the most cramped, foul-smelling spaces Taru has ever occupied. The retainer and the rest of the Savages in their company have been crammed inside of it, door locked from the outside, for days and nights on end. The food has been quite literally rotten, the water sparse, and the companionship less than desirable.

And now a storm is tossing the ship around like some vicious cat batting about its supper before the kill.

After being marched half to death to the shores outside the Fourth City (Savages could hardly be seen deployed from a Crachian city port), they were hustled onto rowboats and sped out to be loaded onto a fleet of ships anchored in the bay. The skies darkened for days, but the full brunt of the storm didn't hit the fleet until almost a week at sea.

Now it seems as though they are paying for not heeding the sky's repeated warning. It is all Taru can do to stay in their rickety seat, so dramatic is the pitching and yawing of the craft around them. The crack of thunder seems to shake the very air. The retainer is soaked to the bone. Every grain of wood seems to be leaking, and the salt water is up past their ankles. They haven't been able to keep a candle lit in hours, but the constant flash of lightning keeps the hold steadily illuminated.

It is at least enough for Taru to see the despair across the features of every face around them.

One of the others falls to the floor in front of the retainer. Frail and old, he claws at his own stomach in agony. He's hardly the first to shit himself to death over the past week on this little jaunt, but that hasn't made Taru any more indifferent.

As they lean forward to render aid, a deafening boom overhead drowns out the man's screams. Taru flings themself against the wall of the hold as the deck above collapses under the weight of the ship's mast, the massive, broken beam crashing through the ceiling of the hold and piercing all the way through the bottom of the ship.

Water rushes inside, flooding the hold in column-size jets.

The panic breaks loose whatever tenuous restraints were previously keeping it in check. Taru can no longer even see the man they were going to help, and now they watch as others jump right into the middle of the sudden tide pool, never to reemerge.

Standing atop the seat their tired rear was occupying only a moment ago, Taru looks across the rising water to the severed length of the mast protruding from the hole in the deck above.

Girding themself, Taru leans into the curved wall of the hull and bends their knees before leaping over the flooded hull and onto the body of the mast. It is as drenched as everything else, but Taru's hands manage to grab hold of the rigging still wrapped around the mast. The retainer encircles the thick beam with their legs and begins shimmying up its length.

It takes long moments, countless splinters perforating their flesh, and several slips back down the mast before Taru emerges above deck. The panic reigns here, too. Wranglers and Skrain all scramble in futile attempts to both escape the nearly capsizing ship and to somehow save it.

Taru rolls from the broken mast onto the deck just as the entire vessel slumps forward, tilting awkwardly in the water, which rushes up to swallow the bow.

The rain is like frozen bits of glass, the wind feels as though it will rip the flesh from their bones, and the thunder seems to be inside their head. Somehow Taru manages to find their feet atop the slick, uneven surface of the ship's deck. Squinting through the darkness, they stumble forward, peering around in hopes of finding a rowboat still tethered to the galleon.

A hard surface collides with the side of Taru's face, clipping their jaw and knocking them momentarily senseless. They are dropped to the broken, slanted deck. Taru finds themself sliding down the sudden incline several feet before grasping the slots in the deck, halting their momentum.

Taru turns their bloody cheek toward the cutting sheets of rain slicing the deck.

For the first and only time, Erazo looms tall above the retainer, clutching the handle of his wooden bludgeon in one hand and grinding its rounded end against the soaked palm of his other hand.

He grins malevolently.

"I guess dying in battle has been taken off the table!" the sadistic wrangler shouts down at them over the gales.

He raises the bludgeon and brings it down toward Taru's skull, only for the retainer to reach up and snatch his wrist in mid-flight, blocking the blow.

"Not yet!" Taru shouts back.

They ram their opposite fist up into the wrangler's groin, lifting Erazo half a foot from the deck. His plump body seizes around Taru's arm, his shriek rising above the sound of the thunder and lightning crashing around the vessel.

Taru unclenches their fist and grips the wrangler's trousers, tightly clutching the wet material. Their other hand reaches for the scruff of his neck, grasping him like an errant puppy.

Standing with a prolonged and primal scream, the retainer hoists the man's entire body above their head, holding him suspended there as Taru carefully balances their feet on the wet, uneven deck.

Erazo squeaks some words of protest, or perhaps pleading, but the retainer cannot hear them above the cries of the storm.

Bending their knees and elbows, Taru pitches forward and slams the wrangler's body down upon a piece of the ship's felled yardarm, breaking his back and silencing him forever.

Gasping for breath after the brief scuffle and massive feat of strength, Taru doubles over, clutching their knees and spitting rainwater at what's left of the deck below.

Half the Skrain vessel is submerged now, and the bubbling maelstrom of water surrounding the ship is quickly consuming the rest. Taru forces themself to stand, and begins making their way to the stern, scouring the portion of the ship still above water for something to use as a makeshift raft.

There is nothing, however. Taru is alone on the rapidly descending end of a sinking ship in the middle of an angry sea.

Lightning flashes close enough for Taru to feel the hairs on their arms rise through the dampness of their skin. A brief yet invigorating charge jolts through their body. It is then they decide not to die here, sucked up by the gurgling mouth of the whirlpool directly below them.

Drawing in the most expansive lungful of air they can manage, Taru leaps over the side of the doomed craft, plunging headlong into the chaotic waters.

THE CHALLENGE

DYEAWAN LIES AMONG THE SCALE MODEL BUILDINGS OF the Capitol, her thin body filling the main thoroughfare that stretches in front of the Spectrum. Her small hands, the inside of each palm crisscrossed with thin white scars from years of dragging the rest of her along the alleys of the Bottoms, are folded atop the woolen gray tunic material covering her abdomen.

Riko is lying in the intersecting street, her heels propped up on a miniature sky carriage tower, her right hand cradling the back of her head.

The two girls' heads are practically touching. They both stare wistfully at the domed ceiling of the map room. The stone is painted to appear as the clouded sky, complete with a sun rendered in gold dust that catches the light from the windows of the room and actually shines.

"I missed this," Riko says quietly. "Lying here, looking up at that gold sun. I used to do it a lot before you made me all fancy and important."

"I didn't 'make' you anything," Dyeawan gently insists. "I just asked for your help."

"I don't feel all that helpful so far."

"We are just beginning," Dyeawan replies.

Riko neither agrees nor disagrees with her.

"Do you mind me doing it with you?" Dyeawan asks a moment later.

"What?"

"This."

Riko shakes her head, smiling. "It's better with company."

It warms Dyeawan to hear that. Riko allows her head to tilt to one side, leaning her temple against that of her friend.

Dyeawan reaches up and idly rubs the ends of Riko's short hair between her fingertips. She's dyed just the straight-cut tips blue to match her gray planner's tunic, and Dyeawan studies the icy shade with fascination.

"So what is it you *really* want to do with the planners?" Riko asks her in earnest. "And how can I help? Besides backing you to the other planners, yeah?"

Dyeawan thinks carefully about her answer, letting the silken strands of hair slip from her fingers.

"I want us to do what Crache has always promised to do for its people. *All* of its people. And we are going to begin with the Capitol, with the Bottoms. Everyone there should have the same kind of comfort and safety the rest of the city enjoys."

"I never really thought about the people there much before you came to the Cadre," Riko admits. "It's easy not to think about them here, removed from everyone and everything. They teach us to think of all the cities as problems to be solved, instead of places where people, real people, live and . . . die."

"I understand," Dyeawan assures her friend, and she means it. "I don't blame you for anything."

Riko barely seems to hear her. The brilliant young girl is lost in her own thoughts.

"I feel like it has to start with purpose, yeah?" she says.

"What's that? What starts with purpose?"

"The people in the Bottoms having what you said, what everyone else in the Capitol has. The Gens live comfortably because they all serve a purpose. People in the Bottoms aren't given the opportunity to have the same."

"How do we give them the opportunity to serve their purpose?"

Riko is obviously thinking intensely about the problem now.

Before she can offer up her solution, Mister Quan glides into the map room, halting before the table and dutifully waiting.

Dyeawan leans her chin forward to peer at him, thankful his stature rises above the skyline of the miniature city.

"Is it time, Mister Quan?"

He bows his head in the affirmative.

Riko sighs. "These planner meetings aren't nearly as fun as I thought they'd be. I imagined we'd talk more about inventing and less about administering ourselves."

"You cannot design a bureaucracy without becoming one, it seems."

Riko grins as she sits up in the model street. "You know, I kind of miss the way you used to talk," she says.

Dyeawan looks at her curiously. "Ignorant?"

"You were *never* ignorant," Riko says.

"Then what is it you miss?"

"I don't know. You sounded so much more . . . innocent, yeah?"

Dyeawan falls silent, contemplating that word.

Riko frowns. "I'm sorry, I didn't mean—"

"No, you're right. I'm not innocent anymore. I can't afford to be."

"I talk too much."

Dyeawan stares hard at her. "Don't ever stop making yourself heard, Riko."

That seems to make her friend feel better, even emboldened.

Riko leaps to her feet, quickly and gingerly darting among the building models and sculpted city features without trampling so much as a streetlight or noodle stand. She hops down from the living map gracefully beside Mister Quan.

Dyeawan sits up. Her tender is waiting at the edge of the lake-size table. She presses the flat of her palms against the table and begins scooting her body along the flawless copy of the city street.

Riko waits, silently and patiently. She has learned not to ask Dyeawan if she wants help, trusting her friend to ask for it as needed.

Mister Quan, likewise, defers to Dyeawan in all matters. He bows respectfully as she reaches the end of the street, and the table.

Dyeawan carefully lifts her legs over the edge of the map table and folds them before lowering herself down onto the platform of her tender.

"Would you like a ride?" she asks Riko with a grin.

"Don't mind if I do."

Riko hops up onto the platform behind Dyeawan, gently resting her hands on her friend's shoulders.

Dyeawan runs her hands over the paddles that look like the armrests of a chair. This is no chair, however. The paddles are connected to the tracks of wheels beneath the tender's platform, controlling the tracks through a system of cords and chains and smaller steel wheels edged with teeth. When Dyeawan presses down against the paddles, they dip forward and roll back in a circle, turning the wheels and moving the tender forward effortlessly.

She guides the tender out of the map room, Riko giggling behind her. Dyeawan revels quietly in the girl's unbridled joy, drawing comfort and strength from it. Surrounded by so much danger, so many lies and machinations, and weighted down by such sudden responsibility, Riko's friendship is fast becoming Dyeawan's sole source of relief.

The tender practically sails through the corridors of the Planning Cadre as if its wheels were on rails. The corridors wind endlessly, gradually inclining like one great, spiraling ramp that ensnares each level of the magnificent, secluded structure. Everything in the Cadre is a concentric circle, it seems, all of them leading to one central point.

That point for Dyeawan and Riko is the meeting room of the planners, the architects and custodians of Crache.

The others are already assembled around their new table as they enter the space. Their silence is as heavy and oppressive as the uniform stares they immediately direct at Dyeawan.

Dyeawan pulls the brake installed in her tender by Tahei the builder, bringing its tracks to a halt.

"This is sooner than I expected," she observes with steely calm.

Riko climbs from the back of the tender, staring from face to face with confusion and increasing alarm. "What's going on?" she asks.

"I know Edger taught you quite a lot," Nia addresses Dyeawan, ignoring both Riko and her question. "One of those lessons should have been that being smart isn't enough."

"No, it's not," Dyeawan says. "You need opportunity."

"You've had yours," Trowel interjects. "I'm sorry to say we remain unconvinced."

Dyeawan cocks her head. "*All* of you?"

She studies the faces of the younger planners, the ones who seemed so hopeful as Dyeawan addressed them all in her first session as their new leader. Those same faces now look defeated and resolute. She knows in that moment she underestimated Nia's sway over the planners as a whole. Dyeawan expected more resistance, and thus more time to maneuver and galvanize her position and enact her plans.

Before he died, Edger said he wanted Dyeawan to succeed him. She took for granted that he'd taught her everything she needed to know to do that. Dyeawan had no illusions there was much knowledge Edger had taken to the grave with him, but she assumed those were largely matters of protocol and procedure and state secrets, all of which she could glean from her new position.

Nia is clearly a thing he did not have time to tell her about nor prepare her to face. Edger no doubt had a plan to transition Dyeawan over time.

She cut that time short when she killed him.

"So what happens now?" Dyeawan asks, genuinely curious. "Do I return to carrying messages and sweeping floors?"

Nia shakes her head resolutely. "You are Edger's chosen. He had that right. As I have the right to challenge you for stewardship of this collective."

"And how will that be decided? By a vote?"

"It is called the Trinity," Trowel haughtily informs Dyeawan.

"A contest?" It is more conclusion than question.

Nia smiles, as if she's pleased with Dyeawan's quickness. "Yes. You and I will compete against one another in three tests."

"What kind of tests?" Riko demands.

Nia remains as calm as her future opponent. "One of the body, one of the mind, and one of the will. The best two victories claim the contest."

Dyeawan furrows her brow. She recalls the last time she took on one of the planners' "tests" and very nearly drowned.

"What are these tests?" Dyeawan asks.

"Chance decides on the test for each, from a field of several options," Nia answers simply. "It's quite fair and balanced for both parties, I assure you."

She's telling the truth. That much is clear to Dyeawan. It is also clear Nia believes without a single doubt that she will triumph in this Trinity of theirs.

That confidence is what gives Dyeawan pause.

"You can, of course, choose not to accept my challenge and simply step aside. There will be no shame. You will be allowed to remain a planner, out of respect for Edger. Your friend will, of course, return to her former duties."

Riko's expression darkens. "I wish I still had my tool belt," she whispers to Dyeawan. "I'd have so many things to throw at her right now."

Dyeawan reaches out and takes Riko's hand, gently and briefly squeezing it. She never takes her eyes off of Nia.

"I accept," she says. "This is a foolish waste of our time, if you do not mind me saying so. But if you are all intent upon this course of action, then so be it."

Nia ignores Dyeawan's assertion, seeming to hear only her answer to the challenge.

"We will table all planning sessions until this matter is decided," Trowel proclaims.

Dyeawan nods, tightly.

"A perfect time for it," she says, dryly.

"What with the violent uprising and all," Riko adds.

"Oh, it won't take long," Nia assures them both. "Particularly if there is no need to hold the third contest."

Riko looks down at Dyeawan with a crooked grin. "It *will* be more efficient if you beat her in two, yeah?"

Hearing that, Nia smiles.

Dyeawan, on the other hand, doesn't find humor in any of this. She stares back at Nia stonily, continuing to study the older woman, more specifically her confident demeanor. Dyeawan considers the way Nia has looked at and talked to and regarded her since Dyeawan became aware of the other planner. Nia hasn't been dismissive, or even particularly condescending, but neither has she displayed any concern about butting heads with Dyeawan, as if Dyeawan is an obstacle rather than a threat.

That's when she realizes Nia is confident because she thinks she has challenged Edger's pet to compete against her, and not Edger's murderer.

If she does not know what I am capable of, Dyeawan thinks, her expression betraying nothing, *she does not know how to defeat me.*

PART TWO

SHARP EDGES

FALLEN KINGDOM

THERE IS A SMALL PIECE OF SOMEONE'S SCALP STUCK TO THE head of the blacksmith's hammer, and Evie can't seem to put it out of her mind.

Kellan, for that is the man's name, rests his scarred and sizeable fists against his hips as he addresses her war council. The handle of the hammer is stuck through the belt cinched around his char-marked apron.

The sight of the hammerhead's stain is not such a gory one. It is little more than a few specks of crusted blood and a shriveled bit of skin.

What distracts Evie so is a single, distinctly red strand of hair seeded in that small, petrified shred of flesh. She finds herself wondering about the owner of that ginger thread, and what has become of them since the blow that removed it was struck. Are they some freckled-faced Skrain recruit, or a grizzled old Aegin with as many white hairs as red? Did they die in the street from that wound? Are they currently stuffed in a hole with the other survivors of the Tenth City revolt lamenting the chunk of their scalp that has been peeled back by the obviously powerful blacksmith?

"Most of the Gen elders are hiding in their circus," Kellan explains. "They probably have a few Aegins in there with them, and mayhap even a few Skrain. They've done their best to seal off all roads leading into the circus. Their barricades are shoddy, but we haven't bothered to test them."

"Figured we're better off," Talma adds. "Let 'em die in there. When the fruits and vegetables in their bazaar rot and their fancy cooks in their fancy stands run out of noodles, they'll begin to know what hunger in the Shade feels like every day."

Talma is the elder who marched their prisoners out through the city gates alongside Kellan to meet Evie's army. She is a rough-looking lump of a woman with long shocks of gray hair and a weathered face. The apron she wears is stained with blood rather than soot, and a meat cleaver dangles from its belt by a leather thong. Evie has learned Talma is, or was, a state-sponsored butcher who cut up what offal and rancid chunks of meat the Tenth City bothered to allot for its poor. She also serves her community as a midwife, and seems to be something of a sage among them, or at least a respected senior member.

In either case, Evie appreciates that Talma has taken the time to clean the blade of her meat cleaver since the battle.

They are all currently met in a tavern, the city revolt leaders and Evie, Mother Manai, Lariat, Sirach, and Yacatek. Bam guards the doors along with Diggs. The tavern sits on the edge of the Shade, which appears to be the Tenth City's version of the Bottoms. It doesn't face the sea as the Bottoms do in the Capitol, but the secluded and neglected streets crowded with shadowy hole-in-the-wall spaces and dirty, forgotten people are a spot-on match.

Evie is struck by how all Crachian cities seem to be copies of one another, with only small details of architecture and landscape differentiating them. Even suffering seems to be doled out in equal measure and with similar organization. It is as if Crache has designed its cities that way.

Blinking to break her focus on that bit of humanity staining Kellan's hammer, Evie looks up at the blacksmith's stony yet surprisingly warm face.

"So, stragglers aside, you've put down all the Aegins and Skrain in the city?"

"Hai," Kellan affirms. "Them that survived are locked in the dungeons. Some we boarded up in their own barracks. I've younglings guarding both. Good boys and girls. Do what they're told. They won't harm or torment them unless one of us tells 'em to do so."

Evie nods. She is struck with an appreciation of the two. Though she hasn't known them long, she is amazed at how Talma and Kellan appear to have rallied and organized their people in such a short time, and after such spontaneous action. She is also impressed by the respect and obedience they claim among their community to be able to achieve those things.

The two of them have recounted to Evie's council how they became the unlikely leaders of a sudden rebellion within the Tenth City. There was obvious unrest after the gates were closed and the city sealed up tightly, with anyone forbidden to either enter or leave. Decrees were posted explaining that an inclement storm threatened the city, but the skies remained as blue and clear as a summer portrait.

To discourage any large-size gatherings or congregating of the people to discuss the matter, the city's Aegins, supported by Skrain soldiers, were dispatched into the Shade. Their increased presence only roused more suspicion and disquiet.

Naturally, as an elder of the Shade, people came to Talma to ask what was happening. At first she tried to calm and placate them, assuring her friends and neighbors that this was nothing more than the usual tamping down of the Shade by the city. However, the questioning not only persisted, but grew more worried and frightened and widespread.

Finally, Talma took it upon herself to directly approach the highest-ranking Aegin and their companion soldiers. Talma began questioning them about the city being sealed. When she demanded to know the nature of the storm that was supposedly swelling in the east, the Aegin, surprised by the seemingly ragged little woman's boldness and no doubt caught off-guard, sputtered something about tornadoes. Talma has seen generations born and live and die in the Shade, and not a single one among those waves of humanity had ever witnessed such a phenomenon.

When she laughed openly in their faces, one of the Aegins struck her with the pommel of their dagger. Talma still wears the lacerated bruise on her wrinkled temple.

That single act proved to be an unexpected spark. The fuse was already in place, grown from years of oppression and neglect and being spat upon by men and women in those uniforms. Watching the same representatives of that city, that nation under whose yoke they'd been crushed for so long finally lit it.

Those who witnessed the assault on Talma seized the Aegins and the Skrain, drowning the armed and more experienced fighters in righteous fury and abused bodies. Those who quickly heard of the events unfolding flocked to participate. The ranks of the sudden revolt swelled quickly and grew hotter with each new soul it absorbed.

Kellan, it seems, only intervened when that initial act of civil disobedience and defense turned into rioting. He seemed, in fact, a rather passive and thoroughly levelheaded individual by nature. His little shop rested on the border of the Shade and drew patrons both from within and outside. Kellan didn't want to see the shops inside the Shade consumed nor the people of the Shade loot the businesses that operated around the confines of the area.

He helped Talma rally the Shade and focus its citizens' ire where it belonged: on the armed enforcers of the state. Though his nature bent toward easiness, Kellan obviously possessed strength and a leader's hand to which the people responded. He and Talma proved a formidable duo.

From what Evie has gleaned, the mistake of the Aegins was underestimating the fervor of the Shade and the threat that boiling anger presented. If they had marshaled the whole of their forces, they could have easily put down the unrest. Instead, they dispatched only a handful of their dagger-wielding peacekeepers to quell the burgeoning riot. When more reports came that the Shade remained unsettled, they sent yet another handful of Aegins and Skrain. They waited hours to finally reinforce that contingent.

By the time the commander of the Tenth City's Aegins and the captain of the Skrain detachment reinforcing them both realized the true breadth of their mistake, it was too late. Their forces were depleted, the rabble they detested was mobilized, armed, and legion, and the real fight was over before it had even begun.

Overcoming the military arm of the city proved to be the only key needed to unlock control over every street and edifice. The citizens of the Tenth City, the Gen members, and those who served them either capitulated or retreated immediately once the revolt spread beyond the Shade. None of them were accustomed to violence of any substance, let alone the fiery brand of rebellion that swept through the streets.

In the end, it was as if the imaginary storm the city had conjured to subdue the people finally manifested within its own walls.

"The Arbiters and Council members have done a better job than the Gen leaders," Kellan continues. "They're all holed up in the Citadel. They've managed to shut it up tight. Breaching it would be a chore."

"Our people would be willing and able," Talma adds. "But it would require a great sacrifice."

"We'll wait until it is absolutely necessary," Evie says. "And when that time comes, my forces will take the Citadel. Your people have done more than enough, and been through more than enough."

Talma says nothing, but it's clear in the way her gray, ancient-looking eyes fall on Evie that she is impressed.

"I have a question," Mother Manai says. "What's the Citadel?"

"It is to the Tenth City what the Spectrum is to the Capitol," Evie informs her.

"It used to be a temple," Sirach notes.

All heads turn toward her. She has been sitting off to the side during this meeting, occupying her own table and her own mug of wine.

"A temple?" Evie asks her.

"Yes. It was where the people of this kingdom kept their gods before Crache finally came for them. Gods of hearth and harvest. Gods of stone worshipped by the masons who built this city. Gods of love and gods of war. Like most people, they had both. They came to the temple to praise and petition in the light of the morning and the first light of the moon at night. Then the Skrain smashed the idols, killed all the priests, and gutted the vestments to make room for their glorious bureaucracy. Anyone who remembered the old gods out loud was murdered. Later, anyone who remembered those people and spoke of it simply disappeared. Just like their gods."

No one else speaks right away. Evie is taken more by Sirach's tone and manner than the content of her speech. The constant gleeful revelry in even the direst of situations and subjects is completely gone from her comrade and lover. Sirach sounds haunted. She *looks* haunted. She is speaking of the thing that creeps in on her in the quietest of moments, and perhaps in her dreams.

"I know nothing of that," Kellan says, hesitantly, though his words are more careful than defensive. "It has been the Citadel my whole life."

"Mine too," Talma adds, and in her voice Evie hears genuine sympathy for the knowledge Sirach carries.

"No one is blaming you," Evie quickly assures them both. "These were things that were done long ago, before our parents' parents were born."

"Not so long to the descendents of those who survived," Sirach says.

Evie aims a stern gaze at her, leadership and practicality overriding her sympathy in that moment. "*Nevertheless*. There is nothing we can do about that. We're here to discuss now. What happens now, and how we move forward."

Sirach stares back at her openly, her face still hung with bitterness and sorrow, but she says no more.

"What of the city larders?" Mother Manai asks. "Are they contained inside this Citadel?"

Evie knows her closest advisor is intentionally leading them down a new path, and she's grateful.

"No," Kellan says. "The big Aegin in charge says they have an emergency store there, and I'd wager the Gen Circus has larders of its own, but the city grain and whatnot are stored separate from 'em both. We set others to guard those too so's they don't get sacked."

"Very wise," Mother Manai replies. "They won't be stocked from outside the city walls for a while, I'd expect."

Kellan and Talma exchange nervous, unchecked looks. Evie watches them without comment, suspecting the source of the sudden shift in their moods, yet not wanting to assume.

"We could barely believe it," Kellan says. "How many you have with you, in that army of yours."

"The Skrain told us the real reason they sealed up the walls," Talma adds. "Hoping to save his skin. But we never expected . . ."

"Does it trouble you?" Evie asks. "We came here for the same reason you did what you did. We're on the same side, I assure you."

"Oh, we believe you, General," Talma says. "We don't worry at your intentions as regards the Skrain and the like."

"Then what concerns you?" Evie says, pressing her point.

Kellan sighs. "As your woman here says, the city stores might not see new feed for a while yet. You've brought a lot of mouths with you."

Lariat snorts derisively. "Without us, the Skrain marching to this city will string you all up by your toes and leave ya to dangle."

Kellan has a reply on his tongue, but Talma intercedes.

"We'll all face what's to come together," she insists. "As you said, General, we're on the same side. We just want to be sure we haven't traded one cruel master for another."

"I'm no one's master, I promise you. Your people have suffered, and they will have all they need. As will the rest of the people in this city who have harmed no one directly. My army will make do with what's left."

Kellan nods. He seems at least somewhat appeased. "And where will your army take shelter? Who will we clear out to make room for so many? The Gen Circus?"

Evie shakes her head. "We'll need to move our forces inside the walls eventually. For now we'll make camp outside the city."

"Lot of our'n won't sit with that," Lariat says. "They've come a long way and fought hard. They need to see some reward from it. A little bit of comfort."

"There are Sicclunans for whom this city is ancestral land," Sirach chimes in on Lariat's heels. "They deserve to come home."

Evie looks from them to Yacatek, the final representative of her army's separate factions, waiting to hear the Storyteller's protests.

Yacatek says nothing. Her eyes and her expression offer Evie more of the same.

"We'll camp outside the walls," Evie repeats. "But we'll give leave to our people in groups to enter the city, one at a time, to enjoy the amenities. We'll also organize patrols to keep the peace and enforce order in the streets, as well as reinforce your guards at the larders, the barracks and dungeons, the Gen Circus, and the Citadel. Is that agreeable to all present?"

Evie makes sure the question has some command behind it, and it appears to be enough to dissuade any further objections or issues.

"Good," she concludes. "As for parsing rations—"

She is interrupted by a Sicclunan soldier, who Bam and Diggs have apparently permitted entrance into the tavern. They all watch the soldier trot over to Sirach and whisper something for her ear alone.

"Good work," she commends the soldier when they're finished. "Keep a constant watch on their movements."

The soldier bows their head briefly and retreats.

Evie and the others wait. Sirach runs her fingers around the sides of her neck, lacing them behind her head, then says: "Fifteen hundred Skrain have made camp half-a-day's ride from the city walls."

"What are they doing?" Mother Manai asks.

"Waiting."

"For what?"

Sirach doesn't speak. She only gazes pointedly at Evie. That devilish grin finally returns to Sirach's lips.

"They're waiting for the rest of the Crachian army," Evie answers for her.

THE BODY

IT'S NOT A MOUNTAIN. IT'S A VOLCANO.

The peak has been the dominant feature of the view from Dyeawan's window since she came to the Planning Cadre. She never fails to take note of the flat hollow that crowns the rocky elevation, but neither did she ever truly understand what it signifies.

The reason is simple. Dyeawan never knew what a volcano was. They certainly have none in the Bottoms of the Capitol. She had, in fact, never heard the word "volcano" before. Though she has expanded her base of knowledge by multitudes in a very short time, Dyeawan only knows what she has read and what she is taught. The subject had simply never come up before.

When Trowel informed her that she was to report to the eastern base of the island's volcano in the light of the next morning for her first challenge, Dyeawan wheeled herself to the library to research the new word. She first read up on volcanoes in general, amazed and humbled by the realization that mountains could spit fire, and enough to lay waste to any manner of flesh, stone, or steel gathered around them.

She then read up on the volcano specific to the Planning Cadre's little unnamed island. Though the outside world had no knowledge of their existence, the Cadre kept meticulous records of their own lives and history since settling there. According to that record, the volcano's eruptions had driven the island's original inhabitants away, melting whatever remained. Fear of it caused ships and potential new residents to avoid and finally forget the island entirely.

Since the time of those cataclysmic events, Dyeawan further read, the fiery mountain had grown cold, lying dormant for many hundreds of years. It stood now only as a monument to the island's past, presenting no threat to the Planning Cadre.

Yet, as Dyeawan rows her tender over the valley at dawn, she sees smoke belching from the hollow at the top of that supposedly barren behemoth.

It is a sight totally unfamiliar to her, even in all the mornings she has awakened to gaze out her window and up at that peak. The spirals of smoke are as black as death. They look like necrotic fingers reaching up to claw at the otherwise calm and vibrant blue of the sky above.

Dyeawan's keen mind attempts to puzzle out not only the reason for it, but the meaning as she moves the tracks of her tender along. The path beneath those tracks is perfectly beaten. Dyeawan is further surprised to find that not only is the path smooth and flat, but it appears to wind all the way to the base of the volcano itself. She can't imagine why such a thing would exist, and wonders if the path has been laid specifically for this challenge, whether just for her or in some time past, whenever this task was originally created.

It occurs to Dyeawan that would be very in keeping with the planners as Edger molded them; creative thought and the drive to transform the improbable into the realized, but aimed at the totally opulent. Though they solved so many practical problems, their philosophy had fallen so deeply into invention without necessity.

Dyeawan wants to win this absurd challenge to change that as much as anything else.

As she approaches the end of the path, her arms already strained from the journey, Dyeawan spots new tendrils of smoke rising in the distance. These wisps are smaller and milky white. Their source is a small cooking pot dangling above an open fire built upon the ground.

An absolutely ancient-looking woman Dyeawan has never before laid eyes upon waits for her at the base of the volcano. Behind her, a small cottage sits on the first slope, constructed from a stony material Dyeawan has also never seen. It is impossibly smooth, the jet-black surfaces of each side gleaming in the morning light.

Though it's a new sight for her, Dyeawan has read about this, too. It is the manner of rock created by a volcano's fiery discharge.

The woman herself is slight and nondescript. Her pure white hair is bound in a loose tail. The skin of her face is clean and bright despite the lines of age present there. She is draped in a warm shawl fashioned from black sheep's wool that covers a simple gray tunic, much like Dyeawan's, though the woman's bears no insignia of any kind.

Dyeawan rows up to her cautiously, watching as she gently stirs the contents of her pot with a wooden spoon. The woman sits on a small, well-crafted chair. Dyeawan notices the feet of that chair are fitted with sprung coils, allowing them to adjust evenly under her weight to the uneven terrain.

"Good morning, young planner," the woman greets her, as if Dyeawan is expected.

The front tracks of her tender reach the path's end. From this point on, the incline of the mountain begins in earnest, first over patches of grassland upon which the woman's dwelling has been erected. Beyond that, sharp, rocky crags overtake the ascent up the volcano with no clear path that Dyeawan can discern.

"Good morning," Dyeawan finally replies. "I did not know anyone lived on this island outside of the keep."

"Oh, I lived there for most of my life. I was once like you. A planner."

"And what are you now, if I may ask?"

"Tired, mostly," the old woman says with a gentle smile. "My name is Tinker. You are Edger's little Slider?"

"Dyeawan."

"Of course. Forgive me. It was once tradition to choose a new name when accepted into the planners."

"I chose my own."

"Wisely, if I may say."

Tinker finishes stirring whatever it is she's brewing, gently tapping the stem of the wooden spoon against the rim of the pot.

Dyeawan briefly sniffs the air. She smells garlic and onion.

"Would you care for some breakfast?" Tinker asks. "I've made soup. You should fortify yourself for what's to come."

"I ate fruit and bread before I set out." Dyeawan now detects some type of game meat as part of the concoction. "Do you hunt out here?"

Tinker chuckles. "No. I keep sheep in a pen nearby. Just a few." She absently strokes at her shawl as she retrieves a nearby clay bowl.

Dyeawan studies her with curiousity. "Why do you live out here like this, if I may ask?"

Tinker begins ladling soup into the bowl. "As I said, I grew tired."

"Of what?"

The old woman shrugs, sipping carefully and demurely from the steaming bowl she holds with both hands. Tinker swallows the hot broth and licks her lips, delighted, before blowing the excess heat through them, almost whistling.

"All of it. I was tired of the problems of the day. Every day. The politics and the intrigue and the personalities of the others. And though I cared for him deeply, I grew tired of Edger in particular. His grandiosity and pomposity wearied me."

"I did not see you at his funeral."

"I mourned him in my own way, privately."

Tinker takes up a spoon and begins eating her soup in earnest. There is something about her manner that Dyeawan finds calming and centering, though her fascination overrides those more pleasant sensations.

"But why are you here? Living like this?"

"Like what, Dyeawan? Simply?"

Dyeawan considers that before answering. "I lived out of doors for most of my life. I do not look back on those times as simple."

"Neither do you look back on them fondly, I imagine. You have had a rough go of it, no doubt. Are you sure you wouldn't like some soup? I do not boast often, but I am proud of both the recipe and my execution."

"No, thank you."

"Please, just a taste. Satisfy an old woman's vanity."

Tinker retrieves her wooden spoon and gathers a sampling of the pot's contents, extending it toward Dyeawan.

Dyeawan eyes the meat and vegetables swimming in the tiny pond of broth. She feels the inside of her mouth salivating all of a sudden.

She gazes over the front of her tender at the uneven ground beyond the path's end and how it begins to gently curve upward.

"Oh, my apologies, dear. How ignorant of me."

Tinker sets her bowl upon the ground and rises from the chair, its springs creaking as they decompress.

The old woman closes the short gap between them and offers the spoon to Dyeawan, her other hand instinctively cradling the air below it.

Dyeawan carefully accepts the spoon and raises the steaming end to her lips. The broth is still hot enough to sting them, but the taste is entirely inviting. She sips at the soup, the flavor livening her tongue, and then slides every bit of it down her throat. The heat is harsh at first, but it warms her stomach in a comforting way.

"Very good," she says. "Thank you."

Tinker smiles, appeased. She withdraws from Dyeawan and returns to her spring-loaded chair and waning cooking fire.

Dyeawan licks her lips once more. The delicious taste of the soup lingers, as does the warmth coating her insides.

She looks up at the peak looming high above them. There is a slightly dizzying fizzle in her head.

"I read in a book that this volcano has lain dormant for hundreds of years."

"Indeed. It would be a dangerous place to live otherwise."

Dyeawan lowers her gaze to the old woman. "For you, here, or for the rest of us in the keep?"

"Both."

Dyeawan considers the peak once more. "If it is dormant, as I read, why is it smoking like that?"

Tinker says nothing at first, nor does her smile betray any particular opinion on the matter. "Why do *you* think it is smoking, Dyeawan?"

At that moment, the ground trembles beneath the tracks of her tender. It is only a slight tremor, but the force is enough to cause the platform supporting Dyeawan to vibrate, sending chills dancing across the surface of her skin. Though she cannot command her legs, she is aware of the bumps raised there.

Dyeawan grips the edges of her paddles to steady herself. Her blood is rushing faster than it was a moment before.

"I have to go up there, don't I?"

Tinker nods. "That is the challenge of the body that was chosen."

"How was it chosen?"

"At random. By me. As an impartial observer."

Dyeawan chooses to accept that. "I am sure you've noticed, but I cannot walk."

"You seem to function ably otherwise."

Dyeawan frowns. "What will accomplishing this prove?"

"To me? Not a thing. As I said, I am only an impartial observer."

Dyeawan's frown only deepens and darkens. "Where is Nia?"

"On the other side of the mountain. She has been administered a paralytic potion to her lower half. She will be ascending the mountain under exactly the same conditions as you."

"This is to be a race, then?"

"If it motivates you to think of it as such."

Dyeawan takes a deep, cleansing breath before asking, "When are we to begin?"

Tinker finishes her bowl of soup. She licks the spoon clean thoroughly before placing it in the bowl and setting them both to the side. She folds her hands over her stomach and regards Dyeawan with what appears to her to be sympathy.

"When the sun finishes its ascent above the horizon, you may begin your ascent. I can offer you no more than that."

"Then I thank you for the soup," Dyeawan says pointedly.

Tinker's smile is renewed. "Any time, dear. I wish you good fortune, if this is what you truly want."

Dyeawan sees no point in questioning her concerning the meaning of those final words.

Gripping the paddles tightly, she urges her tender forward, beyond the path. The way is harder, and the tracks move more slowly, but she is able to row herself up the grassy slope and past

Tinker's campfire. She continues rowing until her tender reaches the edge of the grassy plain at the base of the volcano.

Beyond it, the jagged rocks begin to rise sharply in earnest.

Dyeawan engages the tender's brake, staring up the volcano's length. It seems so much taller from this vantage, reaching all the way to the clouds.

She settles herself and waits on the sun.

OF THE PEOPLE

TEARS STING LEXI'S EYES. THERE IS HARSHNESS UNIQUE TO tears brought on by exposing an onion's innards to the light of day, she finds. Using a sharp paring knife, her hemp-wrapped hands cleanly slice the skin from the thirtieth bulb she's peeled in the last hour. She cuts what remains into several chunks of equal size atop a thick wooden chopping block resting on an upended barrel. It has been her makeshift station for most of the afternoon, established at the end of an alley in the heart of the Bottoms.

For most who have come, she offers the wild onions whole from several carts filled with them, for the people to do with the bounty as they will. However, there are many who are old and weak, and others whose extremities shake due to afflictions. Lexi offers the cut pieces to them, watching as they eat gratefully with hands cleansed in a barrel of fresh water she has also provided.

Though every action Lexi performs is under duress and watchful eyes, she does find respite and relief in witnessing the brief joy of nourishment on every face.

The onions she is distributing have been supplied by Gen Hama, and they aren't all that she's brought with her to the

Bottoms. She has large covered bowls of still-steaming rice from the nearby cookers, the allocation of which was donated by several different large Gens. She also has wedges of hard cheese from Gen Krush, who handle the Capitol's goat herding concession. There are several more barrels of fresh water stacked around her chopping station. Each one is fitted with a tin cup dangling from a chain.

Burr and her Ignobles have many friends indeed, it seems. Lexi can't be certain how many are true allies, and how many more know nothing of Burr's true identity or the Ignobles' plot. It's entirely possible the contributing Gens are simply currying favor or carrying out their end of backroom deals with the Gen Franchise Council member.

Shaheen, the young mother Lexi met curled up around her starving daughter, assists Lexi in distributing the bounty to her fellow Bottoms denizens.

Shaheen looks transformed since that first encounter. Her hair has been washed and brushed. Her skin is scrubbed clean to the point of shine. She has exchanged the tatters she once wore for a new wrap much like the ones Lexi wears. She looks well nourished rather than gaunt and underfed. As noticeable as that, however, is the light that has replaced the pale glaze in her eyes.

Lexi has taken her on as something of an unofficial assistant since returning to her towers in the Gen Circus. Shaheen was so grateful and concerned when Lexi showed up again in the Bottoms after such a long absence that she practically attached herself to Lexi's hip, offering to help her however she could. Lexi was reluctant at first, not wanting to involve the girl in this quagmire. In the end, though, Lexi decided that she might as well offer as much aid as she's able while being coerced by the Ignobles. Thus far she has no plan beyond that, but her mind works toward one more or less every second.

Besides, she enjoyed having help that wasn't assigned to her by Burr.

Char, Shaheen's little daughter, runs about her mother's legs, giggling with carefree glee unknown to the child Lexi and Taru saved from starvation.

Lexi watches idly as Char runs over to the alley wall and begins dabbing with a fingertip at the red paint staining the decaying stone of the building somehow managing to still stand there. Someone has taken the time to create a tableau upon it depicting a flock of dead birds (so distinguished by "X's" drawn in place of their eyes) fallen to the earth. The words "No Sparrows" are scrawled above their upended bodies.

Lexi has taken note of the graffiti on several walls throughout the Capitol. The sight of such vandalism is rare enough, but to see half a dozen marked patches of public stone left untouched is beyond belief. Ordinarily, cleaners would be immediately dispatched by the Spectrum.

One of the first red-stained depictions Lexi saw actually portrayed this "Sparrow General" in a positive light. The rest, however, have derided the unknown military leader. She has seen other tableaus that consisted of giant red birds eating small stick figures that fled in terror from the creature. Another was painted to look like a red wave washing over what was clearly meant to be the Bottoms, and the bird stays atop it.

Shaheen has told Lexi that stories began spreading throughout the Bottoms of a general rising in the east, fighting for the people

Crache has forgotten. Those tales, it seems, were quickly met by contrary ones. New stories began to bubble up that figuratively and literally painted the Sparrow General as an enemy of the people who was slaughtering them en masse.

Naturally, Lexi wonders if Burr has anything to do with it. Though it would be easy to tack any discord being sown in the Capitol to the Ignoble's door, Lexi doesn't think the Sparrow General is part of Burr's plan. It runs contrary to the story Burr and her Ignobles want to tell. They don't want to create a mythic figure of the people. They want the people to see the return of nobility, and their submission to it, as their only hope for a better life.

"Two for each person?" Shaheen asks for the third or fourth time, holding up the onions in her hands.

Lexi nods patiently. "More if they ask. Whatever they need."

Shaheen is a smart young woman, Lexi has found, but entirely unsure of herself. She constantly seeks the approval of her new matron in all matters, despite Lexi's assurances. Not that Lexi can blame her in the slightest. Having taken Shaheen and her daughter in from their former circumstance, it stands to reason the girl would be fearful of losing the newfound stability and be eager to please.

Kamen Lim surveys the proceedings amiably, the flat of his right palm resting against the pommel of the Capitol-issued dagger sheathed in its Aegin's bandolier slung across his torso. He's not tethered to Lexi, officially. Kamen Lim has somehow been abruptly reassigned to patrol the Bottoms, and the route of his patrol just happens to coincide with whatever Lexi's current location in the Bottoms happens to be.

"You know what's good?" Kamen Lim offers jovially. "Chop

up a bunch of that wild onion and mix it in with the rice. Add a little garlic if you can get it. Delicious."

"Perhaps we can open a restaurant," Lexi says brightly, her sarcasm only evident to anyone with ears. It doesn't seem to bother the Aegin in the slightest, if he even picks up on it. He lets out a chuckle, in fact.

"I'd like that. I enjoy cooking. My wife is a fantastic baker, but cooking is usually my domain. We make a fine team! Supper and dessert, that's what we call ourselves."

He laughs softly at that last bit, fondly, and it's clear the endearment genuinely warms him.

Lexi would find it all terribly charming were he not an agent for the secret conspiracy plotting to overthrow Crache and forcing her to do its bidding by threatening the life of her beloved retainer.

Lexi looks down from her chopping board to find what she thinks at first is a small child wrapped in a hooded cloak. Their caretaker is a young, lanky boy barely into his teens who leads the child up to her by the hand.

When he gently pulls back that hood, Lexi is surprised to gaze down at an elderly woman no more than three feet tall. It is as if a child has aged without actually growing. Her face is cherubic, her cheeks drooping and wrinkled. The flesh around them mostly swallows her eyes. Her white hair has either been trimmed close to her scalp, or has ceased to grow.

Lexi places a piece of onion in the woman's small, grubby palm.

As the old woman munches on it, Lexi hands two more whole wild onions to the boy, who stuffs them inside his shirt with an awkward, somewhat embarrassed smile.

"Thank you, Te-Gen," the woman says in an impossibly high voice.

"It is my pleasure. And please, my name is Lexi."

"You are kind to share so much of your Gen's allotment with us."

"This bounty is far beyond my Gen's allotment. Many others contributed to it who wish to see the people of the Bottoms better fed. Who wish to . . ."

Lexi hesitates. She hadn't wanted to think about this part of her task. She wanted to focus solely on bringing food to these people, and on being among them.

"Who wish . . ." she carries on, "to see a return to a time when all the people of a land were cared for, and not just those who successfully petition to oversee things for the state as the leaders of Gens do."

"What time do you speak of, Te-Gen?" the tiny elder asks.

"It's Lexi."

"Lexi," the old woman repeats, with reverence.

Lexi glances back at Kamen Lim, holding his eyes briefly. Lim smiles as if even he is hanging on her words. He gives her the slightest of nods, urging her to proceed.

She turns back to the old woman and what must be her grandson. Lexi steps from around her onion-chopping station, kneeling down on the alley floor to meet the old woman's aged eyes.

"Life . . . life was not always as you know it. There was a time before councils composed of men and women whose names you will never know allotted the bounty of the lands upon which you live and work and die, and who decided which chosen few among you would control all of a city's resources and live in its best quarters.

There was a time when the people had guardians. These guardians were bound to their lands and people by blood. Sacred blood that flowed through their veins, passed down from guardian to guardian, anointing them as protectors of their lands and people."

"Who were these people?" the old woman asks, enthralled.

Dozens have now gathered around. They are all listening intently to Lexi. She stares over the top of the elder's cropped white hair, seeing their faces, dirty and sallow and desperate, but alight with the brief hope and small nourishment Lexi has brought to them.

She cannot recall ever hating herself so much.

"They were called nobles," she says, reaching up and taking the woman's impossibly small hands in hers. "Descendants of that sacred blood. Some of your ancestors might even have counted among them."

"What happened to them?"

"The rule of blood was overthrown by . . . by the jealous. Those who were jealous and ambitious and filled with greed and rancor. They took the nobles' land and created places like the Bottoms."

Tiny tears begin to spill from the meaty burrows of the old woman's eyes. "Are they all gone?" she asks in the meekest of voices.

Lexi forces her lips to smile. She raises the old woman's hands in hers and holds them against her chest, leaning forward and kissing the wrinkled forehead of the elder.

"No," she whispers. "But they have been too long forgotten. We must remember them. We must tell others. Do you understand?"

The old woman nods silently and tearfully, breaking Lexi's heart all over again.

She rises from her knees and returns behind the barrel. Lexi takes up her paring knife, but she can't seem to focus on cutting another onion until she's watched the woman escorted through the recesses of the crowd by her young caretaker.

When she can no longer see them, Lexi blinks away tears of her own and reaches for a new bulb. She's aware of the others, many others like the old woman, watching her intently with the same sunken and desperate faces, the same tiny spark of hope in their eyes. She can feel them wanting to approach her the same way the old woman did, but they remain at a respectful distance, waiting for Lexi to finish her cutting and beckon them forth.

After Lexi has diced the onions, she and Shaheen spend the next two hours handing out the rest of the food they've brought with them to the Bottoms. The people linger, drinking what fresh water remains and gratefully dining on cheese and the mixture of onions and rice (which Lexi begrudgingly admitted to herself was a good idea on the part of Kamen Lim).

"Should I start loading the wagon?" Shaheen asks her after the last grain of food has been served.

"Yes, I'll help you."

As the two of them return the carts and empty barrels to the wagon that ferried the provisions, Kamen Lim begins gently and politely dispersing the remaining petitioners in the alley.

"It was a good speech," he offers Lexi when the alley is empty.

"Thank you," she replies stiffly.

"I have a . . . suggestion, if you don't mind, Te-Gen."

Lexi sighs. "Of course. What is your suggestion, Aegin Lim?"

He glances at Shaheen. Lexi sighs again, turning to the girl. "Wait for me by the horses, Shaheen."

The girl bows her head obediently, quickly collecting Char and shooing her toward the front of the wagon.

"I would leave out how these folk might be descended from nobility themselves," Kamen Lim says a moment later. "It's a cruel untruth to tell them."

"Shall we really quibble over the truth of the words I spoke? Is that a thing you want to explore?"

Kamen Lim holds up his hands in a placating gesture. "I meant no offense. It simply is not the message Councilwoman Burr would wish you to convey. The rest, however, was very nearly perfect."

"What happens if other Aegins who are not sympathetic to your cause hear me spinning tales of lost nobility in the Capitol? What happens when the Protectorate Ministry finds out?"

"You let me worry about that. You're burdened enough." He almost sounds genuinely concerned for Lexi's spirit under the weight she is shouldering. "It was a good first day!" Lim then declares. "I feel good about our progress."

He motions for her to make her way around the wagon, and Lexi obliges with a strained smile.

It is only when her back is turned to him that the rage and pain seeps out through her eyes.

THE RULE OF REBELLION

BRIO'S NEW GAIT HAS A KIND OF INCONSISTENT MUSIC TO IT, a repeated clink and creaking followed by two deep thuds, rhythmic yet off-time. It's like the drunken pounding-of-boots-and-mug-bottoms orchestra that accompanies a slurred shanty chorus sung in a tavern.

His instruments are the copper hinges and leather straps of the harness securing a forged iron peg to the stump of his leg. That peg leg and a cane fashioned from a shaved tree branch provide the thudding crescendo of his gait's symphony.

Brio demonstrates his new ease of movement for Evie in one of several small rooms above Kellan's shop that the blacksmith has offered to the Sparrow General and her officers as personal quarters. Talma was quick to do the same, and while it was equally appreciated, the aroma of state-issued week-old organs and rancid game meat permeating the building in which her shop resided made the choice an easy one for the rebellion leaders (though none of them mentioned the smell to the kindly old butcher, who seemed so accustomed to the odor as to no longer be aware of it).

Evie sits on the edge of a stiff straw cot, watching Brio use his hip to shift his new leg forward, aided in his balance by the cane.

"I guess we both owe the Sicclunan smiths a lot," she says, glancing at her sparrow-emblazoned armor stacked neatly in the corner, its joints and straps freshly greased with pig fat from Kellan's stores.

Brio halts, slightly winded from his enthusiastic demonstration. There is a rickety rocking chair installed in the corner opposite her armor. He begins awkwardly lowering himself onto its seat, one hand gripping the handle of his cane while the other steadies the chair by its back.

Evie quickly rises from the cot. "Let me help—"

"No," he says, gently yet with firmness. "I need to do it myself."

Evie nods silently, but she doesn't sit back down on the cot. She watches him negotiate the tenuous descent into the rocking chair. It takes several seconds for him to configure his new appendage comfortably, as well as reposition his cane, which he almost trips over while sitting, but Brio manages.

After he is settled, Evie lowers her body onto the cot's edge once again, her eyes still filled with concern.

Brio steadily catches his breath, resting his cane across his lap. He smiles warmly at her as sweat stipples his brow. "We're all adjusting to new circumstances," he says, adding, "General."

Evie grins, still slightly embarrassed, and shakes her head as she fixes him with a reprimanding gaze.

Brio arrived that morning with the rest of the Sicclunan forces and civilians who remained behind as Evie's army took the Crachian border crossing. They'd begun making camp alongside the base the rebellion has established outside the city gates, and Brio was escorted to the edge of the Shade to reunite with Evie.

"You've done well here, Evie," he says after she has finished informing him of the events over the past few weeks.

"The people of this city did the work," she insists. "They bled and died taking it from the Aegins and the Skrain, while I spent my time getting dressed in all that ridiculous finery."

"It's good armor for a good general, and you need it just as we all need you."

"So Mother Manai keeps telling me," Evie mutters.

"Where is Mother, by the way? I have yet to see her among your esteemed coterie."

Evie takes up the flat pillow crowning the cot and flings it across the room at him. Brio bats it away with his cane, chuckling at her sensitivity.

"I sent Sirach and her night brigade out to scout," she answers him. "They're going to circumvent the Skrain encampment. We need to know how far away and how many the main force is that's coming to bolster them. Mother went along to assess whatever Savages they're bringing with them. She's the expert, after all."

Brio grows quiet, his expression turning introspective. Evie has several guesses as to what thoughts her words have inspired within him, but she imagines she only needs one.

"They'll raze this entire city to the ground, you know," he finally says. "They'll have the Skrain murder everyone, rebel and innocents alike, if that's what it takes. Not just to defeat us, but to wipe any memory that this happened from Crache's history. The *idea* of what we're doing will be even more terrifying to them than the rebellion itself. They cannot allow that idea to spread any more than it already has."

"The walls are strong, and we'll have our full force to defend them, bolstered by the willing from the Shade," Evie says, though she isn't sure whether she's defending their actions or positing a scenario with the hope Brio will poke holes in its solidity.

He sighs, reclining in the rocking chair. "They will tear these walls down, Evie. They will bring the largest siege weapons the Skrain have ever constructed, and they will knock down every wall protecting this city. It doesn't matter to them how long it takes."

Evie can only nod. She knows he speaks the truth.

"How badly do you think we will be outnumbered?" Brio asks.

There is no attack in his question, only genuine concern. She shrugs. "Five-to-one? Ten-to-one maybe? At the very least, it won't be the full force of Crache. We broke through the middle of the front line, but there have to be legions spread across what remains. They won't be able to recall and organize them in time, not if they mean to begin the siege when the Skrain already entrenched here are reinforced. In any case, we won't know for sure about their numbers until Sirach and Mother return."

"You're fond of her, aren't you?"

"Mother Manai? She's become our little rebellion's greatest asset."

"Sirach, I meant."

"Oh." Evie shifts her weight atop the cot uncomfortably. She'd been hoping to avoid this subject in the face of total annihilation by the Skrain.

"It isn't any business of mine, of course," Brio admits.

"I suppose not."

She studies the kindness writ upon his face. It is remarkable to her how feelings, even those cultivated over a lifetime, can change so drastically. She accepted the mission given to her by Lexi with years of deep and confused feelings for Brio still bubbling in her guts. Much of her remained in love with the boy he was.

Now, looking at the man before her, Evie feels none of that. She cares for him, respects him, and even feels protective of him, but that's because Brio needs protecting. The rest is . . . perhaps not gone, but clarified.

The only uncertainty left within her is reserved for her feelings about the battle yet to come.

"You're different, you know," he says, his tone inscrutable. "Not from the girl I knew as a child, but from the woman who came to rescue me in that Savage camp. You're changed since then, I think."

Evie smiles. "I was just thinking the same thing, in a way."

An impossibly heavy fist that can only belong to Bam begins colliding with the outside of the room's only door. Brio starts at the sudden pounding, but Evie has grown accustomed to it. "Come in, Bam!" she calls out, grinning at Brio's reaction.

The door swings wide and Bam's massive frame presses it against the wall to clear the way for Lariat. He's wearing the barbed and spiked straps across his barrel torso and down his arms and hands that he wears in battle.

"Problem needin' the general's attention," the broom-mustached ex-Savage informs Evie. "I woulda settled it, but you told me not to kill no one unless they was trying to kill me."

"Who says you can't follow orders?" Evie says, commending him.

The old man guffaws, and she is certain she can see every hair in his mustache vibrate.

"Can I be of assistance?" Brio asks from his chair.

"Don't trouble yourself," Evie says.

Brio is already working himself up out of the rocker, however. "I *will* trouble myself, if you don't mind. But you go ahead. I will catch up. Where are you going?"

The question is directed at Lariat, who regards the slender Gen leader's spunk with warm amusement. "Little nothin' of a watering hole down the way," he answers. "Broken mug nailed above the door."

"I will find it," Brio assures Evie.

"I'll go with Lariat," she tells Bam. "You escort Brio."

"Is that necessary?" Brio asks.

"Yes." Evie levels him with a gaze that will brook no argument.

Satisfied when Brio offers none, Evie looks to Bam, seeing a scowl beneath his ragged hood and past the mess of curly tendrils that perpetually shroud his face.

"I'll be fine, Bam," Evie placates her devoted bodyguard. "Lariat is with me."

"I'm faster'n you anyway," he taunts the stoic hulk.

Bam answers that with a solitary grunt.

Grinning, Evie follows Lariat out of the room and down the cramped building's dilapidated staircase. They emerge onto the street a moment later. Lariat falls into step beside Evie, spiked hands never leaving the horizontal handles of the katars sheathed on either of his hips. He retains his usual jovial air, but keeps an ever-watchful eye on Evie and their surroundings, and those that pass them by.

It still makes Evie slightly uneasy, the loyalty and protectiveness they all display toward her. Despite the battles they've won and how far their campaign has progressed from a few rogue Savages, a large part of her still doesn't believe she has earned or deserves their fealty. It is the thought that wakes her up every morning, and drives her to earn that fealty every day, however she can.

Lariat leads her to the tavern marked by the broken mug hung above its door, which is just three uneven boards nailed together and barely hanging from two rusty hinges. He pulls it open easily and steps aside, motioning with a smile and a grand sweep of his arm for Evie to enter.

"Duty's waitin'," he says, low enough for only her to hear.

The smell of stale rice wine mixed with several other foul odors Evie doesn't care to identify immediately sting her nostrils. The cramped interior of the tavern is little more than a hastily constructed bar counter and two equally shoddy tables with unmatched chairs. A stout barkeep protects a shelf of a few bottles and a large jug, along with a collection of cups, most of them chipped. He wears his worry on a thick hung brow as he surveys the scene unfolding in his establishment.

The tavern's occupants are divided into two distinct groups, currently facing off against each other on either side of the confines.

Diggs stands between them. The handsome elder ex-Savage turns the leather-covered head of a mace slowly in one palm.

Though no one seems willing to cross him, there is still plenty of hot blood simmering in the air.

It is no chore to discern the sides. The members of Evie's forces, ex-Savages all, are still branded by the bluish-green runes covering their exposed skin, generated by the blood coins that remain anchored in their guts.

The other group is composed of locals from the Shade, from the look of them mostly beggars who've copped a few coins and menial workers.

The contingents are hurling insults and threatening gestures at one another as Evie walks in, several of them holding smashed cups and broken table legs threateningly.

"What's happening here?" she demands, silencing their expletive volleys.

"I believe you call it a clash of cultures," Diggs tells her. "Agitated by a waning supply of spirits."

He grins mischievously at her. Evie is as susceptible to Diggs' charm as the next warm-blooded creature, but she has no time or energy for it under the present circumstance.

"We wanna be served!" one of her fighters yells, already sounding as though they have been, several times over.

"This is *our* place!" a local fires back at him. "Our mugs get filled first!"

Evie looks with irritation from the two congregations to the barkeep. "These don't seem like insurmountable problems," she says dryly.

"I don't have enough wine for the lot of 'em," he protests. "Just this afternoon I've seen more thirsty gullets than I get in a week, normal. Your soldiers have drunk me out of stock."

Evie sighs, feeling a dull, painful throb beginning to form

between her ears. “Back to camp!” she orders her fighters. “All of you!”

None of them move at first. It’s clear their blood is still raging.

Lariat slaps a leather and steel adorned hand against the katar scabbard hanging from his left hip. “If you missed the general’s words, maybe I need to make them hearin’ holes in your heads bigger!”

That snaps them out of it, or at least enough of them to get the rest moving when they see their fellows begin to depart the cramped battlefield.

“I apologize for the disturbance,” Evie says, addressing the Shade denizens who remain. “It will not happen again.”

“Thank ye, General,” the barkeep offers.

Bam enters the tavern a moment later, nearly knocking the flimsy door off its hinges.

Brio follows in his wake, leaning heavily on his cane, obviously exerted from the effort of the short march. “Have I missed the excitement?” he asks, gazing about the now calm waters of the tavern interior.

“It turns out the situation called for a general, not a diplomat,” Evie explains.

“I see. So glad I made the trip then.”

“I told you not to.”

“You did indeed,” Brio relents.

Evie looks up at Lariat and Diggs. “They can’t go to a tavern outside the Shade?” she asks. “We control the damn city. It’s not as if they’ll be turned away.”

“Here’s where our kind feel comfortable, like,” Lariat says.

"And I don't know that you want them tempted with the finer things this city has to offer," Diggs adds. "You told them no looting."

"Your counselors make salient points, General."

Evie's eyes narrow dangerously at Brio. He stifles a chuckle and hangs his head, leaning his full weight against his cane.

"Would you like one on the house, General?" the barkeep asks Evie. "It'd be an honor to say I served the Blood Sparrow herself."

Her head snaps toward him in surprise bordering on alarm, and then to the members of the Elder Company flanking her. "So it's the *Blood* Sparrow now?" she practically spits at them.

Lariat shrugs, not even attempting to hide his abject amusement.

"These things take on their own life," Diggs offers. "And they *do* paint your armor in red."

Evie points a finger at him, drawing it like a dagger from her hip. "Your clichés do not pass for wisdom with me, by the way!"

She turns, still mortified, and storms from the tavern without another word.

Shared laughter, including Brio's, follows her out into the street. Bam is already waiting for her there. Evie is so used to his presence shadowing her at this point that she scarcely feels the need to acknowledge him, though she does with a reassuring nod.

Her bodyguard follows her back up the shabby little street. It is a hot afternoon, but the sun feels good on Evie's face. Standing once again on the corner occupied by Kellan's blacksmith shop, Evie turns her eyes toward the clear skies, enjoying the calm.

When she returns her gaze to the Shade, Evie notices another slightly troublesome scene unfolding beyond the border of the slum.

Half a dozen B'ors tribesmen are wielding weapons and tools of steel and iron. Such a sight would be rare enough, but these warriors are using those instruments to dismantle a section of the cobbled city street. They have already broken through the thick slab of stone, and are uprooting large chunks of the pocked masonry to expose the raw ground beneath.

Two other warriors are gathered around Yacatek, armed with their traditional weapons of stone and bone, clearly the Storyteller's honor guards. She surveys the progress of the diggers patiently and passively.

Sighing in frustration, Evie soon marches over to the B'ors Storyteller, Bam tromping to catch up behind her.

"I gave orders not to loot or pillage this city in any way."

Yacatek's guards begin to step forward, raising Bam's hackles, but she quickly waves them back with the slightest of gestures. "You did," she affirms.

"Does that not include bashing a large hole into the streets?"

"That is for the great General to decide."

Evie detects the briefest of grins as Yacatek says those words, but she ignores it. "If you want to bury one of your story knives, there are less obstructed spots to do it."

"I am not burying a knife," Yacatek calmly explains. "I am retrieving one."

Confused, Evie turns to watch the small crew of B'ors diggers burrowing deeper into the earth beneath the stone street.

After several minutes, the hacking and hollowing of the dirt ceases. One of the warriors delves an arm into the hole they've created and roots about. When that arm finally reappears, he is holding a slender object caked in dense, dark earth.

As the dirt is brushed away, Evie recognizes a stone knife, its blade still clearly etched with intricate markings.

"Did you . . . bury that here?" she asks Yacatek.

The warrior reverently carries the story knife over to Yacatek, who accepts it with an appreciative nod.

"This dagger is older than us both," she tells Evie as she continues to clean the soil away from its blade. "Do you think me so ancient?"

"Then how did you know it was here?"

"I am a storyteller," Yacatek replies, as if that should be explanation enough.

Evie wants to press her further, finding the whole proposition impossible, but she is also curious as to the origins of the story knife. "What does it say?"

Yacatek traces the characters representing the B'ors story language with a fingertip. "It would mean nothing to you," she says.

Evie is offended. "How do you know that?"

Yacatek looks up at her with stormy eyes. "Because you sit in a room with your people and you argue about who truly possesses this land. You talk of the desecration of your gods as if they created what we see around us now, when it was hands of men and women who shed the blood of those who kept this land long before those same men and women turned their thoughts to a god."

Evie's expression sinks. "Your people lived here before Sirach's, didn't they?"

Yacatek nods. "And before those Sirach's people took these lands from."

"I didn't know."

"You did not want to know," Yacatek corrects her. "None of you do. I ask you, General, what will be our reward if this war is won? What will be left for my people after all of you have had your say about what belongs to you?"

Evie doesn't know how to answer that question, and Yacatek can see it written plainly on her face.

The two women stare at each other until an agitated voice in the distance cuts through their shared silence. "General! General Evie!"

She turns to see two rune-stained ex-Savages carrying a smaller figure between them. This third soldier is draped all in black like one of the night fighters under Sirach's command. The trio approaches from the other side of the street that winds through the rest of the city to its main gates.

Hearing the commotion, Lariat and Diggs hustle over from where they were previously milling in front of the tavern to join Evie and Bam.

As the ex-Savages near, Evie sees that their charge has several long, deep gashes in their black garb. Dark, dried blood is visible beneath the tears.

A new fear begins creeping up Evie's throat.

"What's happened?" she calls to the Sicclunan scout.

"We were moving around their camp," they relate through

broken, ragged breaths stitched with pain. "The Skrain ambushed us. Only I . . . only I escaped. Sirach ordered me to . . . return . . . to tell you."

"Mother," she hears Lariat ominously breathe.

"Did you see what became of the others?" Evie says, trying to keep her voice calm and even.

"Killed," the Sicclunan manages. "All except Sirach and . . . and Mother Manai."

"Did they get away?" Lariat demands.

Evie waits, somehow already knowing the answer.

"No," the scout says. "They took them. The Skrain. They took them both. They have them."

FLOTSAM

TARU AWAKENS TO THE EYES OF A DRAGON SEEMING TO peer directly into their soul.

The retainer rolls away in terror, feeling damp and gritty soil beneath them. Taru stops and falls back against what a part of their brain not currently occupied by panic and confusion informs them is sand. They begin coughing and convulsing violently, the cringe-inducing taste of salt water filling their throat and mouth. Taru hacks up a half gallon of the stuff in short order, the process as terrible as any physical experience they've ever endured.

When it's over, they rest their elbows against the sand and force their head up, blinking against light that isn't particularly bright, but feels very harsh.

Taru is sprawled out on a beach. Waves of clear, blue water are lapping lazily at the shore just a few feet away. They can hear some type of bird squawking in the distance, its call totally foreign to Taru. It might be mid-morning, and the scene is more peaceful and serene than it has any right to be, given the last moment Taru can recall.

They remember the Skrain galleon practically splitting in half.

They remember breaking that insufferable Savage Legion tasker over their knee. They remember swimming for their very life in the middle of a furious storm. They don't remember anything after that.

The creature that was gazing at Taru raises its head, continuing to regard them with curious and gargantuan eyes. The reptilian face doesn't belong to a dragon, but rather the largest turtle upon which Taru has ever laid eyes. It's the size of a rowboat. Its shell is covered in two-foot spikes that look as though they were formed by a volcanic eruption.

"What can you possibly be?" Taru croaks.

"Never seen a spiker before, huh?"

Taru's head whips around, causing their neck and temples and everything connected to them intense pain.

A few yards up the shore, a fisherman is reclining in a beach chair that looks fashioned from driftwood splinters, the long line of their tall, skinny pole cast far into the shallow tide.

He's not Crachian. He's a Rok Islander. Taru has been among them before, immediately before the Aegins took the retainer.

So Taru has washed up on the shores of Rok Island then—the only independent nation to ever successfully resist Crachian invasion.

"They ain't fast, so over time their shells grew them stickers. Makes a thing think twice before setting on 'em, trying to make supper out of what's inside that shell."

"There are . . . there are predators big enough to hunt these things on this island?"

The fisherman smiles. "Size ain't everything."

Taru falls silent, shaking their head to clear the dust and finding that to be another painful mistake.

"Were you planning to help me at any point?" they ask, eyes shut tight to minimize the aching feeling in their skull.

"Your people forbid us from mixing with ye, don't they? I'm a law-abiding type."

"My people?"

"The ants. Crachians."

"How do you know I'm from Crache? Everyone in the Capitol always tells me I don't look like I'm from there."

"You're marked, unless those things on your face are just what happens when you hit the bottle real hard."

Taru crawls forward, peering into a shallow puddle of water nestled in a hole in the sand. The runes brought on by the bloodcoin they forced down the retainer's gullet are starting to propagate. There's one on their cheek, another in the center of their forehead, and yet another branding their right temple.

The rest returns to their mind then. The reason they were being shipped across the nation, Brio and the rebellion, and Lexi, left alone in the Capitol, surrounded by enemies. And now Taru is free, able to return to her. But how? Trying to reach the Capitol as a marked, escaped Savage would surely be impossible.

Rok Island, the only independent nation to ever successfully resist Crachian invasion.

Taru looks to the little fisherman, eyes flashing desperately. "I escaped the hold of a ship that capsized in a storm," they explain, urgently. "It was carrying Savage Legionnaires west to fight the rebellion there."

"You don't say," the fisherman comments idly, as if he's only half listening.

"Did you hear?" Taru demands. "I said there is a rebellion in the east. A rebellion against Crache, made of its own people, its own armies."

"Aye? That must be a sight."

Taru sighs, pressing their forehead into the cool, damp sand. It feels good, refreshing, even replenishing. It aids in them forming a new thought, and with it a new tack.

"Do you know a ship called the *Black Turtle*?" the retainer asks, raising their face from the beach. "It is a Rok vessel."

Finally, Taru seems to capture the fisherman's attention. "Might could be," he answers, measuredly.

"Its captain . . . Captain Staz . . . she knows me. She knew me before—" Taru waves a callused, pruned hand over their facial runes. "Before I became this."

"Oh, aye?"

"Is Captain Staz back on Rok?" Taru says, more than a little exasperated.

The fisherman leans back in his little rickety beach chair. Again, he smiles. "Might could be."

SO HIGH

THE TINY CUTS ARE MULTIPLYING LIKE RABBITS IN HEAT. After three hours, they cover her small hands and thin arms, thin red slivers like gory notches calculating some macabre achievement by her limbs. Dyeawan can only guess at the amount of blood she's left in drops along her way up the stony face of the supposedly dormant volcano.

She began her ascent after sunrise, as instructed. She had ample time beforehand to consider her path, as well as the sharp rocks that would greet her every inch of the way. While there was clearly no real trail to speak of leading up the face, it became like looking down at a maze from a bird's eye view. Her mind began to solve it in that way, finding the negative space zigzagging between the crags, and identifying the best holds for her hands to ferry her along.

She prepared by stripping the padding that covers the platform of her tender and tearing it into wide strips. Dyeawan wrapped the padding around her legs, knowing she would be forced to drag them up those rocks. She considered fashioning some kind of litter, but in the end decided she didn't want to be burdened by the extra weight. She needed to be as light and mobile as possible if she hoped to accomplish this task, let alone beat Nia to the top.

She also tore strips of cloth away from the excess material of her tunic and used them to wrap her hands as thickly as possible while still allowing them to grip tightly. Her final act of preparation was to yank cords out of her tender's construction and use them to lash her legs together so neither would wander dangerously as she ascended.

It was not lost on Dyeawan that this was the second time she's had to disassemble her tender to meet one of the Planning Cadre's ominous challenges.

She can't help wondering if those internal challenges will ever cease.

She can't help wondering if she will ever be enough for them, even as their supposed leader.

Abandoning her tender and feeling the ground beneath her body, Dyeawan's mind is immediately transported back to the alleys and streets of the Bottoms. She never thought she'd long for her tin sheet and stolen pig grease again. She also longed for the steely strength that once permeated her arms, honed by those years of dragging her body along the floor of the Bottoms on that greased tin sheet.

It wasn't as difficult as she initially supposed, at least at the outset. The incline was less steep than Dyeawan ascertained from the mountain's base. Her arms proved stronger and more able than she imagined they would when put to such a daunting task. She moves her body along with relative ease and rapidity, finding barren spaces through which to pull her legs, and, failing those spaces, flat rocks over which to drag them. She covered what must have been fifty yards without even realizing it, and with only her breath and the pace of her heartbeat quickening.

None of that lasted.

After that initial gain, those barren spaces narrowed, the flat rocks grew more jagged, and the incline sharpened dangerously. By the top of the morning, the few cuts Dyeawan had suffered previously became legion. Her arms felt as though they were broiling from within. Her mouth had not been so dry since her longest days on the street without food or water. Her pace was slowed by more than half, and Dyeawan felt herself losing speed with every handhold for which she reached, though she continued to press forward.

That wasn't the most worrisome development, however.

The tremors she'd experienced during her meeting with Tinker began in earnest less than an hour into her ascent. The first shook the mountain just hard enough to loose small pebbles that were little more than granite dust. They rained over her harmlessly. The next time the mountain shivered, however, Dyeawan had to cling to her current purchase and bury her face between the crags to shield her head from the fist-size stones that rolled down in the tremor's wake.

When Dyeawan started out, the smoke trailing from the peak was dark and shot through with slate-gray. Now, as the sun rises high with the afternoon, smoke is billowing from the top of the peak in thick, deathly curtains as dense as the night itself. It is as if the sky is calling the illusory black columns to its breast.

Now, half the volcano's face behind her, Dyeawan's biceps, forearms, and chest are burning, her elbow joints feel like the rusted hinges of a door caught in a gale, and the rock beneath her is seized in a state of constant, violent rumbling that seems to intensify with every passing moment.

Dyeawan's volcano research was thorough. She knows about lava, and about eruptions. She imagines a great molten churning occurring behind these rocks. She imagines the lava bubbling chaotically and threatening to boil over like soup left too long in a stove pot.

Finally, she imagines the mountain's blood washing over her, melting her flesh and turning whatever is left to blackened ash. Considering her current plight, that might very well be a blessing.

Gripping the rocks with her bloody fingers, sweat glazing every inch of her slight body, Dyeawan inexplicably finds herself recalling a conversation she had with Edger. It was shortly after she passed her seemingly lethal test to prove herself worthy of becoming a planner. She'd asked him why it was necessary for her to fear for her life during the exam. She wanted to know why she couldn't simply have been presented with complex problems and proved her ability to solve them.

The problems we solve, Edger had explained, *are very often and quite literally life and death for veritable multitudes. You must be able to see them as such to gain their full weight and measure.*

Dyeawan accepted that explanation then, but what's before her now, what she has been tasked to do here, just seems punitive and absurd.

How does a race up a mountain I'm terrified is going to explode teach me anything? she wonders bitterly.

How does it prove who should lead those who solve life-and-death problems for Crache?

She thinks about her last conversation with Riko before Nia challenged her to this farce. They spoke of what Dyeawan wanted to accomplish sitting at the head of the planners.

Dyeawan recalls saying some impassioned things that she thought worthy at the time, yet now, clinging to the hot rocks of a quaking volcano, she can't remember the substance of any of those words.

Nor can she remember why she should so badly want to sit at the top of the Planning Cadre.

The entire mountain convulses like a dying man. Dyeawan is shaken loose from her purchase and goes sliding back down the tenuous path she's following, contorting painfully to avoid the most jagged features and still slicing her body open at several points before managing to grab another hold deep enough to stop her sudden descent.

Dyeawan concentrates all that she is on that single point of her grip. She wipes the soot from her eyes, only succeeding in replacing it with blood and sweat. It takes several moments of blinking before she can see well enough to locate another hold for her free hand. Reaching for it, she rights herself against the face of the mountain and clings there.

The heat is almost unbearable. The rocks begin to sear through the now filthy wraps around her hands, painfully stinging the last unmarred patches of her flesh. Dyeawan isn't sure she can hang on, much less ascend any farther. Let Nia have it then, if she hasn't already reached the top and returned safely to the base.

A thunderous bursting and a renewed convulsing of the terrain draw her attention away from those defeatist thoughts and agonized sensations.

Dyeawan looks up, to the peak, to that smoking hollow wreathed in fiery light. The shaking of the mountain intensifies in that moment. However, Dyeawan no longer consciously feels it beneath her. The world seems to slow its pace and become eerily quiet. The constant rumbling in her ears ceases, and the whole of her consciousness is focused on that devil's spout crowning the mountain.

The next sound Dyeawan registers is a deep bawling from inside the volcano as it erupts, spewing liquid fire what seems like a thousand feet in the air. Dyeawan has never before seen shades of red and orange so vibrant and alive and terrifying. The lava fills the sky above and begins raining in torrents down on the rocks directly above her position.

Dyeawan looks frantically over her shoulder, gazing down the path she's crawled over. It is futile to attempt to make her way back down. Her eyes search the mountain's face for some possible refuge she can take from the encroaching tidal wave of molten rock, but if such a thing even exists, which she is certain it does not, there is no such haven within a distance she could cover before the rolling fire engulfs her.

Dyeawan stares up at the radiant lava flowing down toward her, almost alive in its leech-like movements. The heat from the oncoming wave blisters the flesh of her face. She looks down and sees the skin atop her arms beginning to steam.

This is the part where you break down and cry and scream and

wait for it all to be over, a voice inside her head casually informs Dyeawan.

The voice sounds less like her own and more like Edger's.

He never knew her, not really, and the ghost of his memory knows her even less. The girl who would've sobbed in pain and fear and helplessness no longer exists. That is one of the reasons she chose to reclaim her name before taking her seat at the planners' table; she knew the person who put on that gray tunic and concentric circle badge was a completely different one from the girl Edger and the Cadre scraped from the streets of the Bottoms.

You've come this far. There is nothing to do but see this foolish task to its conclusion. You have to attempt to solve the problem, wherever it leads.

That voice does belong to her, and it is who Dyeawan is now.

She relinquishes her left hand's grip on its current hold, extending her arm forward and grasping the next rock that will grant her purchase. Every inch of her skin is now searing in agony, the pain threatening to shut down her mind while her muscles shriek at her to task them no more. She ignores it all, willing her thoughts to clarify, to push through the overwhelming sensations and allow her control over what parts of her body still obey her.

Dyeawan manages three more handholds before the lava rolls over her, and now, only now, does she unleash a savage, anguished cry. Her voice is extinguished as her very flesh is seared black and turned to instant tar. After that, the pain exists only inside her head, for scant slivers of moments that seem and feel like miniature eternities.

Strong hands grasp her by the arms, and in the next moment Dyeawan blinks eyelids she believed had just melted to find it all gone.

She is indeed lying upon the rocks of the mountain. Her cloth-wrapped hands are dirty and bloody from the climb. However, her skin is still more or less intact. There isn't a burn mark upon her. She no longer feels pain beyond reckoning. She only feels tired and worn through and confused.

The lava has also disappeared. It is as if not a single drop has ever touched the stone surrounding her.

It is a calm, clear day. Barely a breeze disrupts the serenity.

She stares up into Tinker's smiling face. From there she shifts her cloudy, disoriented gaze to the top of the peak. It is smoking as it did when she first noticed the black exhaust, in thin wisps muddled with gray.

"The smoke is real," Tinker reassures her. "A few simple potions mixed in the appropriate quantities in the heart of the volcano, which lies forever dormant, as you read."

Dyeawan's breathing is still highly elevated, as is the pace of the blood rushing through her veins. She closes her eyes and forces her mind to focus, commanding her heartbeat to slow and the frantic fizzling between her ears to recede.

Tinker's voice invades her self-imposed darkness. "It *is* remarkable what a few simple potions mixed in the proper proportions can do, isn't it?"

Dyeawan opens her eyes, unclear as to why the old woman is reiterating that observation. She looks down to see a needle sticking in her right thigh. It is attached to a bellows, not unlike the one she used to inject Edger's wind dragon, Ku, triggering the mating throes that killed her mentor.

"Don't worry," Tinker says. "It's curative. It has restored you to your natural state."

Dyeawan considers the needle and bellows in silence for a moment, waiting for her breathing to normalize.

"The soup," she says.

Tinker nods, her smile broadening.

"But you ate it too," Dyeawan puzzles, looking up at the old woman once more.

"I inoculated myself beforehand."

Dyeawan reaches down and pulls the needle from her leg, holding it up to the light of the afternoon and scrutinizing it. "How did it make me see what you wanted me to see?"

"I wanted you to see nothing," Tinker corrects her.

Dyeawan frowns. "You know what I mean."

"The potion merely opened your mind to suggestion. Powerfully, of course. You already had volcanoes on the brain. I'm certain you studied them thoroughly. The smoke effect provided all the remaining suggestion you required."

Dyeawan understands, though she is disappointed in her own weakness, regardless of what compounds they tricked her into swallowing. "But I did not reach the top."

"That wasn't the challenge."

Dyeawan is confused again. "You said—"

"I told you an untruth, I'm afraid."

Dyeawan loathes the way those long associated with the Planning Cadre seem unable or unwilling to call a lie what it is, especially when it is a lie perpetrated by them.

"This was never a race," Tinker confirms. "Nor was it the contest of the body."

"It was the contest of the will," Dyeawan concludes.

The old woman seems pleased. "Correct."

A steely calm fills Dyeawan's weary body, soothing her fractured mind. There is anger, but it's a dull feeling somewhere in the background. She quickly dismisses it as useless.

"And how did Nia fare?" she asks the former planner.

"She crawled into the fire. Much like you."

Dyeawan is thoroughly unsurprised. "Of course she did."

Tinker releases her hold and gently pries the needle and bellows from Dyeawan's hand. "I've brought a litter. I'll bear you back down the mountain. There's a hidden trail not far from here."

Again, Dyeawan is thoroughly unsurprised. "Of course there is," she says.

HOSTAGE OF THE MIND

THERE IS NO ESCAPING THE THOUGHT FOR LEXI. SHE HAS been avoiding it since being released back into the world and the Gen Circus by her captors. She avoided it while picking up food in the Gen bazaar to restock the tower's larders, something Lexi has done thousands of times before. She avoided it while walking, for the first time in weeks, through the doors of the tower in which she was born and raised and fell in love with her husband. She avoided it while tidying up the receiving room on the ground floor, where the most scrutinizing observer could find not a single hint that murdered bodies ever occupied the space.

That thought is the simple fact that the towers no longer feel like her home.

Lexi cannot locate what has changed within, much less around, her. She sits in the nook of her familiar parlor window, the one that faces its opposite in the sister tower where Brio grew up. She holds in her hands the reed-of-the-wind that Taru helped her repair after she bashed it over the skull of her would-be assassin. Everything is the same—all the sights and sounds and smells that have surrounded her for the whole of her life.

Yet everything is different. All that is familiar is now completely unfamiliar, or at least it *feels* so.

Lexi wonders if she is merely seeing the entire world through different eyes now, with a gaze that has beheld so much horror and truth. She has delved too deeply beneath the veneer of Crache, perhaps deeper than anyone not conspiring to bring down the nation. Her head is filled with too many plots, too much knowledge of the dark ambitions and actions of others.

She wonders when, not if, the Protectorate Ministry will come for her, to question her, to abduct her, or even, finally, to kill her.

She wonders what Burr will do with her if Lexi lives long enough to accomplish the purpose the Ignoble has laid before her, by whatever delusional standard Burr will consider that purpose achieved.

She also constantly wonders about Taru. Is her retainer enjoying the same treatment Lexi did in another castle in the hidden lands of some other Ignoble, concealed for centuries from the bureaucracy of Crache? Is Taru rotting in a dark and dank dungeon somewhere? Are they even alive? Is Burr merely lying to Lexi, dangling the false hope of Taru's safety and return in front of her to subdue and compel Lexi to commit ultimately heinous acts?

It all feels so futile, yet she cannot bring herself to refuse Burr's demands. Lexi only knows her spirit can ill afford living with the knowledge another person she loves has been taken from her and will not return. After months of resisting the idea Brio was dead and finally learning he is alive, only for his current status to be totally unknown to her, Lexi is compelled to do whatever she has to in order to keep Taru, or at the very least the idea of them, alive and well in her mind.

Her body is weary from the long days spent in the Bottoms. She and Shaheen have developed a routine, a route they follow in their wagon filled with food donated from the allotments of Gens either sympathetic to Burr's cause or secretly held under the woman's conniving yoke. Those donations have doubled in their daily amount since this whole thing began. Lexi reckons there isn't a poor soul left in the Bottoms who is not fed by their hands.

They worship her now. Lexi would like to delude herself into believing Burr's plan has succeeded only in filling empty bellies and fortifying others in need. The truth, however, is that the people of the Bottoms idolize and revere Lexi. At this point, she could order them all to walk off the docks and drown in the sea and most of them would probably do it without question, so assured are they of Lexi's kind nature, altruistic intentions, and genuine affection for them.

It *is* genuine, too. They are no longer some nameless, faceless, unwashed mass to her. Lexi no longer sympathizes with them as a vague collective, or idea of suffering. She knows them now, and empathizes with their plight. She knows their names and recognizes their faces and has learned their stories. She has come to love and trust them, and they her in return.

Yet with every scrap of food she hands out, Lexi also serves them the tale Burr has instructed her to dispense under threat of Taru's death. Lexi spins the grand and glorious web of lies that paints ancient nobility as loving protectors and caretakers of their people. The seeds she planted in a few minds about how much better their lives would be if nobility were restored to rule have blossomed into a burgeoning belief system among the people of the Bottoms.

Lexi told herself she was agreeing to Burr's terms and instructions to bide time. She needed that time to figure out how to subvert Burr's goals for her while saving Taru's life and hopefully her own. Yet she has no plan. She has no allies. She is shadowed every day by Kamen Lim, and is only the tool Burr intended to fashion her into.

Lexi rises from the window, wandering across the soft rug in her bare feet. She absently strums the reed, striking nothing resembling an actual chord. She curls her toes, staring down at them, at the lush threads of the rug protruding between them. Blood once stained those fibers, that of the men who came to kill her. Taru washed it out of the rug. Lexi offered to help, but her retainer refused, insisting to perform the gruesome task alone.

The smooth wood of the reed is cool against her fingers. She holds the beautiful instrument by its reconstructed neck, cradling its wooden belly as she turns it over and over in her hands.

Lexi stares down at the round table in the middle of the rug. There is a chain of bloody memories that lives in her mind, each link forged by the trauma of witnessing and creating violent death.

Upon the table, Lexi sees herself being held down by the Savage sent to kill her. That image warps into one of the other Savage, the lanky spear-wielding man, splayed open by Taru's blade before being sprawled over the top of the same table right before Lexi's eyes. There was so much blood; more than Lexi had ever seen at one time, much less pouring from one person's body. The scrawny murderer's eyes were wide and vacant, devoid of even the slightest spark of life, no longer looking as though they belonged inside a man.

That empty gaze is the next link in the chain of memories. Lexi recalls Daian's eyes as the poison took hold of him. His eyes slowly fell into that same void. She remembers the surprise that preceded that blankness. Even for such a creature as Daian, an unrepentant killer, a madman, the realization of his own tenuous mortality was such a shock.

As was the notion that Lexi killed him, she supposes.

It's not so much living with that knowledge as it is the truth within her. Lexi *wanted* to kill Daian. The plan she affected in her prison quarters within Burr's castle was not one of escape, but of murder. Escaping was only a pretense. Lexi knew even with Daian's help, even if he had provided her all the knowledge of their location and the surrounding terrain and the secrets of Burr's blood garden, she had no chance of succeeding in her proposed flight.

She simply wanted to kill him. She was tired of being their victim, and she hated what Daian was, and what he'd done.

Lexi strangles the neck of the reed with both of her hands. She raises the cherished memento high above her head and smashes it against the edge of the table. The seams where its broken parts have been mended separate as the body of the instrument shatters. She is left holding a neck connected to nothing.

And yes, there is impulsive fury in what she's just done, but there is also a conscious thought, and that is the reed *should* be broken into a hundred pieces. Repairing it was wrong. The stringed instrument represents a time that is not only gone, but was destroyed by loss and malice and violence and death.

Lexi casts the neck of the reed away and drops to her knees. Her tears come in torrents, racking her body. She doubles over, clutching at the fibers of the rug.

That is how Shaheen finds Lexi, on her hands and knees sobbing her pain and frustration into that antique rug, seeing through tear-filled eyes blood stains that are no longer present among its threads.

"Te-Gen!" the girl cries in alarm, rushing to Lexi's side.

"I'm all right, Shaheen," Lexi assures her, roughly choking back as much sorrow as spittle. "I'm all right."

Shaheen lightly grips Lexi's upper arm for support, rubbing the area between her shoulder blades with the other hand.

"What happened?"

Lexi doesn't know how to begin to answer. She rises to her knees with Shaheen's help, sitting against the heels of her bare feet. Her hands cup her face as she inhales and exhales deeply, cleansing herself of the sudden fit.

"I . . . I slipped," she finally manages to say, lowering her hands.

Shaheen is quiet, and it's clear from her expression she doesn't believe Lexi. "It's not," Shaheen stammers. "I shouldn't pry. It's not my place."

The girl begins to stand, but Lexi instinctively reaches out and grasps her wrist, halting her. "No," Lexi says. "I'm sorry. It's not your fault."

Shaheen nods, kneeling in front of her.

"What can I do?" she asks. "What is wrong?"

"I don't know what you can do," Lexi answers honestly. "I . . . I'm just . . ."

The tears begin spilling over her cheeks anew. She feels herself losing her grip once more.

"I'm alone," Lexi says, the admission hurling her back into the abyss. "I'm all alone. I thought . . . I thought I could do this, that I could *show* them I was stronger . . . but I can't. I have no one."

Shaheen reaches out and embraces Lexi, pulling her close.

Lexi allows herself to be held, encircling the smaller girl with her arms. Soon she's clinging to Shaheen, sobbing into the crook of her neck.

"You're not alone," Shaheen whispers in her ear. "You have me. You helped me once. Let me help you."

Lexi is already shaking her head, smearing her tears across the girl's shoulder. "You can't. Not with this. You don't understand—"

"Lexi," the girl bids her gently.

"No, Shaheen, you can't know what's really happening—"

"Lexi," she repeats, loudly, and in a completely different tone.

It is so jarring that Lexi actually pulls away from her, startled.

Shaheen's hands grip Lexi's forearms, stopping her short. The girl's hands are strong, surprising Lexi again. They feel as firm as vises encircling her flesh.

She stares into her ward's eyes. Shaheen's expression has also changed. Lexi sees nothing of the timid street urchin, a mother too soon seeking the Gen leader's approval constantly. The young woman meeting her gaze is filled with confidence. The confusion that filled her eyes a moment before has been replaced by knowing certainty.

"You *have* help, Lexi," Shaheen insists. "All you've ever had to do was ask for it."

Lexi doesn't know what to say. She's completely at a loss to understand the abrupt change in the girl.

At that moment, Char comes scampering into the room, waving a large white lily they allowed her to pick in the Gen Circus garden.

Lexi watches the stern, knowing expression vanish from Shaheen's face, replaced by a warm smile as she turns her head to address her daughter. "Go up to your room, my little mouse," she says, speaking softly. "It's your bedtime. I'll come tuck you in soon."

Char stops waving her flower. She takes in the scene of the two of them there on the floor, blinking with wide, innocent eyes.

"Go on, Char," her mother repeats, more firmly this time.

The little girl hesitates a moment longer, and then turns around and runs out of the room. Shaheen returns her gaze to Lexi, letting her surprisingly strong hands slip from around her arms.

Her expression has not totally transformed back to that severe, unfamiliar visage. It's somewhere between the two; the mother who tends to her child with gentility and warmth, and the assertive young woman who just assured Lexi they can help.

"Who are you?" Lexi asks her.

Without saying a word, Shaheen bends forward and contorts her body, slipping the wrap gifted to her by Lexi from her shoulder and down her arm.

There is a small tattoo inked in pale silver on Shaheen's back. It is an emblem all too familiar to Lexi.

Shaheen, the girl she found starving and ragged in a forgotten alley, is marked by an eagle's eye, the symbol of the Protectorate Ministry.

THE INEVITABLE

THE LONGHOUSE HAS A PERFECTLY THATCHED ROOF AND large windows at both ends to allow the breeze to sweep through its surprisingly spacious confines.

"What do you do in the storm season?" Taru asks their host.

Captain Staz of the *Black Turtle* reclines in what looks like a much better crafted version of the chair occupied by the fisherman Taru met on the beach. The diminutive woman smokes a pipe that looks more like a seashell with one end shaped into a stem. She inhales from its mouth and blows a slightly acrid-smelling smoke into the breeze.

"We sew shutters from soil and grass, held together with woven nets, and seed the soil. The rains water them as they pour. By the time storm season has passed the shutters have all sprouted crops. We plant them in our gardens and harvest supper."

Taru is impressed.

"That is . . . quite brilliant."

"The island teaches you to be industrious."

Taru's large frame is testing the limits of a chair similar to the captain's, both of them arranged around a short table set upon a rug that feels like dry rice under Taru's bare feet. Since being taken to Staz and welcomed into her home, Taru has been given water and plied with several bowls of a steaming hot stew of the freshest fish from the island's bay, cooked in a rich and heady broth the color of arterial blood.

"Would you like more to eat?" the captain asks after Taru has finished their third bowl.

"No, thank you. It was delicious."

"An old family recipe. To Islanders those are as sacred as anything else we have."

"I can see why."

Staz examines Taru curiously. "You do not seem at ease, my friend. You are safe here, you know. I know that by pact with your people we are supposed to expel any Crachian who attempts to escape to our shores, but you must know I have no intention of honoring such things, and no Skrain will be coming after you here. I'm certain they believe everyone aboard your galleon drowned."

Taru stirs in their chair. "That is not what . . . first of all, thank you for that. I mean it. I appreciate your help and hospitality. Truly I do. You have saved me, and I am thankful."

"It sounds like there is more to that thought than gratitude."

"There is, yes. When that ship went down I was being ferried to the east to fight against the rebellion brewing there. Forced to fight, I should say."

Staz takes a long, contemplative drag from her pipe.

"We know about it. We like to keep apprised of these things, from a distance."

"It is that distance I wish to talk with you about."

“Oh, aye? What would you ask of me?”

“What I would ask of all the Rok Islanders. To fight.”

Staz laughs, unfurling smoke in every direction. “Fighting. We are good at that. It’s true. Another thing the island teaches you. But the fight you speak of is not here.”

“It is not. You would have to sail to the eastern frontier of Crache itself.”

“The battles we’ve won against Crache have always been within our reefs. That’s where Rok’s strength lies.”

“I would not presume to tell you who you are, but I have to believe the strength of any nation lies in its people.”

“It is always a difficult thing, to speak of an entire people as one. In Crache they call us here on Rok ‘a simple people.’ I am sure you have heard that before. This is a thing you say about a people when you want to treat them like your children, and rarely kindly. People are never simple.”

“I would agree.”

“Do you know what fate is?”

“The idea that everything that happens is meant to happen.”

“On Rok we do not hold with fate. We do not believe the outcome of events cannot be changed, that what we do cannot change such things. But we do believe in the inevitable. Do you understand the difference, my friend?”

“I am not sure I do.”

“We do not believe our actions cannot change things, but we know that whatever happens, whatever comes from that, we must accept the outcome is what must be.”

“I feel as though you are trying to tell me something without speaking to it directly. I have never been good with veiled speech. More often than not it is lost on me."

"I speak of the inevitable because you have come here to talk of Crache and rebellion."

"In fairness, I did not come here. I washed up here."

"Perhaps that too was inevitable."

"I cannot tell you I see this inevitability you speak of, but I do see opportunity. The rebellion is an opportunity."

"For you?"

"For *all* of us, who live under Crache's yoke and who could be crushed by it."

"Rok has stood against Crache without breaking, and will continue to do so."

"Rok has stood against Crache as it is. What about what Crache might become? The Crache that continues to grow and expand, consuming everything in its path. What of a Crache that is twice the size of the one you have repelled in the past?"

"As I say, Crache is inevitable."

Taru feels frustration and disappointment churning within them, but they do not want to disrespect their host in the captain's own home by disagreeing with Staz further.

"So too then is Crache's downfall," she adds without emotion.

That hits Taru like a fist. They are silent for several moments before speaking again.

"So then . . . are you saying . . ."

"I am saying what comes will come, and we must be ready, but I will act to change things as I can."

Taru can feel an expansion in their chest, something lighter and more hopeful than they've felt since being taken into custody by the Aegins.

"Thank you, Captain."

"Do not thank me yet. As I said, my friend, the people of Rok are not simple. What I believe may not be what my fellow captains believe."

"And . . . if they feel differently about this fight? Where does that leave us?"

Staz smiles cattishly. "We will see. You would be surprised what a pot of my stew can do."

Taru doesn't know what that means, but they cannot deny the captain's stew is delicious.

THE GATHERERS

WHEN BRIO ASKED EVIE HOW BADLY SHE THOUGHT THEIR forces would be outnumbered in the forthcoming battle, she placed their worst odds at ten to one.

It appears she was only slightly off in that estimate.

It looks more like twelve to one, at least from her cursory count of the Skrain in the massive encampment spread below them.

"Their tents are nicer than ours," Chimot observes.

Evie smiles wryly. "They would be."

Three more hooded, black-clad warriors in the upper branches of the vibrantly blooming dragon fruit tree join them. There is a lush and thriving grove of the tall, bountiful trees standing not two hundred yards from the edge of the Skrain camp. It has either been hastily abandoned, or hurriedly ransacked, or both. There are overturned wheelbarrows and smashed crates, not to mention several felled trees.

The leaders of the Gen whom the Franchise Council has granted the dragon fruit harvesting concession for the Tenth City are no doubt sequestered in the Circus of their besieged burg. The workers in their employ who actually tend to and pick the grove are either too afraid to venture out, or too indifferent. In either case, the grove was left for the Skrain gatherers to pick clean and help feed their gargantuan new host.

The small band of Sicclunans, led by Evie, ascended their heightened vantage point just in time to watch the main force of the Skrain army arrive. It was hours simply watching the mounted and marching columns trail into the valley, a seemingly endless snake made of writhing steel armor. It was a sobering if not completely terrifying illustration of how overwhelming their legions are, and how potentially doomed the rebellion may be.

It made them easier to count, in any case.

"We could light a few fires," Chimot suggests. "Or more than a few."

Chimot is the scout who came back. She is one of Sirach's protégés and lieutenants in the Sicclunan special force trained in moving and fighting in the dark of night. Her fellow lieutenants did not return from their mission, and were not taken prisoner alongside Sirach and Mother Manai.

Though badly wounded, Chimot refused to remain behind when Evie conceived their current mission. Evie watched the woman (though she appears barely more than a girl) clean and stitch up her own lacerations, cleansing her other cuts and bruises with some manner of Sicclunan salve that seemed like it scorched her and caused those injuries to steam briefly. All the while she cursed the Skrain who ambushed them and colorfully described the ways in which she would dispatch them upon their next encounter.

She very much reminds Evie of Sirach, in fact.

"Maybe on our way out," she tells Chimot. "That's not why we've come."

"Of course it isn't," Chimot says calmly, a breath passing before she adds, with only the dullest edge of irony, "General."

Evie says nothing. She knows her hold over the Sicclunan forces is tenuous at best, but this small contingent, at least, is united by one factor: their shared love of Sirach.

The Skrain host that has arrived from the west is still establishing camp, which is good for her party and their plans. There is a brief period of preoccupation and disorder, if not controlled chaos, when an army of that size previously on the march settles, particularly in preparation for what they expect to be a lengthy and exhaustive siege.

"Or maybe one *big* fire," Chimot muses later.

Evie shakes her covered head. "I like the way you think, anyway."

The branches below their position in the treetop begin rustling as if seized by an ill wind. Evie's black-gloved hand goes for the hilt of her short sword, but Chimot reaches out to still her. "He's ours," she says. "Did you hear him coming before now?"

Again, Evie allows that nudging in her tone to pass.

She looks down at the blooms covering the branches beneath where the rest of them have posted. A hooded and masked head deftly emerges through it, as if rising from the surface of a calm pool. Barely a leaf or stick is stirred, much less broken, as the Sicclunan warrior practically swims up to join them.

"They're coming," a voice muffled by the cloth of the mask informs them.

Evie and Chimot trade looks through their thin eye slits. Evie nods decisively.

They'd spied the party of anglers as Evie's band crept past the Skrain's own scouts just after dusk. The group was finishing up a long day of fishing several small ponds in the area. The anglers wore no insignia—only the shabby, stinking garb of their trade—but Evie knew they were part of the Skrain's gatherers, no doubt dispatched to catch fresh fish for the officers in the camp who commanded a better meal than common soldiers.

Chimot gives a similar nod to the other black-clad soldiers, and then begins leading them silently down through the branches of the tree.

Evie follows, far less experienced than they in these clandestine arts. She is a quick study, however. She watches their hands and feet, the way they move their bodies, and how all of that interacts with their surroundings. Evie tries to mimic those movements and understand the methodology behind them.

They all drop from the lower branches to the grove floor without announcing their landing. Just as quickly, each shrouded scout merges with the bark of a different dragon fruit tree, practically disappearing from sight in the encroaching darkness of the evening.

Evie stays close to Chimot, pressing her body beside the younger woman's and against the thick hide of a particularly ancient specimen.

"You're getting less slow," Chimot taunts under her breath.

"You're almost the teacher Sirach is," Evie fires back in the same hushed tone.

They wait. Soon they hear the crunch of leaf and blade underfoot as half a dozen people trek through the grove.

From where she and Chimot are concealed, Evie watches the anglers, straw hats drooping over their heads and bamboo poles hanging over their shoulders. Each pair is carrying a heavily burdened basket between them, freshly caught fish of several different sizes and varieties piled above the rims.

They look tired, wearied by more than the day. They're scrawny, the lot of them, underfed themselves despite spending long days harvesting bountiful fare for others. Their clothes are run through with holes and stained with the blood and oils of their catch.

"We don't need to kill any of them," Evie whispers to Chimot.

"Burying their bodies would seem quite rude otherwise," the young warrior rejoins.

Very much like Sirach, Evie thinks.

"They're not soldiers," she says. "They're anglers. Lowly men and women fishing to survive."

"War is not the time to distinguish between our enemies and those who give them shelter and aid."

"It's the most important time to do so," Evie counters.

"Sirach wouldn't hesitate."

Evie's tone darkens. "Sirach is not here."

She hears an exasperated sigh in the dark. "No, and if we tie those anglers up and leave them, and if one of them gets free or they're discovered, we will not succeed in retrieving Sirach. We'll also probably all die ourselves."

Evie steps away from the tree to face Chimot directly, squaring her shoulders and putting as much bass as she can behind a whisper.

"This is neither an argument nor a discussion. I am giving you an order."

Chimot turns to face Evie fully now, hands hanging loosely at her sides, though the rest of her body seems tense.

The position of the other Sicclunan fighters doesn't change, but there is a subtle shift in their postures. Evie senses it more than she sees it.

She knows they are looking to Chimot for guidance and leadership. If it comes to blows between her and Evie, the black-clad warriors won't hesitate to support Chimot.

They remain Sicclunan, and Evie cannot fault them for that.

She waits, quietly digging her feet into the ground beneath them. Apparently it is loud enough to draw Chimot's gaze downward for a scant moment before it returns to Evie's face.

Whatever process of deliberation is occurring behind her eyes happens quickly, at least. Chimot slowly relaxes her posture, leaning back against the bark of the tree.

"We'll gag them and hang them up in the trees, alive," she says, practically grumbling, "It'll take as long as burying them, I suppose."

THE BODY (FOR REAL THIS TIME)

"YOU LOOK WELL," DYEAWAN NOTES OF NIA AS THE TWO OF them sit outside the secreted chambers in the heart of the Planning Cadre.

And she does. Nia appears thoroughly undisturbed by their recent shared experience. Her gray planner's tunic is freshly washed and pressed, and utterly free of creases. Her dark hair with its dull orange and red touches is neatly bound back in a tail. She looks rested, her eyes bright and clear with not a trace of swelling or sagging from a restless night.

Her hands are even free of fresh cuts, whereas Dyeawan's are wrapped in fresh dressings, the insides of which have been treated with healing ointment.

She probably wore gloves, Dyeawan thinks to herself. *Of course she thought to bring gloves. We were called to the base of a mountain. Why did I not think of it as well?*

They were probably thick gloves, too.

Dyeawan has to consciously suppress the frown that threatens to overtake her lips.

The only sign Nia even undertook the same climb is a pebbly

magenta welt raised on her right temple, probably from failing to dodge a falling rock. The welt and its color even seem to complement her appearance.

Nia, for her part, responds to Dyeawan's observation with the slightest bow of her head. "You look well also," she says a moment later.

Dyeawan briefly dips her chin in kind.

Neither of them looks directly at the other. They are, both of them, keeping their eyes fixed on the closed chamber doors across the corridor in front of them. A gap of nearly five feet separates Dyeawan's tender from the nondescript chair on which Nia sits, backed against the wall. They each keep their backs high and straight, their chins slightly raised.

Dyeawan is aware they are posturing, but she can't seem to make herself stop.

Those closed doors are equally baffling. There aren't many doors in the Planning Cadre to begin with. The majority of the keep's design is open, with broad, accessible arches.

In addition, these doors are not of the typical Crachian aesthetic. Quite the contrary, they are both forged from solid-looking steel rather than carved from wood, and each is adorned with wrought iron rungs held in the mouths of giant ants forged and sculpted from the same material.

Those thick, heavy metal circles recall to Dyeawan's mind the God Rung, and she is less than grateful for the reminder.

The cut of the doors themselves is also foreboding. Tall and wide enough to accommodate a wagon, their edges are flared at their narrowed top, almost like serrations in the spine of a camping knife.

She has no notion of what lies behind the doors, but it is apparent whoever fashioned them wanted petitioners to wonder, and did not want their guesses to be hopeful and bright.

Realizing that, Dyeawan begins to find the silence in the corridor increasingly oppressive.

"Do you know which task has been chosen for this challenge?" she asks Nia. "Assuming this *is* the challenge of the body."

"Of course I don't." Her tone belies neither irritation nor impatience. She is merely a stating a fact that she seems to feel should be obvious to both of them.

Dyeawan lets the matter rest. She tells herself she has already spoken to the older woman too much. They are opponents, opposites. Nia is attempting to remove Dyeawan from her position—one that Dyeawan, who has decided despite her moments of doubt under volcanic duress, still wants and from which she can still create much needed change for people remaining mired in the circumstances from which Dyeawan was saved.

She can't resist, however. A question presses heavily on her mind, and Nia is the only other person with the reference to answer it. "What did you think? When you saw the lava flowing toward you?"

Nia draws a slow, deep breath, her shoulders squaring back before she releases it. Dyeawan cannot discern whether the other planner's gesture is born of annoyance or contemplation.

"I thought," she answers carefully, "that I must be hallucinating."

Dyeawan believes it, not because Nia is more intelligent or astute, but because she has been among the Cadre and the planners far longer. Nia knows how they operate, and how they test people.

Of course she would be more able and quicker to arrive at that conclusion and proceed accordingly.

"What did you think?" Nia asks, surprising her.

Dyeawan finally turns her head toward the other woman, hoping her own expression remains neutral. "I thought I was going to die," she answers honestly.

"And still you climbed?"

"Yes."

Nia nods, continuing to stare straight ahead. Her expression is unreadable to Dyeawan, who continues to study her openly in the silence that follows.

She finally gives up, returning her gaze to the ominous doors awaiting them.

When the air between them finally starts to feel settled, Nia disrupts it anew by saying, "Then I suppose you should have won."

Dyeawan's head snaps around to regard her with unmasked shock. Nia betrays nothing. She continues to passively consider the doors before them, subtly cocking her head.

Dyeawan opens her mouth to speak, but she is completely unsure of what words are lingering behind her tongue and quickly seals her lips. She turns her gaze away and is left to puzzle over Nia's words, their meaning, and their sincerity.

Dyeawan is still puzzling over all of those things when the doors finally begin to yawn open, their metallic edges echoing sickly through the corridor. Firelight spills out at Nia's feet and Dyeawan's wheel tracks.

There is no one to greet them, or usher them beyond the

threshold. That absence only increases the feeling of underlying menace beneath the whole affair.

Nia rises from her seat, politely gesturing Dyeawan forward. "After you."

Dyeawan says nothing. She is more than slightly annoyed by the older woman's constant restraint and formality. It seems to run so contrary to Nia's purpose in all of this.

Taking as deep a breath as she can without making a show of it, Dyeawan maneuvers her tender in front of the other planner and rows herself through the doors.

The room beyond is less sinister than she thought it might be. It is a circular chamber with low ceilings held up by four bare columns, the torch-filled sconces affixed to them the source of the firelight, and block walls composed of a differently colored stone than the rest of the keep. Dyeawan surmises this chamber is older, more original to the structure as when it was first erected. The floor is fashioned from glossy black obsidian, probably harvested from the island's volcano ages ago, reinforcing Dyeawan's suspicions.

Tinker is waiting for them inside, bereft of her sheep's-wool shawl. Her faded gray tunic remains unadorned, though she has freed her milky white hair from its tail.

"Greetings, you two."

Neither Dyeawan nor Nia feel compelled to reply, though they both bow their heads with varying degrees of depth and enthusiasm.

"It is entirely strange for me to find myself back between the walls of this keep," Tinker muses, casting her gaze about the confines of the space, "much less in this awful space."

"You are generous to agree to oversee these proceedings, Tinker," Nia cordially tells the old woman.

Dyeawan chooses not to voice an opinion on the contents of either woman's statement.

"Generosity doesn't enter into it, I promise you. I find this whole thing quite silly, to be honest."

Dyeawan drops her head, though her hair is not quite long enough to conceal her grin.

Nia is thoroughly unruffled. "Then may I inquire as to your motivation?" she presses Tinker.

"Respect for Edger, who was also quite silly at times, but to whom I owed much and cared for deeply despite his flaws."

Dyeawan finds, oddly, she can appreciate that sentiment. Though she has currently lost interest in the brief exchange between Nia and Tinker. Her focus is on the only visible piece of furniture in the chamber. It is a small obsidian table, almost like an altar, rising up from the floor itself like a frozen wave upon a shining black tide. It resides in the center of the space, beside Tinker, with two obsidian stools fixed on either side of it. The surface of the table has handles on it, two of them, set into its top in opposing diagonal corners.

It is also supporting two square objects draped in white silk.

"You both succeeded in the first contest, a measure of the will, with equal aplomb," Tinker says. "As it stands, in terms of scores, the challenge is a draw. The winner of the next two events will determine the outcome of the challenge as a whole."

"And if we end up drawing twice more?" Dyeawan asks. "Or each of us wins one contest?"

"Don't worry," Tinker bids them with what seems to be her usual unperturbed smile. "This contest in particular will be decisive."

Dyeawan quickly decides that statement cannot bode well for either of them.

Tinker motions to the table. "Please, sit. Both of you."

Nia readily complies, striding forward and slipping in between the table's edge and one of the stools. Dyeawan rows forward, turning her tender alongside the obsidian protrusion and inching as closely as she can steer her conveyance.

"Do you require assistance?" Tinker asks her.

"No," Dyeawan curtly replies.

She leans over the side of her tender and grips the edge of the table, laying her other hand flat against the seat of the stool. Dyeawan slides herself from one surface onto the other with practiced ease, despite the awkward angle and the intense smoothness of the obsidian. She lifts her legs with her hands and fits them carefully beneath the tabletop, comfortably adjusting the rest of her body.

Lacing her fingers atop the table, Dyeawan stares briefly at Nia before gazing down once again at the two squares covered by silken cloths between them. Clever as Edger once declared her, Dyeawan has not a single guess what's under those cloths or what purpose they will serve.

"The contest is simple enough," Tinker announces. "In fact, it is one of the oldest contests we have, dating all the way back to the beginning of civilization."

Short of fire, Dyeawan cannot conceive of what from then would still be useful today.

"There are cave paintings found on this very island, in fact, that depict ancient men and women engaged in the contest you two are about to undertake against one another."

"I recall less preamble before you sent me up the mountain," Dyeawan blandly remarks.

If Tinker is offended, she doesn't show it. She even chuckles warmly at Dyeawan. "I admire your wit and your frankness, my dear. I purely do admire it."

Dyeawan feels entirely uncomforted by the compliment. She waits, silently if not impatiently.

Tinker shakes her head gently at Dyeawan. "Wrist wrestling," the old woman says. "There are fancier names for it, but that's what it is, essentially."

Dyeawan stares up at her with a furrowed brow, and then she looks to Nia. Even the challenger to her title seems mildly befuddled by Tinker's proposition.

"It is quite simple," Tinker continues. "Elbows of your dominant hand on the table. Your other hand will grasp these convenient handles. You will press your wrists together. You will attempt to force your opponent's wrist down upon the table. The first contestant whose wrist touches its surface is declared the loser."

Dyeawan is not outraged. She is merely offended. "This is somehow even more ridiculous than having us climb a mountain after poisoning us to believe it was exploding."

"I agree wholeheartedly," Tinker assents without reservation. "I did not create the tasks. They have existed for hundreds of years. I simply chose one in each category at random."

"What purpose is this meant to serve?" Dyeawan demands.

"What does this have to do with planning beyond the base prejudice of the able-bodied?"

The retired planner shrugs. "I believe the thinking behind it was something along the lines of: Control over one's mind is paramount as a planner, and by extension control of one's mind over one's body."

"I cannot control the whole of my body," Dyeawan replies. "Am I still thought lesser for it as I was when I first came here, when all those with such seeming limitations who live here were deemed fit only to clean and cook and serve your meals?"

"You are only required to use the upper portion for this challenge. Having spent much of your life with your arms compensating for your legs, I would imagine you might even have an advantage."

Dyeawan is appalled by that statement, and by Tinker's attitude toward her in general. More than that, she is deeply disturbed at how they have all treated her, whether with outright disdain or gentle dismissal, as if she were a pet. Dyeawan begins to understand she has tolerated it in her life at the Planning Cadre because being treated like a pet was an improvement over being treated like an unwanted cur in the streets.

She knows now she should not have to settle for one situation or another because of where she comes from or the condition of her legs.

"I believe you are a genuine and kind person," Dyeawan says to Tinker. "You may be very smart, as well. But your years here have not relieved you of ignorance."

For the first time since meeting the old woman, Dyeawan sees

Tinker frown. "I sincerely apologize," she says, earnestly. "I spoke thoughtlessly and with unwarranted presumption."

"Thank you. I accept your apology. It does not make this contest any less absurd."

"You can quit any time you wish," Nia reminds her, almost sounding helpful.

The gaze Dyeawan fixes her with could melt steel.

"It is always worth asking yourself if you truly want what you are pursuing," Tinker comments.

"I never asked for any of this," Dyeawan says, still looking at Nia.

That is not strictly true, and Dyeawan knows it. She may not have chosen to come to the Cadre, but her actions since then sought this outcome.

The two of them don't know that, however.

"Very well," she says. "Let's get this over with and done, then." Dyeawan grasps the stone handle rising from the table's surface to her left. She plants her opposite elbow and holds her wrist high.

Nia nods, and Dyeawan can't tell whether it's a gesture of satisfaction or simply continuation. Gripping her own handle, Nia digs her elbow into the tabletop and presses her wrist against Dyeawan's.

She can feel the pulsing of both Nia's lifeblood as well as her own pulse pressing against that vital throb in the older woman's wrist.

Dyeawan cannot recall the last time she was so aware of the steady, rhythmic thrumming of the blood in her veins.

"If you intentionally break contact with your opponent, you lose."

Dyeawan merely stares back at her opponent. Nia might as well be the cover of a book left blank.

"Begin," Tinker instructs them.

The pressure of Nia's wrist and arm comes so fast and so furiously that Dyeawan is taken almost completely by surprise. She is not overpowered. She is simply unprepared. Nia's wrist quickly drives hers toward the table.

Only at the last moment is Dyeawan able to tense the muscles of her arm and stop the momentum of its fall.

She grunts, balling her fist tightly and reversing the pressure against Nia's wrist, slowly forcing their conjoined appendages away from the table.

Nia is stronger than she would've anticipated, and Dyeawan is still sore and depleted from her climb, but she also has to believe her opponent is, as well.

They lock eyes, and Nia appears to be staring through her rather than at her.

As they grapple, Tinker leans over the side of the table. "I'm sorry to have to do this," she says to both heated opponents in the throes of their contest. Tinker rips away the silk cloths from both rectangles occupying the tabletop.

The corner of Dyeawan's gaze registers what has just been uncovered, and her jaw falls silently open as she struggles to maintain her wrist's position and pressure.

The cloths were concealing small clay boxes with no covers. Inside each box, a large, thorny-haired spider resides. They are very much alive, as indicated by the continuous flexing of their many legs. The bulbous bodies of both creatures are adorned with a star-shaped pattern of red and green and black.

The boxes are positioned on either side of their wrestling

match, directly on the spots where either Dyeawan's or Nia's wrists will fall.

"Their bite won't kill you," Tinker calmly informs them. "By now you've both realized none of the challenges or tests constructed by the planners are truly lethal. But their bite will cause agonizing pain, and that pain will last quite a while."

Dyeawan's jaw snaps shut. "Why?" is all she can manage through her grinding teeth.

"Motivation?" Tinker responds vaguely. "These challenges were designed generations before my time. Who knows what they were truly thinking. I believe this is meant to test your control over your body's fight or flight response as much as your control over your opponent."

Her serene and conversational tone is a macabre juxtaposition against Dyeawan and Nia grunting and hissing. They are evenly matched as Dyeawan peers over their red and white wrists and hands, seeking Nia's gaze.

"We could both stop this," she blurts out.

Nia's face has turned as red as the flesh of her competing wrist at this point. She shakes her head definitively.

Angered and frustrated by that impenetrable stubbornness, Dyeawan refocuses on their locked wrists, doubling her already considerable effort. Slowly, she begins to force the older woman's arm down toward the table and the embrace of the poisonous creature housed in its miniature pen there.

"We . . . could both . . . *stop this*," Dyeawan repeats.

"No!" Nia practically screams.

Dyeawan watches as the physical strain peels back the layers of control and stoicism Nia has trained herself to impose on her expression. She sees desperation in Edger's former protégé. Desperation, and a terrible fear of failing.

Still, the back of her wrist is now barely an inch from the top of that lidless box. The spider inside begins crawling against the walls of its pen. An inch becomes a scant few millimeters, and still Nia will not relent.

Dyeawan's frustration boils over. "You . . . are . . . so . . . *irrational!*"

With a very uncharacteristic cry, she breaks contact, pulling her wrist from atop Nia's and leaning back from the table.

"Interesting," she hears Tinker mutter to herself.

The two competing planners cradle their tormented wrists against their chests, panting and gasping for breath as they stare across the obsidian table at each other.

"Congratulations, Nia," Tinker says to her. "You've triumphed in the challenge of the body."

Nia ignores the old woman. She stares with a mixture of bewilderment and anger at Dyeawan.

"You could have won," she all but spits.

"Won what?" Dyeawan fires back.

Nia has no answer for that, or at least she doesn't voice one.

CRACKING SHELLS

TARU IS FAST LEARNING THAT WHEN ROK ISLANDERS gather to make important decisions, it is less like a summit of leaders and more like a family feast, and the family doesn't necessarily like one another.

The food is fantastic, however.

Taru sits cross-legged on a luscious grass mat that feels as soft as silk. They've just about taken down their second bowl of fish soup, a towering pot of which Staz cooked up the night before.

Beside the retainer, the diminutive captain of the *Black Turtle* is bundled in the heavy coat that has protected the elderly woman from decades of harsh gales and biting sea breezes.

"The soup is delicious," Taru states before sucking in the last spoonful.

"It's my grandmother's recipe. The secret is to roll the conch in crushed difta root. My sister uses tort seed. She is an idiot."

Taru laughs, more loudly than they would've preferred, but the old woman seems to do that to them.

They are gathered, perhaps two hundred Rok Islanders and the retainer, in a longhouse that seems to Taru to stretch half the length of the Capitol's Spectrum. Every group in attendance brought with them a bounty of whatever dish they felt best represented their cooking skills and family recipes, and from what Taru has observed, proving their superiority, and arguing loudly about the inferiority of their neighbors' offerings, appears to be the central item on their agenda for the evening.

Taru thought they were there to discuss going to war.

As Staz has explained it, the Rok have no rulers or bureaucracy, as a Crachian would understand the concept. Anyone can convene a gathering to discuss an issue they feel affects the island as a whole, and anyone who wishes to speak may have a voice. Islanders tend to let the captains of Rok ships speak for their crews and the villages from which they originate.

"That seems highly chaotic and disorganized," the retainer had told Staz.

The old woman had only shrugged and replied, "It seems to work out well enough."

Taru has spent a week under the Islander captain's roof as her guest, and in that short time, the retainer has decided Rok is the island of their heart. They have never felt so at ease or readily accepted in a place and by its people before.

Taru almost feels guilty about asking Staz to convene this meeting, but they cannot abandon their friends to the chaos and war in Crache without trying to aid them.

The repeated thud of wood pounding against wood rises above the scattered conversation and arguments over spices. A woman only slightly younger-looking than Staz steps to the middle of the largest gathering, holding a staff made from a beautiful piece of polished driftwood.

"Let's get to the meat of this thing!" she declares. "We're here to talk about the ants and their in-fighting!"

"That's Captain Florcha of the *Razor Fin*," Staz whispers to Taru. "Bigger idiot than my sister."

"My position is simple!" Florcha proclaims.

"Much like the woman herself," Staz adds.

"The time has not yet come!" Florcha insists, voice booming to the longhouse at large.

"Our fleet is ready!" another voice shoots back.

"That is *not* the point!"

"Your metal is as weak as your brine soup!" an elder voice complains.

Florcha waves her driftwood staff. "My brine soup is as sour as it needs to be, you fillet-butchering hag!"

"You were saying," Staz cuts in, a surprising amount of bass and power in her voice for such a tiny, aged thing.

"Yes!" Florcha answers, getting back on track. "Our power has never been in our fleet. Our power has and always will be this island. Once we leave it, we are no longer fighting our fight. We will be fighting theirs. We will be fighting the way of the ant."

A great many in attendance appear to nod while others outright holler their agreement with that position. Those are met with the dissenting Islanders, and in a few moments a more heated argument than any of the ones over cooking techniques has erupted throughout the longhouse.

Taru sighs, certain this is all going nowhere, and it may still take forever to get there.

The sniping and yelling prattles on for another few minutes before Staz, who has remained relatively quiet, appears to have had enough. She rises from her grass mat, slowly, standing to her full five feet. Taru is surprised to find the incessant clamoring die down almost immediately. It's clear their new friend commands respect far beyond the deck of her ship.

"This island is parent and partner to us all," Staz tells the abruptly silent Islanders. "It is also a pile of rocks and timber. Rok's grit is not in its sand. It is in its people. In us. Crache did not learn to fear an island. They did not fail to tame an island. Crache learned to fear the Islanders of Rok. But it is a lesson they always seem to forget. They will forget again."

"Then we will defeat them again," Florcha says. "*Here*, where we are strongest."

"For how long? How many times? They can afford to attack and be repelled a hundred times, a thousand. Ours is a battle that can only be lost once. Just once. If the shores of Rok are ever taken, they will be lost. This has always been true. We will finally and forever become part of their great eating machine. And all of your worst fears, Florcha, all of those things knotted in your guts that are making you want to stay here where you feel safe, they will *all* come true if that happens. This island will not save you. It will not save any of us."

Taru watches Captain Florcha, and then scans the faces of many in the crowd. They look truly shaken and taken aback by these words.

Eventually, Florcha musters a retort, pointing directly at Taru. "You ask us to go to war on the word of a stranger."

"You have never sailed your ship into a Crachian port. I have entered the bay of their Capitol a hundred times. I doubt I would have lived to speak of it without this one and their masters and mistresses."

"And if you are wrong?" Florcha demands.

Staz cocks her tiny head at her fellow captain. "Why do you ask questions with obvious answers? If I'm wrong, we all die."

That sets the crowd to chattering again, and that begins to boil over into the same battle of voices shouting over one another.

Staz sighs, and it is more like a low growl that rumbles in her throat. "I am tired of speaking. This is my final word. There will never be a better time than now for Rok to strike against our greatest enemy. This rebellion of Savages will not come again if it is defeated. You are wrong, Florcha. This *is* our time. Right now. At my age, the next great battle I choose will be my last, live or die. *This* is the fight I choose. My crew joins me. Those of you who captain ships may also join us as you choose. If I have to go alone, so be it. I promise our old enemy will remember my name long after I am dashed on the great reef."

With that, Captain Staz of the *Black Turtle* tucks her tiny, withered hands back inside the seemingly endless folds of her coat. She glances down at Taru and the retainer swears they see the little old woman wink at them behind her shades.

Taru watches Staz pad slowly across the crowded floor of the longhouse, apparently heading for the nearest exit. The retainer quickly rises from their own grass mat and strides to catch up.

Taru follows their Rok Islander host out into the night, hearing the voices rise high and hotly behind them inside the lodge. "What do you think will happen now?" they ask the Captain, somewhat breathless after the last few minutes.

"They will argue for another few hours," Staz answers calmly. "They'll drink. Fists will probably fly."

Taru waits.

"And then?" they press.

"They will agree to go to war with the ants," Staz replies, smiling in the moonlight.

FIRE OR THE KNIFE

THERE IS A DELICATE PERCH THAT SITS ATOP THE STONE archway above the main entrance to Xia Tower. A small oriel window there looks out over the bridge leading to the towers and the bazaar of the Gen Circus beyond.

When they were children, Lexi and Brio could both kneel upon the perch and watch the goings-on of the day. They would see Brio's father, clad in the one fine new tunic he allowed himself every year, converse with the noodle makers and sellers in their little stands. They would watch Lexi's mother shop for groceries. Their parents would both be largely ignored by the members of the other Gens, who looked down upon the lowly Gen Stalbraid eking out their existence in the Circus, serving as pleaders for the wretches of the Bottoms.

Now, as an adult, Lexi can scarcely manage to balance atop that same perch alone. She has to crouch to fit far enough inside the oriel window in order to see outside.

It appears to her to be yet another way she has outgrown these towers.

From her vantage, Lexi watches Shaheen. Her "ward" walks among the fruit and vegetable stands pockmarking the edge of the bazaar. The handle of a basket is cradled in the crook of her left arm. She didn't fully explain her plan to Lexi; Shaheen merely told her a needed distraction would be created in the bazaar.

Lexi cannot spot the Aegins loyal to Kamen Lim and Burr whom Shaheen has assured her keep a constant vigil on her tower. She has no doubt they are among the many Aegins patrolling the Circus. She studies each one she can make out from her window, strutting and preening or shuffling along tiredly in their green tunics and dagger-bearing leather baldrics.

Lexi finds she truly loathes them, all of them, whether they are in the pocket of the Protectorate Ministry, as the ones who attempted to kill Daian, or that of the Ignobles, as Daian himself was. At best, they are the cheap, purposeless thugs who tormented Taru in public for pleasure.

Shaheen, meanwhile, stops to admire a pyramid of dragon fruit erected atop a pallet outside one of the vendor's stands. She selects a particular sphere of the rainbow-colored delicacy, examining it for freshness and bruises, testing the firmness of its skin.

Satisfied, the young mother places the piece of fruit in her basket, preparing to move on. She pauses, however, appearing to reconsider. She reaches back into her basket and removes the dragon fruit, considering it anew.

It all looks perfectly natural and forgettable to Lexi, just an indecisive young person changing their mind in their selection of groceries. Shaheen replaces the dragon fruit among its fellows and makes her way from the fruit stand. The whole dull business passes in less than a few seconds.

Perhaps because of that, it is even more surprising when, a few more seconds later, the pyramid of dragon fruit explodes.

There is no fire, only a sudden, thunderous booming and enough concussive force of some unseen origin within the pyramid to send every piece of fruit flying. More than half of it is reduced to a hail of shredded peel and pulp.

The noise more than anything is the catalyst for the ensuing chaos. The patrons of the Gen Circus bazaar in their fine, colorful tunics and wraps are sent scattering. One would think the rebellion itself had come to their staid little market.

Lexi watches them flee and wilt in panic. She wonders if she was ever truly that docile and afraid and so deeply unfamiliar with the violent and the chaotic. She no longer remembers a Lexi who didn't know all the things that can and do go hideously wrong in the Capitol, and in Crache as a whole.

Every Aegin in the vicinity rushes into the bazaar to both investigate the event and attempt to calm and control the crowd. Shaheen, for her part, has disappeared among the thick of the confusion. Lexi can no longer spot her in the bazaar, or on the edges of the Circus common.

"May I help you down, Te-Gen?"

The voice startles her to the point of nearly toppling from her perch. Lexi strains to peer over her shoulder, finding a ghostly Protectorate Ministry agent gazing up at Lexi from the foyer, black cape draped over one shoulder of her equally black tunic. The woman is gaunt and remarkably pale. More accurately, she's white as a corpse. Her hair is only a shade lighter, and cropped high and tight to her scalp. Eyes the blue of a glacier, sharp and clear, swim in the middle of all of it.

Her eagle's eye pendant gleams in the light pouring in around Lexi from the oriel window. It is enough to blind her for the briefest of moments as the reflection streaks across her face. She didn't even see the agent enter her tower.

"I'll manage," she replies calmly.

The agent bows her head respectfully, taking several paces back.

Lexi clambers from above the entrance's arch in a most undignified way, descending the features of the masonry with unrefined practice. She touches down on the foyer floor and turns to scrutinize the features of the Protectorate Ministry agent.

"I know you," Lexi says.

A moment later it hits her that she is indeed looking at a ghost.

"You do not, I assure you, and you never will. That is what I am, and what we do."

Lexi stammers, taken aback. "No . . . I . . . I watched you . . ."

A sudden darkness overtakes the agent's expression. "Yes?"

Lexi shakes her head. "It's impossible."

Shaheen rejoins them in the tower, carefully peeling a dragon fruit and biting into it. Lexi watches the girl stroll through the main entrance with the most carefree of airs. If nothing else, her presence breaks the spell of memory that has been cast on Lexi.

The agent seems willing to let the moment pass, as well. "Thank you, Shaheen," she commends the girl.

Shaheen bows respectfully. "Only to serve," she says, as if reciting the lyrics of a poem.

The agent returns her attention to Lexi. "Is there somewhere we might speak comfortably and privately, Te-Gen?"

Lexi manages to nod. She still feels rattled and unsure of her own voice.

They adjourn to the receiving parlor. As Lexi walks past the two to escort them, she notices the handle of the Protectorate Ministry agent's dagger. It has been carved from obsidian, complete with its pommel.

"I seem to remind you of someone," she says as they enter the comfortably furnished space.

"I must be mistaken," Lexi insists.

"My name is Strinnix," the agent stonily informs her. "You may find it interesting to know my twin is also an operative of the Ministry. They have been missing for quite a while now. In fact, they vanished around the precise time you chose to take this mysterious sojourn of yours to parts unknown for what I'm certain was rest and recreation. I hope you attained plenty of both before returning to us."

Lexi's breath feels trapped in the center of her throat. The beating of her heart seems to have doubled with every word spoken by the pale woman. Ginnix. That was the other one's name.

Lexi remembers now. She is gazing at the mirror image of the Protectorate Ministry agent Lexi watched Daian duel and kill in this very room. Though no less stricken, at least she knows the woman is not a ghost.

Strinnix lowers herself into one of the plush parlor chairs, gloved hand encircling the obsidian-handled dagger sheathed at her belt. "We were adopted by the Ministry as babes," she explains, though Lexi did not ask. "We were raised there for the whole of our lives. We have always served."

"You must be . . . very close."

Strinnix smiles, but there is no joy in the expression. "In our way."

Lexi has no idea how to proceed. Fortunately for her, the Protectorate Ministry agent does.

"You have, I imagine, many questions."

Lexi demurely seats herself on a chaise facing the agent's chair, regaining her composure. "All I do these days is ask mysterious people many questions about mysterious affairs I don't understand, it seems."

"Not *all* you do," Strinnix remarks.

"I do not take your meaning."

The agent spreads her arms magnanimously. "You are the matron of the Bottoms. You spend your days feeding the underfed and tending to those in need. Full days, from what I have heard."

Strinnix glances up at Shaheen, who stands removed from the two, silently and patiently attending their discussion. The girl smiles gratefully, bowing anew.

"By the way, didn't you announce your plans to become the new pleader for the Bottoms?" Strinnix asks Lexi.

"I became sidetracked, unfortunately."

"And yet the Gen Franchise Council has stopped hounding you and Stalbraid. Did you make some new friends, Te-Gen?"

Lexi frowns. "I feel as though you are asking me questions to which you already know the answers."

"They are, I am afraid, the only kind I ask."

“Then how do you ascertain new information?”

“Generally, I demand it.”

Lexi feels a churning in her stomach. “I see.”

Strinnix offers her nothing else, at least for the moment.

“How did she come into your service?” Lexi asks, speaking to Strinnix yet boring her gaze into Shaheen. “That is my most searing question at the moment, or at least the one that baffles me the most.”

Her ward stares back openly, offering no defiance nor appearing defensive because of the accusation laced into Lexi’s question.

“You brought Shaheen to us,” the agent tells her. “The Ministry has had you under our own surveillance since you returned and long before you disappeared. We received a full report on your first encounter with young Shaheen here. You were quite taken with her then, by all accounts.”

“I didn’t know—” Lexi pauses, her head spinning slightly. “I did not know how people like her lived, not really.”

“Yes, well, as it became apparent your status among the rabble in the Bottoms was increasing, as well as galvanizing the populace there, it became incumbent upon us to monitor you closer than on a surface level. Naturally, placing an operative in your service seemed the best way to accomplish this. I would have preferred to enlist your retainer, but they did not seem . . . amenable. Even to my methods.”

“You are correct about that.”

“I took Shaheen and her daughter from the Bottoms myself. We indoctrinated her, put her through some intensive training.”

Lexi studies her ward. She appears to take no issue with terms like “rabble” and “indoctrinate” being applied to her.

"She appears to have progressed very far very quickly," Lexi observes with disdain.

"We are quite adept at producing needed assets from raw materials, and rapidly. The Ministry has perfected the process over centuries."

"She was coerced then? You mucked about with her mind?"

"I have as much freedom of will as you, Te-Gen," Shaheen insists. "Now, anyway."

"We do not control minds, Te-Gen. We simply recondition them. With someone as young and desperate and intelligent as Shaheen, it proved quite easy. You would think intelligence would inhibit such a process, but quite the opposite is true."

Strinnix sounds as though she's discussing a unique feature of the seasons rather than retraining a person's entire being.

"In any case, the situation . . . deteriorated before we could effectively place her. After the murder of several Aegins acting on our behalf, and learning you were harboring a rogue Aegin as well as sensitive information in the form of certain documents, the decision was made to bring you in. That obviously didn't work out."

Lexi says nothing to that, and hopes her face offers the same absence of information.

"That rogue Aegin disappeared. The documents disappeared. You disappeared. Only one of those things has since resurfaced."

Lexi feigns sympathy. "I am sorry your carefully laid plans were so upset."

"No matter," Strinnix reassures her. "Your return gave us the opportunity to realize Shaheen's full potential after all."

"And what have you learned from her?"

The Ministry agent shrugs. "Nothing we did not already know. But gathering information was no longer her primary purpose."

"Oh?"

Strinnix nods.

A new thought strikes Lexi. "You say 'was' her primary purpose."

"I did," the agent confirms. "She has accomplished it."

"And that purpose was?"

"Why, bringing the two of us together, of course. I told her she simply had to wait for you to be ready. I assured her the weight you are carrying would inevitably crush you to earth."

"You were right," Shaheen says.

Strinnix smiles her mirthless smile anew. "Yes, dear. Thank you."

"You know about Burr and the Ignobles," Lexi concludes, though she can't believe it herself.

"Of course, we do. The Protectorate Ministry has known the Ignobles are far more than bitter relics of a bygone age for some time now. We are fully aware of Burr's little antique hideaway where she costume-plays a noble lady from that era."

"But if you know, why—"

"Why don't we arrest her? Because we do *not* know the breadth of the Ignoble organization. We also do not possess the names of everyone in it, let alone those regular citizens over whom they exude influence in the Crachian government. Arresting Burr at this point would create more problems than it would solve. Her removal would publicly disrupt the Spectrum due to her position on the Gen Franchise Council, and she would only be replaced at the head of the proverbial snake by someone whose identity we may not know."

"But Burr could tell you all of these things you don't know," Lexi points out.

Strinnix feigns a small laugh that is as joyless as her smile. "Burr is a fanatic, Te-Gen. She is a misguided madwoman. I doubt she would allow us to take her alive, and even if we did, we have calculated the probability that her body would succumb to our interrogation methods before her mind did. And personally, I find such methods thoroughly unreliable. Even the most refined torture is still a blunt instrument."

Lexi thinks of Burr, running through their interactions in her mind. She was always struck most by the Ignoble's certainty, her pure, unwavering belief in her sacred rite of ascension by blood and the superiority of nobility.

Strinnix is correct about her.

"Besides, we do not need Burr in order to uncover her hidden co-conspirators and assets," the agent says. "We have you now."

"Burr is the only one I know about, the only one I've met," Lexi says.

"For now."

"Why would she tell me anything?"

"Because you are an integral part of her glorious mission to return nobility to power in Crache, Te-Gen."

"I'm just a tool to her."

"A hammer can drive a nail," Strinnix replies. "It can also crack a skull. Circumstance is everything."

Lexi doesn't want to do either, yet she knows telling that to the Protectorate Ministry agent is futile and meaningless. "What would you have me do?"

"Continue to serve your purpose. You have proven so adept at bringing the populace of the Bottoms willingly into your embrace. Burr can see that. You've become her line to them. Tell her they're ready to embrace the returning nobles as well, but that the idea is no longer sufficient to rally them. That they need faces and names to raise up as their new protectors."

"She will never believe I'm willingly helping her plans come to fruition."

"You discerned how to capture the hearts and minds of your flock by the sea. Do the same with Burr."

"I can't pacify her with a wheel of cheese. You said it yourself—she's a madwoman."

"Find out what her wheel of cheese is, then."

"And if I can't?"

Strinnix leans back in her chair, letting a brief yet oppressive silence settle over them before deigning to answer Lexi's question. "You will be alone again," she says. "*All* alone."

Lexi is forced to swallow the rock quarry in her throat in order to respond.

"You tried to kill me once," she reminds Strinnix carefully. "You tried to abduct me in my home. You kidnapped my husband and sent him off to die on some mud-covered battlefield. Why in the names of all the forbidden gods would I be better served by you than Burr?"

"Fair points, all," Strinnix admits. "As I said, Te-Gen, circumstance is everything. When those actions were undertaken, we viewed you as an enemy of Crache in pursuit and then possession of damaging state secrets."

"And now?"

Strinnix shrugs. "You are a potential asset, and the Ministry has developed larger problems than knowledge of the Savage Legion and how its ranks are filled becoming public domain. There is a rebellion to the east, and in dealing with it we can ill afford to be undermined here in the Capitol by these deluded Ignoble creatures."

Lexi actually believes that part. "So what's to become of me after, assuming there is an after? And what of Brio, if he's even still alive?"

"If he *is* still alive, we can arrange to have him returned to you. The Ministry will allow the two of you and your Gen to resume your capacity as pleaders . . . under our supervision, of course."

"We would work for you?"

"Call it a collaboration."

Both words taste equally foul in Lexi's mouth.

"It's better than the alternative," Strinnix continues. "There is no end to your current scenario that does not involve Burr either murdering you or having you murdered. She cannot have a commoner leading the commoners she wishes to rule over. Even if the Ignobles did somehow succeed in deposing us, your popularity among the people would make you a threat to her."

"This is like being asked to choose fire or the knife to remove a boil," Lexi states plainly. "No offense intended, of course."

"Why would I take offense? I am not the boil in that comparison, am I?"

Lexi can't decide if that is meant to be humor.

She doesn't trust Strinnix, and she will never forgive the Protectorate Ministry for what they've done to her Gen and her kithkin, but Lexi sees no alternative.

"I'll do what I can," she finally says. "It will probably get me killed far sooner than Burr intended, but I don't see that I have a choice."

Perhaps Strinnix is pleased, but she does not show it outwardly. "Very well then," she says. "You will communicate with us through Shaheen. Burr and her people see her as nothing more than an urchin and a lackey, so they are not watching her as they are you." Strinnix rises from the parlor chair. "I will let you retire for the evening, Te-Gen."

Lexi watches, brow furrowed. "How will you leave without being seen?"

"Easily."

Lexi is only more confused. "But Shaheen's gambit . . . in the bazaar—"

"That was for your benefit," the agent explains. "I wanted to remind you that the Ignobles are not the only ones who can manipulate matters to achieve their goals. The Protectorate Ministry was shaping Crache from the shadows long before these blood-obsessed throwbacks began scheming and plotting against us."

Their endless games weary Lexi as much as they terrify her.

"I see. Good evening, then."

Lexi rises and begins to walk to the parlor entrance to see the agent out.

"Te-Gen," Strinnix bids her.

Lexi sighs. "What now?"

"I have a query unrelated to the current state of these matters. It is one for my own edification."

Lexi waits, girding herself for what she knows is coming. "Yes?"

"Agent Ginnix. Assigned to your case. Is she dead?"

There is no emotion in her voice, only a matter-of-factness that Lexi doesn't believe for a moment.

She wants to lie to Strinnix, but after everything the pale woman has told her and considering the situation as it stands, Lexi can't conjure a reason not to tell her the truth.

"Yes, she's dead," she admits.

Strinnix nods. Her expression remains unchanged. "I see. By Aegin Daian's hand?"

"Yes."

"And what is *his* status?"

A new knot forms in Lexi's stomach. "He's dead too."

"How did he die?" Strinnix presses, her mood dipping only slightly.

Again, Lexi can think of no legitimate reason not to simply tell her the truth. She just does not want to say it. "Curiosity," she answers.

To her surprise, Strinnix smiles. "I see," she says. "We'll leave it at that, then."

Lexi is grateful to watch the Ministry agent leave her parlor, uninterested in whatever circuitous route she plans to take from the tower. She has become accustomed to the line between unexpected guests and intruders in her home blurring beyond recognition.

"Do you need anything else tonight, Te-Gen?" Shaheen asks her, pleasantly.

Lexi stares into the girl's eyes. They seem totally unaffected by the content of her conversation with Strinnix. "Please don't speak to me anymore unless you absolutely have to."

Shaheen seems to take no offense at the request. "As you wish," she says, leaving Lexi alone in the parlor.

Lexi watches her go, thinking that whatever the Protectorate Ministry did to Shaheen, it was, if nothing else, very effective.

SHE NEEDS YOU MORE

THE LAST TIME EVIE INFILTRATED A SKRAIN ENCAMPMENT, it was alongside Mother Manai, and they were both clad in the heavy plates and mail of Skrain armor.

This time, she is wearing the hole-filled secondhand rags of a put-upon angler, stained with dried blood and guts and reeking of fish both alive and long dead. They also wore clothes several sizes too large for her.

She is more comfortable this time, at least.

No one pays any heed to the lowly congregation of fish purveyors as they ferry their baskets filled with the catch of the day. They entered the camp without incident, strolling past the posted sentries, only noted by one of them who gleefully snagged a medium-size tuna from the top of one of their loads.

Now the Sicclunan scouts and Evie find themselves lost in the bustle of the evening. Tents are still being erected. Latrines are being dug. Kitchens are being outfitted. Weapons, armor, and equipment are being cleaned and greased and stored. Siege towers are being constructed. Those not tasked with a particular errand are gathered around small campfires talking and eating and gambling as soldiers do.

Their plan is to dump their aromatic fare in the first empty tent they come across, *after* locating where the Skrain keep their prisoners. Until then, carrying their burdens and pretending to look hurried and late in delivering them is a better show to put on for the enemies surrounding them.

They manage another several dozen yards of winding through the sea of tents and wagons before it happens.

"You there!"

It is clear to all of their ears that the voice cutting through the din of the crowd is addressing their little coterie.

They stop walking. Evie turns calmly to take in the Skrain soldier decked out in full regalia, eyeing his lieutenant's stripes. Chimot glances pointedly at her, and then down at the basket they carry between them. The majority of their weapons are concealed beneath several layers of steadily decaying fish.

Evie subtly shakes her head.

The Skrain lieutenant stalks over to her and smartly knocks the straw hat that was swallowing most of her head and part of her face.

Evie tenses, her grip on the basket's handle tightening. She knows there is no chance of fighting their way out of the camp at this point. They've journeyed too far into the heart of the beast.

The lieutenant leans in until they are virtually nose-to-nose. He's an ugly man with a permanently squinting right eye. "The senior staff has been waiting for these!" he barks into her face, his breath stinking of rice wine and garlic. He jabs a fingertip toward the fish.

Evie's body immediately relaxes, and she drops her gaze subserviently. "Hai," she replies meekly.

The lieutenant steps back, shouting at the rest of them, "Get this lot to the officer's field kitchen for scaling on the double! And there better be a good amount of yellowtail in those baskets!"

Evie and Chimot both nod like eager puppies, prompting the other undercover scouts to do the same.

Evie reaches down and retrieves her borrowed hat from the ground, re-covering her head and face with it. By the time she has corrected her façade, the Skrain lieutenant is already seeking another target for his pompous ire and has marched away from them.

Evie and Chimot look at each other, the Sicclunan actually chuckling while Evie can only breathe a sigh of relief.

They trudge on through the rows between the tents and wagons and equipment. Even the non-military servants scurrying about the camp pay them no mind. The Skrain host is far too large for every lowly page and cook and stable worker to know one another.

"They'll probably be keeping them in cages or pens, not tents," Chimot suggests.

Evie agrees. "Maybe we should put some of the more sun-turned fish heads in a bowl and tell one of the officers that we're to feed the prisoners and we're lost."

Before Chimot can comment on that plan, she is interrupted by an oncoming commotion that rounds the bend in the row behind them. A rush of heightened activity begins surging around them, throngs of Skrain soldiers all moving as one in the same direction, which seems to be toward the center of the sprawling tent city. Evie and the Sicclunans have to tighten their formation around their baskets to keep from getting swept along by the crowd.

"Is it payday?!" Chimot asks over the cacophony surrounding them.

Evie just shakes her head, a sinister feeling swirling somewhere between her chest and stomach.

"It looks like they're all gathering," Chimot continues. "That means big sections of the camp will be cleared out. It'll make it easier to search."

Again, Evie shakes her head.

She could not explain why if Chimot asked, but the strong impulse to track the source of all this excitement fills her with inexplicable dread in that moment.

"Come on!" she orders them, practically dragging Chimot forward by her end of the basket.

The Sicclunan scout shouts some form of protest, but Evie can't hear. The force of her pulling on the basket and the need to maintain their cover is enough to keep Chimot moving, and that means the rest of the Sicclunans follow.

It takes several minutes of muscling their way through packed bodies, many clad in steel armor. Evie finally reaches the choke point of the throng, where the surge forward has stopped. They are now all contracting excitedly around a central point.

The swollen crowd is too thick to permit them to see what is happening at the epicenter of its focus.

"Wait here!" Chimot instructs the disguised Sicclunans.

She and Evie drop their basket and discreetly make their way up onto the top of a supply wagon. The vantage is not exactly inconspicuous, but it allows them to see above the helmeted heads of the Skrain. Besides which, everyone's attention appears to be focused forward.

A crude arena has been constructed in the center of the monstrous military encampment. Wooden panels that look as though they were stripped from the sides of wagons are arranged in an expansive octagonal wall that encloses a space just large enough for two people to move freely about. Tall, blazing torches have been staked into the ground along the makeshift fencing every few feet. They have even raked the ground inside flat and bare to facilitate whatever activity that patch of earth is about to support.

Skrain soldiers armored in various states of completeness are lined up a dozen deep behind the walls. They are enjoying a riotous celebration, chewing on hunks of cooked venison, biting the heads off smoked fish, and downing copious amounts of wine. Many of the soldiers have paired off (or formed small groups) to lustfully grope and tongue each other.

It takes some time, and even portions of the Skrain in attendance begin to shift restlessly, but finally a section of cheers erupts on either side of the arena walls.

As Evie and Chimot look on, two women are hurled from those opposite sides into the center of the ominous, fire-lit circle. They both land roughly on their hands and knees, but quickly and forcefully arise to face each other.

They are Sirach and Mother Manai.

Seized by outrage and instinct, Evie takes a step forward, reaching under her stinking borrowed shirt for the dagger she has secreted there.

Chimot is quick to halt her.

"We can do *nothing* while they're both in the middle of all of that, with a thousand eyes on them."

She is right, of course. Evie looks on helplessly as her friends turn to take in their audience.

Sirach and Mother Manai have been stripped of their armor and weapons, and apparently their clothing. They are each draped in what looks more like cloth sacks than garments, and not clean sacks either. Their feet are bare. They have both sustained a decent beating. Whether in battle or interrogation or simply for fun, Evie can't know. Each woman wears cuts on her lips and bruises on her cheeks and temples. They appear to be no worse for the wear, however.

The spike that ordinarily compensates for Mother's lost hand has also been confiscated. The stump of her wrist is bare. Evie has never seen Mother without some type of weapon adorning that limb. The older woman has always been very particular about exposing it in mixed company. What remains from the cut that took her hand is withered and gnarled and petrified.

Evie is outraged all over again that the Skrain have deprived Mother Manai of the leather hood she used to cover her stump, exposing it without her consent. That seems to Evie the grossest violation of all somehow.

A Skrain captain steps between the two prisoners, resplendent in his armor stamped with the Crachian ant. He drunkenly waves an ornate goblet, rice wine splashing across Sirach's face as he ceremoniously addresses those in attendance.

"Welcome to tonight's entertainment, soldiers!"

His greeting is met with raucous cheers from the Skrain, as well as most of their servants.

Evie watches Sirach calmly lick the wine spatter from her cheek with a murderous grin. Her spirits have not been outwardly diminished, it seems.

"The rules are simple!" the Skrain captain announces, speaking to Sirach and Mother Manai, but booming his voice for the benefit of the audience. "There are none!"

That draws the drooling, sadistic laughter he was clearly seeking.

"But there is a prize for the winner," he goes on. "The one of you that kills the other gets to take the loser's body back to your Sparrow bitch as a taste of what's to come for her and the rest of you rebel scum!"

The soldiers around them absolutely erupt at that proclamation.

Evie watches as Mother Manai and Sirach stare darkly at each other, seeming to almost forget the thousands screaming for their blood.

"Fair enough, isn't it?" the captain says to the two forced combatants.

He draws two short, rusted swords that are more like machetes from either side of his belt, dropping them on the raked ground between Sirach and Mother Manai.

"Give 'em a good show, ladies!"

His drunken laughter is sickening.

The Skrain officer leaves them to it, practically dumping the remainder of his goblet's contents over his face as he climbs out of the octagon.

Evie and Chimot exchange uneasy looks, neither of them knowing what to say or how to react. They can only watch.

Sirach is the first to crouch low and retrieve one of the blades. Her gaze is stony on Mother Manai as the Sicclunan shifts easily into a fighting stance.

Mother hesitates, but finally takes up the remaining weapon.

Evie watches the pair circle each other hesitantly with their rusty blades held at their sides.

At first it appears as though neither unwilling combatant will strike first. Then Sirach lunges forward, surprising her older opponent, and draws the edge of her machete's blade across Mother's cheek, spilling several tear trails of her blood.

Just as quickly, Sirach leaps back, holding her arms akimbo as if to challenge the older woman to retaliate.

The wine-soaked Skrain lap up the theatrics.

"She's goading her," Evie says knowingly. "She wants Mother to kill her."

"I've never known her to be sentimental," Chimot says, and though she is clearly trying to hide her feelings, her concern is evident.

Waiting for a counterattack that doesn't come, Sirach finally steps forward again and prods Mother Manai in the chest with the flat end of her machete.

This time, however, Mother bats it away with her own blade and smashes the younger woman's face with the stump of her arm. Sirach is sent stumbling backwards with a bloodied nose and a surprised look on her face that quickly morphs into anger.

"Shit," Evie hisses, recognizing her lover's expression.

Sirach charges forward in earnest and now the two of them lock horns for real, bodies becoming a mess of flailing, blade-wielding limbs and screaming heads. They manage to keep each other's sword arms restrained, but each lands several body and head blows to the other.

Evie is lost as she takes in their struggle. There is no answer to this riddle. She cannot hope for any outcome. She cannot choose between watching her lover or her best friend die.

The flurry ends when Mother Manai purposefully ties up Sirach's arms, doing her best to restrain her younger, stronger opponent.

In the next moment, both of their chins drop to their chests, hiding their faces from view. They continue to jockey for position, but it appears half-hearted to Evie. She suspects they are talking to each other, and though she cannot hear that conversation, she can venture a terrified guess.

The embattled conference ends with Sirach letting out a feral cry and shoving the older woman violently to the ground.

Rather than rain blows down upon her, Sirach steps back with an agonized expression. The pain splattered across her face isn't physical, Evie is certain of that.

Evie looks over at Mother Manai to see her closest advisor achingly sit up.

Mother looks to Sirach, and the Sicclunan stares back, unwavering in her resolve.

Despite the noise and the waves of metal and flesh moving chaotically between them, Evie can see Mother Manai clearly in that moment.

She can even see in her friend's eyes that the choice has been made.

Evie begins shaking her head, as if to dissuade Mother Manai from her chosen course of action, but neither of them can see their Sparrow General from inside the mock arena.

Mother rises from the dust raised around her prone form. She stares across the circle at Sirach with grim determination etched in the weathered lines of her face. Sirach stares back, uncertainty written in her posture and expression.

"She needs you more!" Mother Manai cries.

With that she surges forward, rushing Sirach and flinging herself onto the Sicclunan's blade.

Sirach attempts to backpedal, but the fury and force of Mother's charge catches her off-guard. The pressure created by their two bodies coming together so vigorously drives even her dull, decrepit makeshift gladiator's blade deep into Mother Manai's gut.

The killing blow sends the crowd into a frenzy, and shatters Evie's heart into a thousand rough shards.

Mother grips Sirach's shoulder with the hand she has left, encircling the Sicclunan with the stump of her other arm. Sirach carefully lowers Mother onto her back, still clutching the handle of the machete whose blade is buried in the other woman's abdomen.

Evie can see Mother Manai's lips still moving, though she doesn't think any words are brought forth. Mother's eyes are wide open, the light from the torches dancing inside of them, creating the illusion of life where life is quickly draining away.

Sirach clings to her until Mother's lips stop moving, and that light from the torches is all that remains of the woman's spark.

Sirach finally releases her hold on the machete's handle. Mother Manai's blood has run over her hand and down her arm. She stands, staring down at the wide-eyed corpse of the elder ex-Savage. There are no tears from Sirach, no blubbering of sorrow or fits of rage. The two women were convenient and ultimately temporary allies, not friends. The kill only hardens her expression, from what Evie can see in the firelight.

She does not look triumphant, or even relieved.

Evie does shed tears, as silently as she can, letting them spill over her cheeks while the rest of her remains as stoic and stiff as possible.

Chimot's hand touches her shoulder, and Evie turns with a start.

"There's nothing more we can do," she urges Evie. "Not now."

Sirach's second wears a stony expression, but Evie sees very real sympathy in her eyes. Seeing that more than hearing her words anchors Evie. She knows Chimot is right again.

Evie allows herself one last look back at Mother Manai, the woman who taught her how to be a general, lying there in dirty rags with a rusty blade defiling her body.

She will never be able to make Crache pay enough. Evie knows that beyond a shadow of a doubt.

PART THREE

RECALCULATIONS OF THE TONGUE

THEY'RE COMING

"AND WE'RE NOT READY," EVIE SAYS TO THE OTHER LEADERS of the rebellion she started what now feels like a lifetime ago.

They are gathered around an ornate marble meeting table in the headquarters of the Tenth City's Aegins, currently one of the most deserted structures in town. Its armory and larders have already been raided for the cause, but it remains a convenient place to host a large group in privacy and comfort.

It certainly smells better than any building in the Shade.

Evie occupies the head of the table. She has donned her full set of Sparrow General armor, complete with its accursed cape. Ordinarily she would never bother with armor for a meeting such as this, but she found herself compelled as she dressed that morning. Perhaps it was because the last lecture Mother Manai subjected Evie to concerned the importance of the armor's symbolism, including the damned cape.

Brio sits to Evie's left, hands resting atop the knotted wood head of his cane. He watches her with the same look of sympathy and worry he's had for her since she returned with the Sicclunan scouts from infiltrating the Skrain encampment.

Sirach and Chimot congregate to Evie's right. The cuts on Sirach are beginning to heal, the bruises shifting in tone from almost black purple to a sickly yellowish-green. She and Evie have spoken very little since Sirach was released from the Skrain camp.

Evie feels no anger toward her. Sirach seems to have taken it upon herself to retreat from her, and Evie either hasn't had the time or can't seem to deduce how to reach out to her. They have communicated largely through Chimot, hence her presence on the war council.

Yacatek faces Evie from the opposite end of the marble slab. They haven't spoken since that day on the street, when Evie watched the B'ors unearth an ancient ancestral knife buried there before those who massacred their people settled and built the city.

Evie remembers Yacatek asking her what the B'ors' reward would be if the rebellion won. She still has no answer, but Evie knows Yacatek didn't truly expect one.

Kellan and Talma join the rest as the leaders of their own private rebellion. Neither of them can fully appreciate the personal loss Evie and the others have suffered, but it is clear they've noticed the mood among the war council has changed drastically since taking up residence in the Tenth City.

What remains of the Elder Company, once the most battle-tested senior members of the Savage Legion, hunker together in one corner of the room. They look much as they did when Evie first laid eyes upon them. It was at the first Revel she attended, the night before her first battle, all of them huddled around their drinks and pleasure workers, laughing raucously.

She remembers her very first glimpse of Mother Manai from

that evening, a mug of wine in her hand and a pretty young bare-chested man on her lap. She remembers a squat, ugly woman with terrible bowl-shaped hair who was so full of life and passion and strength despite her bondage and conscription into the Savage Legion.

The Skrain captain was true to his word after all. Sirach returned to the city with Mother's body in tow. Though clearly a drunken sadist, the man either had a hidden and effective methodology or happened upon one that night. The sight of Mother Manai being wheeled through the city streets, even covered by the cloth Evie draped over her, demoralized her makeshift army deeply, particularly the former Savages.

Talma keeps a truly wretched garden in a patch of mostly infertile soil barely larger than a Skrain's shield in the alley behind her butcher's shop. It seemed as good a place as any in the city to bury Mother. Evie wished to find her people and return her body to them, but it was a fleeting, futile thought. It is very likely all of them will be buried here soon.

And if not, Evie would always know where to find Mother Manai.

The ceremony was brief, but everyone seemed to feel that it was appropriate. Yacatek and the B'ors attended, to Evie's surprise. The ones who fought as Savages alongside Mother Manai respected her as a warrior, and the rest had heard stories of her fierceness and valor from their Storyteller.

Though she knew her for the shortest time among the rune-covered warriors of the rebellion, it was left to Evie to speak over the ground to which they committed Mother Manai's body.

"I hope something beautiful grows here," she'd managed through the tears strangling her voice. "Something that thrives where it shouldn't, too tough to wilt. She would've liked that."

Evie didn't have it within her to say goodbye, and so she left it at that.

Looking at the survivors of the Elder Company now, bereft of Mother Manai's light and energy and leadership, they simply seem like sad old men to Evie.

Lariat, ever the loud and brash master of ceremonies, looks as though someone has let the air out of a bladder. He curls his thick lips under that overgrown broom mustache of his, gaze shifting about grouchily.

Bam has retreated even further inward than he usually resides, hugging his colossal mallet the way a child might clutch a straw-stuffed doll.

Diggs is foregoing greasing every moment with his customary charm. Even his admirable coif of increasingly salty hair is neglected and out of place.

Evie can't help feeling she has failed them every bit as much as she failed Mother Manai.

"We're not ready," she repeats to her battle-hardened war council. "And we won't ever be, no matter how much time we have."

"Then what's the answer?" Chimot asks. "Is there even one?"

Sirach says nothing, though for the first time in days she looks directly at Evie.

Evie suspects she already knows what's coming.

"We have to leave the city," Evie announces. "We have to

march on the Skrain host now, before they begin siege preparations outside the walls."

None of her comrades speak at first. Several of them look uneasily at one another.

Kellan and Talma are the deepest struck. They seem totally lost in the news.

"I suppose," Sirach says, "for the sake of discussion, I'll be the one to point out that marching on the Skrain is tantamount to suicide. Not that I'm objecting, you understand."

Evie thinks she spots the ghost of a grin threatening Sirach's lips. She'd like to feel bolstered by it, but there is only fear and regret presently bubbling within her.

"Why would we leave the safety of these walls after we fought so hard to claim them?" Talma asks, fairly.

"I'm neither ordering nor asking you and the people of the Shade to do anything. You fought for yourselves, not for us. We may be natural allies, but I will not attempt to conscript you into anything. It's *for* your people our forces need to fight on the field, and not in these streets."

Evie glances at Brio, who nods somberly.

"If the Skrain lay siege to the Tenth City," she says, addressing them all, "they will destroy it and everyone in it."

"I can't contend to be terribly moved by that," Sirach replies, and then looks to Kellan and Talma. "Nothing against you two, personally."

"Of course not," Talma replies with mock sincerity.

"I agree with the Sicclunan, for once," Lariat rings in gravely. "But not because I don't give a spit for the Shade. It's the rest of 'em I don't give a spit for, all them well-fed Gen types and all them parchment-pushing arbiter types in their marble palaces."

"They aren't exactly rallying to support us, General," Diggs adds.

"There is no separating the two," Evie insists. "The Shade, the Gen Circus, the Citadel, they are all part of the same city. The Skrain won't distinguish when they're leveling every building in sight with their siege weapons and hurling fire over the walls."

"I wasn't distinguishing either," Sirach informs her.

"Do we condemn the people of the Tenth City to die out of spite?" Evie asks her coldly. "Because *that's* what we'd be doing. We have no hope of holding this city, or breaking a Skrain siege. Will what's left of the Sicclunan forces come to rescue us, Sirach?"

"No," she admits readily.

"*No one* is coming to help us," Evie tells them all. "There will be no resupply, no reinforcement. Even if we can successfully defend the walls somehow, what happens when hunger sweeps through the city? When the people start eating one another? What we have, this army we've assembled, right here and now, this is it. This is the only battle we'll ever fight. If we seal ourselves inside these walls, we turn this city into a tomb."

None of them, including Sirach, seem willing or able to argue with that.

"What's your plan, then?" Sirach asks her.

"We will rally and marshal our forces in the night and attack them at dawn."

"They're watching every move we make, day *and* night," Chimot says. "We have no hope of taking them by surprise."

"No, but we're a lighter and faster army. We can use that. We can rally and strike before they have time to field their full strength. They are *expecting* us to wait here for them. They think they have all the time in the world. They're building their siege towers and drinking themselves stupid. We saw that with our own eyes. They are not preparing for a frontal assault, much less one hitting them right now. We can catch them off-guard enough to split their force and fight them in waves. It's our only chance. If we can fight our way to the camp we might be able to send them scattering."

"If they hold our initial attack long enough to give the rest of the host time to mobilize, we'll be annihilated."

"Then we don't let them hold us."

Sirach still looks unconvinced. Evie shifts her gaze to Chimot.

"You wanted to light some fires. Let's fight our way back into that camp and give you your chance."

Chimot grins despite herself. "I see what you like about her," she mutters to Sirach.

"You can put as much verve behind it as you can muster," Sirach says. "This has a one in a thousand chance of succeeding."

"We only have to break their line!" Evie insists. "That's what Savages do."

"I'm not a Savage," Sirach replies. "And Sicclunans have learned the value of striking and evading. We only meet the Skrain when absolutely necessary, and never with our full force. As you said, this is all we have. If we are defeated here, then this thing you've created is defeated. And my people will be too weakened to recover."

"I understand," Evie says after a moment. "And if this is as far as the Sicclunans go with us, I understand that as well. You can still retreat."

Sirach's eyes soften on hers. "We could all retreat."

"No," Evie says. "I won't abandon the people of the Shade."

"Crache is our home," Lariat tells the Sicclunan warrior. "For better or worse. It's where we belong. We'll take 'er back or we'll die here."

Evie stares across the room at the giant of a man, her heart going out to him. "You're with me, then?" she asks.

"You're thinkin' like a Savage," he says. "Can't ask more'n that."

Beside him, Bam nods in agreement beneath his hood. Diggs, however, hesitates.

"I never really figured on seein' a hundred battles, anyway," Lariat tells him.

"I did," Diggs says, protesting.

"Well, you're a good-lookin' idiot," Lariat fires back.

Diggs seems to think about that, and then he begins to laugh. "Savages, then," he says.

Emboldened by their support, Evie rises from her seat and leans over the edge of the marble slab.

"This is where we are," Evie states firmly. "And this is the only course of action I can see that has *any* chance of moving us forward. If we stay within these walls, we'll last a little longer, but we will die here *without question*. And we will cause the deaths of countless people in this city who are not our enemy, who've done nothing and do nothing but try to live, as all of us are trying to live."

"And if you're defeated?" Kellan asks. "We took this city, but we can't possibly hold this city without you. They'll come for us next."

"Thank you for saying 'if,'" Sirach remarks brightly, drawing a chortle from her lieutenant.

Evie casts her a reprimanding glance, and then looks to Kellan and Talma. "If we're defeated, then you can at least surrender without further bloodshed. It's the best alternative I can offer you."

"The Skrain might only execute the leaders," Sirach says to the two, trying to sound helpful.

"If any of you want to join with us in the field," Evie adds, ignoring Sirach, "we would be proud to fight alongside you."

Kellan and Talma exchange wary looks.

"None of us are soldiers, General," Kellan says to her.

"Neither were we," Evie replies.

Kellan nods, accepting that.

Evie looks to Yacatek.

"Will the B'ors take the field with us?" she asks the Storyteller, who has remained silent throughout the proceedings thus far.

"It is the only way the B'ors know how to fight," Yacatek says. "And we have nothing to go back to."

Satisfied, Evie turns her attention back to Sirach, the last holdout among her council. "Will the Sicclunans continue to stand with us?" She does her best to mask the desperation and longing lurking behind her voice.

Sirach glances at Chimot, who stares back briefly before dropping her chin to her chest.

"All or nothing, then," Sirach declares, mustering her usual bravado while still managing to sound none too happy about the decision.

Evie can't help but sigh in relief, hanging her head for a moment before recovering.

She looks up and moves her gaze from face to face around the room. "Thank you all," she says.

Brio smartly taps the bottom of his cane against the floor several times in rapid succession, as if applauding her. Evie looks back at him to find a sad smile forced upon his otherwise grim expression.

She knows he agrees this is the best of the bad choices before them.

Evie turns back. She addresses her war council one final time, hoping she sounds like the leader they've elevated her to be.

"All right," she says. "We attack at dawn."

THE MIND

"I CANNOT *BELIEVE* THEY MADE YOU THINK YOU WERE being melted by lava!" Riko exclaims. "And wrist wrestling over poisonous spiders? What *is* that? I mean . . ."

As absurd as it may seem considering the subject matter, Dyeawan finds her friend's indignation amusing more than anything. She doesn't quite laugh, but it does bring a smile to her lips.

"Edger spoke often of the Planning Cadre being too stuck in the past," Dyeawan says. "I think these contests might be one of the things he was talking about."

Her small room is filled with the blue light that reigns between the rule of darkness and the rise of dawn. They let the last of the candles burn out hours ago, sitting in the darkness and not much minding. Their conversation provided illumination enough.

It is the same humble room Dyeawan has occupied since her first night in the Planning Cadre. She has never seen any reason to take a new one, though Edger offered her many far more spacious and lavish options in the keep.

Even after replacing him as head of the planners, she chose to remain here. Her bed, not much more than a cot, is the softest surface upon which she's ever slept. She has her single window with its narrow view of the island's lush greenery, towering peak, and blue waters. The roof is intact and consistent and keeps out the rain. Her little chair in the corner, where she has read nearly every book in the keep's library, many of them multiple times, is as much a friend to her as Riko.

It is the best, the *only* home Dyeawan has ever had or known, and she can't imagine anyone needing more.

She could not sleep the night before the final contest of the challenge. Dyeawan intended to simply read through the small hours, but as the moon rose high and full in the night, Riko knocked at her door.

She entered holding a bowl filled with plump red grapes, beautifully and freshly picked and seeded.

"From Makai, in the kitchen," Riko explained. "They are all rooting for you so hard down there. You're their hero."

Dyeawan was warmed by that, if not also filled with a sense of guilt and doubt. But she was grateful to the cranky old cook, whose lack of vision has never impaired his ability to produce delicious fare, just as her lack of control over her legs has never impeded her.

She and Riko sat up together the rest of the night eating grapes and talking about everything except the challenge and the politics of the Planning Cadre. That proved to be the best gift Riko could've given her.

"You know what's strange?" Riko asks her in the predawn.

They are sitting on opposite ends of Dyeawan's bed, their legs entwined like a skinny log raft.

"Many things," Dyeawan answers, quite definitively.

"You are hilarious!" Riko proclaims with jovial sarcasm. "No, it's just . . . sometimes I think about being someone else and maybe doing something else, yeah? Something more simple."

"What do you mean, exactly? And why would that be so strange?"

"Because we're here! I get to design things that . . . I can't even believe it every day, what I get to help build. But at the same time, there are moments when I think about maybe like, having a tinker's shop in a city somewhere. Fixing things for the people there. Little things. And maybe making toys for their kids. I have so many ideas for toys! But everyone here says they're impractical and useless."

"When I lived in the streets," Dyeawan tells her, "I used to collect little things. Nothing that mattered to anyone else. Broken pieces of clay and glass. Odd bits of string. Once I found a whole cork. That was my favorite. I didn't understand why at the time. I didn't really think about it. Since coming here, everything I've learned, all the reading I've done, I know now I did it because those little things were mine. No one would take them from me. They made me feel as though I had control over *something* when I had no control over anything, even my own life."

Riko has such a look of pain and sympathy on her face as she listens to her friend's story.

"That's so sad," she says, hugging Dyeawan's right foot against her chest. "But also kind of hopeful, yeah? I guess?"

"My point is, *toys* are important, Riko. No one feels more powerless than children, particularly poor children. Toys give them power and a sense of themselves."

Riko is clearly taken aback. "I never thought about it like that."

Dyeawan smiles. "I doubt most people do. In any case, I know you'd build amazing toys. And you should."

"I'll show you my designs, yeah?" Riko says, delighted. "After all of this with Nia is over, and you're leading the planners without her in your way, we can build some for the kids where you grew up, in the Burrows."

"The Bottoms," Dyeawan says, gently correcting her.

"Right! Them too!"

Dyeawan giggles, something she doesn't do much of anymore.

A soft pale gold ray of light falls across her face then. Dyeawan looks to the window, seeing the first beams of sunlight cresting the horizon. Her good humor quickly fades.

Riko watches her, turning equally somber.

"Is it time?" she asks.

Dyeawan nods.

Riko sighs resolutely. "Okay then."

Gently moving her friend's legs aside, Riko clambers from the mattress and steadies the tender awaiting Dyeawan beside it.

"One last ride?" Riko asks, mustering her brightest smile.

"Of course," Dyeawan says, drawing strength from her.

She pulls herself forward with her still aching arms and crawls onto her tender.

Once she is settled, Riko hops up onto the platform behind her, resting on her knees and gently gripping Dyeawan's shoulders.

Moments later they are sailing through the corridors of the Planning Cadre as they have dozens of times before, laughing virtually the entire way, choosing to forget everything else and live in those few moments of joy and companionship and freedom from the weight of the world in which they exist.

When they reach the planners' meeting room, it is empty save for Tinker and Nia.

"I wish I could stay," Riko says as Dyeawan brakes the tender so that her friend can disembark.

"I do too," Dyeawan agrees.

Riko reaches out and grips Dyeawan's wrist lightly. "I'll see you on the other side, yeah?"

"Whatever happens," Dyeawan confirms.

Riko blows her a kiss while backing away, lingering as long as she can before turning and leaving the space in earnest.

"I haven't been in this room in ages," Tinker remarks, glancing about with obvious nostalgia. "It shouldn't exist, you know. Architecturally speaking."

"The fascination wears off," Dyeawan replies.

"This table is new, isn't it?" Tinker asks, brushing a hand over its smooth surface. "What happened to that ridiculous, you know . . ." She trails off, swirling her fingertip in increasingly smaller circles.

Dyeawan doesn't answer, but shoots a pointed glance in Nia's direction. Her opponent retains her usual stoicism, though Dyeawan thinks she catches a flash of irritation tweaking Nia's features.

"In any case," Tinker says with a sigh, "this business between the two of you began here, and it will end here, one way or the other. And as this is the room in which the planners have solved so many problems with keen minds, it seems fitting this is where the contest of the mind will take place."

Dyeawan can't tell whether or not the old woman means those words facetiously.

"You will both be injected with a series of potions," Tinker explains. "The effect will be similar to what you experienced at the volcano. However, these will induce an inside state rather than an outside state. You will retreat within your own mind, and that is where the contest will take place. It will be much like a dream in which you retain your awareness.

"I will speak to you both while you are held in this state, introducing problems and scenarios. You won't be aware of your physical surroundings, or me, and your bodies will remain locked in thrall, but your minds will create worlds within your own heads based on my words. That is where you will meet your challenges."

Dyeawan has had more than enough of the Planning Cadre poisoning her and altering her perceptions, and vows inwardly that this will be the last time.

"How will you judge who wins?" she asks.

"Think of it like navigating a maze within your own head," Tinker says. "The first one to make it through, and back to consciousness, will be declared the winner."

"What if we get lost in the maze?" Dyeawan asks.

"Don't get lost," Tinker advises her, quite unhelpfully.

"Shouldn't we lie down?" Nia inquires.

"You may sit. Your bodies will stiffen under the influence of the potions and be held in place until your control over them returns."

"Sounds restful," Nia says in a rare display of humor.

"At least your physical exertion in these contests is at an end,"

Tinker says, consoling them. "I will need a moment to prepare the injections. Please get comfortable."

She walks away, leaving them alone for a time.

Dyeawan watches Nia take a seat at the head of the table. She does so without pomp, and Dyeawan isn't certain whether or not it is meant to be a symbolic gesture. In either case, she rows her tender over to the opposite end of the table, settling herself in front of it.

They stare at one another in silence, waiting for Tinker to return.

"I want you to know something," Nia says unexpectedly.

Dyeawan blinks at her opponent, the surprise evident on her face.

Nia draws a slow, deep breath, exhaling before she speaks again. "It's not jealousy."

"What isn't?" Dyeawan asks.

"I am not challenging you for leadership of the planners because I'm jealous or bitter or resentful. I once thought I would be Edger's choice to succeed him one day, that much is true. But his choices were his own, and it was his right to make them. You became his choice. I accept that. Truly."

It is the first time, not counting the end of their wrist-wrestling match, that Dyeawan is able to read the older woman. Nia is telling her the truth.

"Then what is it?"

"You aren't ready," Nia states flatly. "Edger never meant for you to succeed him so soon. You are brilliant, Dyeawan, there is no doubt about that. Your mind consumes and processes knowledge on a plateau few will ever reach. But that is not enough. Books are not enough. Edger's lessons weren't enough. You lack the experience necessary to guide the planners, and by proxy the whole of Crache."

Dyeawan can deny neither the truth nor wisdom in those words. She thrust this upon herself when she still had much to learn about leading and planning from Edger.

She could not live with nor let him continue to pursue his atrocities, however. She will never regret her choice in that.

"I was raised from a babe in this keep, as part of the Planning Cadre," Nia continues. "I have served as a planner for almost ten years. I know what they need, and how to achieve it. I agree with much of your aims and philosophy, as I agreed with Edger's notion that we must move on from the past. But I am the superior choice to do so."

"Why did you not say this to me before?"

Nia's shoulders rise in an almost imperceptible shrug. "Would you have abdicated your position to me?"

Dyeawan considers that. "No," she says.

"Will you now?"

Dyeawan thinks about Riko, and about the toys she wants to design and build. She thinks about the children like her she left behind in the Bottoms to collect their bits of string and broken glass.

"I can't. I'm sorry."

Nia nods as if that is the answer she expected. "I merely wanted you to know," she says.

"I appreciate that," Dyeawan replies, sincerely. "Thank you. I never wanted to be your enemy."

"You aren't my enemy now."

Dyeawan doesn't know why she is so grateful to hear that, but she is.

Tinker finally returns, bearing a clay tray supporting two rows of small needles attached to bellows lined up across its surface.

"Are we ready to begin?"

"I am ready for this to end," Dyeawan says.

Tinker seems to take that as a "yes."

She places the tray down upon the tabletop in front of Dyeawan, beginning with her. "I've heated these needles just so," she explains. "It should ease their passage, but this will sting a bit, I'm afraid."

"I am almost certain I've had worse."

"To be sure," Tinker says noncommittally. "Tilt your chin forward just a bit for me."

Dyeawan does as instructed, though she tracks Tinker's movements warily from the corners of her eyes.

Tinker steps behind her with the first needle and bellows.

"Is that going—" Dyeawan begins, but her next word gets caught in her throat as Tinker jabs the tip of the needle into the back of her neck.

Dyeawan winces and tightly shuts her eyes. Her fists clench upon the tabletop.

The pain is brief, and a moment later she's able to open her eyes again, the rest of her body relaxing as well.

She doesn't feel any differently at first. The table still spreads out before her. Nia still sits at the other end, studying her curiously. Tinker continues to hover about Dyeawan's shoulders.

Dyeawan opens her mouth to ask when the first potion will

begin to take effect. No words come out of her mouth, however. Instead, her tongue melts down her chin and onto her chest in a pink, milky torrent.

There is no pain now. There is no feeling at all. There is only a detached curiosity as she stares down at her tongue, which looks like melted butter run down the front of her tunic.

Dyeawan considers whether or not she should attempt to lap her melted tongue back into her. She then realizes she lacks the tool to perform that action.

It's absurdly funny to her, and she would laugh if she possessed the means.

Unfortunately, the moment's good humor is shattered as the world in front of her abruptly crashes into her eyes. Dyeawan cannot decide whether she is suddenly hurtling forward at a great speed or whether everything in her field of vision has been sucked through her eyeballs.

In either case, it all becomes a blur.

Then there is only nothingness, and the brief feeling of intensely accelerated motion ceases.

Dyeawan experiences the sensation of floating for what may be five minutes or five hours. Time becomes rather meaningless. She can no longer feel any part of her body, nor command any of her senses. She is a thought in an endless void, and somehow it is oddly soothing to exist in that state. Dyeawan would've thought it torturous were it explained to her secondhand.

Then it is as if someone sparks a torch. That void becomes illuminated, and she is reconstituted in a physical world once more.

It is not the world she left, however. Dyeawan finds herself back upon the platform of her tender, tongue firmly ensconced inside her skull. The planners' meeting room, Tinker and Nia, and the keep are all gone. There appears to be no ground beneath her feet, and nothing surrounding her for miles except the shifting colors of a far-off horizon.

Dyeawan contemplates those colors, as well as the absence of any other physical environment, for some time.

"So this is what the inside of your head looks like," a sinister, troublingly familiar voice says, interrupting. "I wondered."

Dyeawan maneuvers her tender around to face the speaker, dread creeping through what she is aware is her imagined body.

She finds Oisin staring at her across the formless ground, giving the most self-satisfied smile she has ever seen stain the severe Protectorate Ministry agent's icy lips.

"Not what you expected to find in here, I am certain," he says to her.

And indeed, it was not.

NEW HOUSES

DURING THEIR CLANDESTINE CONVERSATION, AGENT Strinnix colorfully employed an analogy involving hammers to eschew Lexi's insistence that she was merely a tool to Burr and the Ignobles. Strinnix told Lexi hammers can drive nails or they can crush skulls. Circumstance determined their importance as well as their impact. That was the Protectorate Ministry agent's less than subtle point, anyway.

Lexi remembers thinking she wanted nothing to do with driving nails or crushing skulls.

Though it was a metaphor at the time, after a full day of actually swinging a hammer, she's finding her distaste for the tool is also a literal truth.

On the sky carriage ride home from the Bottoms alone, she picked three half-finger-size splinters out of her palms, which were already dully aching and throbbing.

As she walks through the Gen Circus beside Kamen Lim, Lexi is forced to use her teeth to pull a much shorter wooden sliver from her fingertip.

With the help of Shaheen and several willing and able recruits like her ward was when they first met, Lexi has begun construction on an eating-house in the Bottoms. Obtaining the land wasn't an issue; there are so many disused, vacant, and barren lots in the Bottoms forsaken by all but those who occasionally sleep on the ground there. The timber is once again being supplied by a Gen loyal to Burr, all of it funneled through seemingly proper channels within the Spectrum. They also provided her with a builder knowledgeable in matters of such construction.

The house will be open to all and its fare will be provided at no cost. It seemed the next logical step, and part of Lexi will be glad not to have to cart food and water down to the Bottoms by wagon at dawn every morning and distribute it in stinking alleys.

She'd never cut a board or driven a nail before in her life, and though the labor is less than pleasurable, Lexi is finding it feels good to build something from the ground up.

"Try soaking your hands in lily oil," Kamen Lim suggests in his torturously congenial way. "My wife absolutely swears by it, for everything. She tried to soak my entire head once to cure an ache in my temples!" He laughs heartily at that.

"Perhaps she was attempting to drown you," Lexi mutters irritably.

"Perhaps," Lim agrees, nodding soulfully. "There have been many suppers when I saw a certain menace in the way she held her sticks as she looked at me." He laughs again, remaining maddeningly impenetrable, even by the most vicious of her barbed words.

Yet a thick skin is necessary, she supposes, moving through

the evening patrons of the bazaar and the noodle stands. All of the Gen members in their finery either ignore her or cast open disdain upon her with their looks. None offer her warmth, let alone a formal greeting.

It is not simply the way Lexi looks at that moment, her work clothes covered in dust and wood shavings and various other muck. Her hair is disheveled and her face dirty. Yet she wears her Gen pendant, the same as the rest of them.

The others in the Circus have always looked down on Gen Stalbraid. Those Gens have their lofty operations, agriculture, and various other concessions, performing important and bountiful functions needed and lauded by the Spectrum. They count large numbers among their ranks and employ huge staffs, enjoying their opulent clothing and larder allotments from the state. They could never understand why any Gen would choose to remain so small, clinging to familial traditions, let alone accept a concession pleading for the lowliest ranks of the city.

In truth, Lexi cares nothing for their collective or individual disdain now. They are barely even real people to her anymore. Most of them know nothing of the world as it truly is, only seeing what exists in this polished and pristine circle where they are protected and provided for in exchange for their service. They could not fathom the depths of Crache, or what really dwells there.

They reach the short bridge to Gen Stalbraid's shabby little towers.

"Thank you for escorting me," Lexi says to Kamen Lim, as she always does.

"Of course. I will bid you good evening, Te-Gen," he says,

as he always does at her door. "Until the morrow. We'll see about getting those ceiling joists sorted, hai?"

"Actually, if you could come in for a few moments, there is a private conversation we should have."

Lim peers down at her in very real surprise. "An invitation inside?" he asks, a pleased smile spreading across his lips. "How could I refuse?"

Lexi nods, leading him over the bridge and to the main entrance of Xia Tower.

"I'm afraid I have nothing to offer you," she says as they walk through the foyer. "Shaheen is gathering supplies in the bazaar."

"So busy feeding others, you forget to stock your own larder?"

"Something like that."

"No worries, Te-Gen," he reassures her pleasantly. "I'll reserve my appetite for supper at home with the family."

Lexi nods. "Very well. Please join me in the parlor."

She feels herself slipping back into her old role of the formal hostess, receiving and greeting and attending to guests Brio was petitioning for some meager show of support or contribution for the Bottoms.

Lexi leads the duplicitous Aegin into the same room in which she recently conspired with the Protectorate Ministry to spy on Kamen Lim's benefactors. She offers him a seat, and Lim gratefully obliges, holding the handle of his sheathed dagger instinctively as he lowers himself into one of the plush, high-backed chairs furnishing the parlor.

Lexi occupies her usual spot on the chaise.

"Would you like the opportunity to freshen yourself before we speak, Te-Gen?" Lim offers, ever the gentleman.

The state of her had slipped Lexi's mind. Her hands reflexively go to her dirt-streaked face, and then smooth back her already matted hair.

"No, thank you," she says.

"Proceed then," he urges her with a smile.

Lexi inhales deeply. The beginning is crucial. She knows she has to seem reluctant. She has no hope of convincing any of them if she appears to be readily offering to advance their cause or give them aid in accomplishing their goals.

Burr and Lim have both come to know her too well.

"I'm concerned . . . for the people," she begins. "The state that we've . . . that *I've* whipped them into. I worry it is coming to a dangerous boil." She quickly adds, "For them."

Lexi hopes if she makes this entreaty about the people in the Bottoms, Lim may believe it, and thus convince Burr. They know she truly cares for the folks she has been feeding and helping for so many weeks.

"It is a primer for things to come," Lim says in a pacifying tone.

Lexi rubs her face with her aching, bloodied hands. "Yes, I know, and that's just it. They may be too primed too quickly."

"How's that?"

"They're growing . . . restless with my stories and with my rhetoric. Of course, they rally to the notion of the Crachian bureaucracy being replaced by people who truly care for them and will improve their lives, but they see no path to it. The problem is I'm telling them grand tales with no real heroes or heroines. Without that, they're beginning to see my words as fantasy. Unattainable. I can see it beginning to have the opposite effect Lady Burr desires."

"You fear they'll turn on the notion of nobility?" Lim asks her.

"No," Lexi says quickly.

"You fear . . . they'll turn on you? Have you grown so attached to their affections? It's understandable, certainly—"

"It is not me I'm worried about," she insists. "And it is certainly not your cause I fret over. Your mistress is coercing me into furthering it."

"Fair enough."

"My fear . . . is that they will turn their frustrations inward, upon themselves. I fear they'll lash out and riot against the Aegins before the Ignobles are prepared to support them. If that happens, the people of the Bottoms will suffer greater than they will even if your plans do come to fruition."

She studies Kamen Lim's face, his reaction. Her words seem as though they are sinking hooks within him, and he is genuinely mulling over the worries she has just voiced.

"What do you suggest then?" he asks. "Do you actually have a suggestion, or do you wish me to simply convey your general concern?"

"I do," Lexi ventures, carefully.

"I am all ears!" Lim proclaims, reclining in his chair and crossing an ankle over his opposite knee.

"They need to see a noble, in the flesh," Lexi proposes. "If you truly wish this to work, they need to meet one. I understand Lady Burr cannot expose herself. She is too important to your cause.

But there must be other Ignobles who could begin revealing their ancestry and intentions to the people of the Bottoms . . . in secret, of course."

Lim's expression takes on an unusually serious pallor. He appears to be weighing the notion.

Lexi feels she needs to press the issue to tip him over the edge in her favor. "If you truly wish to rally in the name of nobility, to the point at which they will openly revolt against the Capitol, then you must give them nobles to rally around. I am only a messenger. I have made that clear to them."

"Of course," he says. "Of course that . . . limitation is inevitable, I suppose. We do not want them popping their cork prematurely, if you will."

"I certainly don't want that," Lexi affirms, again adding, "For them."

Lim appears thoughtful. "I will take up your concerns with Lady Burr and pass along your suggestion."

Lexi feels her heart lighten just a hair. It is all she can do to hide her immense relief. "Thank you, Sir Kamen."

That brings the smile back to his face. "That is the first time you've called me that. Thank *you*, my lady."

He rises from the chair, spryly and jovially. Lexi quickly stands, as well.

"And thank you for your honesty," he says. "I know you carry many doubts about a return to nobility . . . but you will see, it is what is best for the future of Crache."

"I think only of the people," Lexi reiterates.

"As well you should," he says with a respectful bow.

Lexi returns the gesture curtly.

As Lim turns to exit the room, he comes face to face with Shaheen, standing in the parlor archway, cradling her basket of groceries.

"Shaheen!" he says warmly, displaying not an ounce of surprise or accusation. "How long have you been standing there, my dear?"

She watches Shaheen caught off-guard for the briefest of moments, Lexi's breath catching as she hopes Lim took no notice of it. Fortunately, a radiant smile quickly forms on her lips. "I just walked in, Aegin Lim. I'm sorry if I'm interrupting."

"No, no, I was just making my way home for the evening."

Lexi hears nothing save the usual fatherly kindness in his tone.

Shaheen nods, playing her role of the eager, unsure interloper into the world of the Gen Circus.

Lim bows again, to Shaheen this time, and begins to stroll past her.

At the last moment he pauses, staring down into her basket.

Reaching inside, Lim retrieves a piece of dragon fruit, inspecting it closely and giving it a good squeeze.

"Oh, that's a good one," he remarks, dropping the fruit back in the basket and gently mussing the hair atop Shaheen's head. He departs then, whistling cheerfully as he crosses the foyer and exits the tower.

Shaheen maintains her youthfully ignorant and friendly visage until she is certain he is long gone.

"How did it go?" she asks Lexi, her tone shifting to that of the undercover Ministry operative.

"He believed me, I think," Lexi says. "Whether or not Burr will believe *him* is out of my hands."

The look in Shaheen's eyes makes Lexi think she is unconvinced.

I've only been a spy for a day—what do you expect? Lexi thinks, but she does not say it aloud.

In a way, Shaheen frightens her more than Daian did.

PARTERS AT THE GATES OF DAWN

FEW THINGS BRING PEOPLE BACK TOGETHER LIKE FACING their shared and collective death. Perhaps that is why Evie and Sirach spent two hours fucking each other like animals immediately following the rebellion's final war council before their attack on the Skrain.

They were meant to be behind closed doors discussing the Sicclunan role in the sudden assault. And they did, in-between ragged breaths and devouring each other's lips, tongues, and various other fleshy areas. The only preamble had been Evie dismissing the rest of the council while requesting Sirach remain behind for a moment, ignoring Brio's knowing gaze all the while.

Sirach, for her part, had instructed Chimot to return to their soldiers without her and begin dispensing marching orders.

Chimot's gaze was beyond knowing. Her eyes were absolute founts of silent wisdom on the subject of what was about to happen when the rest of them left the room.

Neither one of them spoke about their rejoining, or what came before that divided them. They merely fell upon each other the minute they were alone and began tearing away pieces of their lover's armor while trading thoughts on troop deployments, tactics, and speedy, stealthy mobilization methods.

By the end of it, they were sweat-soaked and glazed in each other, lying naked upon the marble table side by side. The taste of Sirach lingered deliciously on Evie's tongue, and she never wanted to stop feeling the cool stone beneath her bare back.

They were silent for as many more moments as either of them seemed to feel they could steal from preparing their forces.

"Tell me you aren't staying because of me," Evie bid her, though it was clearly more of a question.

"I'm staying because of you," Sirach answered without hesitation.

"You are such an asshole," Evie chided, despite the grin that came to her face.

"Apologies, General. You should reprimand me for disobeying a direct order."

Evie reluctantly peeled her damp body from the tabletop and turned to her side to face Sirach, leaning against a slick elbow. "Tell me you aren't staying *only* for me," she said.

Sirach closed her eyes. Her expression remained glowingly serene. "I am not staying only for you. I am staying because, for the first time in my life, I am home. I never imagined I would be able to say that. And I am only here because of you and your born-again Savages. I want the rest of my people whose ancestors were purged from your other cities to feel that as well."

"And if we all die tomorrow?"

"Then that is what we died for—to go home," Sirach insisted, her tone and expression unchanged. "It can't just be about survival.

There is no future in that. And without a future what are we surviving for?"

Sirach opened her eyes, looking up at Evie with more unvarnished love and openness than she'd yet seen from the woman.

"You're doing the only thing you can do," Sirach said. "*We* are doing the only thing we can do. It is as you said. Don't damn yourself for holding two piles of shit and dropping the heavier one. That is what being the leader of an army at war is more often than not. This campaign was very likely doomed from the start. Yet here we are."

Evie nodded, somehow breathing just a bit easier in that moment. "Here we are," she echoed.

That was the last they spoke of it. Evie and Sirach forced their sapped bodies from that table and quickly re-dressed and collected their armor pieces to go ready themselves separately to depart the Tenth City.

Evie missed having Mother Manai to assist her in preparing to take the field, and it was all she could do as she once again donned her Sparrow General armor and tied back her own hair to keep thoughts of the woman from breaking down the high walls she'd built since returning from the Skrain encampment to dam that pain, at least for the time being.

It was decided at the end of their war council that a vanguard composed of their thousands of former Savage Legionnaires would push on ahead of the rest of the rebellion force at speed to do what Savages do best. They would hit whatever resistance the Skrain muster to defend their camp while readying the remainder of the Crachian host to join in defending against the unexpected assault.

Evie had not arrived at that decision easily, no more so than settling on the assault itself. There is little chance many of them will still be fighting when the rest of the rebellion arrives. However, even Lariat and the others agreed it was their best hope of having any success on the field. They would hit the hopefully incomplete Skrain line as hard and fast as they could, and with a not inconsiderable amount of luck they would push enough of their ex-Savage ranks into the camp itself to begin creating chaos and sowing fear and discord among the Crachian troops.

Evie parted with the last surviving members of the Elder Company at the city gates, feeling as though ten pounds of gravel weighted down her guts.

"I feel as though I should be going with you," she'd said to Lariat as he readied to lead the rune-covered company out alongside Diggs and Bam.

"That's not a general's work," he very knowingly replied, adding with less bravado, "That's what Mother'd tell you, anyhow."

Evie couldn't stop the tears from welling in both of her eyes. "I'm sending you to die," she said quietly, as if she had to admit that out loud to herself.

"Most of us, I reckon," Lariat said dispassionately and without hesitation. "But that's what we do, little sparrow. I mean, General."

He chuckled at that last.

Evie shook her head. "I'm no better than the Skrain, then. I'm using you as they did."

Lariat sighed, looming over her largely and sympathetically. "It's our choice now," he told her. "Most of us have no homes to go back to. We'd rather die fightin' than bein' gutted or dragged back by our tender bits from some blood coin hunter's rope."

He cupped her cheeks briefly with his impossibly large, callused hands. "This is the fight *we* chose," he insisted one last time.

Lariat peered down at the blade-and-barb-encumbered leather straps crisscrossing his bare torso and shoulders and extending down his arms to skeletal gauntlets encasing his wrists and fingers, each with their own curved and sharpened metal teeth.

"I'd give ya a squeeze, but I'd stick you good," he'd said to her.

Instead, Lariat stroked the top of her head and gently pressed his rough lips to her forehead. "I have daughters like you somewhere," he'd whispered. "At least, I hope they're like you. If you ever run across 'em, tell 'em the old man went out of this world trying to get back to them."

Evie was forced to swallow hard before answering. "I will if I have to. But don't make me if you can help it, all right?"

For the first time since learning of Mother Manai's death, a piece of the brawny brute's usual jocularity returned to him. He unsheathed his twin katars smoothly and held them aloft in a heroic pose.

"They're gettin' a weapon, not a man!" he boldly proclaimed, laughing raucously. Returning his triangular blades to their scabbards, he favored her with a wink before turning to depart.

"Tell me something," Diggs said to her on the heels of following Lariat.

"What's that?"

"Are you simply not taken by handsome older men, or . . . ?" He trailed off then, grinning down at her.

Evie laughed, playfully shoving him down the path Lariat was still beating. "Good luck, Diggs. Never change."

"The same to you," he said, backpedaling. "On both counts."

Bam lingered, arms folded sullenly across his bulbous chest, the haft of the mallet hanging over his shoulder laced through them. He stared at her forlornly through the veil of his gathered hood and hanging hair.

Evie had looked on him with such gratefulness and sympathy in her eyes.

"You have to go with them, Bam," she'd said, firmly. "They need you more than I do now. Keep as many of them on their feet and fighting for as long as you can, will you? And don't fall yourself, if you have the choice."

Bam nodded obediently, as he always did.

Evie reached up and placed her hand against his chest.

"Thank you," she said. "Thank you for always watching over me."

He nodded again.

"You're nice," he said in his surprisingly gentle voice.

Evie smiled up at him, a juggernaut on the battlefield she had witnessed commit so many truly brutal, even grotesque acts.

"You're nice, too," she said, and she meant it.

Evie has been parted from her gruff companions and comrades-in-arms for less than an hour now, but she feels the absence of them deeply. They are as much family as she has known in her adult life.

Mounted atop the best battle horse in their makeshift army, Evie performs a final check of her weapons and armor, finding every instrument and tiny fastener is held perfectly in place. Sirach's mount trots up beside hers, her lover removing a pair of leather gloves from her belt.

Evie turns and peers at the ranks assembled behind them, ready to march at double-time pace to strike at the massive beast that is the Skrain host.

"Where is Chimot?" Evie asks.

"I sent her ahead with a party of my own scouts," Sirach answers casually, fitting the worryingly thin gloves over her hands.

Evie is surprised and confused to the point of alarm. "With Lariat's men? In the vanguard?"

Sirach shakes her head.

"Then what?" Evie demands, invoking her General voice.

Sirach chuckles quietly. "Relax. Chimot told me about her idea of setting a few fires in the camp. They're going to slip in *ahead* of your rough-edged friends and make a few sparks before the battle begins. Why fight through the hordes to get in the camp? When the Skrain alarms sound, it'll be even easier for them to pass into that tent city than it was for you."

Evie stares at her with her jaw practically hanging. "Why didn't I think of that?" she asks herself aloud.

Sirach's newly gloved hand reaches over to lightly pat her cheek. "Don't worry, dear. Just look pretty."

Sirach blows her a kiss, and it is all Evie can do not to pop her in the mouth with an open palm.

She's just so damned pleased Sirach is on their side, though.

A rising clamor beyond the threshold of the city gates sharply draws her attention. Evie sees the light of burning torches and hears the rattling of steel and the shouting of ramped-up voices.

For one wild, desperate second, she fears the Gen Circus or the Citadel or both have chosen this moment to storm from their barricaded havens and take the city back. She can almost see the remaining Aegins and Skrain coming for them in the receding darkness.

Instead, Kellan leads an armed assortment of men and women from the Shade out through the gates. They must number in the thousands, all of them strong-looking and able of body. They're carrying appropriated Skrain weapons and wearing Skrain armor with Aegin daggers held in Aegin baldrics slung across their chests.

Kellan's hammer is much larger than when Evie first met him, forged distinctly for battle.

"Permission to join the war, General!" he calls out to her as they approach the formation. She can see his friendly smile by the light of his people's torches.

Evie breaks away from Sirach and her forces and quickly gallops over to meet him.

"What is this?" she asks, still in shock if no longer feeling the quick stab of fear.

"We thought you could use the help," he says.

"What about the city?"

"Talma will stay behind with enough of us to keep the Gens and the arbiters in their holes until we return."

Evie stares down at him gravely. "You're sure, Kellan?"

The blacksmith glances back at the men and women behind him. It is clear most of them have never worn armor or held proper weapons before, yet they look neither uncomfortable nor unsure of themselves. Their eyes are hard. Their postures are tight and sprung and ready.

They want a fight. Evie can see it scrawled in the features of every face lit by the torches.

"Again, I thank you," she says to Kellan. "Fall in behind the Sicclunan soldiers. We have to move fast."

"We'll keep up," Kellan assures her.

At his back, the people of the Shade unleash a chorus of assenting battle cries, raising their hard-won weapons high in the air.

Satisfied, Evie rears her mount and rides back to where Sirach is waiting with a strange grin on her face.

"What is it?" Evie asks her.

"You'd almost think we're not all going to die," she marvels, watching the Shade's battalion file out to join them.

Evie follows her gaze, the hardened faces she just stared into becoming a blur as her new recruits fall into formation.

"Almost," she says grimly.

THE TRUTH

"THIS ISN'T RIGHT," DYEAWAN SAYS FOR PERHAPS THE FIFTH time in a row. "You should not be here."

Oisin's irritation finally boils over.

"Please cease your mewling," he says with open disdain. "That word is meaningless, in any case. 'Rightness.' It is invoked by the weak to relieve themselves of fault in a chaotic world. There is no right, young one. That would imply a prescribed order to things. There is only the order we impose."

"That is what *you* do," Dyeawan tells him.

"That is what we all do. That is the purpose of both the Protectorate Ministry *and* the Planning Cadre. That is the thing at the head of which you currently sit. And that is why Edger's former little pet is correct—you are not fit to lead."

"I know this is all happening in my own mind," Dyeawan says, speaking more to herself than the Ministry agent. "I know my body is back sitting at the planners' table."

"And so?" Oisin sounds terribly bored.

"Then am I imagining you, as well, or are you the one speaking to me back in the keep?"

"I am a construct, in either case. If my corporeal form truly is with yours, whispering to you back in the keep, then that form cannot hear your questions. Your mortal body is seized in a state of total paralysis. Therefore, if you ask me a question here, it is only your imagined self that is asking your image of me that question. Any answer I give you will, in fact, be coming from *you*, as well."

Dyeawan is certain she'd have an ache in her head if she were not so starkly aware that the head atop her shoulders at that moment did not truly exist.

"Perhaps I am only your mind interpreting another's words spoken to you in your unconscious state," Oisin offers.

Dyeawan has her doubts about that. She cannot explain why, but even through the smoke and past the mirrors constantly created by the Planning Cadre, this feels wrong to her.

She begins to notice that those swirling colors in the far-off distance have grown much larger and closer as they've talked. In fact, they are like a wall made of the aurora rising tall directly behind her.

"Why are you here?" Dyeawan asks the agent.

"Was this situation somehow not fully explained to you? You seemed to have a perfect grasp upon it only a moment ago."

"Why are *you* here? You are hardly impartial, are you? Where is Tinker?"

"I am here to carry out the orders you issued me in your role as the esteemed leading mind of the Planning Cadre," Oisin informs her, making no attempt to hide his sarcasm.

The latter question he outright ignores.

"My orders? Which ones?"

As if in answer to her question, the colors that were previously swelling larger in the corners of her vision now expand to surround them both.

Starting, Dyeawan instinctively rows her tender forward just a hair.

Oisin appears unconcerned.

"What's happening?" she demands.

"The truth," he answers.

The walls of color close in around the two until they finally contract, enveloping them both and filling Dyeawan's field of vision with rolling waves of vibrant hues.

When the color recedes, she finds the two of them occupying Edger's office. The hour must be late, for the candles in the room have all burned down by more than half.

Oisin is standing beside her tender. He is also sitting in a chair across from Edger himself, alive and well and holding one of his neutral, conversational expression masks up to his perpetually blank face. Neither of the men engaged in conversation pay her or the Oisin beside her any heed, as if they are not even there.

"What is this?" she asks the Oisin accompanying her.

"You know, this is an illusion," he replies, ignoring her question. "You could walk if you wanted to. You have no need of that contraption here."

Dyeawan frowns darkly at him. "It is always the mistake of people like you to presume people like me wish only to be 'cured' of what you see as our weaknesses."

Dyeawan glances between the two Oisins, realizing they are in a memory; not hers, but one being described to her back in the world of mortal flesh where she left her body.

Edger breathes his voice through the bony pipes of the wind dragon attached to the head of the Planning Cadre's throat, addressing the other Oisin.

Seeing Ku, the little creature that enabled Edger to speak, causes a brief pang in what Dyeawan imagines to be her chest.

"She is progressing at a rate of acceleration beyond anything I could have anticipated."

The Oisin to whom Edger is speaking dismissively waves a black-gloved hand.

"For a street urchin, perhaps," he says.

"For any mind in this keep, including mine," Edger insists. "Her mind is like a sponge. It soaks up any information to which she is exposed. Her knowledge, her vocabulary, her imagination—they are growing by leaps and bounds daily."

"Again, impressive for a street urchin."

Edger lowers his current mask in exasperation, retrieving and replacing it with another mask sculpted into a furious face. "You do not understand what she is, or why she is remarkable. And it is not my own vanity. I have guided Nia with my own hand from the time she was a babe, and I say to you that Dyeawan, with no formal education and no nurturing to speak of, has a more impressive mind than Nia has ever displayed. She is the one, I tell you."

Oisin laughs bitterly. "This is a matter of engineering, and you speak of it as if it were prophecy."

"I use one to create the other," Edger informs him.

Dyeawan looks up at the Oisin who apparently conjured this place for her.

"What does he mean?" she asks him. "I'm the 'one'? One of what?"

"We haven't gotten there yet," is all he tells her in response.

Just as quickly as they materialized in Edger's office, Dyeawan and Oisin are standing at the bend of an alley in the Bottoms.

She recognizes it immediately. It is one of the more secluded arteries she once used to get around without being seen or bothered.

A familiar sound accompanies the familiar sight, drawing Dyeawan's attention up the alley. It is the unpleasant, intermittent scraping of metal over stone, and it is a chorus she still hears in her dreams at night.

She sees herself from not so very long ago. That Dyeawan is gaunt, underfed, and dirtier. Her dark hair is like tiny slicks of grease hanging around her head. She holds a stone in each filthy rag-wrapped hand, grinding them against the alley floor and using them to pull the rest of her along atop her sheet of tin.

Dyeawan isn't sure how seeing herself from that time makes her feel. There is sorrow and sympathy for the girl she was. There is relief and pride in the one she has become. There is also a strange sadness for the loss of that other girl, despite the terribly sunken place in which the younger version of her dwelled.

Two large figures stride past Oisin and the Dyeawan who is only an observer in this world. The two are clearly cut from the worst element of the Bottoms. Dyeawan recognizes their ilk, and remembers avoiding them like the plague.

She knew them by their eyes more than anything. Their eyes always gave them away. Their eyes were sinister, and always seeking weaker prey.

Today, as observer Dyeawan watches the men, their eyes spot her younger version rowing her way through the seemingly empty alley.

One of them smiles, hungrily, barely a tooth left inside his head that is not withered. He nudges his fellow, who nods in agreement.

The brutes strike out up the alley, clearly pursuing Dyeawan and her tin sheet. One of them pulls a rough-hewn blade from inside their clothes.

This cannot be a memory. Dyeawan does not remember either of the men, and she certainly does not remember being attacked at knifepoint. She wonders if this is a problem she is meant to solve? And if so, how?

The brutes quicken their paces, closing the gap between them and the younger Dyeawan's back.

Her older self is about to call out in warning, forgetting she and Oisin are only observers, but she stops short as two more figures emerge in the center of the alley, behind the malicious pursuers.

They are Aegins. They appear from one of the many discarded-looking doorways the Dyeawan of old just slid herself past along the alley.

Both Aegins have their daggers drawn. They seize the brutes deftly and expertly, clamping hands over their mouths full of rotted teeth to silence them before plunging those state-issued blades lethally into their backs.

They cradle the would-be attackers until both cease their struggling, and then quickly the Aegins haul the life-slipping bodies back inside the building, out of sight.

The Dyeawan sliding along the alley floor on her tin sheet never even notices the fracas that unfolds behind her.

Dyeawan of the present looks up from her tender at Oisin, as confused as she has ever been in her life.

He looks down on her, reading with disdain the question written in the features of her face.

"Did you *really* think you survived for so long down here, a crippled girl on her own, without being murdered for the coin or crust of bread you begged that day? Or beaten to a pulp for fun? Or violated in a far worse way? And how do you imagine you never once found yourself yanked from the street by Aegins until so late into your life?"

Dyeawan says nothing.

"Not that you didn't suffer, I suppose," he says with less harshness in his tone.

Their view of the alley is replaced by one of a nearby street, one of the Bottoms' main arteries connecting the docks to the rest of the city. It is the top of the afternoon, and the action of the day is at a pitch. Merchants and shoppers and beggars and drovers all choke the space with their bodies. Aegins ominously move among them. Fishmonger carts nearly collide with wagons ferrying cargo from ships in the middle of the thoroughfare.

Another pair of men soon steps in front of Dyeawan and Oisin. At first she takes no notice of them as they blend in against their surroundings, but a strange flash of black marking one of their faces draws her attention. Once Dyeawan actually looks up at the pair, she cannot look away.

The men are Edger and Oisin, ten years younger and wearing the garb of simple merchants who operate in the Bottoms.

Dyeawan glances back at the Oisin of the present, who offers her only a shrug and an unreadable expression.

Dyeawan studies Edger. His hair is darker. There are fewer lines in his brow. More remarkably, however, he wears half of a black, leathery mask over one side of his face.

The other side is still expressive, its muscles twitching and moving in the heat of the afternoon.

This must have been before the affliction that stole his ability to emote fully took hold.

The younger Edger and Oisin are silently, but with intense interest, watching a little girl chasing an errant rat up the sidewalk. They say nothing to each other, but Edger in particular appears intensely interested in the child for some reason.

Dyeawan knows that raggedy little girl with a smudged face who wears a cut-up sack instead of proper clothes. She watches the child's small, thin legs move fast and free as she pursues her quarry, giggling despite the muck in which she dwells as she easily weaves around the bodies of adults who ignore her utterly.

The girl is Dyeawan.

She watches herself as a child keep the rat firmly in her sights, clapping her hands as if this is a game rather than the pursuit of rare meat to nourish her and help keep her alive for another week.

The rat is both fast and clever. As its pursuer draws near, the rodent slices quickly to its left, leaping from the sidewalk and disappearing momentarily beneath a passing fish cart.

Child Dyeawan halts, the soles of her bare feet skidding across the walk. She frantically scans the street, spotting her quarry as the rat emerges from the passing shadow of the cart.

Though she knows the stomach of her current form is only a product of her imagining, present Dyeawan feels it churn.

This scene *is* a memory, she realizes. She remembers this day. Not Edger and Oisin's clandestine presence, certainly, but she remembers chasing that rat.

She also remembers what happens next.

Child Dyeawan smiles triumphantly, leaping from the sidewalk to pursue the rat into the busy street. The creature skitters anew, making for the other side of the thoroughfare.

The little girl avoids the bustling traffic as easily as the sea of oblivious passersby on the walk, at least at first. As she reaches the middle of the road, however, one of her dirty, bare feet catches a loose stone and she trips, falling forward onto her stomach.

It knocks the wind out of her. Dyeawan remembers that, too.

She never saw the wagon that is now barreling down on her younger, prone form.

Present Dyeawan looks up at Edger and Oisin. The side of Edger's face that can still move is contorted in sudden, dark concern. It is a striking thing for her to see, Edger looking on her, any version of her, with such passion and worry and obvious affection. It also makes no sense because he did not know her then.

Did he?

Edger actually takes a step forward as if to intercede in the events they are observing from afar.

Oisin, the younger version of the agent, bars Edger's way with a firm arm.

Edger looks back at his companion in alarm, and the younger Oisin shakes his head, eyes flashing a warning.

A clear desperation fills that remaining expressive portion of Edger's face. He does not continue moving forward, but there is anguish as he continues to watch the little girl.

The child that was Dyeawan manages to avoid being trampled under the hooves of the horses drawing that wagon, but she cannot wriggle away fast enough to avoid the wagon's wheels.

Those wheels she does remember seeing.

Present Dyeawan is filled with the impulse to scream. She closes her eyes, not wanting to watch what occurs in the next moment.

When the scream comes, it is her childlike self lying in the street who unleashes it, and the pain contained within that shrieking is beyond measure.

Dyeawan only opens her eyes again after that screaming ceases.

The busy street is gone. Edger and Oisin the younger are gone.

Dyeawan's tender, the Oisin of the present standing beside it, is resting on another street, a much quieter street.

Rising in front of them is a shabby, state-run orphanage on the outskirts of the Bottoms. It is the same building Dyeawan once escaped as a child even younger than the one struck by those wheels.

The clacking of shod horse hooves and the lash of a buggy whip rises in the distance.

The buggy that rears behind them a few moments later is nondescript, but its windows are shrouded in thick, black curtains. Its driver is as nondescript and forgettable as the buggy itself.

Dyeawan glances back to see the buggy's door open and a woman of middle age climb out, bearing a large basket. The woman is familiar, if not immediately recognizable.

Dyeawan watches her ferry the basket past them without notice, walking up to the door of the orphanage. She carefully places her burden at the step of that door, pulling apart the loose weave of the basket's rim to peer at its contents.

The woman smiles then, and that Dyeawan recognizes more than anything.

The woman is Tinker, nearly twenty years younger than when Dyeawan first encountered her at the base of that volcano.

Tinker reaches inside the basket, briefly giggling to herself. Then her smile turns sad as she regards whatever is inside. Dyeawan thinks she sees reluctance in the woman as she stands, staring disdainfully at the door before finally turning away and walking back over to the buggy.

The door opens and Tinker climbs inside without a look back at the burden she has unloaded at the orphanage step.

Dyeawan's gaze lingers on that door after the buggy doesn't immediately pull away. Those black curtains ripple, and then a gloved hand pulls them back. The face that peers out doesn't belong to Tinker.

It is Edger, a young man with a handsome, somberly expressive face. The half-mask is gone. Not a trace of paralysis afflicts his features.

Edger stares across the road at the step of the orphanage and the basket that has been left for its cruel administrators.

For the first time, Dyeawan attempts to read his face. His brow hangs heavily, but she cannot discern whether it is concern or curiosity Edger is expressing. In either case, he is clearly attending to business of the most serious and personal nature.

After a time, he replaces the curtains and the buggy driver cracks their whip, urging the horses forward. Edger's expression never changes, and Dyeawan is left wondering how he felt about what just happened, clearly under his orders.

Oisin offers nothing when Dyeawan looks to him. He only shifts his gaze to the step of the building in front of them.

Filled with a virulently spreading sense of dread, Dyeawan looks from him to the basket still waiting at the foot of that door. She begins to slowly row her tender over to the orphanage entrance, employing her conveyance's brake and climbing forward to the edge of the tender's platform.

A soft blanket lines the inside of the basket as she peers down at it. Dyeawan reaches from her tender and begins to unravel its cottony folds. She starts as a plump little hand and impossibly tiny fingers grip one of her digits from within the basket.

Dyeawan pulls the final piece of the swaddled blanket aside to peer into the face of a pulpy-headed baby, not long out of the womb.

Somehow Dyeawan knows the baby is herself, even if she cannot fully accept that as a fact.

The infant looks so healthy and clean and innocent. There is purity in their unknowing gaze. Those eyes represent so much possibility and hope and promise. At the same time, they also project so much ignorance of the harsh world into which they've been born.

The baby knows nothing of what awaits them, how dark and hungry and anguished and fearful the long nights will be.

She knows her tears are not real, but Dyeawan sheds them all the same, watching as a salty droplet falls upon the baby's soft little cheek.

Oisin approaches them. "Edger seeded many of you," he explains, his words barely managing to penetrate her understanding. "However, it wasn't his seed that truly mattered. Edger was convinced your raising was the key to the whole endeavor, the way and manner in which you all grew up, as well as the location and circumstance. He wanted to see how those differing circumstances would affect the development of both your minds and who you became as people. He placed some of you here, in the Bottoms, given nothing to build upon. Some were raised by the Skrain to be soldiers. Some, like Nia, were raised in the Planning Cadre."

Dyeawan wipes the nonexistent tears from her eyes, swallowing a nonexistent lump. Her mind is racing, and as a result the world around them seems to visibly quake.

"What do you mean, he 'seeded' many?" she asks, her voice trembling as violently as the imagined street beneath them.

"You know precisely what I mean," Oisin says coldly.

Edger was your father. You killed your own father.

Dyeawan recalls their first meeting, after she woke up in the keep after falling asleep in a dungeon. Edger was so curious about her. It seemed so sinister to her at the time. She remembers how stricken and surprised and amazed he was when she showed him that first light box she constructed. She remembers his many lessons, the effort he put into teaching her Crache's secrets and machinery, and how hard he pushed the other planners to accept her.

It all seemed so random to her then.

She wants to tell Oisin it's impossible, but Dyeawan knows it is entirely possible. It is, in fact, who Edger was. Life was a raw resource to him, to be manipulated and tested and forged as he saw fit to serve his purpose.

He wanted an heir, a new mind to push the Planning Cadre forward after him, and this was his method. He spawned her and put her through hell just to see what kind of person doing so would produce.

The world around them ceases to quake, and begins to grow cold. Soon, snow is falling and blanketing the ground. Snow never falls in the Bottoms.

"I was an experiment, then," she says, dispassionately.

"A failed one, in my estimation."

Dyeawan nods, refusing to deteriorate into a tantrum in front of the odious man, construct or no.

"Who was my mother?" she calmly asks.

Oisin shrugs. "There were many of them. They were chosen because they were good breeding stock, not for their personalities. I truly could not tell you which one gave birth to you. Records were not kept. Edger wanted it that way. They were not to be involved further in the process. They were well compensated for their contribution, and they had no knowledge of their progenies' fate or purpose."

Good breeding stock.

No records.

Process.

Well compensated.

Dyeawan becomes aware of her fists, balled so hard against the paddles of her tender that her knuckles have turned stark white.

"You wanted to know," Oisin reminds her, watching her steadily break down. "You *ordered* me to tell you, in fact."

"Then why didn't you? Why didn't you tell me when I asked?"

"I was under orders not to. From Edger. In a keep filled with the greatest secrets of Crache, your origin, and the origin of those like you, was Edger's most closely held secret, even from the majority of the other planners."

Dyeawan's gaze furiously bores into him. "Then why tell me now?"

"Because no one will ever know I did," Oisin answers simply.

It is all too much. Dyeawan cannot harden her heart or steel her mind against it any longer. She screams, savagely, and the building behind her explodes as if it were made of glass. Oisin is blasted across the street from the force of the combustion, but Dyeawan and her tender are unaffected.

The echoes of her scream linger long after her lungs are exhausted, and Dyeawan doubles forward, gasping and crying and pounding her fists against the tender's paddles.

Slowly, the world around her begins to crumble, not the walls and objects made of stone, but the very air.

Dyeawan's image of herself crumbles along with it.

The world contracts and she is once again staring across the planners' meeting table at Nia, who stares back at her, seemingly frozen in place.

Dyeawan tries to move her head, then her arms, and finally just blink her eyelids. Her entire body is held, motionless and out of her control, by the lingering effects of the potions. She can't even move her eyeballs about in their sockets.

From the corner of one of those eyes, Dyeawan spies Oisin standing beside the table, very much in the flesh. He watches her with a reserved yet clearly sadistic glee.

From the corner of her other eye, Dyeawan sees Tinker, or rather the old woman's body.

She is lying on the floor on the other side of the table, dead, her life's blood emptied in a pool around her from a slit throat.

Tinker's wide, empty eyes seem to stare up at Dyeawan from the floor. She has such a look of surprise on the rest of her face.

Even through the terrible shock and the horror creeping within every inch of her, Dyeawan can't help having the thought that it's so incredibly strange to see the woman without the constant, assured expression she always wore, as if Tinker was always in possession of a secret only she knew.

"You're back, aren't you?" Oisin delightedly observes. "I can see you in there once more."

The Ministry's Cadre liaison leans casually against the edge of the table, sweeping his half-cape aside and folding gloved hands in front of him as he regards her. "Well then," he says. "Congratulations. You've won."

He casts a glance back at Nia, who shows no sign of renewed awareness.

He grins at Dyeawan, who continues to strain futilely to regain control over the upper half of her body.

"So, now you know." Oisin leans down to seek the level of her fixed gaze. "Do you feel better, or worse?"

Dyeawan has neither the time nor the energy to ponder that question just now. She is more concerned with the murdered body at the base of her tracks and sharing Tinker's fate in the immediate future.

"Edger should have listened to me about you," Oisin laments with false sincerity. "He would have lived much longer."

He stands away from the edge of the table, moving closer toward her. As he does, Oisin's gloved hand closes around the hilt of his sheathed dagger.

Dyeawan's heart is racing now.

"But now the failed experiment finally ends," he seethes at her with open contempt. "I am sure he would take comfort in that now."

Dyeawan becomes aware that her tongue is once again rolling inside her mouth. She can feel and taste the acidic saliva of her own fear. She strains again to move her lips, feeling them part slowly and with great effort. The rest of her remains locked in its immobile state.

"Oh, you wish to speak?" Oisin asks her with mock sympathy. "Please, grace me with your final words. Make them as smart as Edger was always so certain you were."

Dyeawan's eyes dart frantically from Oisin's self-satisfied expression to Nia, still a monument in her chair.

"What," she forces past her lips. "What . . . about . . . her . . ."

Oisin glances back at Nia, and then offers Dyeawan a shrug. "She wants what I want," he says. "That being *not* you."

Oisin draws his dagger, brandishing it at his side. His gloved fingers flex disturbingly around the handle as he looks down upon her. "I have no desire to see your body suffer. This will be painless and efficient."

Dyeawan begins to sense a tingle in her shoulders, and then down her arms. She begins gently rocking side to side atop her tender platform. Feeling is slowly returning to her fingers, as well.

"And worry not," he says. "I have no intention of harming your little friend. She will be there to mourn you."

Dyeawan is able to grip the ends of her tender's paddles, but it's too late.

Oisin is finally done talking. She can see that in his eyes. Dyeawan still cannot close hers to avoid watching the strike come, however. She only hopes he is telling the truth about Riko, and that her friend will go on to fashion the toys of her dreams.

Before Oisin can rear back his dagger-wielding arm to strike, two large needles with bellows attached to them are plunged through each of his cheeks by steady hands.

The Protectorate Ministry agent shrieks and whirls away from the table, staggering frantically around the back of Dyeawan's tender as he wildly swings his dagger at the naked air.

The steady hands that drove the needles into his face belong to Nia.

Dyeawan looks up to see her standing where Oisin was when he drew his dagger. Her shoulders rise and fall rapidly with the quickened pace of her breath.

Nia looks back at her with a clear anguish in her eyes.

Dyeawan is finally able to command her arms to row their paddles. She backs her tender away from the table as quickly as she can, turning it to face Oisin.

The Ministry agent yanks one needle free of his cheek, and then the other. His own breathing has become ragged and enraged.

He focuses on Dyeawan with infernos in his eyes, though they are clouded by the residue of the potions those needles contained. His already swollen cheeks are crying tears of blood diluted by that same residue.

Dyeawan watches a single drop fall and splatter upon his eagle's eye pendant.

She has no plan. She thinks if she can somehow circumvent him and guide her tender out of the room, she might outrun him in the corridors long enough to call for help.

Dyeawan also realizes escape is a goal, not a plan, and the path to accomplishing that goal is beyond her capacity to see at that moment.

Oisin is hunched over and seething, but the dagger is still clutched firmly in his glove.

He stammers, "You little . . . you accursed . . . little . . . I'll . . ." before lunging forward to advance on Dyeawan's tender, raising the dagger above his head.

Unfortunately, in his diminished state and hurried step, the sole of Oisin's boot slips messily in the pool of Tinker's blood.

Both of the Ministry agent's feet are swept high into the air and he plummets to the floor beside her body.

Dyeawan watches the back of his head smack against the hard stone masonry.

Though he flails, Oisin makes no immediate attempt to get back up.

In a rare instance of abandoning all conscious thought, Dyeawan rows her tender forward furiously, pumping all the strength her arms can muster through those paddles.

In seconds she closes the gap between them, Oisin sprawled out before her on his back. Dyeawan cuts a sudden, hard turn, jostled on her platform as the right tracks roll up and over Oisin's neck, pinning it to the floor.

He thrashes beneath the tender, sputtering and cursing and almost unseating her as he stabs harmlessly yet fanatically at the tender's wheels.

Dyeawan grits her teeth as she struggles to steady herself, gripping the edges of both sides of the platform.

A conscious thought finally breaks through the survival instincts driving her. Dyeawan releases the edge of the platform's left side and shifts all of her weight to the right side. She clutches the top of the wheel track tightly and pushes against them until her rump has lifted clear up off the platform.

Holding herself like that for just an instant, Dyeawan steels herself and then smashes her full weight against the right side of the platform with Oisin's throat stuck beneath its track.

His thrashing ceases. There is an audible crunch, followed by a sickly wheezing, and finally Oisin's body goes still.

Dyeawan leans away from the edge of her tender and tries to will her frantically beating heart to slow and breath to replenish her depleted lungs.

"Are you all right?" Nia asks her.

"I don't know how to answer that question," she admits.

Through it all, the pain of her body and the shredding of her mind by Oisin's revelations, a disturbing idea bubbles up inside Dyeawan's head.

"How long were you conscious and able to move before you

decided to act?" she asks Nia, trying very hard to make the question not sound like an accusation.

Nia considers her in silence for a moment before answering. "A while," she admits.

Dyeawan already suspected as much. "What made you decide to help me?"

"In the end?" Nia pauses, and then says with little emotional attachment to her words, "Because you are my sister, I suppose."

Dyeawan gapes at her in surprise. "Oisin showed you, too?"

Nia looks down at his body, still contorted beneath the tender's track. "I already knew," she says. "Edger told me long ago."

Dyeawan wants to laugh, bitterly, but there is no laughter left in her. "We weren't his daughters," she assures Nia. "We were his projects."

"I owed him no less in either case."

"I did," Dyeawan says stonily.

Nia has no counter for that.

Dyeawan peers over the edge of her platform at the portion of Oisin's exposed body that is visible from that angle. She carefully rows her tender backwards, removing the track from his neck and leveling herself.

"What did he mean?" Nia asks her.

Dyeawan can only shake her head to indicate she does not take Nia's meaning.

"When Oisin said if Edger had listened to him he'd still be alive," she presses. "What did he mean?"

Dyeawan has no answers for her, but judging by Nia's reaction, Dyeawan's silence, or possibly the look on her face, is enough.

"What will happen now?" Dyeawan asks, hoping to relieve the pressure of that subject for the time being. "What do we do about him? And us?"

Nia considers both Dyeawan and the dead Protectorate Ministry agent.

"I don't say this often," she admits. "But I have no idea."

TURNABOUT

IN HER DREAM, LEXI IS MAKING LOVE TO BRIO IN THE BED HE has not shared with her for what feels like months beyond count. Most of the time, in her waking hours, she is too preoccupied to think about how much she misses both the closeness of their sex and the pleasure, release, and escape it granted her.

She dreams she is astride his thin yet strong body, her hips grinding down upon his, thrilling at the sensation welling up from that central point of their coupling. The light from the torches in their bedchamber fills his eyes and dances across the skin of his bare chest.

He always looks up at her face, holding her eyes with his. She likes that. He always reaches up and rubs just the ends of her hair between his fingertips. She likes that even more somehow. He has always fit inside of her and against her as if his body is tailored to hers, and she likes that best of all.

Afterward she sees them lying in bed and eating segments of dragon fruit that Brio cut up himself before they retired for the evening. That happened often, too.

"I wanted to be a sailor," he says, prompted by nothing.

"What?"

"Since I was a boy. I didn't want to follow my father or become a pleader. I wanted to be a sailor."

"You never once told me that."

"I always imagined you would find it a silly thing to want to be, particularly for me."

"I would never think that. And 'silly' is not a thing you are. You have always been too serious, if anything."

"I could have been a serious sailor. There are serious sailors, are there not?"

"Why a sailor?" Lexi asks him, giggling to herself.

"When Father would take me along with him on his excursions to the Bottoms, we would visit a Rok Islander vessel in the port, the *Black Turtle*."

"They have black turtles on Rok Island?"

"I don't know," Brio says, as if the thought never even occurred to him before. "In any case, its captain was a little puffball of a woman. She was harder than a Skrain sword, though. She liked me. She let me run around the deck, pestering all her hands. I would watch them scrub that deck and tie their rigging and mend and fly their sails. I never actually saw them upon the water, but I would stare out at it from the deck, and it seemed like such an escape."

"Why did you want to escape?"

"Who does not want to escape now and then?"

"And would you have taken me?" she asks, poking him in the ribs none too gently.

"You don't care for the water," he answers with a wicked grin.

She begins lightly pummeling his chest with the flats of her hands, and he laughs, pulling her to him to quell her outburst.

Lexi is calmed in their embrace. She leans her forehead gratefully against his and stares into his eyes anew.

A part of her knows then that this is indeed a dream. More than that, it is a memory she is reliving while she sleeps.

Brio begins singing softly then, yet the voice is not his own.

Lexi leans back with a start, staring at his face. His eyes remain the same upon her, filled with love and affection and comfort in the history they share.

His lips, however, seem to move independently of the rest of that. He sings a song she has never heard, a children's lullaby, in a different man's voice. Though it is not his, Lexi thinks she recognizes that voice all the same.

She wakes from the dream in the dead of night, sitting up in the same bed.

Lexi can still hear the singing. It drifts into her bedchamber from somewhere down the stairs beyond.

She rises and grabs for a silken, multi-colored dressing gown nearby, covering herself with it. Her body is slightly damp from the intensity of the dream, and her breathing more than a little elevated from its content. Lexi retrieves a flint striker she keeps near her bedside and uses it to light the head of one of the torches in a freestanding sconce. When it's blazing, she removes it from the cradle and strides off across the room to her bedchamber door.

It is already partially open, which is why she was able to hear that voice coaxing out its song. Lexi slips through and descends the familiar steps of the tower, torch held aloft to light her way. The singing begins to grow louder and she tracks its source, and she begins to understand the words.

You are the lily atop the pond
You are the frog that hops upon
You are the croak the frog yelps out
As they hop about
But a frog wants only the flies
Its tongue flicks out to find
It hops to seek its prey
The fly buzzes to get away
But the frog needs only one
And not all of them are won
And so both the frog and the flies
Live 'til morrow's sun does rise
In the morn it begins anew
And now you know what frogs do

She reaches the bottom of the staircase to see rippling firelight dancing across the floor of the foyer. She can hear the fire in the hearth of the receiving parlor crackling loudly.

That is where the lullaby is coming from.

Lexi slowly drops her foot from the last step onto the foyer, stiffening as she feels a sudden, warm wetness rise around the edges of her sole.

There is more than firelight staining the stone floor at her feet. There is quite a bit of blood, as well.

Lexi lowers the head of her torch to examine it. The blood is spattered across the floor in a broken trail. She follows where it leads slowly and with rising terror, her bare feet careful to avoid the rich, red viscous liquid as they pad toward the main entrance, where the trail abruptly ends in an ever-widening pool.

New drops are falling in the center of it from above.

Somewhere behind her, the singer of that gentle lullaby continues their recitation unimpeded, only adding to the ghastly mood of the scene.

Her sense of dread approaching its crescendo, Lexi raises her torch from the foyer floor to light the doorway.

Shaheen hangs from the perch below the oriel window by her bound wrists. Her chin is slumped to her repeatedly pierced chest. Lexi's gifted wrap is hanging in bloody, shredded tatters from her body. Her eyes are neither open nor shut; they appear to have been plucked out. Though her tongue hanging from her mouth is more than enough to convey the tormented expression with which she died.

Her feet are bare, and the blood continues to drip from the very tips of her toes.

Lexi is too stunned and horrified even to scream. She merely covers her mouth with the fingers of her free hand. Her hand clutching the torch trembles violently, and finally loses its grip. The haft slips away. The torch tumbles into Shaheen's pooled blood there at the front of the door with a brief clatter.

Its light is dimmed upon impact, and slowly the fire encompassing the head of the torch begins to die out, leaving Lexi in the darkness beyond the glow of the receiving parlor arch.

"Do join us when you are finished, my dear!" an elderly, feminine voice calls to her from the parlor.

It doesn't belong to the singer, for they've yet to cease their concert.

She could run, of course. But where would she go, in her bare feet and dressing gown? Whom would she go to? The Circus Aegins, who may or may not be controlled by the Ignobles? Will she run to the tower of another Gen who spits upon Stalbraid? Will she flee all the way to the Bottoms, and hope the ragged masses of desperate, barely fed people will swarm to protect her?

"There is very little to consider, my lady!" Burr shouts in a more severe tone after Lexi hesitates.

Balling her fists against her hips, Lexi slowly turns and forces her feet to begin covering the space between the foyer and the receiving parlor. She can feel every step she takes leaving a bloody footprint upon the stone.

Entering the field of light spilling from the archway, Lexi finds she is even more terrified, something she wouldn't have thought possible, about what is waiting for her in the room beyond. She expects a scene even bloodier and more menacing than the one to which she has just turned her back.

Instead, she finds Burr sitting cozied in a plush chair near the blazing hearth of Tower Xia's receiving parlor, sipping from a small clay cup of what smells and steams like strong, hot tea. Near her, straddling Lexi's favored chaise, Kamen Lim gently bounces Char upon his knee with a smile while singing his song about the frogs in the pond to her.

Shaheen's daughter looks unharmed, at least physically, but her eyes are wide and staring into seemingly nothing. As Lexi looks on her, the girl barely blinks.

Did she watch? Lexi wonders with frantic and renewed horror. *Did they make her watch?*

Burr formally greets Lexi. "Good evening, my lady."

"Oh, look, Char!" Lim nudges the girl enthusiastically. "Te-Gen is here! I told you she would be down soon enough."

"So sorry to rouse you from your bed at this unseemly hour, my lady," Burr says.

"W-what have you done?" Lexi brokenly sputters at her. "What . . ."

"Why, I have made new friends." Burr gestures to the traumatized little girl in Kamen Lim's lap. "Just as I hear you have been making new friends."

She sips her tea demurely, allowing her words to sink in.

"Who was it?" Burr asks a moment later. "From the Protectorate Ministry, that is to say. And I don't mean your little . . ."—she pauses, gesturing with her cup—". . . hanger-on out there."

"Strinnix," Lexi says, no coyness or duplicity left in her exhausted and tormented body.

"Ah, of course! You should feel honored, my lady—that dried-up albino is among the highest-ranking officials in the entire Ministry. We must really be worrying them. That, or she has taken the disappearance of her twin personally. I suppose she loved her, in her way. Ginnix was the soldier of the two. Strinnix is the brains. It's a shame Daian didn't kill her instead."

"They know about you," Lexi tells her, desperately, hoping to appease or alarm the Ignoble enough to deter her from further bloodshed. "They know who you are. They know where your castle is."

"And I know who and where they are," Burr says, sounding thoroughly unsurprised and unconcerned.

Lexi hangs her head, deflated. Her knees feel impossibly weak. She is, in fact, uncertain how she's still standing upright.

"What did Strinnix want, precisely?" Burr asks her. "We have our suspicions, of course, but I want to know for certain. The girl wouldn't say. Her conditioning ran quite deep, and I saw no need to prolong her questioning, knowing you would volunteer the only information I really need."

"Strinnix wanted to know the names of the others. She wanted to know who the other Ignobles are, the powerful ones like you, who would replace you if you fell."

"I see. Very good then."

Lexi watches her twist her teacup upon its saucer as Burr regards her, the slow grinding of clay upon clay sounding impossibly loud in comparison to the crackling of the fire.

Lexi waits, tensing, wondering if her time upon Kamen Lim's dagger has come.

"I did see value in your suggestion, however," Burr informs her.

They are not going to kill you, not yet. Lexi's weary body relaxes as she breathes slightly easier.

"I agree the time has come to escalate our rallying of those dwelling in the Bottoms. Words can only push them so far, after all. Are you listening, my lady?"

Lexi becomes aware that her gaze keeps drifting anxiously from Burr to Char. She blinks her eyelids hard, shaking her head quickly and trying to focus her attention on the Ignoble. "Yes," she says fearfully. "I am sorry."

"No matter," Burr says. "As I was saying, at the end of this week you are to give a speech, among the newly minted bones of your charitable feeding house to be in the Bottoms."

"A speech?"

"Yes, my lady. One of your signature rousing oratories, such as the impassioned performance you gave in the court of the Arbiters that first galvanized the lower folk. We've already dispatched operatives in manufactured tatters to pose as homeless indigents and spread the word among the other rabble down there. We want to ensure you have a vast audience for your public address to all of your grateful petitioners."

"But . . . why? To tell them what?"

Burr shrugs. "It matters very little to me at this point. All I require is for you to be present, beloved by the masses, which you already are, and to reinforce precisely what you've been telling them for all this time. An indifferent bureaucracy strangles Crache, and the return of nobility would see all people cared for and well fed, including them. We will take care of the rest."

Lexi swallows what feels like rose thorns. "May I . . . may I ask what the rest is?"

"Quite frankly, I am not certain I can trust you with that information, my lady." Burr sips from her cup, staring pointedly over its rim at her.

Lexi says nothing.

"Simply play your assigned role," Burr instructs, licking her lips.

"What if—" Lexi begins, but she is unable to continue.

"Yes?"

"What if . . . *they* approach me again, before the end of the week? What am I to tell them?"

"Tell them whatever you wish," Burr says, beginning to sound impatient.

"And if they stop me from speaking? If they take me, as they attempted to do before?"

"If that happens, know that your service to my house has been greatly appreciated," Burr relays to her in a formal tone.

It doesn't matter, Lexi realizes. They've built her up to be the symbol among the people of the Bottoms that Burr desires. If Lexi disappears now, they can turn her into a martyr for their cause, even without a body, and use her to rally the people that way.

"Sir Kamen will continue to see you to your daily rounds," Burr says. "If you should want to preview any of your ideas for your speech to him, feel free. He is quite verbose."

"It would be my pleasure, Te-Gen," Lim seconds.

"Oh, and for the remainder of the week before your address, food donations will be double. We want your admirers well fed and feeling indebted. Obviously distributing the bounty will be harder with no help, but I know you will manage. You're quite resourceful."

Burr sets aside her now empty teacup and smoothes the legs of the trousers matching her tunic.

"Do not bother yourself with the disarray at your door," Burr instructs her, rising from the chair. "My people will see to it, clandestinely. I swear, but this little tower of yours collects its share of dead bodies, doesn't it? You should be very careful not to become one of them yourself."

She folds her hands within the sleeves of her tunic and turns from Lexi, puttering out of the parlor.

Kamen Lim gathers Char sweetly up in his arms before rising from the chaise to follow Burr.

"Please," Lexi quietly begs. "Please, leave her with me. Let me take care of her."

"Oh, you needn't worry, Te-Gen," Lim kindly assures her. "I have seven of my own. I'm an old hand with them, I promise."

Burr pauses in the archway, turning back to favor Lexi with a radiant smile. "We will take good care of her, I promise you. I am always in need of good, strong stock to keep my castle and lands. In fact, I recently had to discharge my gardener, and after a lifetime of service. Such a waste, wouldn't you agree?"

Burr again turns away, leaving her with that macabre implication.

Kamen Lim cradles Char's head against the crook of his neck and bows respectfully to Lexi. "Good evening, Te-Gen," he bids her before following his mistress out of the parlor.

Lexi is left to stare into the light of the roaring fire, her insides twisted into strands of barbed wire, haunted by the new ghosts that have been added to the inside of her head.

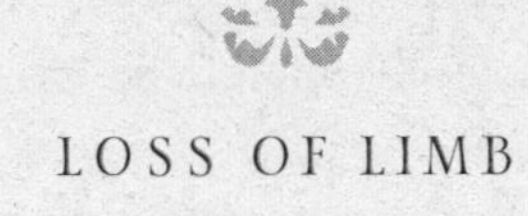

LOSS OF LIMB

THE BODIES ARE GONE FROM THE FLOOR, AND NOT A TRACE of blood remains.

Dyeawan watched Mister Quan clean up the latter with his own hands. Though he said nothing, it was clear he'd have it no other way. Dyeawan wasn't sure why. It may have been out of respect for Tinker, who was clearly close to Edger, Quan's former and longtime benefactor. He must have known Tinker well. It may have been out of respect for the meeting space of the planners as a loyal and devoted servant of the Cadre. It may simply have been to spare Dyeawan the horrific sight as quickly as possible.

In any case, as she watched his towering frame crumpled upon the floor, bucket beside him and a rag in his large hand, Dyeawan was struck by how sullen the stoic man seemed. It was perhaps the saddest she had ever seen him, even at Edger's funeral, even immediately after learning of Edger's sudden death.

It was impossible to keep the murder of Tinker and Oisin's death a secret, even if Dyeawan had wanted to make it so. The events have shocked and devastated the whole of the Planning

Cadre. There has never been violence within the keep, at least none that was recorded in their histories or spoken of publicly.

They have yet to notify the Protectorate Ministry, formally. Oisin was the only uniformed agent on the island. Dyeawan considered the possibility the Ministry has clandestine agents among the Cadre members themselves, and she has determined it is far more than a possibility. Yet if such operatives wish to inform the Ministry, there is little any of them can do about it.

Dyeawan is more concerned about any hidden provocateurs retaliating on Oisin's behalf, or trying to finish what he began. Somehow she finds that possibility negligible. Informants are one thing, Dyeawan reckons, and assassins another. If Oisin had the latter available and at his command, surely they would've dispatched her themselves, or at least been involved in the agent's attempt.

The most important question, at least at this early stage, is whether or not Oisin acted alone. Neither Dyeawan nor Nia have been able to arrive at any conclusion on that aspect of what happened.

If Oisin was under Protectorate Ministry orders, or even if he simply had Ministry approval, the entire hidden world of the Planning Cadre may now be at stake. To willfully sanction the murder of a former planner as well as a current planner is an act of war.

If that truly is what has happened, it changes everything.

Dyeawan and Nia share the head of the table as the rest of the planners file into the meeting room. Riko sits to Dyeawan's right. Every time she glances at Dyeawan, Riko looks as though she's about to throw her arms around her friend's neck and squeeze her gratefully, relieved that Dyeawan is still alive.

Riko has sworn she will never forgive herself for not being there when Dyeawan was in the direst need, despite her friend's insistence that she might've very well been the one who was killed if she had been present. Besides which, Riko was forbidden from attending the contests of the challenge.

The rest of the planners convene in somber silence. The elders among them look stoic, while their younger counterparts are more open with their obvious concern.

Dyeawan feels for them all, in a way. None of them have any experience with their entire world changing overnight, whereas she is quite versed in how such events can upend your mind and put you at a terrible loss as to how to proceed.

"Before we begin," Trowel addresses them both, "and recognizing the gravity of the other matters before us, I feel we must establish who is leading this meeting, *and* this sacred body."

Dyeawan and Nia exchange looks. They both expected this, but their eyes seem to agree that the man is so damned wearying.

"Well?" Trowel demands. "What is the result of the challenge?"

"It was a draw," Nia informs him.

Trowel sighs in frustration. "Then how will it be decided? When is the next contest?"

"There won't be one," Dyeawan says. "We're done competing against each other."

The old man can't seem to comprehend that statement. "Then who will lead?" he asks.

"Neither of us," Nia says. "Both of us. All of us. It is past time for this collective to truly become a collective."

"We wish to move forward with equal say in *all* matters," Dyeawan adds. "Everyone seated at this table will have their vote on any course of action we take, and only with a majority will we proceed."

"You cannot do that!" Trowel practically shouts at the pair of them.

Dyeawan remains perfectly calm. After what she has endured over the past weeks, and in the past few days alone, Trowel's anger is nothing to her but an ill breeze.

"I was under the impression we ruled Crache," she says. "We can do anything we want."

"This body as a whole guides Crache's path, yes," he explains patiently and with obvious and intense irritation. "But its own internal structure has long been set forth so that rules govern its function."

"Then we are changing the rules," Nia proclaims.

Dyeawan is closely studying the reaction of every planner seated around the table. The next generation of their contingent seems energized by Nia's and her apparent union. More than that, they seem reassured.

And except for Trowel, she believes the old guard has been shaken deeply enough to consider this paradigm shift with open minds.

But they need Trowel. She knows that, too. He is the most dominant personality among the planners' elders, and obviously their loudest voice.

"We vote on many matters," Nia says, attempting to reason with the old man amicably. "We vote on new candidates to join our ranks. Dyeawan and I are simply proposing to extend that practice to all resolutions offered up at this table."

It is so very strange for Dyeawan to hear Nia speak of them in tandem, as collaborators.

Sisters, she called them.

Dyeawan isn't certain how deeply Nia has taken that sentiment to heart, even if she has agreed to combine their efforts. She still has clear suspicions about Dyeawan's involvement in Edger's alleged accidental death. But Nia is nothing else if not practical. Dyeawan has learned that about the woman. And she knows the problems of the planners loom larger than their personal struggle for authority.

"What if I do not vote in favor of your proposal?" Trowel sarcastically asks, and then casts a glance at the other planners his age.

Nia sighs, hanging her head and rubbing her forehead with the flat of her palm.

"Edger wanted your submission or your resignation," Dyeawan very plainly tells him. "He used me to force your hand in choosing one or the other. You still have that choice. You are wise enough to know you will never lead this body, Trowel. That much is clear. You must therefore be wise enough to understand when I say we have neither the time for your dissent nor will it be further tolerated. If you wish to leave this table, then leave it."

"Tinker's cabin is unoccupied," Nia reminds him, her tone grave. "You could take up residence there."

Trowel is struck by her words. The old man seems for the first time to fully comprehend Nia's and Dyeawan's union, and what the ramifications of his opposition to it might mean for him.

He looks to the others of his ilk. Few of them choose to gaze back at him. That more than anything else seems to take the steam out of the elder planner's protests. He sits back in his chair, falling silent.

Satisfied, Dyeawan gestures to Nia to move on.

"Our first task is to reexamine the Protectorate Ministry," Nia informs them. "Dyeawan and I have determined that they have become a much larger problem than they solve."

"The Protectorate Ministry . . . is the arm of the Planning Cadre," Trowel says, being more careful and reserved and respectful than he had been only moments ago.

"People lose limbs all the time," Dyeawan responds, pointedly.

"We can't know the extent of their involvement in what occurred here, if they were involved at all."

"That is true. And we must know for sure whether or not they were aware of Oisin's plans before we decide how to proceed. But in either case, it is clear the Protectorate Ministry has grown beyond their original mandate. They have a taste for ruling, and they grow weary of us telling them what to do."

"We can ill afford division at this moment in time, with the rebellion in the east," Trowel reminds the two of them.

"You dismissed that same rebellion, did you not?" Dyeawan asks.

"I spoke . . . prematurely," Trowel admits.

"We have not forgotten the rebellion, I assure you," Nia says.

"But it is the Ministry that keeps the bureaucracy in line." Trowel sounds worried now. "The bureaucracy keeps in line the Gens and the Skrain, and the Gens and the Skrain keep the rest of the people pacified and productive. That is how Crache operates.

That is why we are the most prosperous and elevated society that has ever existed."

"Our mission is to safeguard that prosperity for *people*," Dyeawan insists, "not the idea of a society. A Protectorate Ministry agent spilled blood in this house. If we are not safe, no one is safe. If no one is safe, that elevation you speak of becomes a descent into chaos."

"The Planning Cadre is not a military body," Trowel says helplessly, sounding absolutely lost now. "We are not warriors. We cannot defend our own house. We cannot win a war with the Ministry."

"We do not need to be warriors," Dyeawan firmly replies. "If I learned anything from Edger, it is the power of viewing the world around you as composed of resources. That is all Crache is, as it exists now. It is a collection of resources being shuffled around and reallocated and repurposed. We create and command those resources, whether those we've placed in charge of them know us or not. And we can marshal whatever resources we need to accomplish whatever task to which we set ourselves."

She looks directly at Trowel, who offers up no further protest, either because her point has been made or he has simply run out of fuel.

"We are not suggesting we go to war with the Ministry," Nia says. "What we must do is what we have always done in the face of a dire problem, and that is learn. We must gain more knowledge of their intentions and plans. We must learn."

"And prepare," Dyeawan adds heavily.

Nia nods in agreement.

"Do we all agree the Protectorate Ministry has become a problem to be solved?" Dyeawan asks the table. "Show of hands."

Riko volunteers hers first, smiling brightly at Dyeawan.

Every gray tunic seated around the table, their hands rising in a wave that ends with Trowel, follows her.

Dyeawan bores her gaze into the old man, who looks back at her with the last dying ember of his defiance before dropping his chin. Slowly, inevitably, his hand goes up.

"Settled," Nia proclaims.

She does not sound triumphant, but Dyeawan has come to know her new comrade well enough to recognize the subtlest of victories in Nia's voice.

She grins sidelong at her half-sister, hoping there is more of that to come.

"Now," Dyeawan says to the rest of them, lacing her fingers in front of her, "let's return to the subject of the rebellion in the east."

SUNDOWNED

EVIE GALLOPS PAST THE FIRST BLOODY, RUNE-COVERED body a hundred and fifty yards from where the Skrain have re-established their line.

Her ex-Savages managed to catch the enemy off-guard and push them back. She can scarcely believe the gambit worked. She can, however, believe the cost of that very small victory evidenced around her.

In between the army Evie led out of the Tenth City gates before first light and the Skrain defenses is the abandoned killing ground of her advance force's pre-dawn assault. It is small comfort to her that for every rebel body laid low there are also five Skrain bodies littering the battlefield, but it does bring a spark of hope to the rebellion's main force.

Evie is not leading them into a meat grinder, not yet, anyway. She is leading them to bolster her rebels, who have the enemy retreating, if only by yards.

What remains of the former Savage Legionnaires continues to stab and slash and smash their bodies into the Skrain shields that have fallen back to re-form a line less than half a mile from their camp.

The tent city of the Skrain host sprawls impossibly in the near distance behind their line. A third of those tents appear to be on fire.

She saw the smoke rising in dozens of separate, distinct white columns as Evie's force crested the top of the valley in which the Skrain have erected their massive war machine. A mile later, she could see the wreaths of flame crowning hundreds of tents on the edge of the encampment.

Chimot and her stealthy Sicclunan band succeeded. Evie can't know if they survived the effort, or what other disruption or menace they managed to engineer for the Skrain host to cope with, but they succeeded in lighting the enemy's home ablaze.

That is another boon for the rebellion's fleeting chances in this fight.

The chaos of the camp can be heard by the Sparrow General even over the pounding of her own horse's hooves and the gory sounds of the battle raging ahead of her. Her deepest hope is that panic, and perhaps even fear, is spreading through every armored body and helmed mind in that sea of burning tents.

Behind Evie's mount, her army's double-time march has become a full-out charge. The hypnotic, choral battle chants of the Sicclunans are underscored by the intense rattling of their shields and spears and swords as they bolt over the open terrain of the valley.

The Tenth City volunteers, as well as the refugees who joined the rebellion at the Crachian border, sprint at the rear, screaming their own form of incoherent combat chorus with bloody fervor.

The warriors of the B'ors dash ahead of the rest of their forces. Many of them are somehow outpacing Evie's mount. She looks down to watch their arms and legs pumping in steady, blinding rhythm. They look as though they could run like that all day without tiring. None of them whoop or yell. They keep their eyes forward, silently, a stony menace galvanizing their sun-kissed features.

With every dead ex-Savage Evie rides past, she spares a glance downward, looking for Lariat, Diggs, and Bam. It may be absurd to think she can spot them in all this madness, but the fact she hasn't seen any one of their faces brings her a shallow comfort all the same.

A wave of black splinters is launched from somewhere beyond the fray ahead. The Skrain archers must be firing from behind their line, attempting to weaken the secondary force advancing on them like banshees.

She looks up, slitting her eyes against the bright light of the morning sun to see a storm of arrows reaching the apex of their arc. They seem to hold their own in the midst of that blue sky, hovering thoughtfully as if they might somehow deny falling and take off in flight of their own. Perhaps that is just Evie's mind trying to find poetry and meaning in the midst of violent madness.

"Shields!" she cries over her shoulder, hearing both the warning and the order repeated throughout the ranks.

The Sicclunans raise their shields on the run, as do those among the Shade volunteers who carry such implements and have enough sense to hear and respond to the call.

The arrows fall like needles spilled from a weaver's basket. Evie jerks her mount from one side to the other to avoid clusters whose descent she anticipates, ducking and feinting individual arrows that surprise her field of vision. Somehow both her horse and she avoid absorbing a single pinprick. She looks over to see that Sirach has also come through the volley unscathed.

The tribal warriors keeping pace with her steed's gallop only continue to charge headlong, their course never deviating. Their collective gaze remains focused solely on the line of enemy soldiers ahead of them. They might not even be aware of the hail of arrowheads threatening from above.

Evie casts a glance back at her forces to see bodies falling off the charge, mostly belonging to people from the Shade who either had no shields or lacked the training, experience, and wherewithal to protect themselves with one.

Beside her mount, Evie catches sight of an arrow sticking out of the bloodied shoulder of a warrior of the B'ors who doesn't appear to notice they've been struck. The warrior continues charging at full speed, the same grim determination on their face as when the charge began.

Evie wishes there were ten thousand more of them. She supposes they do too, for much different reasons than winning a single battle.

She hesitates for only a moment as they approach the Skrain line, focusing on the ex-Savages still fighting so fiercely to break it. Evie is worried the poor, brave souls will be trampled as their own reinforcements crash into the skirmish behind them.

There is no time and no recourse. The battle will be fought and won or lost right here and now. Any indecision from Evie in this moment would be the greatest betrayal of the people who have already died for her and the rebellion that day.

Evie urges her mount forward at the beast's top speed, drawing her sword from its scabbard.

She glances over at Sirach, whose deeply curved blade is twirling hotly in her hand. "I'll see you in the Skrain captain's tent tonight!" Evie shouts at her, hoping she sounds confident.

"All or nothing!" Sirach yells back at her with a carefree grin before breaking away on her steed.

Evie faces forward just in time to watch the Skrain shields disappear under the front of her horse. She pulls back on the reins and digs her heels into the beast's flanks, causing it to leap into the air over the Skrain's line. As she feels the air rush up around her, Evie swipes her sword against the blur of armor and flesh beneath it.

Her blade rings against steel, and then she is struggling to stay astride in her saddle among the thick of the enemy.

The key to handling the chaos of melee battle, she finds, is making your world smaller. Evie sees and hears only what is around her horse. The first Skrain soldier who charges within that sphere meets the tip of her blade with his right eye. The next lets out a howling war bellow as she raises an ax above her head, ready to cut a steak from the flank of Evie's mount. The Sparrow General silences the woman's feral cry by ramming her sword down the Skrain soldier's throat.

Evie manages to cut down several more from horseback before a searing pain seizes her. She looks down to see the back of her left calf slashed through her boot by the edge of a lance as it pierces her mount's hindquarters. The horse whinnies in anguish and rears powerfully, throwing Evie clear from the saddle. She manages to hold on to her sword, narrowly avoiding landing atop her head as she hits the ground, instead taking the brunt of the impact between her shoulders.

The landing jars her all the same, but Evie decides to feel the pain later. She recovers to her knees, taking the tsuka of her curved blade in both hands and slicing clean through the right leg below the knee of the first Skrain that closes within striking distance. Standing, Evie is very nearly bowled back over as the flat of a Skrain shield is thrust into the side of her body.

Evie stumbles, but she rights herself and replants her feet just in time to raise her sword, blocking the enemy blade held by the soldier with the shield. At the same time, she fumbles to free her ax held in its steel ring from her belt. Evie stops several more ferocious blows of the Skrain soldier's sword before bringing the handle of the ax to her other hand.

Her opponent raises their shield as she steps her back foot forward and brings the ax head down against it. The Skrain soldier is unprepared when Evie feints and moves the top of that same shield with the hooked beard of the ax's blade, yanking it down hard and throwing her opponent off balance. Evie shifts her footing once more to drive the point of her sword up under the soldier's chin, impaling them through their tongue and the roof of their mouth.

Evie meets the next foe that seeks her, and then the next, until she couldn't count the Skrain who have fallen to her sword that day. At some point, she loses her ax after swinging its spike into the groin of a soldier whose body pulls it from her hand as they flail about as if they have been set on fire. She takes up a dropped shield to compensate, but only until the top of it is split down the middle by the blade of a horse-cutting spear. Evie chops the haft of the spear in twain before piercing its owner through their guts.

She cannot be certain how much time passes before the fighting begins to thin. Evie only knows she is splattered in blood that's not hers, the leg that was slashed has begun to grow numb, and every muscle in her body is searing as if it is being cooked. She takes no pause until she dispatches yet another enemy and another one doesn't immediately rush in to replace them.

Gasping to find her breath, Evie keeps a tight hold on her sword's tsuka and keeps her body locked in a defensive stance as she peers around her. Bodies are stacked three high in many places, most of them wearing Skrain armor. The line Evie rode against has firmly collapsed, and the majority of those she sees still standing around her belong to the rebellion.

The Skrain forces have begun to fall back again.

Have they pushed the Crachian army to the edge of their camp already? Will they really be able to storm into the burning tent city itself?

Evie cannot fully accept that the much larger army hasn't already ended her day. She turns back to take a quick tally of the rebellion's force that remains fighting.

As Evie holds aloft her blade, a reflection moving through the length of it beneath miniature tableaus of blood catches her eye. Turning, a new darkness consumes her, blotting out the sun. She gazes to her right and left, seeing the same thing occurring across the battlefield. Expansive columns of shadow are drawn among the stained and crushed blades of grass and boot-torn earth.

Evie's gaze tracks the source of those shadows, staring up into the afternoon sky.

The Skrain command, in their panicked desperation and bid to buy more time to field the rest of their forces, have ordered a dozen half-finished siege towers wheeled to the edge of the battle. They are lined in a perfect row, spaced a dozen yards apart, bringing a premature night to the trod-upon grassland around Evie and the others.

It makes no sense to Evie at first. Siege towers are built to combat high walls, not armies on the field. She sees no catapults or monstrous crossbows attached to the incomplete wooden monoliths, no weaponry to launch at the rebels. A wild thought occurs to her that the Skrain might be sending more archers up through those towers to pick Evie's people off from above the fighting, but the efficacy of such an endeavor seems small even to her, and there is no doubt they would hit their own soldiers if anyone.

She sees no archers, or anyone else filling those siege towers. They appear to be totally empty.

What Evie does see is horse-drawn wagons, dozens of them, tethered to the middle and very tops of the skeletal towers by long, thick braids of rope. The wagons charge hard and fast over the battlefield. The soldiers inside make no move to strike out at the rebels fleeing their path. The only mission of the Skrain in the wagons appears to be to defend the drivers and keep the wheels rolling.

Evie feels the hot acid of fear rise in her throat before the realization fully hits her.

By then, the tops of those massive monuments of heavy lumber are already pitching forward.

Evie turns frantically, yelling at the top of her lungs, "Stop those wagons! Cut the ropes! *Cut the ropes!*"

But it's too late. Most of the wagons have already drawn their tethers taut, and those dozens of building-size wooden stacks are toppling like ancient trees felled by the single swipe of one divine ax blade.

Those farthest back from the thickest of the fight turn to run away, but the bulk of the rebel force is caught directly beneath the arc of those falling giants, as are many Skrain soldiers.

Evie flees the shadow of the tower looming above her. She manages to avoid the deafening, earth-shaking crash that comes a moment later, but she is bowled over by the wind and debris the falling siege tower creates as it shatters upon the battlefield. The sound of the ensuing, collective boom is deafening.

She loses time, aware only of the ringing in her ears and hacking and choking on the dust kicked up by those apocalyptic crashes.

It feels as though a Skrain soldier just buried an ax in her skull as Evie regains her grasp on the world around her. An eerie silence has overtaken the field in the wake of the siege towers making landfall, punctuated only by the distinct and anguished scream of someone maimed or dying.

Her head hasn't been pierced, she discovers. The pain is welling from within. She sputters and spits as she attempts to clear the suffocating dust from her mouth and nose. That same dust and debris make it difficult to see anything but the sun's harsh glaring.

Evie attempts to move, finding it not only impossible, but also painful. She is pinned to the ground by the remnants of a large beam. Evie's hands are free. She can't seem to recall what became of her sword, and certainly cannot locate it now. She pushes futilely against the beam, only succeeding in shifting it to further compress her already mashed lungs. There are walls of smashed wood surrounding her on all sides.

Eventually she gives up.

It shouldn't matter, particularly at that moment, but the taste in her mouth is awful. There is a chalky mix of sawdust, dirt, and blood coating her tongue. Despite having sweat away half her weight this afternoon, Evie isn't even thirsty. She simply wants a slug of water to wash that taste out of her mouth.

A new shadow falls over her, not nearly the breadth or depth of the ones cast by the towers, but not that far off.

Evie watches big, strong hands close around the edges of the beam atop her and easily lift it away. The air rushes back in to fill her lungs. She blinks until the ends of messy tendrils of muddy curls and a bulbous sock puppet's nose stained by bluish-green runes come into focus for her.

It's Bam, his hood peeled back and half his face covered in enemy blood and bits of brains mashed by his mallet. He slips those powerful hands beneath her arms and lifts Evie up like a babe, planting her gently on her feet.

She has to grip his shoulder for several moments before she is certain of her footing, and even then standing feels like being stabbed through both sides by long, serrated blades.

Evie has never been more grateful to see anyone in her life, however.

Bam uses a single fingertip practically as thick as her chin to brush away the stained, stray strands of hair from Evie's muddy and bloodied face.

She smiles up at him weakly. "I missed you, too," she says.

Bam says nothing, but his big, hound dog eyes tell her enough.

"Lariat?" she asks him. "Diggs?"

Those eyes droop low, and Bam ominously shakes his head.

The smile perishes on Evie's lips. It takes a moment for the implication to completely close in on her. She feels as if another beam has fallen on her chest. But there is no time to mourn now.

She turns and gazes out over the sudden junkyard. All the bodies strewn over the battlefield are buried beneath several layers of broken wood. All around her, rebels and more than a few Skrain who weren't crushed by the towers are emerging from the wreckage.

There is a clambering above them, shifting the debris and raining arm-size splinters at their feet.

Bam takes up his gore-adorned mallet from where he set it aside, and Evie draws the flared dagger still in its scabbard on her belt.

They relax as Sirach hunkers down atop another colossal beam overhead, peering down at them with a weary grin. The bridge of her nose has been split open badly, staining her lips and chin. Otherwise she looks no worse for the wear. "I don't mean to interrupt, but I wanted to make you aware of developments."

Evie's heart feels just a shade lighter seeing her alive, but it doesn't last.

Sirach points behind them with the tip of a Skrain sword she has commandeered somewhere along the way.

Evie turns, and her heart sinks into the acid pool of her stomach.

A wave of Skrain rises above the wreckage of the siege towers far ahead of them. It is like watching thousands of armored termites crawl through the husk of a gargantuan chewed table leg.

The enemy soldiers are fresh, unsoiled, and ready to bowl over what remains of the rebels.

And they are legion.

Evie sweeps her gaze back and forth across the new line of enemies scrambling over the heap. They continue to grow and sprawl and propagate exponentially. It looks as though the Skrain have finally mustered and fielded the rest of their host, at least what remains of it. And what remains of it appears to be more than enough to annihilate the survivors of their siege tower gambit.

"I meant 'all or nothing' more as a rallying cry, you know," Sirach says darkly.

She could order the rebels who are left to fall back, Evie thinks, but fall back to what? They would never make it to the Tenth City before the rest of the Skrain host bore them down. And even if a few of them did survive to flee inside the gates, they would create the same problem they took to the field to avoid.

There is a short sword hanging from Bam's belt that he carries as a back-up weapon. Evie reaches out and takes it by the handle, drawing the blade from its scabbard.

She reaches up to cup Bam's cheek with the other hand.

"Are you ready to go home?" she asks him.

Her devoted bodyguard nods, hefting the haft of his mallet.

Evie nods in kind, holding his eyes for a moment before looking to Sirach.

Evie's gaze asks her the same question she just posed to Bam.

Sirach offers her a shrug, but her own eyes say far more. There is a sadness and longing and acceptance there that both bolsters Evie and breaks her heart.

Sirach rises tall and strong from the beam and fixes the sword in her hand, at the ready.

Satisfied, Evie turns and begins climbing over the collapsed

Skrain towers to face their enemy. She finds solid footing atop an only slightly tilted platform that survived the fall.

All around her, the surviving rebels are finding their feet for one more go.

Evie looks up at the sun hanging high as the afternoon reaches its peak. At least she won't die in the shadows.

"Evie!" Sirach excitedly shouts at her.

The tone of her voice, so uncustomary in its naked awe, is enough to distract their General from her thoughts of rapidly impending death and defeat.

Evie looks to Sirach, following her lover's wide-eyed gaze a mile west, to the ridge of the valley.

That ridge had been empty when the battle began. As far as Evie knows, their two armies are the only large pockets of humanity to be found for leagues in every direction.

The ridge is no longer empty.

There must be thousands of warriors, and there is no mistaking that is what they are, standing shoulder-to-shoulder along the summit. The armor they wear isn't recognizable to Evie as steel or even leather, but armor it is. Most of them are holding aloft large, machete-like blades that curve forward from the hilt rather than sweep back. She has never seen the shape of weapons like them.

Hundreds of what look like war chariots line the bottom of the ridge below the main force of the army. The basket of each chariot is fashioned from the hollowed and upended shell of a Rok island turtle like something from a children's story. It is large enough to fit five standing or three sitting, its exterior as black as volcanic glass. Razor-edged spikes cover the baskets' exterior.

Each chariot is lashed to a team of what looks like gargantuan pigs; Evie realizes they are wild boar. Though she's never seen one, she's heard stories about them, and knows their tusks are sometimes illegally imported from Rok and sold as trinkets or ground up as aphrodisiacs.

"Those are Rok Islanders," Sirach marvels. "I can't . . . we've made overtures to them for years . . . so many years . . . but they've never . . . they wouldn't . . ."

"It doesn't look like they're here to sell fish," Evie says breathlessly, a slow but thundering swell of hope beginning to rise through her chest.

She almost can't accept it. It's like something from a story she would've heard as a child, the kind of stories about battles and heroes Crache doesn't include in any text or teaching about their history, tales only whispered between the old who heard them from their elders, traveling backwards in time for generations. In those stories, the heroic army would find itself at the brink of defeat by their evil enemies, facing overwhelming odds that were surely impossible to overcome. At the last possible moment, a great cavalry would ride in and aid them, saving the day and winning the battle for the side of right and good.

Evie can't believe she is living right now in that moment. She hadn't even prayed, not to the forbidden gods of the stars, not to any gods. Yet here was an answer to the deepest desire of her heart. It's salvation. It's victory for the rebellion of which she has been given charge and a moment ago was certain she'd failed. She was ready to die fighting futilely, but now, blessedly—

"Um," Sirach says beside her, the awe gone from her voice,

replaced by something dark and deeply concerned. "What are they waiting for?"

Evie is shaken from her grateful and tear-inducing reverie.

She blinks, refocusing on the ridge and the army waiting there.

The army *still* waiting there.

The Rok Islanders haven't charged, and it does not in that moment look as though they are preparing to do so.

Evie looks away from the ridge, across the wreckage in front of her soldiers. The Skrain are advancing quickly now, massed in rows of bodies that stretch all the way back to their camp. They're closing the gap between their ant-embossed armor and the surviving rebels.

Still, thousands of Rok Islanders who are clearly outfitted for battle and far away from their home across the sea, having invaded land upon which they are forbidden to even set foot, are making no move to join the fray.

Darkness creeps into every corner of Evie's heart, reaching a shadowy claw up to grip her mind.

"They aren't here to help us, are they?" she asks in the voice of some forgotten ghost, not really expecting any answer.

Shake it off girl, Mother Manai shouts inside her head. *You're the Sparrow General! Lead! Lead until there is no one left to hear your commands! Do it now! They're coming!*

Evie grits her teeth and turns from the ridge, summoning every ounce of will to banish the sight and thought of the idle Rok Islanders. She grips the sword she's holding with both hands.

"Square up!" she barks at those standing around her, listless and defeated and confused in the face of their almost salvation. "Form on me, dammit! Now!"

"You heard your General!" Sirach growls beside her, fixing Evie with eyes trying desperately to mask the fear behind them. "Form up!"

Bam is quick to close ranks beside them, and in the next moment, dozens of others follow, a line forming with Evie and her comrades at its center. It's a broken line, filled with holes that should be plugged by rebels who can no longer stand and fight, but what's left of it rallies with weapons in hand, crying out like the Savages who were once dashed upon shields without a thought given to their lives.

Bloody and outnumbered, they turn to face what comes.

CRASHED UPON THE ROK

"WHAT ARE WE WAITING FOR?" TARU DEMANDS, THE ANXIety and eagerness and frustration filling their throat like bile.

"The battle to end," Staz casually informs the retainer.

Taru could scarcely believe it when they began offloading the chariots from their ships once the armada reached the Crachian coast. Horses are not native to Rok Island, and thus Rok Islanders do not ride. But Taru can't help thinking the war chariots are a match for any army's mounted cavalry, if not better than most assembled on horseback.

Now the retainer finds themself installed directly behind the driver of one such contraption, Staz seated to their right.

The *Black Turtle*'s captain reclines luxuriously as if the trio is simply out for a holiday stroll through the countryside. She has traded her puffy sailor's jacket for the light armor worn by the Rok Island forces that is apparently made from some type of large predatory fish's skin, as well as the hardened shells from smaller creatures found on the island. Despite the costume change, the armor swallows the small elderly woman only slightly less than her signature jacket does.

Taru is aghast at their friend's words. "What are you talking about? Look at what's happening! What's left of the rebels are about to be slaughtered!"

"They're fierce fighters, from what we've seen," Staz comments, again sounding as if she's speaking about a squabble between gulls on a beach. "They should cut the rest of the ants down by a third at least before they're done. We should roll over them easy after that."

Taru can feel their heart pounding between their ears. The retainer's breath comes in quick, ragged, panicked gasps as they say, "You said you'd chosen this fight!"

Staz looks up at them for the first time, genuine confusion straining the many wrinkles of the captain's tiny, withered face.

"I have. I've chosen to fight Crache. All of that down there is Crache. Why would we stop the ants from eating themselves? This is how we are going to win."

Taru grips the shoulder plate of the little captain's shell armor. "The Savages and their allies are fighting *against* Crache!" the retainer practically pleads. "We are on the same side!"

Staz casts her eyes down at Taru's hand, then up into the retainer's face. "You can join them if you like," she says, a stony undercurrent in her tone. "If you're still alive when we charge, you're still welcome to fight on our side. It is your choice."

Taru feels as though all the blood is draining from their limbs. They release their hold on Staz and fall back against the side of the chariot basket. "You lied to me."

Staz doesn't get angry. She looks up at Taru with the sentimentality of a grandparent watching a very young child learning hard truths about the world.

“You convinced yourself that your way is our way,” she says to Taru. “You lied to yourself.”

The retainer turns helplessly from the Rok captain, staring across the valley at the massacre moments from igniting.

The Skrain bear down on the pathetic remnants of the rebel line, ready to engulf the emancipated Savages and their allies in steel.

Taru can no longer hear the violent symphony of the clashing armies filling the valley. The only sound in Taru’s world at that moment is the tearing of their own heart.

MARTYR'S LAMENT

THERE IS NOT A SINGLE DOUBT IN LEXI'S MIND THAT BURR plans to have her killed tonight.

She arrives at that conclusion as she stares out across the conglomeration of faces surrounding her. Lexi has never seen such a gathering in the Bottoms, not even when she has brought a wagon to heel full of food and fresh water for them. Burr worked her dark magic well. The Ignoble rallied them all to this place, as she promised.

She also watches the Aegins. They are the key to everything that happens at this level of the Crachian machine, she has fully come to realize. They are the instruments of power in these lowly, broken streets. Most of them sell their allegiances so easily, it seems, and whether it is the Spectrum, or the Protectorate Ministry, or the Ignobles pulling their strings, the Aegins dance their corrupt dance of oppression and brutality and pacify or agitate the people of the Bottoms at the will of their true masters and mistresses.

Lexi sees Aegins who are confused and concerned, some angry, some terrified. These are mostly the younger baldric-wearers, more than likely new recruits who've barely donned their green tunics.

Perhaps some of them will prove to be honest, forthright, and fair. But Lexi suspects it is only that someone has not approached them willing to buy them.

The older Aegins are the ones allowing the congregation to flourish and keep growing as more residents of the Bottoms are drawn to the event. They merely make certain the crowd is contained and corralled appropriately for Burr's purposes.

Lexi wants to believe that purpose is simply for them all to hear her speak and be inspired to support the Ignobles' cause. However, there are no soldiers, Lexi notices. There is not a single Skrain in sight. Perhaps that is because they are all in the east, fighting the Blood Sparrow, who is either a devil or a mythic liberator, depending on the graffiti one is viewing.

Lexi's suspicion is that Burr does not want soldiers there. Soldiers might quell any unrest that crops up too quickly and efficiently. And as Lexi has observed, in the Bottoms it begins and ends with the Aegins. They are the targets of these people's immediate ire. The Aegins represent their oppressors in a way no faceless, nameless bureaucrat who has never stepped foot in the Bottoms can, though they ultimately decide to keep these people mired in their strife.

Turning the people of Crache against the Skrain will come later, probably much later.

Right now, Burr simply wants the Bottoms to erupt and lash out at the Capitol's Aegin population. That is how you begin to destabilize a city. To accomplish that, an inciting event will be necessary. Having her secret knights in Aegin's tunics simply begin bashing the people wouldn't be enough. Those in attendance tonight have been beset by Aegins their entire lives. It is part of their every day.

The only thing that has changed for them is Lexi. She has become a previously unknown hand reaching down from the rest of the city that shuns them, offering to elevate every soul.

What if their newfound savior was sacrificed before their eyes? Lexi asks herself. *What would they do? How much blood would they spill in their grief and rage?*

The answer to those questions is how Lexi knows they are all here to watch her die. That's what Burr wants. Lexi's use to the Ignoble has run its course, particularly with the Protectorate Ministry pulling at her. This is the last, the only way in which her life can benefit Burr's cause.

Dozens of paper lamps adorn the wooden skeleton of the building-to-be around her. Lexi hung them from the beams of the eating-house's frame and lit them all herself. The pale pink have always been her favorite, and they dominate the jade greens and crimson reds mixed among them. The glow their collective light casts is warm and inviting, and it fills the open sawdust-covered space around her, the curtain of illumination ending just beyond so that the rest of the muck and decay and neglect of the Bottoms remains in darkness.

It is quite beautiful in its way, she thinks, but that notion only leads to more sorrow for her now.

She spent the rest of the afternoon building a platform for herself out of the timber that is meant to construct the floor of the building.

Lexi has discovered she has something of a talent for building. Though she hated the exhaustive labor at first, she has found respite and escape in it these past days. With every nail she drives and board she cuts, Lexi imagines herself to be part of a crew working for one of the many Gens responsible for city construction. She has no responsibilities beyond the raw materials she fashions into something useful. She has no cares beyond keeping her belly fed and her taskmasters happy.

Most luxuriantly, Lexi the Builder has never seen a young girl butchered and strung up at her door. That Lexi does not have to live with her last image of that girl haunting the space behind her eyelids when she closes them at night.

Kamen Lim supervises the finishing touches Lexi is putting on her stage for the night. She hears him draw in a deep, cleansing breath, apparently enjoying the night air despite the constant stink in this part of the city.

"Are you ready, Te-Gen?" he asks her, cheerfully adding, "Because they are certainly ready for you, I should say!"

Lexi stares up at him in abject horror, so stricken is she by witnessing his good humor after knowing what he did to Shaheen.

"What manner of creature are you?" she asks, beyond fear and silence at this point.

Lim appears charmingly befuddled by the question, taking no umbrage at its implications. In answer, he says, conversationally, "If you deviate from Burr's instructions when addressing these fine people, I'll have to kill you. Good luck!"

He offers the well wishes with a radiant smile and a gentle pat against her upper arm.

But you're going to kill me either way, aren't you, Sir Kamen?

Lexi can scarcely conceive of such a man. Daian, at the very least, made sense to her. He was a duplicitous killer who reveled in murder and mayhem, thriving on the pain of others. She sees no duplicity in Lim, despite the fact he keeps his allegiances to the Ignobles secret. His warmth and manners seem utterly genuine, and completely contrary to the cold acts of violence she has witnessed him perform.

She wonders what has become of the meat and bone that used to fill her knees, because at that moment they feel empty and useless. Lexi forces them to carry her up onto the makeshift stage regardless, trying to control breath that is threatening to mutiny within her throat.

They are all awaiting her, a thousand ragged and dirty faces turned up to gaze reverently at Lexi.

She has given little thought to what she is about to say to them, only deciding the best course is to start with the truth.

"Every day," she begins, "I feel your gratitude and appreciation. I have met many of you face-to-face, and I make it my duty to truly look into the eyes of every one of you who comes to nourish yourselves, to know you as well as I can."

Her introduction is met with murmurs of appreciation and agreement from the crowd.

Lexi takes a deep breath. "But your gratitude and appreciation also pains me deeply. You should *not* feel grateful for a scrap of cheese, or a sip of clean water. You have a right to all of these things, and so much more. Every belly in this city should be fed, and can be fed. Every child should feel warmth and safety at night. That you are denied these things to allow the rest of the city to enjoy its lavish wonders is abominable. It is the worst betrayal possible by those who are entrusted to rule."

Those first murmurs of the people now turn to raucous cheers of approval and savage cries of rage.

Every word thus far is the truth, at least to Lexi, and it feels good to speak it. It makes her feel almost free.

"I want that to change for you, for all of Crache. But it will not as long as this great engine built by our founders continues to spin its wheels unabated, with so many of its people caught between them."

It seems as if every voice in attendance is now joining together to shout their assent.

"I have told many of you there is another way," she says, forced to speak above the rising ire of the crowd, "harkening back to before that great, sacrificial engine was built. I have told you stories of those who once ruled over the people and the lands of Crache, descended from higher blood. I have told you of the nobles."

The rage of her audience takes on a new fervor of hope and want. They grow even louder and more restless. Lexi sees the formerly static bodies crowded around the skeleton of the house begin to shift and writhe.

She sees the Aegins begin to move among them too. The way they are dispersing is odd, to say the least, but clearly deliberate. Many of them are slipping in through the crowd, mixing themselves among the audience where it is gathered the thickest. The Aegins are not moving in teams, or even in pairs, but as individuals. If the crowd turns on them, these Aegins will be utterly exposed and quickly consumed.

Perhaps that is the point, though. Perhaps they are Burr's sacrificial lambs, offerings to the mob she is trying to raise.

Lexi is also aware of Kamen Lim closing in behind her, lingering just at the edge of the platform. Her blood feels ready to pound through her veins, her very flesh. She knows she has to make a decision. The rest of this address may be her final words, but more than that, they will represent the final action she chose to take in her life.

Telling the people of the Bottoms the truth did indeed feel good.

Lexi decides to end her speech as she began it.

"I have told you the return of the nobles is the only thing that might save us all!" she shouts above the cacophony, raising her voice to its highest pitch as she all but screams, "And I have lied to you!"

Those seemingly simple words are enough to quiet the near riotous crowd. The murmuring returns, and now those murmurs are confused.

"Crache brands their ants on everything because that is what you are to them, what they want you to be. The would-be nobles do not see you as ants . . . they see you as cattle."

Lexi spares a backward glance to see perhaps the first frown she has witnessed gracing Kamen Lim's face. His hand goes to the hilt of his sheathed dagger.

She turns back to the crowd, quickening the pace and raising the urgency of her words.

"They, the nobles, have herded you together to stampede at their behest! And even if you crush those they see as enemies or obstacles in their path to rising again, the nobles will slaughter and consume you all, just like cattle!"

The crowd's confusion begins turning to anger like hot water becoming steam. Behind her, she can almost hear Lim's blade clearing the leather of its sheath.

"Look at the Aegins around you! They *want* you to attack them! They want you to rise up and throw the Capitol into chaos so their secret masters, the nobles, can claim whatever remains! They don't care how many of you die to give them back their glory and power! Do not take their bait! Do not sacrifice yourselves! Your blood will only replace cruelty with more cruelty in the Crachian engine!"

The crowd's protests are almost afraid now. The confusion and revelation has overtaken their rage.

"The nobles will kill you all to feed themselves," Lexi concludes as Kamen Lim closes in behind her. "*And this is their knife!*" she cries out just before he rams five inches of razor-sharp steel through her back.

It does not hurt as much as she expected, not at first. There is pain, yes, but greater is the surprise. Despite provoking Lim to strike, Lexi was still unprepared for the force and intrusion of the blade entering her body.

Then she truly registers the feeling of the sharp edges turning within her, and the pain is beyond anything she imagined.

The people of the Bottoms are rapt by the same shock as Lexi, if not her pain. They crowd desperately around the stage, appalled by the attack and terrified for the life of their matron. The freshly nailed wood planks beneath her feet begin to violently quake as the owners of those confused and concerned voices rush in, surrounding her makeshift pulpit. The jostling only helps Lim's blade find a hundred new angles of agony in her back.

"That was very disappointing, Te-Gen," he whispers in her ear, hidden malice welling up from within. Hearing that is almost gratifying.

Finally, gratefully, the blade is pulled from within her. The relief Lexi feels is fleeting, replaced by entirely new and even more severe pain.

Lim gives her body to the crowd, thrusting her forward from the edge of the stage.

Dozens of ragged hands reach up to embrace her. Those she has fed cradle Lexi. She hears their disturbed and distressed and pleading voices in her ears as they pass her along over their heads. Numbness begins to spread through her body from the point where the Aegin dagger struck her.

Lexi peers over the crowd from the corners of her eyes, finding it impossible to move her head. The people of the Bottoms are not attacking the Aegins in retaliation. They are not raging and pulling down the beams of her eating-house in their grief. They are not descending into a hungry mob devouring everything around them to salve their pain and need.

Instead, she sees glassy eyes and tear-stained cheeks watching her and reaching out to comfort and aid and protect her, or merely to reverently touch her.

Lexi cannot see Kamen Lim, but she hopes his continued disappointment is gnawing at his guts.

Letting her eyelids fall closed, she thinks of Brio, and she thinks of Taru, and she thinks of her mother, who taught Lexi to be as strong as she needed to be without turning her heart hard to the world.

We are not flowers. We do not wilt.

No, but we do die like flowers, Lexi thinks. *We die and we return to the earth, just like flowers.*

And then she thinks no more.

ACKNOWLEDGMENTS

THE REBELLION CONTINUES, AND I'M GRATEFUL TO STILL BE here chronicling it for you all. While not much time will have elapsed between the first and second volumes of the Savage Rebellion series for you, the journey to get to this book has felt much, much longer to me, I assure you. Thank you for taking that journey with me, and I hope you've got the gas to reach the third and final book (I hope I do too).

There is always a village to acknowledge and thank. My editor, Ed Schlesinger, who joined the rebellion late and did his best to storm the walls with me. My agent, DongWon Song, who planes a mean edge regardless of whether that edge is made of wood or a writer's existential terror. My wife, Nikki, who is the burning engine of my entire life. My mother, Barbara, who personally hand-sold more copies of *Savage Legion* than anyone, and I'm sure will do the same for this book. My master of webs, Jack "Helljack" Townsend, who keeps my web presence from being the embarrassing mess it would be if I were in charge of it. Chris McGrath came back and created another phantasmagorically amazing cover illustration for us, and I can't imagine this series without his artwork accompanying it, complemented by the design talent of John Vario, Jr. Navah Wolfe will always be the spiritual matron of this series, and I miss her and wish her the best. I'd also like to thank my copyeditor for this novel, Lauren Forte, and everyone at Saga Press: Joe Monti, Lauren Jackson, and Madison Penico—thanks for making this all a reality.

Matt Wallace
Los Angeles
November 24, 2020